T5-BPY-924

Shadows of Silence

A Novel by
ARTURO AZUELA

Translated by Elena C. Murray

UNIVERSITY OF NOTRE DAME PRESS
Notre Dame, Indiana 46556

Copyright © 1985 by
University of Notre Dame Press
Notre Dame, Indiana 46556
All Rights Reserved

Manufactured in the United States of America

Library of Congress Cataloging in Publication Data

Azuela, Arturo, 1938-
Shadows of Silence.

1. Mexico City (Mexico)—Riot, 1968—Fiction.   I. Title.
PQ7298.1.Z77M313   1984   863   84-40361
ISBN 0-268-01716-6

DQ
7298.1
.Z77
m313
1985

PART I

At Loggerheads

261169

I

TIRED FROM THE TRIP and impervious to the noises from the plane and the delays that insured a late arrival, Gabriel was trying to sort out his memories. He could not, even by biting his lips, ease his agitation. Within a few minutes, down below, caught between feelings of rage and foreboding he would be confronted by a great melée of sounds and images: the roar of cars at intersections and the catcalls of vagrants, the sirens of patrol cars and the rumble of trolleys through the dusty streets. From the window he could see that the plane was approaching the forsaken enclaves and squalor of the people piled together on the hillside slopes. On that June afternoon, the shock of the murder once again aroused his long harbored qualms.

Leaning toward the window, Gabriel tightened his seat belt and began to think about his own destiny and the destinies of others. He saw himself walking inside some match factory or wandering among abandoned boxcars along the railroad tracks. He focused his attention on the outskirts of the city, as though he were going to be flying for hours more, reflecting that the city would bring a whole new set of sounds, different reverberations; there the whirring of airplanes would mingle with the never-ending drone of steam shovels and cranes. He improvised answers as he went along, the chronicles of his dead uppermost in his mind, but he was unable to fathom the undercurrents of the crime.

Dry-mouthed, and with one hand resting on his knee, his thoughts returned again to that morning, a few months back, when, upon reading one news report after another, a host of characters had paraded in his mind. As their voices mingled together, their stories interwove, their visages suspended in mid-air. After three years, countless images and recollections had now collapsed together in a matter of a few hours. It was inconceivable to him that José Augusto could be a murderer. It had been an absurd, callous crime, apparently committed at point-blank range and completely unpremeditated, save perhaps for the state of turmoil that pent-

3

up feelings of loneliness and jealousy had brought to a head. Suddenly, Gabriel riveted his gaze on the horizon: its clarity collided with his inner confusion. Now he mulled over his own particular hassles during the last days prior to his departure, when he had felt so screwed up by frustration and slander.

. . . "Come on, you dumb son of a bitch! Cheer up, and don't sweat the small stuff, Gabriel," José Augusto would say to me as we walked along Bucareli Avenue. Sometimes he would fall silent, burrowing in the dark cubbyholes of his mind. And he seemed able to talk only to the smoke from his cigarette. He was tall and ungainly, with the eyes of a lynx. He possessed what he called the natural habit of abstraction. José Augusto Banderas lived in front of the Lux Movie Theater, a few blocks from the pool hall on the Ribera de San Cosme. He was much too blunt and rarely listened to anybody else. We would wander in every which way—along the banks of the Río Consulado or the dusty soccer fields, over by the La Raza Monument. I was just a damn kid when I met him and we spent our time roaming around the city. Often, I would wait for him in front of the grocery store on Serapio Rendón Street, among the market stalls and fruit stands. His dark eyes were always alert, as if eager to pick out any given point in the distance. I think even then Banderas knew how to be derisive by using his silences. He also knew what he was up to. He was nobody's fool . . .

A mass of clouds and the meager vegetation of endless hills were fading into the background. Surrounded by the odors of a plane trip lasting more than fifteen hours, Gabriel paid scant attention to the cabin lights or to the bored yawns from some of the passengers. He made fruitless attempts to sort out the mirages of the past few years, but was unable to extricate himself from his own contradictions, nor could he avoid transposing the sequence of so many past experiences. Now the sewage of the Grand Canal, thousands of water tanks, gray, flat rooftops, clotheslines and the shabby outskirts of the city lay but a few kilometers away. He recalled the knife-sharpeners' whistles, the clay-colored, emaciated faces, the foul mouths and the crowds in the Zócalo.

All his answers were either left dangling or merged with the other enigmas of those lives close to his own. Gazing at the contours of the Ajusco, he thought back to Laura's indifference and to the interminable debates with Banderas. Below, the empty lots and the roadways in the

4

harsh barrios came into view as the plane continued its route. Bodies that had completely surrendered themselves to apathy and youngsters waiting in turn for their water buckets could be seen amidst the garbage dumps and dust bowls. While transposing the scenes in his mind—screams in the dusk or a procession of silences—he dwelt, for a few moments, on how they used to greet the dawn with alcohol and cigarettes.

At last, amid twisted alleys and old abandoned churches, there, in miniature, he recognized the neighborhood where he was born. In his eagerness to reconstruct lost images, he conjured up, one after another, the late nights in San Juan de Letrán, the brothel on Arandas Street, the newsroom, and the dimming midnight lights along the Nonoalco tenements. Few of those buildings still remained, those too-familiar ramparts, the rooftops and basement rooms corroded by misery and decay. With a flock of images stored away in his mind he could find no place to rest his gaze or focus his thoughts. The events of so many years were interwoven with his own quest for the mythical scheme in the universe.

Gabriel found it hard to believe that José Augusto was running scared—brooding over his futile obsessions, more alone than ever and perhaps getting ready to cross the border or take refuge in some hole in the Peralvillo district. In some newspapers, the reports were devastating: "It was a political crime and an infiltrator—one who knew too much and who, at any moment could turn informer—was silenced."

All these speculations were either magnified or tangled into knots of melancholy: a long string of vilification which in turn gave way to new queries. He knew that he could not relinquish the privilege of coming face to face with himself, of seeing his image reflected in the mirrors of his inner self and in the changes that had taken place in others. Again the familiar faces clustered together in countless settings: in the cafés in Tacuba, on Chilpancingo Square, near the old buildings on Miravalle Plaza. The faces would linger, shout, scatter rumors, or be engrossed in disjointed monologues.

I lost touch with José Augusto for several years. I heard he was a good columnist and had worked for several publishers. When I saw him again, he acted as if we had never been out of touch. We met in the newsroom. He was as skinny as ever, but had grown taller and he moved his fingers around all the time, as if he always had a lot of unfinished things on his mind. Then, after trading the same old puns and rehashed stories, we began to take stock of all the years lost in aimlessness and procrastination. I noticed that the supercilious expression was by now clearly defined in his long face and that he had become shrewder. At least he didn't look as gloomy as he had in the past. We laughed about the brawls against the Santa Julia gang, about the Saturday nights in the brothels, and our bawdy insults to the taco vendors of the Lagunilla. Though he expressed himself without those long, silent pauses, he still smoked furiously. And now he was more known as Banderas than as José Augusto. Everyone referred to him as "our friend Banderas," "our pal Banderas" or "Banderas the nut."

According to the news stories, the murder took place in Laura's apartment, in a building near Miravalle Square. Two shots had been fired point-blank and the gun had been left lying at the victim's feet. "The criminal—José Augusto Banderas—is a member of an underground organization. As a result of a trivial argument, but, in fact, acting in accord with a perfectly preconceived plan, the subject in question killed a man whom he had found in the apartment of his former mistress. Banderas' escape was witnessed by some of the tenants of a four story building on Sinaloa street, half a block from Oaxaca Avenue. He fled under the cover of night and his whereabouts are unknown. In view of the murderer's previous record, as well as that of his ex-mistress and the dead man, it is most likely that the matter at hand is a serious political crime and that third parties are involved."

This then, was a profile of José Augusto—he of the multiple and contradictory personalities, of the husky voice, always ready to leave his mark regardless of the cost. Here was the tireless instigator, and the José Augusto of the abrupt metamorphoses. Gabriel poured over the news reports again and again, asking himself whether this were really true, if what he had read in the Consulate really involved people he had known for so long. Their bonds and stories, the seemingly endless time they had spent together, their first experiences in politics—all came back to Gabriel's mind. He shifted back and forth from the frustrations of his unfulfilled goals to the dalliances in bedrooms, to women holding maggoty corn in their hands, to the absent stare in drunkards' eyes.

"It looks like we're going to be late in landing. There's probably a lot of traffic at the airport," said someone from one of the aisle seats.

Gabriel drew nearer to the window. Rubbing his hands together and holding his breath, he looked down on what had been waiting for him for such a long time: the streets and squares that he had so often remembered, recreated from afar, and idealized in the process. Beyond the intersections

6

and the landfills there loomed in the distance a dark splash—a spot that gradually was made brighter by the afternoon light.

Apparently by police request, the first news report of the crime made the headlines. For the next two days, it was front-page news, then half a page, and finally it was relegated to page four. The following week it gradually disappeared among the movie and theater announcements. The last item was succinct: "José Augusto Banderas has left the country without leaving a trace. It is alleged that he landed at the Milan airport from where he subsequently departed for Czechoslovakia on his way to North Korea." Gabriel felt that everything was entangled in an interminable skein of loose ends and knots still to be unraveled, with imaginary murals and phantoms defaced with curses. He realized that very soon he would have to transform his own reality, *to resort to the disputes concocted by so many individuals, to my unfinished tales and to the repetition of old scenarios, where I will have to breathe life into other characters, debase them and ennoble them and cram them into every single one of my senses.*

. . . We used to spend hours drinking coffee. Our time was still our own, as if life would never change. We would discuss our first printed articles and revile against all mankind. One day, I don't even remember when, the meetings started. We would talk ourselves hoarse and our aspirations were boundless. We were dedicated to building dreams and Utopias. "What the fuck—" José Augusto would say, "One must live with the world open." And it was true: we were incurably optimistic. We questioned everything, believing at the same time that we could transform it all. One Friday, we went all the way to Andrea's, which at that time was to hell and gone—in Coyoacán. Andrea Chacón was our first confidante, our ally in the ups and downs of our lives. A promising actress and the epitome of frankness, she claimed that of all the deadly sins, there was only one that she was really guilty of: lust. To tell the truth, I don't know how she ever put up with us. After a few months, we had completely taken over her house. We were the world's biggest pains in the ass, but she bore it all with a generosity that tolerated all our whims. Little by little, Friday nights became a ritual. There we would remain, in that house in Coyoacán, drinking and talking for hours on end. At dawn, José Augusto and I would walk all the way to Insurgentes Avenue. We never tired of strolling, of smoking, or of squeezing the city into our veins and into our eyeballs. "I'm just sizing you up, you big jerk," José Augusto would say after tossing out one solemn phrase

7

after another. "Why don't you go and size up your grandmother?" I would counter. "Because I only size up the living," he would retort, at last, as the street lights grew dim . . .

Down below, as the plane took a slow curve, some of the clearings in Chapultepec Park and a lengthy stretch of the Freeway were lighting up. It was one of those Saturdays in June when the people take over the parks, squares and promenades, when open spaces—those near the dung-heaps or in the slums—become puddles while the sand pits turn into mud pits. Gabriel picked out the large buildings, the colonial stamp of the downtown area, an aqueduct in ruins and the last traces of the cracked land of the Texcoco Bowl. The city had been washed clean by the rains, down there where so many epochs had merged together in a single neighborhood, in a scant few blocks, on the slopes in the hills or the cavities in the volcanic rock.

Gabriel breathed deeply and the rhythm of the violent sequence of past events slackened. "It is necessary to start from scratch," he thought, "to give up hopeless goals and put some balls into the written word."

Feeling a need to take in everything passing beneath him, he continued to gaze out the window. He recognized several buildings near Insurgentes Square, and even managed to see some enormous holes and a miniature trolley car on Chapultepec Avenue. His thoughts turned at once to Domingo Buenaventura in his apartment on Sinaloa Street, and to the conversations amid piles of books and photographs of the Spanish Civil War. He focused on Domingo's angular face, on his hairless chin, his strong voice, white hair and the smell of tobacco from his pipe.

Most likely, Buenaventura would be writing; perhaps later he would be listening to others converse or feel like taking a walk, wandering to the usual places looking for other night owls. Gabriel imagined him strolling along Miravalle Square and then sitting beneath the tavern lights, a few blocks from the building where Laura and José Augusto had lived, where the political meetings, of one sort or another, had taken place for several years, where the discussions seemed to pause only long enough for acceptance or rejection of a particular point. An irrepressible rebel, always controversial and self-assured, Buenaventura was the only one of the group who had experienced prison and persecution first hand. His principles were far from abstract; they had been forged in his own witness of degradation and abasement.

. . . Every afternoon, Domingo Buenaventura would be in his apartment; we would drop in and talk for hours. Switching back and forth

8

from reality to reading his manuscripts, he made us participants in his vagaries. Thanks to him, we gradually got rid of the habit of waste, of leaving everything for our next diatribes. From him we also learned not to be on the defensive, not to fall back on useless explanations. Before long, the living room would be full of cigarette smoke, and by the time we opened the windows, Sinaloa Street was already dark and deserted. We always used better language with Buenaventura, and we didn't overdo it with lies or doubts. Domingo would compare the political events of the past few years with those we were living through. At that time, we hadn't the slightest idea of what many of us were to undergo, nor of the events that would radically alter our expectations a couple of years after my return . . .

It was nearly mid-afternoon and the sun, leaning against the city, with its glare traced the outlines of the shadows, the concrete cubes, the graveyards, the expanse of new housing developments and the newly-built towers of Nonoalco-Tlaltelolco. From the athletic fields of Magdalena Mixuca to the entrance of the Cuernavaca toll road, from Madereros to Balbuena, cars came and went, swarming in all directions and jamming the freeways. Recognizing a few buildings at the National University, Gabriel was reminded of the bus strike, of the rallies in front of the rectory building, and of the first genuine demonstrations.

He tried to locate some landmarks near Coyoacán, where Andrea lived; perhaps he could go see her that same afternoon. His thoughts reverted abruptly to the pile of newspapers, to the moment when he had read the shocking news—to the dead man's photograph and to José Augusto's alleged criminal record—where slander and prevarication were enmeshed with the enigma surrounding those characters who had been a part of his life, whom he had haphazardly judged without full knowledge of the facts—with the recklessness and stupidity typical of rash judgments.

Gabriel recalled the moment when he finished reading the last newspaper, that last item that shook him to the very core and forced him to get up and rush out of the Consulate, and lose himself in a Paris more weatherstricken than ever. In the Trocadero on a cold, damp morning, overflowing with drowsiness and disenchantment, Gabriel felt the relentless urge to reject all tortuous entanglements and falsehoods. He had not yet realized that the life stories of José Augusto and Laura were only a pretext; that everything was the result of an unexpected encounter with their own labyrinths, the first revelations of so many incongruities, of so many suppressed doubts and pent-up feelings.

9

. . . The last time I saw José Augusto before I left the country, he was with Laura. Although they were already going through some initial trepidations, and were not yet living together, I was certain that everything would work out beautifully for them. I had always believed that she was made to order for that lunatic Banderas. Neither cunning nor arrogance were any longer apparent in his recurrent sarcasm. Distant and sparse of words, Laura had a peculiar smile: at times her mannerisms were brusk and she seemed to be always on tenterhooks—waiting for something indefinable to happen.

"All right, you son of a bitch, make the most of everything dangling in front of you . . . go whole hog, you bastard. And have a ball," José Augusto told me as we said our goodbyes in a coffee shop on Hamburgo Street. He never answered a single one of my letters, and later I found out that after he and Laura had broken up, he wandered around the city like a zombie, sinking to the lowest depths, and speaking to no one. I also heard that his articles had become more and more belligerent and that he was just about to be fired from his job at the paper. I pictured him in some kind of tenement, completely disheveled, refusing to see anyone . . . I've always been convinced that none of us were born at the right time—that we were all doomed to be excluded from everything. No one can deny that we're a stubborn bunch, and, all in all, that we know how to put up a front, as if we didn't give a shit about adversity . . .

While surveying the conglomeration of fences and buildings, of pavements and dust bowls, Gabriel thought about the jumble of predictions that had come true, the nightmares that had materialized, and the corrosion that was relentlessly gaining ground. He shifted his thoughts from the movie house balconies to the raucous bellows of the *pulquerías*, from the corridors of government buildings to the measured steps of the guards at one of the gates of the National Palace. He would add any bizarre touch that came to mind: a buffoon dancing on the main balcony of the National Palace, the serpent and the eagle devouring each other; he would dwell on the insidious leer of a politician embracing his cronies and on the statue of a seated hero pointing the way to his country's destiny.

Dung heaps and smokestacks, empty lots and junk yards continued to unfold before him, giving way to the inexorable erosion of the old valley and the upheaval of the surrounding areas in the background. It did not occur to Gabriel to think about the date or the time, nor to wonder about the new courtyard in the Museum of Anthropology.

10

He chose a spot at random—the TV antennas or the bougainvillea-filled patios, the palm trees in the boulevards or the pine and jacaranda gardens—there, where the afternoon was more visibly waning, every trace of harmony dissolved.

At last, the plane veered toward the airport, the sun's rays boring down on the squalor of Ciudad Nezahualcoyotl and the shimmer of the Palacio de los Deportes. When he spotted Zaragoza Avenue and the excavations for the construction of the metro lines, he fancied himself the sole owner of the air and the buildings, of the streets, the apocryphal figures, of the city, ruptured by sham and pretense.

In any case, he belonged here, and only here—to its forsaken enclaves and to the chronicles of their dead. Little by little, the past gradually faded among blurred shadows and distant words, and, as Laura's and José Augusto's traces and Buenaventura's rebukes also vanished, Gabriel felt all the more lonely, believing himself once again to have the rooftops, the basements, the earth and the entire world—silences and all—to himself alone. When the plane reached the airfield, he sensed that other challenges were barely beginning.

II

IT WAS NEARLY MIDNIGHT and it had rained for more than three hours. José Augusto swallowed the last mouthful of coffee and, as he placed the cup back on the saucer, he spewed forth a few choice curses. Once again, with emptiness as his sole companion and steeped in indifference, he stared at the spots on the table and at the circular marks left by the glasses, occasionally dwelling on the grooves etched in by time. He was left without cigarettes, without spirits and even without the slightest desire to see what lay beyond the window, to focus his eyes once more on the lights shimmering against the sidewalks. Once in a while, he lit a match and then would let it flicker out in the middle of the ashtray.

On that last Monday in November, with its dreary rain and skies dense with clouds, the Paseo de la Reforma was deserted. The raindrops hammered against the statues in the boulevards, making the pavement glisten all the more. Feeling like an idiot, resentment welling up in his throat and hardened stare, José Augusto slid one of his hands along the edges of the table. Who knows how many times he had railed against the rivalry with his father—old man Banderas, long since dead and forgotten—and those goddamned memories that kept coming back again and again and lately had been brought to the fore like an incurable disease. A few garbled words reached him from the last table in the corner while the waiter, sitting behind the bar, counted the minutes, unperturbed.

"I like your article," the news editor had told him that same afternoon, "although I'm not sure we can publish it. You pull no punches, and to tell the truth, you're risking your neck. In any case, we'll see . . . "

"Oh, Hell, it's nothing to make such a fuss about, I barely spoke a few plain truths," José Augusto retorted, although, "in this shitty, absurd country, there are only a handful of people who don't follow orders, word for word, from the powers that be. Here, one must learn to read between the lines and guess at hidden meanings, we have to realize that we manipulate each other and shit on each other every waking moment."

He gazed at the backdrop beyond the rain, and as the drops trickled down the windowpane, the silhouette of a beggar gradually faded away. It could be the image of Laura that lay at a distance, beyond his own diatribes, his fits of anger, those rages which would capture, perhaps at a moment's notice, his consciousness once more. As if he were willing to settle for only a few puffs, he took a cigarette butt, examined the yellowish filter and lit it slowly. He felt an acrid, parched taste in his mouth—the taste of insomnia, of daybreak and loneliness.

As he moved the match toward the ashtray, he saw himself a few years back, walking by the National Lottery Building, *Whiling away the time to my heart's content; each day held new wonders, there were no fixed goals, no crap of any kind. I was an out-and-out bully, always quick with the wisecracks and ready for a fight. I never had a red cent, but I held the whole goddamned world in my hands.* He saw himself at a movie house—the Savoy, the Alameda, the Palacio Chino—and remembered his first awkward attempts to make out—his hand on a breast and his tongue touching another tongue. As he stubbed out the cigarette butt, he blotted out those images with one stroke, and then, with his left hand, felt the far end of the table.

"Good old Spindleshanks, always up to the same old shit. You have a new load of crap up your sleeve every day. You could bull anybody." He remembered the voice but he had forgotten the face amid all the faces he had seen in the rickety old grocery store opposite Santiago Tlaltelolco Park, more than twenty years ago, when the list of nicknames was interminable and the absurd was an everyday occurrence.

"I'm not that bad," José Augusto would answer, although deep down, he knew that the enigmas at his core were always there, vying within him, churning up his self-indulgence and his obsessions.

After gazing at the empty coffee cup, he looked out the window and his mind pieced together a montage of memories: the Angel of Independence, several generals from the Revolution, and enthusiastic shouts from thousands of fans in a football stadium all came back to him. He recalled the Saturday visits to brothels, and the tedious nights spent in semi-darkness. He remembered early Sunday mornings smacking of rum and sweaty palms. Other vignettes followed: cheap perfume and hair oil smeared on coal-black hair, stentorious belches and the spittle of drunkards on the pavement. Tired hips, incapable of generating lust of any kind, swayed to and fro to the rhythm of a *danzón*, their trappings bent on a speedy penetration. There they were, the flaccid torsos and jaded expres-

13

sions, the feverish panting, repelled by the hasty last pawings from a client. *"What the hell, let's go to any old flophouse, you little bastard and let's see if the sweet Lord steered us toward a good lay."*

José Augusto looked at one table after another—then at chair legs, the tile floor, an ashtray, and the spoon—as if he were piecing a jigsaw puzzle together. He imagined the voices of Gabriel and Sebastián and remembered some of the times he had been in this very place—wedged between Buenaventura's innuendos and Andrea's rantings. He excluded Laura from being part of that particular tableau; he always pictured her alone, always facing him. Even though he had not seen her for several months, he held her constantly inside himself in every hollow of his memory and in the lines of his hands.

He knew that with Laura everything had been special and unhurried; that in her presence the boredom and cynicism disappeared. Before he knew it, her voice, her body, her perfect thighs had led him away from the odors of the motels and the beds of the rooming house in Buenavista. For as long as he was with her, all of the ambivalence, the one-night stands, the fruitless searches and the constant lying had vanished. Laura had come into his life at a point when he thought that his ennui was a permanent condition. His cynicism, pettiness and chronic complaining dissolved as she overwhelmed him with her lust. Then he had barely enough time to look forward to the following night, to the movement of her legs and her soft moans. Perhaps for the first time in his life he had been obsessed by a woman. "I'm hooked through and through—to the marrow, to the eyeballs, to my very pores." Perhaps for the first time he had experienced true fulfillment.

Seated at the foot of the bed, her hands touching her thighs, her knees glowing, and the anticipation of pleasure in her eyes, Laura seemed to obliterate all else. Then she would undress, smile, and light a cigarette, get between the sheets, and, without saying a word, ask José Augusto to come closer, as if she were always eager to explore new positions, to discover a new tremor behind each gasp and behind each grazing of their hands, of their hips, of their navels.

As the rain fell at a humdrum pace and the window misted over, José Augusto conjured up a white screen—the silent films his father never tired of watching: first, the soldiers in the railway depots, and then, an explosion on the battlefield, the camera lingering on the photographs of the murdered *caudillos: Look at them closely, they really knew how to risk their lives, not like the bastards nowadays who hold seats in Congress or the toadies in the*

Ministry. Yes, sir, those men you see there were either outcasts or born rebels, or crusaders for social justice, but, in any case, hats off to them, they were legend, and, after all, they built up the little that we have now. Indeed they did, even if you sneer at them. And wipe that goddamned smirk off your face—I'm sick and tired of it!

For years he had been fed up by those scenes—the hangings, the executions, Carranza's profile, and the death of President Madero—but, in spite of everything, in spite of his apparent aversion to them and to his father's constant harping, every single time he had glanced casually at them, a lump formed in his throat and his fists clenched; he was also beset by silent rages and a loathing for phony heroes. When a flash of lightning flared between the tree branches, he returned to reality—to the rain, the cigarette butts in the ashtray and the voices at the far end of the bar.

José Augusto shifted his gaze to the shelf behind the counter where the dirty dishes and the pop bottles were stacked, and went back to his article—the only meager satisfaction he had had in the past few weeks. He rewrote it in his mind, one paragraph after another,—the truth, as he saw it—an uncompromising and unadulterated denouncement of the sacrosanct lies and paragons of history. Then, touching the edges of the spoon, he reverted to his disassociations, to the endless contradictions, to his longing to be elsewhere or to talk to many familiar faces. He also wished, at this particular moment, to cut time short, to blot Laura out once and for all, to accuse her of deceit, and to expose the whole farce of that trumped-up charade to make him leave the apartment in Sinaloa. Little by little, the apparent stagnation of his surroundings—the waiter's dark face and the atrocious still-life hanging on his side of the wall—made him feel that he was in no place at all, not able to live in the past or to be alone in the present. For a moment, he felt as if his whole body was that of a discarded marionette.

"Whether you like it or not, you are too much like your father, much more than you can ever imagine," friends and relatives had told him over and over again.

It had been more than a month since he had seen his mother—an old lady now well over seventy who had always denied her widowhood in the apartment on Miguel Schultz Street by reading the paper or drinking her cup of tea every afternoon, and feeling all alone among the dusty paintings and photographs in the parlor. José Augusto pictured her waiting for his phone call or waiting for him, chattering about nothing in particular, and reverting—again and again—to the invisible presence of old Banderas and to the faded yellow books on a shelf in the corridor. He could hear her complaining about her backaches, blaming the dirty city air and the constant racket from the people leaving the market or the cantina. There she was, an old lady in her worn rocking chair, striving to do away with old grudges, wind up all unfinished projects and put an end to the dilemmas that had wandered into her mind.

José Augusto longed to see in the steamy window an affectionate gesture from his father, to achieve a reconciliation that could never be: to make the most of his procrastination, to forget his frustrations and his premature gray hair. He felt like approaching the table at the far end and talking to a couple of strangers, surprise them, take them off guard. He could easily make up a few stories and argue over the blunders committed by the new regime, the Vietnam war, or political prisoners. Since he could not see their faces—one had his back to him and the other was behind a pillar—and he could only catch a glimpse of their dark jackets and their gesturing hands, he imagined them with wrinkles, rings under their eyes and double chins, and had them arriving in the city that same afternoon. He surmised they were a pair of losers, so he put them up at a seedy hotel on Aquilas Serdán Street, supplying them with smug grins and the typical mannerisms of the pimp. He squeezed the filter of a cigarette butt with two fingers.

What a long way he was from the goals mapped out for the boy wonder Banderas who just a few years ago had everything going for him. Then he was editor-in-chief of a magazine. In shirt sleeves, his brow furrowed and his fists clenched, he dictated editorials, scanned one article after another, selected news items and assigned interviews and news stories. Dark-haired and bushy-browed, always nipping at his cigarette, he would dissect the last issue of the magazine, talking to himself or to others, and hurling all sorts of insults at them for their blunders. He could not abide ignorance, indolence or ambiguities. "Here, either things are done right from beginning to end, or you can go to hell," he would say with a certain tone of self-confidence. He was used to smoking a couple of packs a day, his dark eyes bloodshot and the blood rushing to his head from the endless inquiries on new subjects or interviews. José Augusto had taken charge from the very moment he and Domingo Buenaventura had first set foot in the dreary office on Morelos Street. The rooms, closed up for several years, had been subsisting on their own cobwebs and decay.

Despite everything, despite his ability and ambition, within two months problems had begun piling up: *there were always threats; there were*

16

problems among ourselves and there was no end to the squabbling and infighting that screwed up the works. Besides, money was short and the printing job got tougher and tougher each day.

One Thursday night, while he was going over some galley proofs and Domingo was writing an article on the death of several politicians in a bizarre plane crash, four armed men in dark glasses and gangster outfits stormed in and destroyed everything in sight. Their anger exploded not only in the crashing of sledgehammers but in their insults and political tirades. *There was nothing we could do, our fists were powerless. We surveyed the wreckage, the office in ruins, and something I will never forget: a yellowish moon, like a blob of dung, could be seen through the broken windows. I don't know how we managed to keep our spirits up despite the fact that there was no stopping the bastards; they told us that we were asinine ultra-radical, dangerous extremists without the faintest notion of political reality. We had no choice: in less than six months we had to close down.*

Just a few weeks ago, Buenaventura had urged him: "Let's get it going again. Times are changing and we have better chances now." But José Augusto, impassive, as if he were already in another world, did not reply; perhaps he doubted his own capacity for self-control. More likely, he lacked any enthusiasm for bringing dead goals back to life.

He now debated as to whether he should ask for the check or smoke another cigarette. As he folded his hands together, his gaze rested on the waiter, on his angular face where benevolence merged with stupidity, on his gape, directed nowhere in particular, conveying the impression of an aimless existence. On impulse, he began comparing similar places—the cafés on Motolinía and Hamburgo Streets, the one on Serapio Rendón, or the one in the Américas movie theater—on similar wet afternoons, the potholes overflowing with puddles, traffic jams on the crossways and depressing lights at dusk. He magnified the disjointed conversations and imperviousness to the passage of hours.

Little by little, almost before realizing it, with Laura his fantasies had crumbled, his lies dwindled into hackneyed expressions. Later, when the quarrels became more frequent and surprises few and far between, dispassionate, he felt encased in the ludicrousness of the situation and his feigned patience; he felt hardened, fed up, wavering between his urge to clear out or to say nothing until the following day. Then apathy set in with its self-conscious indifference and the proverbial scenes; his finding any excuse to let off steam, his relish in her pleas, and their stilted voices and recriminations.

But in spite of everything—day after day or night after night—on the rug or on the bed or on the sofa, their love making soared to new heights. However, once the rapture was over, they reverted to insults and pretenses.

"It's hard to believe a single word you say." Laura would say coldly, despite the rage that smoldered in her throat.

"Goddamn it! With that attitude, we won't get anywhere!" José Augusto would bristle, enjoying the quarrel, which, like a disturbing rumor, triggered in him even more wonder and more lust.

"I knew it! Well, it looks as if you can't wait to leave right now. You know that I can manage on my own, so you can start packing," Laura would add, extending her arm so that it pointed to the closet door. She was well aware that she was showing the suggestive curves of her body, perhaps brimming with anticipation until she felt again her knees clasped near José Augusto's mouth.

During this primeval game, when all conversation verged on the bizarre, he was never sure if he should glare angrily at the folds of the sheet that covered her breasts and her thighs, or if he should slowly rise from the bed, get dressed without uttering a word, usher himself out to the half-lit staircase and listen to his own footsteps—those squeaking sounds that he would never forget. Then, he would remain silent and laugh it off, reflecting that there was no way to start over. He gazed at her as she slept, and smoked wearily, unable to enjoy even the drifting smoke. He would turn off the living room lights, go back to bed, and stretch out on his back, thinking about another woman whom he would see the following Saturday, about exploring another body that might make him forget the one so near him, or the face that watched over his sleep. But when he slammed the door for the last time, when after several months of hesitation and despondency he finally walked out of the apartment for good, he could not disentangle himself from the memories of those steamy nights spent behind those four walls. As days went by he did nothing else but think of her and dream of opening her up, of *envisioning my hands around her waist, penetrating her as never before, smelling her scent once more, her breathing next to mine, to harden it again, to gaze at her through half-closed eyes, to look at her dark tuft awaiting me, her body lying crosswise on the green blanket over the carpet.*

Finally, shedding a voice from the past that called to him from a bar on Bolívar Street and straining the tendons of his neck, he savagely crushed the empty cigarette pack, asked for the check and looked at the waiter as though he were inspecting an object. He left a bill on the table and yearned for a greeting, for the everyday hubbub and the familiar voices in the café.

18

Outside it was midnight, sluggish and damp. He began to walk slowly back to the apartment on Chilpancingo Street. He saw a numb figure lying on the opposite sidewalk amidst the trickle of the raindrops into the sewer and the splashing puddles as cars sped by.

More annoyed at the wind than at the raindrops, he left without figuring out certain snatches of conversation and unable to distinguish the faces of the people in the dark jackets. His anxiety flared up and he braced himself for the next few hours of insomnia. He started walking faster, casting aside all futile obsessions. The silhouettes of the enormous glass casement on the next corner—a showcase for an airline company—and the sheer emptiness of the windows and balconies gleamed all the more. His sole thought was to keep going, to buy cigarettes and to turn at the next corner. The murky skies seemed to deaden the sounds of the rain, embedded in the depths of the night. Brazen and relentless, they splashed sidelong against the walls, only to drown in the dungheaps at their base. His brain and stomach throbbed in unison and the taste of bile lingered on his tongue.

He began to hear the rain everywhere—beyond the square, on the marquees, behind the parking lot facing him. He pictured it drenching the steeples of the Cathedral and the dome of the Monument to the Revolution. He kept on walking, incapable of limiting himself to any single memory. Once again, resentment welling up in his veins, he had the sensation that the rain was dirty and the buildings shabby.

III

AS HE WAITED FOR Domingo Buenaventura opposite the building on Sinaloa Street, Gabriel once again examined the implications of the crime. Jumbled ideas kept crossing his mind in a helter-skelter fashion, and everything was still confused. That afternoon he had checked into a crummy hotel half a block from Aquiles Serdán Street, right in the midst of the noise from the parking lots and streetcars, the steam shovels and drills that never stopped. He had been walking for countless blocks, taking in all the unexpected changes and the snide remarks from passersby. There were no pressing matters to attend to, no particular feelings of weariness, no promising solutions. The images intermingled constantly: everything he had seen en route from the airport to the Zócalo and on his stroll through San Juan de Letrán and Juárez Avenues. After three years, he found himself once again at the very scene of so many meetings, the dim light of the street lamps on the sidewalks, the solitary balconies and the gray walls. It seemed to him that everything had been abandoned to the dust storms and downpours.

"We're jinxed," he had heard a voice saying a couple of hours earlier as he passed a cantina on a squalid street in the Guerrero district where the stench from the sewers clung to the street corners and oozed into the tenements.

Gabriel had also seen several dull-eyed women with flabby bodies and cheeks thick with makeup. As he gradually picked out the different sounds and places, he was taken aback by the new thoroughfares that had been added to the old avenues and by his encounters with faces very much like his own. He had spotted people from a wide variety of social strata in the parks, on the street corners, at the entrance to movie theaters or restaurants. Engrossed in sorting out his impressions, he inhaled the dirty air, reeking with the smell of burnt gasoline. He reflected that he had been promising himself this June afternoon for a long time.

20

First he had rung Buenaventura's door bell several times, shifting then from one corner to another. He selected the more recent sequences, with Laura and José Augusto's voices still ringing in his ears. He would momentarily submit to flights of fancy or to delusion, as if he could gain full control over time, as if everything had stopped still; but the inconsistencies and the feelings of guilt always came back. He surveyed the setting where he had been part of so many arguments. He recalled the animosity and harsh looks elicited when, during the recital of hypothetical heroic exploits, someone or other would then proclaim a nonexistent victory. He was, however, at loss for new words, and found himself incapable of recreating the feelings of confusion between what he had invented and what he had actually experienced.

. . . It was always difficult to challenge José Augusto's statements. There was a period where he read anything that happened to fall into his hands. Some people declared that he was doomed to be a blight on other people's lives, while others predicted that before long he would be somebody to reckon with. Once he and I went into a bookstore on Hidalgo Avenue. "Hey, you, return that book you stole—immediately!" yelled the owner, just as we were about to leave. José Augusto turned, and without a word, took out the book he had hidden in his jacket. He returned it at once to the shelf in the corner. It was an eighteenth-century medical text, full of spots and beautifully illustrated. The old man, all set to insult him, restrained himself as soon as he saw José Augusto's expression. I'm not quite sure at what precise moment—after a series of feigned apologies— they began to discuss authors, dates, and publishing houses. The conversation lasted more than half an hour. At last, when the old man had been won over and we were again just about to leave, I noticed that Banderas had undergone a transformation. What impressed me most was the change in both his voice and his facial expressions. We were barely half a block away, and almost up to Alameda Park, when all of a sudden he took out two other books he had hidden in the other side of his jacket. "Tactics, Gabriel. . . . This one is yours," he said without saying anything else. I have kept that book to this day—the very first novel on urban slums by some poor unknown bastard. When we reached the Sorrento Café, Banderas discarded his expression of perennial contempt and became José Augusto once more. There is absolutely no doubt that already, way back then,

21

many of us imagined there were several Banderases and only one José Augusto . . .

Gabriel left himself open to any and all memories—to the crowds on the street corners, to the floods at the Nonoalco Bridge, to his own laughter in the brothel at Xola Street. Another character kept slipping into his flashbacks: Sebastián Cardoso of the endless line of crap and of boundless imagination: one day he would be absolutely down in the dumps and the next, sitting on top of the world. A master of all-night binges and the only one who could put José Augusto in his place, Sebastián was an extrovert *par excellence*—with the body of a whale and the face of a night owl, constantly shifting back and forth from total abstinence to complete debauchery, from caustic wordplay to the rhetoric of the visionary. A mad poet, Sebastián was perhaps the only figure completely devoid of hypocrisy. Despite his bullshit and his straightforward, no-nonsense manner of driving people up the wall, he always knew how to be himself. A man perfectly suited to profound truths, he possessed a lucid mind and was a connoisseur of the local dives, whorehouses and the best all-night bull sessions in town.

Gabriel stared at the window where Laura and José Augusto had lived. He reconstructed the furniture in the living room, piece by piece: the standing lamp, the copper ashtray and the oval mirror by the side of the bed. He had been there a number of times, dropping in for coffee after hours of discussion at Domingo Buenaventura's apartment.

He compared afternoons and mornings—even the mid-afternoon sunlight with the gloom of any of the dives. He could see the expressions of those who felt endowed with stamina enough to cross any barrier. They all seemed to maintain the same degree of optimism and to be impervious to the flaws in their illusory enthusiasms. In a strange way, they were rooted in reality yet determined to encompass the absurd, with all its consequences.

Suddenly, he remembered a huge dance hall by Regina Square, couples dancing one set after another, their sullen expressions, the knife at the belt, the silver heels and the faces where perspiration and contempt were partners. Incensed, he thought about some of the streets that he had just walked through—the enormous tunnels and the mud heaps on the sidewalks. He cursed the businessmen and the hucksters of the city, telling himself over and over again that they were the most perfect sons of bitches ever produced by the scum of the earth.

22

He set aside Sebastián's tirades and Laura's silences, concentrating instead on Buenaventura's window. He imagined every step of the route José Augusto had followed, the astonishment at Andrea's, and the misinterpretations regarding the motives of the crime that would appear in the newspapers. Gabriel harbored not the slightest doubt: all of them were fated to come face to face with those impressions day after day.

"Fuck off, Goddammit! You know damn well what you want, so don't give me that bullshit. You have ants in your pants, so start packing. The world keeps spinning around, time marches on, and fair-weather friends come and go," Sebastián had admonished Gabriel one night as they were leaving the cantina on Artes Street. Later, more ruthlessly, he broached the subject again in his shabby room where cigarette butts were strewn about the floor and empty rum bottles, like corpses, were piled up against the wall.

"See here, Carcass, clear out of here tomorrow if you can, and prepare to meet life headlong. We will give your silence a proper Christian burial," exhorted Sebastián, who by this time was glassy-eyed, saliva dribbling from his mouth. That particular incident took place a few days before his departure, before he had said his goodbyes to Domingo Buenaventura, right there, behind that very window he was gazing at. He had no desire to recall past frustrations nor to track down the sources of slander against him. He had only been told that his articles were not worth a damn. One reporter had added that he was a fifth-rate beginner who just didn't know the ropes.

. . . One night we had been playing dominoes for hours. We were in the top floor room where Sebastián lived—amidst the rattling water tanks and the dust blown in from the wind. I had been winning one game after another; Sebastián insisted that it was my lucky night, and José Augusto wanted to keep on playing. We kept on until we realized it was four o'clock in the morning. The son of a bitch Banderas wouldn't give up: he kept clenching his fists, intent on the chips. The rage that exuded from his pores was unmistakable. By and by, Sebastián commended us to the devil and said he was worn out. "No longer am I the man I was," he muttered. He threw himself on the bed and in no time fell sound asleep. After half a dozen games or so, my luck petered out, with José Augusto chalking up more and more points. When he finally caught up with me, I suggested we leave it at a draw. But his stubbornness knew no bounds and he insisted that we play a bit longer. Once he had gotten way ahead of me he was satisfied and smoked a cigarette at leisure with the airs of a sybarite. With Sebastián still snoring like some kind of beast, we suddenly realized that it was already morning. As we stumbled upon the silence on Colima Street, José Augusto looked as if he had slept all night. All of a sudden, quite near the sidewalk, I spotted a rat and managed to throw a stone at it. "Have more respect for life!" he said coldly. Two days later, I happened to see a whole bunch of disinfectants and packages of rat poison in his kitchen. I didn't say a word and neither did I mention the pistol he had hidden in a desk drawer: I could only think about his great victory at dominoes and the stone that I had hurled so wide of the mark . . .

Still facing the building at Sinaloa, Gabriel felt shaken by the thousands of long-buried memories, as if the invisible had materialized into the concrete. He firmly resolved not to churn up his anxieties and exasperation. That same afternoon he had gone by Bucareli Street and had looked up at the windows of the newsroom where he had spent so many hours glued to his typewriter, where they had wrangled over this article or that editorial. *You haven't the slightest news sense. You, Gabriel, are all over the place. You create too many problems and stir up too many people. We don't need you here any more so it's time to find a replacement for you. And listen, just so you don't think I'm trying to starve you to death and have you turn into an ass-kisser, the only thing I can do for you is put you in touch with a news agency.*

He had been unable to come up with a suitable retort, and a few hours later, still unable to think of one, Gabriel had gone to see Sebastián and talked for hours. Lashing out against his loneliness and boredom, he found solace in alcohol and trivial anxieties. He had to start from scratch somewhere else, shrug off the backstabbing and muster up enough macho to move toward new horizons.

Suddenly, half a block from the building, on Oaxaca Avenue, as the traffic lightened and the street lights glared even more intensely, he heard an almost nasal voice warbling snatches from old corny songs, like those he used to hear around the Nonoalco district when he first began to hang around, had his first puffs of marijuana and began his dalliances with the daughter of the hardware store owner. *Get with it, you clod, as if you were such a lover-boy, Hell, you're still pure as the driven snow, innocent little lamb, shrinking violet—it's about time you deflowered her. Once and for all, why don't you make it with that chick and cut out that faggy stuff?—running back and*

24

forth from one corner to another, sneaking free rides on the back of the trolley cars.

As the nasal voice died down, he reflected on how shadows had accumulated, on ill-fated reminiscences and erstwhile pleasures, dwelling on silences and on drinking, on the first woman he had ever slept with—a prostitute, her arms extended, opening her flabby flesh to him, her too-wet—perhaps even dirty—vagina, her waves of perspiration while showing him a scar on her abdomen, and the futile travesty of lust.

He returned to the vague, distant, smiles, to the confounded whys and wheres of his daily existence, to those splendid days of the rhumba dancers in the old black and white movies, with their magnificent, inaccessible thighs, their hips a cross between vulgarity and overwhelming sensuality.

Almost as a reflex action, he rang the bell once again, knowing that nobody would answer. He imagined its sound reverberating throughout Buenaventura's apartment, only to be muffled by the piles of books and yellowed photographs. He shrugged his shoulders and as he crossed the street he experienced a sudden indifference toward the future.

He was sure he could locate Andrea, that he could go to the other end of town and share his homecoming with her in the house in Coyoacán. He was well aware that he was barely at the preamble, at the preliminary stage of experimenting with new emotions and with the hare-brained ideas that one of the many Banderas was imposing on his consciousness.

. . . We had already left the tear gas smoke behind. I think that was after the Bay of Pigs demonstration. Our eyes still smarting, we first took refuge in a hotel lobby, and then walked along Juárez Avenue until we reached Bucareli. José Augusto wouldn't stop talking; in his customary manner of explaining things—furrowing his brow, raising and lowering his hands, his imperious tone—he would switch back and forth from the Industrial Revolution to the hotbeds of insurrection in remote jungles. He would quote certain writers, presenting examples from the past century and transplanting them to the present. Squinting, he would move his clenched fist at arm's length. Once we reached the Havana Café, after nodding to several familiar faces and settling down at a table in the back, Laura arrived and we began to talk about other things. All of a sudden, we were approached by a fellow who was completely drunk and who greeted Banderas effusively. They recalled God knows how many adventures they had been through together on the border, from the shacks on the sand dunes to raids on the wetbacks. A few minutes after the drunk had left us in peace, an extremely peculiar character came up to us— scrawny, pock-marked, with thick-lensed glasses and a quivering hand. He spoke to José Augusto about mysterious numismatic matters, about an International Society of the Occult and about Extracosmic Liberation. They decided to move to another table and spent a long time talking. When Banderas finally came back to us, he was detained by a beardless revolutionary who requested statistics on discrimination against homosexuals during the Victorian period. By this time, Laura and I had just about had our fill and had made up our minds to leave that screwball Banderas, and ask him to join us later on in the apartment on Sinaloa. José Augusto, however, felt completely at home, paying great attention to whomever happened to approoch him. When we decided to step out into the street, the "Great Madman," as Sebastián called him, was explaining to a reporter the significant role played by the Buenavista Railroad Station during the Carranza period. We turned toward Morelos Street, where José Augusto caught up with us. Laura smiled resignedly, and we then proceeded to hurl insults at the authorities for having suppressed the demonstration. Once we arrived at the apartment, I asked José Augusto why he wasted time in such an absurd fashion. He replied at once: "You haven't learned a thing, Gabriel. You're completely screwed up; honest to God, you're still a simpleton. If you call *that* absurd, why, I hope I always waste my time so absurdly. . . ."

From a phone booth on the corner of Oaxaca and Monterrey, Gabriel rang Andrea's home three times and no one answered. He felt as if every voice had fled him, as if he had been left with only the decaying buildings to keep him company in his brooding. He started toward the tunnels on Insurgentes Square, toward the rumble of the machines and the tireless labor of anonymous men half-buried in the ditches, their arms drilling the earth night and day, tearing down columns and hauling gravel and concrete.

A number of houses had been reduced to rubble: twisted beams, sticks and pieces of wood piled up against corners. Unable to reconcile the past with the present, he couldn't even manage to summon up an expression of rage. It was as if he was treading on something that no longer existed. Nor did he try to picture the way it had once looked or anything else that was irrevocably dead. He walked beyond Chapultepec Avenue, where he visualized, in the not too distant future, a cluster of towers jutting out against the sky and clouds. Through half-closed eyes, he distorted their flickering lights and the gleaming window panes.

Gabriel recalled his very first feelings of emptiness, his first heartaches. He had not thought about them for a long time; a woman, several years older than himself, who had left him without warning. He had spent only a few long nights, just a few times, with that extraordinarily vibrant body, those nipples between his lips or brushing his legs, the soft moans, magnified by the ensuing midday fulfillments. For a few weeks after the last dawn they had spent together, it seemed impossible to him that he could ever accept her rejection. It was the first time in his life that he had come face to face with anguish. As it turned out, he emerged from that experience open to other attachments; ready to learn not to take himself quite so seriously and to laugh at himself, *realizing once and for all that what the hell, one must learn to keep one's cool, and above all, to handle it when dealing with these particular matters.*

"Don't lose your way in an endless tunnel, full of puddles and rocks. Life is hard, but what can we do if a woman's bun is such a tasty tidbit?" Sebastián ventured, in an attempt to fill up the void.

Since he had no desire to keep walking straight ahead, Gabriel returned to survey the demolitions and the rubble. He strolled among the twisted metal and the discarded rails, trying to take pleasure in the figures that sprang up suddenly between the trees on Oaxaca Avenue. The dark fountain of Miravalle Square loomed in the background, with its abandoned benches and the furtive caresses of a few couples. Little by little, he traced in his mind the features of José Augusto's mother—Old Banderas' widow—and tried to imagine her first reaction to the news of the crime.

When he perceived the scent of ashes in the wind, he eased the tension in his jaw and neck muscles. He kept on walking, from one end of the block to the other, on the opposite side of the street, through the passage leading to Sinaloa Street and past strange, unfamiliar doors, solitary doorbells and balconies. He decided then and there to find Sebastián no matter what.

And, as the city made way for the bustle of its nocturnal pleasures, it dawned on Gabriel that many of his phantoms were no longer hollow; there was no longer any doubt that the shadows had a long story behind them.

IV

IN ABSOLUTE DISBELIEF, THE old widow had received the telephone call early one April morning, a few hours before reading the papers. The voice she heard was real, the voice José Augusto used on rare occasions, a disspirited, stunned voice. He dispelled none of her doubts, tumbled out his words, rambled on about the wholly inconceivable affair, while taking care to absolve himself of any blame.

The widow recalled each and every word in precise detail, comparing it to the new stories, weeding out the contradictions and half truths, questioning José Augusto's sketchy version and rejecting the newspaper interpretations. There was no concrete explanation, no single conclusive fact, nor was there the slightest clue as to how he had escaped.

Austere, forthright, her mind still as sharp as ever, old Banderas' widow glanced fleetingly at the faces she saw through the window — teenagers embracing, nonchalant cyclists, children running back and forth across the street, scrawny salesmen and pregnant women; and then she focused on the room around her and the fifty-odd years she had lived there since the first day of her marriage, some thirteen years before José Augusto was born. Straining to retrieve long-forgotten memories, she began to feel overwhelmed, as if the hours had lengthened, the waiting become interminable, indefinite. Her thoughts returned to the phone call, to the vague, perhaps deceptive words which clouded rather than clarified.

Amidst the rising suns and the clouds on the Chinese fans, the pleats of the folding screen and the porcelain vase, the old widow sat in her armchair, resting her feet on a stool. She relived one episode after another: her husband Banderas arguing with her father on the steps of the Chamber of Deputies, or the Banderas who was born in the Hospital de Jesús, the same Banderas who was now in hiding, the Banderas of the always detached and perfunctory farewells. She went on to compare the similarities and differences between the son and the father, dwelling on the interminable personality clashes, wounding comments and long-standing rift between them. "I can't stand that bastard any longer," old Banderas would grumble. "One of these days, he's going to do something really asinine. First, it was the carousing around, and now the so-called revolutionary craze. What with all those oddballs he runs around with, he isn't going to get anywhere," the old man had snorted many years before he died, as if he visualized his son hanging around the bars in the Merced market area or the whorehouses on Vizcaínas Street.

The old man never tired of his warnings, which only served to gnaw further at his dwindling expectations. Then he would gleefully resume the quarrels, the subterfuges, his many guises—now gentle, now harsh—and his apprehensive or petty tactics. At this point, his wife, who had not seen José Augusto for months, and who welcomed any excuse to know more about the life he was leading, would not utter a single word, preferring instead to reflect quietly on José Augusto's eccentricities, broodings and arrogance.

Despite the constant shifts in fortune they had undergone in the remote past, Mrs. Banderas scoffed at her own family's purported gentility. She recalled the elderly gentlemen relatives who had been educated in London in the mid-nineteenth century, the fortunes of dubious origin obtained during the period of Political Reform through real estate transactions involving formerly owned Church property in the Clavería and Narvarte districts, the bankers from the Porfirian period who negotiated with financiers from Paris and Berlin, and the others, the *bon vivants*—the first to introduce the automobile and the *zarzuela* to Mexico. She could only think back wistfully on that old house on Villalongín Street with its shade cast by the trees behind the greenhouse and the trellis covering the walls. She was born here and this was where she first discovered how fortunes were frittered away and where family grudges eventually were brought out into the open.

Then came the "rabble, the mob, the Indian scum who seized everything, those inferior beings who eat like animals, who coarsen everything they touch; that riffraff who should be in the mines, in the fields or in the dungeons," as her father described those who forced them to go into exile in San Antonio. Although when "The revolution was over, and the Villistas and Carranclanes petered out," he managed to secure a position in the Monte de Piedad Pawnshop "so as not to starve to death; after all, these apocalyptic times will be over soon enough, and any day now we will be back in power." By that time, the house on Villalongín had changed hands and his daughters had married "members of that very same riffraff," who, little by little, had settled in the old neighborhoods and had taken over the government jobs.

José Augusto's mother began her married life caught between a past that constantly clashed with the present, between the bewildering Victorian moral code and anticlerical struggles, mazurkas on the piano and anonymous *corridos*, coming and going from her cherished heirlooms to devastated streets. In her mind, she still found herself going back and forth from the noise of automobiles to the smell of detergent, from plastic knick-knacks to old fashioned oil lamps, from staring at the marquees over the neighborhood movie theaters, to television screens or a still life on the dining room wall.

After gazing at her turn-of-the-century photographs and finishing her cup of tea, the old widow pondered over the long separation from her husband several years after José Augusto was born, when old Banderas decided to go North and publish a newspaper there. This was the period when he used to bellow at the drop of a hat, his brown eyes giving off sparks of sarcasm, or his black moods conveying his rage, his pent-up fury. He left without offering many explanations, with a perfunctory farewell, and perhaps with a secret impulse to slam the door. It was the first time she had ever experienced loneliness; it permeated her body, her nights, her days. Little by little, she came face to face with frustration and the determination to gather her strength, to carve out a future for herself at any cost. This was at a time when apartment buildings were springing up all over town, and market-stalls, crammed together, and businesses of all types appeared overnight—from drugstores and taco stands to general stores and pool halls, from music shops to seafood places. The day old Banderas came home still weaving his grand schemes and sporting a new smile and an addiction for tobacco, she welcomed him back as if nothing had happened; she stifled her resentment. The only thought that came to her was that José Augusto's puberty was already a thing of the past.

> . . . I saw Mrs. Banderas lots of times; I remember seeing her at the haberdashers, in the market or on the steps of the San Rafael Church. There's no denying the fact that she belonged to another world, a world far removed from ours. I never fully understood her relationship with José Augusto; he never spoke of her and never invited anyone over. Several years later when we were both working on the same newspaper, strangely enough, he asked me to come

along with him to visit her. As a matter of fact everything was just as I had imagined it. The furniture was very much like what I had seen in other apartments in the same neighborhood: huge loveseats, lace curtains, old-fashioned mirrors, oval picture frames and latticed windows. On that particular occasion, she reminisced about the period before her marriage which was about the time when the old paper currency was replaced and Carranza rose to power. Then she remarked in a good natured way on José Augusto's sullenness. They lived on what José Augusto made from his articles and on the pension old man Banderas had left them. Sometimes they had to pawn or sell assorted personal effects: 19th century tablecloths, the Sevres china, old coins, and, now and then, a rare book. Creased with wrinkles around her eyes, the veins jutting out from the backs of her hands, her face lightly powdered, the old lady still retained a certain air of grandeur, a kind of pride in regarding herself as well born. Holding a magnifying glass between her fingers, her voice feeble, with her Grecian profile and her dark eyes like José Augusto's, she complained of failing eyesight. As she sat in her armchair, her head thrown back condescendingly, she told us that we were naive when it came to politics, that "everyone is cannon fodder, even those who reach the top." At no time did José Augusto, with his mixture of understanding and skepticism, resignation and familiarity, ever contradict her. Before we left, she asked him not to be so fickle and to come see her more often. Once we were out in the street, after a long silence and without further explanation, he said: "Look, Gabriel, I don't know if you understand me. Whenever I go over there, my father's shadow still bugs the hell out of me. I don't know who the hell is to blame. Anyway, there's still a lot of unfinished business in this goddamned shitty life."

After leafing through a book—a strange piece written by a distant uncle, the old lady recalled her husband's voice, his intense political activity, his strolls throughout every corner of the city, and his incredible isolation after years and years of unflagging enthusiasm. The staunch, resolute nature he had displayed during his younger years had given way to compromise, pretense, and finally to boredom, perhaps even to memories of cursory love affairs or some unrequited passion.

"Lázaro Cárdenas was Lázaro Cárdenas! but I wouldn't give you a nickel for a whole barrelful of Cardenistas. They can go to hell!" he would

31

bluster, cocking his head to one side and snapping his fingers. Sometimes he would pace up and down the corridor, running his fingers through his whitened temples and talking to himself.

Little by little, old Banderas began to detach himself from material things, to restrain any motivation, as if he were perfectly content to bask in his failures. Finally, the day arrived when he had no further need for his many facades; he preserved only one till the end—stony, impenetrable, perhaps in the belief that his digressions could not be revealed. "This city!" he rasped, and then, "Who knows what we're coming to!" She never saw him argue with his friends anymore. In the old days he would raise his hands imperiously in defense of Calles and Obregón, and attack the counterrevolutionaries with explosive fervor.

Old Banderas was buried in the San Joaquín cemetery on a Saturday at high noon, with the sun blazing down on the cypress and eucalyptus trees bordering the paths. Only a handful of people followed the coffin. On the way to the grave, a grim-faced José Augusto was deeply immersed in his own conjectures. As he gazed at the parched earth and the dilapidated tombstones, he felt more outrage than regret. He had a sense of desperation and defeat, that vital issues remained unresolved. Often he had thought that some day they would meet halfway, that one Sunday the two of them would laugh over their past quarrels and banish all trace of the antagonism that had existed between them. He disliked funerals and he found it hard to accept that this was, in fact, a corpse before him; that a cold body, eyes closed, hands rigid, was slowly being moved toward the grave. He remembered his father smiling on the corner of Madero and Bolívar, in the barbershop on Saturday mornings, or among the pine trees in the Desierto de los Leones. He saw him sitting, watching television, smoking a cigarette and scratching his beard, his thoughts far away. Then, old Banderas was standing beside the rocking chair in the living room, once more deep in silence, raging at the whole world, moving only his lips and causing the metallic grating of his dentures. It seemed to José Augusto that this last farewell was grotesque, unacceptable; the old man could not possibly just turn into ashes without squaring accounts, speaking plainly for once in his life and settling their differences so as to lay the groundwork for later imaginary quarrels and make-believe conflicts. As the last handful of earth fell on the casket, another impossible notion came into his head: he thought of turning himself into the kind of person who could simply obliterate his memories.

"I did have the opportunity to become acquainted with Old Man

Banderas. At that time, he worked in *El Nacional*. He was, I swear to God, a real man. It was just a matter of listening to him, of having a little bit of patience with him. He was very much a character of his time; didn't say much, but when he did the things he said carried weight. Then he became a first-rate columnist, and in that respect, José Augusto can't hold a candle to him. Later, he grew bitter—some said it was because of one of those love affairs that comes at the wrong time in life. There are plenty of women who harbor a grudge forever. Maybe it was politics, or this shitty country—who knows?" Sebastián declared, eager to sort out José Augusto's roots and probe further into the inner turmoils of the Great Lunatic.

It seemed to the old widow that as far back as she could remember, ever since she lived in the house on Villalongín, Sunday afternoons were always the longest. A rush of thoughts flooded her mind and her distress was reflected not only in her face, but also in the movements of her fingers. Every sound seemed to gather more and more momentum: the noise of trolleys screeching to a halt half-a-block away, the honking of horns in front of the movie house, and the cries of the street vendors were all jumbled together. She would stand and look out the window, listen to the news on the radio or polish the glass cabinet in the dining room with a flannel cloth. She was reminded of her mother's aquarium, the noiseless fish that seem to drift around in silence. She pictured herself waiting for her brothers as they arrived from anywhere, listening to their quarrels or the bragging about their conquests, as she sat on the courtyard steps watching a dark moth flitting in and out among the wooden slats. And ever since that phone call, Sunday afternoons became even more unbearable. She became obsessed with going over the conversation word by word, looking for José Augusto's body, eyes, gestures, movements, in those anonymous faces that shifted from one side of the street to another.

Her loneliness dragged on and the irrational sentences haunted her again and again, overlapping as if they could touch other more distant phrases and link themselves to other echoes, to age-old noises from the cellars and rooftops. Three weeks after the fateful news, in a few moments of clearheadedness, she adopted a definite vow of silence. She strove in vain to sum up both of her lives and to maintain a reasonably pleasant smile.

She wandered back and forth along spacious avenues, cobblestoned streets and solitary parks, pressing her lips as she panted or gradually succumbing to fatigue. Relentlessly, she mulled over the accounts in the newspapers, the photographs of José Augusto, beardless, expressionless, his hair cut short, the thick eyebrows, the carelessly-knotted tie. The interpretations of the crime were all there: Laura issuing her statement, perhaps perjuring herself, perhaps doomed to live in a vacuum for a long time to come.

Growing wearier by the minute as she kept turning the news over and over in her head, the widow was ultimately able to reproduce the whole sequence from beginning to end, straying off, as she did so, into more and more tangents. Although she could scarcely believe her ears, it seemed to her that she could almost hear old Banderas' attacks against Vasconcelos and Lombardo, his aversion for the new rich and for corrupt leaders. And she could almost see José Augusto right behind him, without the slightest trace of down on his chin, playing with his pick-up sticks or doodling in one of his rectangular-shaped notebooks. She relived the anguish she had felt when she saw the two of them target shooting in a field on the Toluca highway—the father teaching the son to shoot straight, to hold the gun steady, and to take aim without flinching.

As the days slipped by, the neighborhood—from San Cosme to Sullivan and from the British cemetery to the street formerly known as Ramón Guzmán—underwent a sudden transformation. "Things speak for themselves. The Monument to the Mother is the symbol of the new era," old Banderas had said once, in reference to the eyesore that had been built not far from Paseo de la Reforma on the spot where the Colonia railroad station had stood for so many years.

Little by little, as her surroundings became increasingly unreal, she envisioned herself in braids, leaving the French Lycée, her books pressed to her chest, or bending her adolescent face forward—among many other faces, other smiles, opposite a long banquet table. She was engrossed not only in magnifying the past but in striving to reject the idea of José Augusto's guilt. One thing she was certain of: very soon she would be getting a letter.

One endless Sunday afternoon, overwhelmed by doubts and showing visible signs of decline in mental powers and in her nervous system, the widow began transposing countless images in desperation at not being able to move her arm and to see no further than the rug, the screen and the window.

A few days later, the demolition crew set to work, night and day, widening the Ribera de San Cosme, dismantling the rails from the tramways and tearing down old buildings. By a curious coincidence, the hammering on the sidewalks and walls ran parallel to her loss of movement,

34

the advance of arteriosclerosis and her disjointed thoughts. She died one Thursday morning, the same day the drilling began on the tunnels for the metro line now part of Tacuba, which ends in Taxqueña. She was buried alongside her husband's grave in the San Joaquín cemetery with only the servant, a neighbor and a couple of relatives present. Barely a week later, a letter arrived at the abandoned apartment; it was later returned to the address of the sender—from which José Augusto had long since vanished—a letter that no one read, written in dark ink, feverish handwriting and prophetic tones—a message searching for clarity and guidance, an effort that slipped by unnoticed and was ultimately buried, like a flickering ember, among the thousands of other envelopes and papers bearing made-up return addresses.

V

AFTER A GREAT MANY inquiries and unsuccessful phone calls, I finally managed to locate Sebastián at the home of one of his brothers. The tone of his voice on the phone filled me with a sense of foreboding as did his penchant for distorting, at whim, the most irrelevant facts. My return shook him out of his self-contemplation, and must have triggered off his imagination. The sweeping statements, friendly banter and same old refrains were an unmistakable sign that Cardoso was in a snit, with the kind of hangover that lasted for days and warped his sense of reality. Nevertheless, he could hardly wait to savor the latest piece of news; as he himself told me once, "Yes, indeed, Gabriel, there is no greater high than the apocryphal reconstruction of our biographies."

At first, I had the feeling that he was holding back, that he really didn't give a damn if he ever saw me again. But once he started quoting, "It is I who, of yore, recited naught but the azure verse and the profane song," there was no doubt in my mind that sooner or later we would take up where we had left off. Besides, his words seemed to transcend the commonplace and convey a certain air of arrogance as if he always had the upper hand, as if, at a moment's notice, he could undergo any given metamorphosis: ruler of the universe, clairvoyant, cryptic and demoniacal poet, old hand at detecting our phony games, and incorrigible theorist when it came to any new organization.

Around eight o'clock, I waited impatiently for Sebastián at the bar on Artes Street, a couple of blocks away from the Monument to the Revolution. While I drank my beer, I observed the domino players with their restless fingers, their self-humoring jokes, and their total absorption in the game. At the far end of the bar there was a fellow drinking all alone; he seemed to be muttering insults to himself or perhaps he was just brooding over some long-lost love. He kept peering at his glass of rum, caressing it, cursing it as if fed up with his loneliness and his daydreams. Once in a while, a few office clerks would drop in, toss down a couple of drinks and leave without even noticing the other patrons of the place.

Finally, Sebastián arrived more than an hour late, grumbling about the traffic, the rain, the floods, this damned city that had been the backdrop for his entire life. At first, he avoided my gaze by signalling to the waiter, stretching his arm, sniffling or staring at the dominoes. It was obvious from the start that he was putting on an act, playing at being aloof and reluctant to stir up old memories.

A couple of stock phrases were followed by a few choice expressions on the "scum of the earth" and his numerous pet peeves. He was wearing a gray jacket and a white shirt, his dark, wavy hair reaching down to the nape of his neck. His owl-like face was sharper, his whale-like body considerably thicker than I remembered. He extended his enormous hands, swinging them up and down and then remained still, with a scornful glance toward the bar which seemed to say that he was a cut above everybody else and that no one there was worthy to touch the cuff of his pants.

"Well, here I am, you knucklehead, the Declining Empire itself," he said, apropos of nothing at all, and taking out a pack of his perennial Faro cigarettes. As always, he licked the Faro rice paper before ordering his drink.

When he finally settled down, I realized that he was showing off his wide assortment of gestures. But he had no control at all over those owlish pupils of his which never failed to reflect every single one of his moods. He licked a cigarette and it seemed to me that his initial half-smile was strained, and that this tableau could well mark the beginning of one hell of a night.

Sebastián rambled on in the same vein, his sentences disjointed. The rage in his eyes throbbed in his temples and seemed to spread to the very flame of the match he was lighting. He smoked leisurely, motioning for his usual drink, acting for all the world as if he owned the place. He ranted on about the cutting, rainy wind of the past few days.

"Why the fuck did you come back? I really think you've run your course. Yes, Gabriel, your coming back is nothing but a miserable waste of time," he said, without further preamble. When the waiter placed the glass of whiskey on the table, Sebastián held his breath, and before taking the first swig, cried, "Cheers, Carcass!" by way of acknowledging my presence. Then I was able to take a closer look at him—the bearing of a sybarite which had been his trademark for several years, the round cheeks, the bulging nose, the half-grown beard and the first traces of wrinkles on his forehead.

"I told you straight out just before you left. Here we live from day to day, and we're still slinging the same old shit, buddy, and going from bad to worse. We're done for, going downhill fast, and tearing each other apart—and now, what with the Supermadman, the Grand Marshall flying the coop, that's the clincher. Don't play dumb with me, you know it as well as I do," he went on, his suppressed anger gradually mounting. He touched the glass and fiddled with an ice cube.

"Well, what do you know! At least, when you insult someone like that, it means you're on the same wave length," I blurted out, as Sebastián was guzzling his second drink.

I was well aware that I had to summon up all my patience to listen to his lame excuses for the same old bullshit, the same old blind spots, the far-fetched reasons for past blunders, the pompous invectives against the times we were living in, and the exaggeration of truth and falsehood alike. And, as I gradually found myself having to put up with all those trite rationalizations, I realized that Sebastián had always clung to his mirages, to what he called our real years. In just a few moments, I was convinced beyond reasonable doubt that Cardoso, for all his charisma and great talent, was in an extreme state of withdrawal and on the verge of collapse. Years ago we still hadn't the faintest inkling that the real years were barely approaching. While he spoke of certain legendary figures, I thought about his shabby room where we had said our goodbyes three years ago, about his sudden outbursts and the sour aftertaste of those long nights. I reflected on Sebastián's speculations about his own death and the inscription on his tombstone, his constant denial of his own inconsistencies, news of his twenty-year-old son living in New York, memories of his two trips to Paris, the effects of his debauchery on future peak years, and of the chances of his altering the course of his misfortunes.

Meanwhile, as the whiskey soothed his throat, clearing his raspy voice and his inner turmoils, Sebastián was warming up for a detailed account of half the city, the chronicle of all the different places where he had lived through the years. He expounded on particular neighborhoods or districts rather than to indulge in any sarcasm that might betray him, avoiding the slightest slip of the tongue that could expose his painful scars. There was no doubt about it: he persisted in erecting supposedly impressive barriers of pretense on the flimsiest of foundations.

He began with the "homely, barren room" on Colima Street, amidst

38

the laundry hanging out to dry and the screeches of the servant girls, the stench from toilets and the noise of transistor radios that started blaring at dawn. He spoke of the femme fatale who allegedly visited him there, an "incredible nymphomaniac whose two erect domes" barely fit in his hands and which he never tired of kneading, squeezing, nibbling, and enjoying in all their splendor.

"In spite of these conquests, I feel that everything is coming apart at the seams. My immortality has breathed its last and I am presiding over the wake," he asserted, with a certain dose of good humor, fervently intertwining his fingers.

He then proceeded to describe the gnarled old trees, the splendid house that had been torn down on Alvaro Obregón Avenue and been replaced by an apartment building so hideous as to be beyond belief. There were no ladies there, no orgies, not one single wild weekend. From there, he moved to a second floor apartment directly opposite the Freeway, with an unbearable din from traffic, smog bumping against his window and families sprouting all over the rooftops and tenement buildings: "Just picture a great flock of crows smudging up the blue heavens."

After downing his first drink, smoking a couple of cigarettes and pounding the table with the back of his hand, he went on to tell of the back rooms of a house near the bullring, bordering on the Mixcoac district, where he had to put up with the stingiest landlady in the world and her son-of-a-bitch kids who lived in the front part of the house and did little else but play on their limp, sugary string instruments and taunt him as if he were a broken down old fatass.

By this time, I could barely get a word in edgewise, so I let him weave his lastest myths so that he felt free to launch into the creation of his own image. Abruptly he referred to his imaginary scorpions, and to the "benevolence of those magnificent arachnids" who followed him from place to place, lightening his burden, particularly during his long, solitary nights or when some stray freeloader just happened to drop in. He dwelt at length on the last woman who had made a wreck of him—the one who made love to him with all sorts of artefacts and who was adept at assuming all the positions imaginable, her firm round buttocks glistening with eau de cologne and the very finest perfume from Paris. It dawned on me then that the old liar was outdoing himself, since by now he thrived not only on his own exploits, but on the vanity and lasciviousness of others as well.

"That woman is something else: full hips, full breasts, a navel that is a feast for the eyes and hands and for the mouth that craves it. You have no idea, it's indescribable."

The fellow who had been sitting at the other end of the bar sauntered over to our table carrying his drink and his hangups with him. He ignored the domino players and wound up sitting next to Sebastián, greeting him as if they were lifelong friends. Without warning, he broke into Sebastián's description of a hangout for hoodlums near the airport with a harangue on how goddamned shitty life is: "Listen, you haven't the slightest idea of what it is like to have a cross nailed here, right in your chest, to feel insulted up to the balls, alone except for my spirit and this poor fucked-up brain of mine, bored, so bored, overwhelmed by so much bullshit." Sebastián stared at his eagle-like profile, gripped his glass and rapped out: "Hey. If you want to wallow in scum get the hell out of here. We don't have to listen to all this sniveling from a corpse. So lay off, because we're not on your trip, buddy—let us alone and take your sackcloth and ashes somewhere else."

The fellow hardly opened his mouth. He glanced at Sebastián out of the corner of his eye, puckered up his face and got up, as if nothing had happened. I had to hand it to him, Cardoso had already become an expert at handling this kind of situation and also in using it to his advantage when it suited him, even at times when his own shouts seemed to pierce the walls, damage telephone receivers, or when he greeted the new day with his futile merrymaking. Many a night he had even shouted curses at street lamps.

Sebastián rambled on. More houses, more neighborhoods, more dens of iniquity came and went: the shabby Escandón district, full of markets and businesses of all kinds; the residence of a politician friend of his in San Angel where the best French wines flowed freely; a boarding house in Churubusco that was a veritable pandemonium with wild parties attended by rowdy drunks. Then came the repeated and exaggerated references to his hallucinations, to his disgust at all those bloated faces and the slobs who were always there. He gave an unexpected twist to his short-lived infatuations and to his erratic personality changes. Gritting his teeth, he then ventured an explanation for the baffling victory scored by the corrupt.

"You know what you can do with patriotism. But I'm fed up to the gills with this goddamned fucking country where everything rankles, where everything is expressed through defiance, or better said, through seething outrage."

Undoubtedly it would be Sebastián's quest for the unattainable which would ultimately plunge him deeper and deeper into misfortune, into reconciling his hatreds with his nostalgia and to working out gleefully the details of his own funeral and the wording for his epitaph. Perhaps for the first time I was beginning to understand Sebastián – the Sebastián ten years older than I, my partner in leisure, the Great Cardoso of the endless stream of words steeped in fantasy.

"See here, you clod, never lose sight of the sage counsel to move on to new horizons and seek one's fame and fortune in new lands. I can remember every word, but I am the worse for it, because if you merely move from place to place without changing your lifestyle and habits as well, you never really get anywhere. That's why things have turned out the way they have for me. I only change places, I am a formless shadow, I am a contradiction. . . ."

He began by extolling the joys of living and then he talked about the whorehouse in the Narvarte district where he had lived more than three weeks. He explained that under no circumstances should he be mistaken for a common lecher. He ordered another drink and I was tempted to go back in time, to retain those instants in my mind in which little by little, his entire face, his body, his elbow on the table and his fingers stroking each other, were lost in thought and transported to the climate of apathy that prevailed in every one of those places he described.

"What happened to José Augusto? I'm sure you must know a great deal," I broke in later, after the waiter took our order, amidst shouts from the domino players. I had asked the question spontaneously, attempting to draw him out of his moodiness and make him forget his meanderings and phantoms once and for all. Underneath all that shrewdness one could detect the longing to take himself seriously.

The malicious grin, the slow, deliberate movement of his cigarette, the glitter in his eyes and the furtive grumble proclaimed that we had arrived at one of his favorite subjects. Muttering, "Aw, what the hell," he sank back into a different kind of silence. He started cramming a series of images together, endowing them with endless symbolism, reconstructing past events and torrid love affairs as if he had the power to turn himself into José Augusto Banderas. At the same time he was getting up enough steam to launch into his own interpretations, mostly to satisfy his own ego. He made a point of converting any nuance into a veritable saga, endowing it with mysterious inferences. He scratched a couple of hairs his jowls could not hide and licked another cigarette with even more relish than

41

before. "It's been over a month since I saw Laura. I swear to God, her face has gotten so hard," he said coldly.

Stroking his fingers with his thumb, Sebastián called for another drink and chuckled to himself. Each of his gestures—the vehemence in his fists, the way he inhaled the cigarette he was lighting, the renewed intention to live each moment to the hilt—were all unmistakable signs that betrayed his state of hallucination. It was most assuredly not in his nature to acknowledge the silences of others; for it was only his own fears that emerged. Contempt colored his language and he assumed the airs that supposedly corresponded to his status.

As he touched upon José Augusto's life, the old liar once again fell back on every possible device: long-winded sentences, precise adjectives, inadvertent contradictions; his voice was tempered by each new episode as if he had the capacity to interpret the inner conflicts of each of his characters. Banderas, he claimed, could have risen above mediocrity, and escaped years of isolation and self-absorption, but his personality gradually underwent a change. He learned to come on strong, to leave his mark on each and every situation. He was well aware of his powers to influence and transform those around him. He went from the unknown to the concrete, from fear to the courage of his convictions. He was always drawn by the persistent magnet of action but firmly rooted in his own mettle and character and so invulnerable to any kind of underhanded attack.

"Because you see, Carcass, José Augusto wasn't swallowed up by trivia; he wasted no time on second-raters. Even if he was shocked at himself for killing that guy, he managed to measure his fear and ward off any pursuit. Can you picture José Augusto jumping from one rooftop to another, mustering up the guts to plan his escape without leaving a single clue, letting his pursuers know that he had carried out a master stroke? Because that's just what his flight was: a masterpiece of cunning. He left no loose ends, made not one single mistake, you get that—not one single mistake! On the other hand, he made us think about the brutality we all keep hidden deep down and which can flare up at any moment. I'm not trying to justify anything—to understand is not to justify. Listen to this carefully, old buddy, I know where he is, I know damn well what route he took to leave the country—that confounded pilgrimage taken by his other personalities. But this secret will never leave me; my lips are sealed forever. So that's the story, Bones, whichever way you look at it and I'm certain that I'm the only one who knows this secret, and even under the worst possible circumstances, no one, absolutely no one, can worm it out of me. Prick up your ears and don't forget it, shithead. Now, just so you'll stop bugging me once and for all, let me tell you that yes, it's true, I love to get pissed and I can't resist a bit of skirt—in other words, "Life goes by with too much haste, so why should my smile just go to waste?"

Almost before he realized it, Sebastián had finished three more drinks and had stubbed out several cigarettes. During an unexpected lull in the conversation he leaned his head on the table, feigned a look of concern, gave a half-smile, scoffing not only at me, or at Sebastián Cardoso himself, but also at the waiter, at the dominos, the bets, and at the announcement from one of the players that he had won twenty games in a row. He mumbled several unintelligible phrases which were followed by, "Here the future holds naught but sloth and indolence," and "the inner flame scorches all; only thus does one triumph over rancor and death." After asserting that he always saw life through crimson-colored glasses and that in the blossoming lips of women there lurked a lethal poison, he ordered another drink, screwed up his lips, snorted in disgust, and divesting himself of all further speculation, crouched down in his chair as if he were hugging himself.

"And Laura? She's guilty too. To what extent, I don't know, but she's also guilty," he said harshly, as if he wanted to bring the discussion to an end, or maybe just to a pause.

"And what about us?" I asked, eager to be heard for the first time all evening. I doubt whether I was or not because from that moment on he got going on a whole string of inconsistencies, of oblique phrases, on the absurd game of threading his insults together, of probing into every single innuendo with his usual bombastic assertions.

When I asked for our check, he went so far as to insult the people at the other table, just at the precise moment when a blank domino closed the game. It could have been a voice from beyond the grave, for all the attention they paid him.

As we left, he asked me to leave him alone, suggesting that we postpone our helluva night for another time. For a long while, I watched as his enormous figure grew smaller and smaller behind the statue of Christopher Columbus, his arms flaying while he cursed buildings, his shadow, his sense of here and now and everyone living in it.

I walked in the opposite direction and a few minutes later I managed to spot the brightly-lit columns of the Monument to the Revolution. Just when the lights of the dome were going out, I believed for a moment that the dark sky was on the verge of lighting up, that the real years were hovering over us, and that perhaps they would be with us for a long time to come. I also reflected that to continue revolving around the symbols of fake exploits, in the very core of our own pettiness, was becoming more and more intolerable.

VI

OUT BEYOND THE WALLS, the night and rain died away slowly. José Augusto lay on the sofa remembering the last morning he had spent at the Sinaloa apartment. The moment he caught a glimpse of his reflection in the window, he became aware of the rancor building up inside of him. He had spent the whole morning in a tense monologue, his eyes blazing, his expression strained. Now he roamed around the darkened room amidst dank cigarette smoke, his own curses and his misgivings. His imagination in high gear, he darted back and forth from his father's tirades to Laura's breasts to the shouts of thousands of demonstrators, to the hideous faces he had seen near the Nonoalco Bridge. He hadn't the slightest idea then that in less than five months he'd be running scared, running away from himself and from others, the prelude to a long absence that would generate the most inconceivable myths with the most vile and preposterous interpretations imaginable.

José Augusto was in no mood to indulge in reminiscences about those early days with Laura, nor to recreate the sensations they had shared in the past—words and images dating back to the moment when his hands first became adept at wandering over her soft skin, his eyes recognizing her in the semi-darkness, their feverish breathing and her incomparable thighs. From time to time, he would rise to his feet and run his fingers across his temples, only to return to the sofa and ask himself: "*What the fuck good are all these memories to me? Just one is enough to get me down. It really screws me up to keep imagining, year after year, the one woman whom I ever cared about. It's a different story when you have memories of at least a few loves to choose from: Fantasies become less unreal and the sense of loss is not so irrevocable.*

Over and over again José Augusto had refused to admit the sheer hopelessness of his situation—the fact that Laura was gradually receding into the past and that he would never again see her naked body in the mirror. Most likely, she had no longer been able to cope with the same old clichés, and longed for nothing more than to rest her clear-eyed gaze upon another body, to rediscover her own voice in another, different voice, to free herself of his complicated rationalizations, of so many bonds, to escape from all that anxiety, from all those phantoms.

José Augusto lay back on the sofa again and stretched his legs, indifferent to the darkness around him and incapable of putting some order into the events of the past few days. He found it hard to believe that he was actually there, totally isolated, in that tiny hovel on the corner of Chilpancingo and Huatusco near the Viaducto freeway, where he had done nothing but curse at his own feelings, his mounting despair and the unbearable waiting which prolonged his sleepless hours. Everything was in a jumble: his self-contempt, his neglected mother, his frustrated political schemes, and his role as night owl turned reporter. Again and again he returned to those years he had wasted among shysters and pen-pushers, and then to Laura, always Laura, to her scent, to her magnificent legs spreading for someone else, to their jealous rages and to their goddamned, imaginary infidelities. He felt nauseated by the taste of the cigarette, his mouth sour and furry. The very idea of roaming through one more street repelled him; he didn't give a damn whether or not it was still drizzling outside.

After a while, he lost all sense of time. He wandered aimlessly into the bathroom and switched on the light. He was stunned by the face in the mirror, the conspicuously deep circles under tense, restless eyes, his hair matted and rumpled. He spat, swore a couple of times and then, with mixed feelings of distaste and apathy, proceeded to take a long, close look at himself, trying in vain to admit to his moodiness and the dissociations of his personality. For a moment he was convinced that Laura too felt the same anguish, that she too was subject to silent moans and inexplicable guilt. He knew she could not discard him easily and that for a long time to come they would both be haunted, not only by their conflicting drives, but also by the happy times they had spent in so many places, by their intensely erotic experiences and by each other's too familiar bodies.

He turned on the faucet, letting the water slip through the palms of his hands, rubbing them against his forehead, the circles under his eyes, and his mouth. Once again, he recalled a particular night at Buenaventura's apartment. His first sight of her had remained fixed in his mind forever after, a few images repeated ceaselessly—her slow, deliberate speech, her erect body, her firm, sinewy legs and her distant gaze. Underneath her blouse and skirt, her lingerie—unfamiliar to him then—had been waiting

46

for him, for his hands to explore those mysterious regions and the hollow between her breasts. That was the first night they spent together, a few hours before their first sunrise in the apartment on Sinaloa. It was the beginning of their life together; it had been a quiet, rainless night.

He shut off the faucet and after turning off the light he returned to his world of sheets and slumber and perspiration. It was only then— in his dreams and his nightmares—that he truly possessed her; it was only then that he could envision her so genuinely and intensely that she seemed to permeate his very marrow, and even the pores of his skin. As he lay there without her, he could feel the anxiety welling up in his throat and in the pit of his stomach. He smoked one cigarette after another, touching his hands now devoid of her scent. At times he longed to cry aloud just to listen to his own voice; he was unable to pull himself together or even to revive his crumbling, short-lived self-confidence.

During the past few weeks he had learned to curse her, to distort the past—with his cigarette as his sole companion, he extracted from its smoke a series of negative speculations on the years he had spent with her. It was always the sounds that ultimately betrayed him in the end. The screeching of trolleys, echoes in the stairways outside, or the whistles of the night watchman: all brought him back to Laura, to a once perfect, harmonious setting, free from delusions of any kind. He was aware that at any moment the images and words, the unbearable pain, the goddamned feelings that refused to die—not yet having exhausted the full range of past experiences—would be twisted out of shape. Over and over again he imagined himself walking at dawn, gazing at his reflection in the glass showcases and cats blinking at him through the shadows. José Augusto seemed to hear himself shouting at Laura; incapable of extricating himself from this last bedrock where his anguish had taken root, his self-condemnation reverberated throughout the room as he addressed the bare walls.

He discarded his shoes and jacket and let his thoughts dwell on his days with Laura. They were all pretty much the same, with no fixed schedules and very little company. He remembered thinking that he had finally deciphered the meaning behind her intricate words and sullen gestures. Every single effort, every sign of optimism had come to nothing. Suddenly, his thoughts were shattered by the noises outside and far-away faces, as if he were a shadow, a mere wanderer immersed in his own quandaries, in his own misery. He muttered meaningless phrases to himself, and barely summoning up the strength to curse to his heart's content, he confronted his own decline and his inner turmoils.

47

He was certain that by now Laura's body was open to new pleasures and that someone else was marveling at her nipples, stroking her thighs and learning to caress her soft skin and half-closed eyes during their lovemaking. Perhaps, at this very moment she was sleeping fully satisfied, and with the mirror—again the mirror—reflecting arms that had just embraced her and given her new alternatives, new outlets. Finally, José Augusto realized that the rain had stopped dead. His mouth was sour and his tongue more parched than ever. He threw himself on the bed and fell into a half-sleep.

After a couple of hours, when the first morning papers were piled up on the corner and the street lights were growing dim, he went down to Chilpancingo Street. He stuck a cigarette between his lips, put his hands in his pockets and started walking north. All traces of his former bravado, of his swaggering, had gone, as if he had lost all hope of retrieving the past. He waited patiently for the café on Insurgentes to open. Its regular patrons were, for the most part, impatient bureaucrats and people who had nothing to do. The ragmen and loaders sleeping around the barracks in the San Cosme market—a tableau from his early childhood almost thirty years ago—suddenly hit him like a bolt, sending his thoughts into a spin. After the first few sips of coffee, he grew tired of watching the street sweeper, the wan faces and the lonely figures on the street. He turned up the lapels of his coat to cover his neck, tried to breathe easily and sought refuge in the daylight.

During the long pauses between each cigarette and each cup of coffee, punctuated by the listless voices at the next table, he had tried to erase the images from his mind: his father's hard, dead, unforgettable face, the relentless afternoon rains driving the rats away from the sewers', his mother sitting in her timeless rocking chair, dreamy-eyed, her voice faltering. Other impressions also gradually melted away: Laura, and his yearning to take her in his arms, to embrace her, to see her naked, to meet her with his tongue, her breath on his, to see her eyes brimming with desire.

He stared at a marquee in front of him, all the while uttering a long monologue, going round and round *the legends you arbitrarily built up around yourself—the hard-boiled know-it-all. You had to go and play for the highest stakes, didn't you? You could't even manage to cover up your ruthlessness and your conceit. You've made up your own life, and worse still, you've done a shoddy job of it; you've wound up being nothing but a phony in a rut where nothing can possibly satisfy you. You thought you were a big shot, the greatest, and you've made a career out of faking it. Worst of all, you've never even learned how to laugh at yourself.*

Once back in the apartment on Chilpancingo, he re-read his article which had been published right in the middle of the editorial page, no less. He started weeding out the news, choosing a new topic from the items on hand. The images were blurred, tumbling out one after the other before his eyes: massacres in Indo-China, the strike at the University, the President's ominous statement, a peculiar train accident, a bank robbery here and there, a case of sabotage and a lone explorer reported missing on a remote island off the Atlantic Coast. He could, of course, go downstairs and call Laura, he had repeated her phone number to himself thousands of times, drumming it into his brain to the point of exhaustion. Perhaps, at this very moment she was working at the publishing house, smiling to herself, stopping to examine periodicals or browsing among the shelves. Sweat started trickling down his face and neck and he went back into the bathroom to splash water once more on his mouth and forehead, clenching his fists even more tightly.

Around nine o'clock, as traffic grew heavier in the streets and light streamed through the window, he was gradually overcome with fatigue and got back into bed, sprawling between the sheets to gaze at the curling smoke rising from his cigarette. Then he fell asleep, flat on his back, hands stretched out, palms open, his head burrowed in the pillow. He could vaguely hear the janitor sweeping the steps, one by one, and the sounds from the downstairs floors, the rooftops and the jacaranda branches. But no noise was capable of shaking him out of his nightmares or his despondency. He lay motionless, like a ramrod or a lifeless piece of wood nestling in a dark cave.

A few hours later, still in a half-stupor, he was awakened from his bizarre dream world by the janitor: He had a phone call. He went downstairs to the telephone on the first-floor landing to answer the call. It jolted him back to reality. The voice was firm, the threats piling up in rapid succession. He trudged up the stairs and opened the window to drain out the air that reeked of his own odors. For the last time, he glanced at his article and left it lying on the table next to the typewriter.

The sun had been shining on the piles of books and on the ashtrays overflowing with cigarette butts. A light breeze blew into the stuffy room; its walls were by now well accustomed to the invectives of its voluntary prisoner. He was utterly perplexed by the words spoken over the phone, and found it hard to believe they were the result of the article that had appeared that very morning. A few minutes later, he stubbed out his cigarette with his shoe, ignoring the dark stain it left on the floor. He let his arms go slack, sensing that his surroundings had recovered their proper dimensions. As his anxiety increased, the objects around him fell into place once again; the sky beond the new building across the street was dull and metallic, no different from any other sky on a November day.

He thought of calling Sebastián. "A mere trifle," he would probably scoff. "We've all been subject to this kind of thing at one time or another; it's best to pay no attention." Then he would surely evade the issue and lecture him on the virtues of mundane logic, or the ever-standing accuracy of rationalism, only to launch into his theory of violence and conclude with a long drawn-out historical explanation of authoritarianism.

As he lit another cigarette, Laura's body seemed to emerge among the folds of the sheets. Then he gazed absently at a point somewhere beyond the floor boards, drumming his fingers on the desk, wondering what to do next: whether to go back outside, wander through the city's streets and get it out of his system once and for all, or sit in some restaurant looking at old people's canes, tourists' phony smiles and waiters' indolent faces.

By this time, noon rush hour was in full swing on Chilpancingo Street with its honking school buses, racing engines and lines of chattering servant girls waiting for the garbage truck. He noticed dust on his fingertips— fingerprints on fingerprints, ashes creeping into his conscience. He put out his cigarette on a pile of butts and walked to the bathroom, feeling the gusts of wind whirling around the mirror. Abruptly, as he shaved, he remembered the pool halls in San Cosme, the swigs of rum between each turn, and the face of a cripple sitting all alone in the shadows, all set to hit him with his crutches without José Augusto's ever knowing the reason. As the razor grazed his face, the soap skimming along his chin and cheeks, he remembered that particular afternoon when that very same cripple, a loutish freak with burly arms and a misshapen face, had beaten him Lord knows how many times—on his forehead, his back, on one leg. The incident had left him totally dumbfounded and for a long time afterward he had hallucinations about those crutches which terrified him. About a week later, José Augusto had taken his father's gun, and without anyone's knowledge, had threatened the cripple. It only took a few seconds to intimidate him for good. José Augusto also knew that in his blind fury he had expressed the utter repugnance he felt for the cripple.

He left the razor on the edge of the basin, washed his face and went back to the room. He looked behind him, toward the door, the bed, the books on the floor, at the litter that kept piling up day after day. He closed the window, thinking about his lost dreams and the gradual fading of his aspirations. He persisted in walling up his thoughts, in clinging to them, certain that he could never again recapture the gift of sensuality. He squinted, running his hands over the nape of his neck, grappling once more with a series of muddled scenes.

Finally, he put on his shirt, slung his jacket over one shoulder, feeling the light from the window warming his back. He decided to go out, to hear familiar voices in an attempt to dispel his anguish, to defy it and to store it away in the farthest corner of his mind.

The slamming of the door scattered dust all over the apartment, and before going downstairs he stared at the gathering of particles as if they were a figment of his imagination, like the clouds of dust that gathered on the stairwell in the building in Sinaloa where the walls were perennial witnesses to the quarrels between furtive couples and the bitter outbursts of lonely outcasts. He recalled the basements from his childhood days; he remembered cubbyholes in closets and the places near the Buenavista station where hoodlums hung out. He stopped briefly before reaching the last step, imagining Laura's smile upstairs—the echoes drifting either way— only to melt away in the corridors. He jerked open the door looking for the sunlight and the bustling activity in the streets, the teeming city and perhaps, hidden between a gap in the clouds, a streak of blue. He turned his back on Chilpancingo Street and turned on Huatusco.

He barely had time to catch a glimpse of the windows across the street before he found himself hemmed in by four thugs who quickly over-powered him. It was two o'clock in the afternoon and the rooftops of the automobiles remained impervious to the damp autumn wind, the dry jacaranda leaves and to the silence of José Augusto, encircled by strange, menacing eyes.

51

VII

THE FOLLOWING EVENING I waited for Domingo Buenaventura's familiar figure to come along at any moment. The silence had been broken by the screeching brakes of an automobile and a belching drunk across the street. Once again I found myself standing opposite the building on Sinaloa Street. My headlong encounter with the city had unleashed a series of bewildering sensations, an endless jumble of sequences, one after another.

At last I spotted Buenaventura on the corner. I greeted him warmly, feeling the need to say what I felt: "Here we are again ready to take the world on. I guess that being so far away, my imagination must have been working overtime thinking about all of you."

Still engrossed in his own thoughts, Domingo weighed his words carefully: "For Christ's sake! Imagine your turning up here like this! You could have at least let us know you were coming back!" He shook my hand and then we walked down the empty street just as we used to on the way back from Andrea's more than three years ago, when, of one mind and for no reason at all, we would head for some other place. I sensed that before long dozens of vague memories would come flooding back to us.

Gesturing wildly and blurting out the words, I immediately started to explain my reasons for coming back: "I just couldn't take any more of the Parisians' *dolce far niente*. It was one continuous scene of anything goes. Besides, I had problems wherever I went. I lived from hand to mouth and didn't have much more to learn. At the news agency, things went from bad to worse." When Domingo opened the door to the building I broke off to look at the feeble streak of light barely flickering against the bannister and the first couple of steps.

For a few moments we stood still as if listening to distant echoes streaming out of the walls—from the smoky glass skylight to the grime on the tile floor, from the dogs' antics in the basement to the balancing act of a cat on the top floor. Gray walls, squeaky hinges, cracked beams, clouds of dust and clandestine lovers seemed to merge and then fade away along the stairwell, as if this particular empty space had the power to record age-old vignettes and provide different endings to current episodes.

As we climbed the creaking stairs, each squeak reminded us of the occupants in the apartments we passed—the bureaucrats, the Spanish refugees, the couple who met in their love nest twice a week. Other scenes came to mind: the first tenants who arrived during the Religious Persecution, the British engineer who ranted on about the oil expropriation, and the wizened, impassive face of the old maid with the shriveled legs. She had been found dead after several days and left to rot in the stench and decay of her own corpse.

. . . At that time, Domingo Buenaventura was still an unknown writer. His first short stories were pretty sordid, to say the least, and were a considerable departure from the prevailing taste of the time. Practically all his characters were decadent and morose loners who lived in slums on the fringe of society. I can still remember his description of the life of one of these outcasts in the Moctezuma district. The character spent his time rambling all over the place making fun of everybody—including God and his own mother. "Around here, life just drags on and on—like a treadmill. I don't know where people get the idea that living has some kind of divine spark about it, since only a handful of humans actually get anything out of it," he grumbled as he watched the planes come in at the airport. This guy was a cross between a down-and-out pimp and a truck driver without a penny to his name. At first, he was a singularly repulsive individual who gave the impression that life was just a big fiasco. But as the story went on, his other facets began to emerge: past and future were woven together simultaneously and somehow he got to you. By the middle of the story, it was impossible to give up on him. In his search for a mistress, whether tarnished or pure, and his habit of wandering through the steets he projected such a zest for life that you actually wound up liking the guy. After a series of comings and goings, the hero finally wound up in a rundown old Turkish Bath out by the Peñón spa, where he died, bathed in sweaty dreams . . . Buenaventura never stopped writing, even when the going was rough. Many times, when he seemed distracted we knew that he was actually writing, that in his mind he was recreating the atmosphere and images from the past . . . Of course, at times our criticism of his works was extremely harsh, especially when he went overboard in his descriptions of the groans of patients in the leprosariums or the brutal facts about an institution for syphilitics. Yet we lived to see the day when we had to eat our own words . . .

On my way upstairs I surrendered once more to my sense of fabulation, and the image of Laura flashed across my mind—worried sick and waiting up for José Augusto till all hours: "What the hell are you coming back here for if you can have your fun somewhere else? There's no point to it!" I thought of Laura, ready to return to her lonely life and to seek her pleasure elsewhere—the pleasures she had experienced up there in her room, with her swelling breasts, her avid mouth, her eager tongue.

The faint sounds of a melody played on electric instruments floated out of the last apartment on the top floor, the one nearest the roof. The long wail of the trumpet and the shrill chords of the double bass slashed into the apparently imperturbable silence, seeping into the dingy floor-boards and even into the light bulb's vain efforts to brighten up that space.

Domingo reached into his pocket and took out his key—the same key he'd had for over twenty-five years. Those hands had darted from one manuscript to another, had lovingly straightened up the photographs of beaten demonstrators and hunted visionaries. "Well, here we are, same as always," Buenaventura remarked as he turned on the lights, revealing the shelves crammed with books, the same worn cushions on the sofa and the old Remington typewriter right in the middle of the desk.

The carpet and a picture of his daughter Isabel on a small table were the only additions I noticed. The photographs of the Spanish Civil War and the tattered posters from different countries were still at the back of a couple of dusty shelves.

"Make yourself at home, Gabriel, you know that around here you can do as you please," Domingo said indulgently and with a gesture that always meant things were going well for him, that his spirits had not been depressed by his problems and disappointments.

"That's where I always used to sit," I observed, pointing to a wooden chair next to the sofa. Then the lampshade hanging in the middle of the room caught my eye. The lamp must have rocked like hell when the shots came from upstairs, just above the beams and the ceiling where we were standing.

Buenaventura took off his gray jacket and sat down on a chair in front of his typewriter, his back reflected in the window. I started comparing the photographs in the background with the present: his wide shoulders, white hair and rumpled collar—the leader of the masses and the frustrated dreamer.

"Now fill me in. You know you can tell me anything that's on your mind," said Domingo gazing impassively at a corner of the room as if suddenly a series of timeless scenes had flashed through his mind.

"I don't know quite where to begin . . . There's so much to tell . . . Maybe you can clear up a few things for me. We could probably start with Laura and José Augusto. What ever happen to her? Where is that lunatic Banderas?"

"Well, as you can imagine, that's a hopelessly entangled mess. Besides, you know as well as I that in these dog-eat-dog circles nobody survives . . . You may not believe it, but I've been very skeptical about the whole thing. Naturally, there are many logical explanations . . . Even so, we still can't get away from the malicious gossip and the rumors . . . I saw José Augusto a couple of weeks before the murder. He was a total wreck. I swear his anger was all bottled up inside him, he was crazy with jealousy and that goddamn pride of his . . . On top of that the wildest stories are going around."

"Who helped José Augusto make his getaway?"

"We haven't the faintest idea. I'd just barely gotten home when I heard the shots. At first, I thought it was those noisy neighbors upstairs quarreling again. But then, I heard the staircase creaking and by the time I got outside, José Augusto had already fled. To tell the truth, no one knows for sure what really happened. Laura left me in charge of her apartment while she stayed over at Andrea's for a while. As for José Augusto, well . . . we've had absolutely no word . . ." Domingo explained. All the while, I kept thinking it was inconceivable that all these riddles had remained dangling in mid-air.

Abruptly, Buenaventura stood up and took a pipe from the rack. He lit it slowly, as if it could help him sort out his thoughts. Perhaps he was trying to figure out the most plausible answer to the whole business, or perhaps he was deploring José Augusto's fate.

. . . On Saturdays, when he was free from political commitments, Domingo Buenaventura liked to stroll through the old downtown neighborhoods and browse, alone, in the bookstores. Then he'd board a crowded bus and ride through long stretches of the city surveying the sights: the colonial churches, the Plaza de Santo Domingo and Donceles Street. After that, he'd go from one newsroom to another, dropping in on old friends. He'd stop at the Statue of El Caballito to gaze at the afternoon clouds and the brand new neon signs on the National Lottery Building, after which he would spend a couple of hours in a café on López or Independencia Streets. Sometimes, he was asked about his experiences in the jails of Morelia or Bogotá or about the Battles of Ebro and Teruel. Although his replies were always noncommittal, there was a strange glint in his eyes, a glint of aversion and restlessness. He tried to talk about his latest writings but no one would listen. Then he'd fall silent, reflecting that what is really important is not expressed out loud; it flows through your thoughts and your senses. He'd always look closely at people's hands because hands reveal even more than voices: they can accuse, show despair and very seldom are they still. After half a pack of cigarettes and several cups of coffee, he would have his fill of the carping about various government officials, arguments about General De Gaulle, or the serious crisis provoked by Nationalist China. Once all the tables were full, he would wave a languid goodbye and leave the deafening chatter behind him to cross the street and have a beer. There he would sit near the bar, ignoring the more boisterous customers and would stare absently at the sawdust on the floor. Somewhat perked up, he would set out resolutely, nodding to a stray ragpicker on the way. Almost automatically he would head for Andrea's house across the city that his imagination had transfigured. No sooner would he arrive than he would invariably dominate the conversation, punctuating his shifting moods with phrases that seemed to flow naturally and that concentrated, for the most part, on the confounded perplexities of daily living and on his own loathing for all kinds of injustice . . .

We dropped the subject of the murder for a while. Pipe in hand, Buenaventura readjusted his glasses and proceeded to express his pessimistic views on the political situation. "Political groups come and go. We're constantly falling prey to infighting and factionalism. It's been the same old story for years—a lack of talent and not much drive."

I hung on to his every word, struck by his vehemence and the belligerence of his opinions. This was the Domingo who minced no words, his fist set firmly on the table—the Domingo who was born on Mesones Street, the idealistic fireband, the same Buenaventura who, sometime in the thirties and shortly after his twentieth birthday, sailed from Veracruz to Cádiz. From there he went on to Madrid and Oviedo. This then, was Buenaventura, the dyed-in-the wool radical who abhorred old age, stagnation and dogmas.

Domingo inhaled lazily, pausing between each sentence, keeping his usual distance from material things. He made constant efforts to bolster his optimism as the anecdotes poured from his memory. He spoke then about his war—the Spanish Civil War—of his wounds and of the International Brigades. "In those days I had the chance to give everything I had. Over there we really learned to toughen ourselves up and to know the meaning of helplessness."

I listened to him more and more intently as he described some places in Cuenca, Valencia and Barcelona, thinking all the while that those two pugnacious hotheads—José Augusto and Sebastián could well be over there right now. Part of the room was reflected in the window and countless shapes seemed to emerge, as if after a long gestation under its polished surface. Domingo recounted the experiences of several of his expatriated friends and the final defeat, describing in detail the now legendary massacres, the treacheries and the accusations. Then he switched to his travels through Colombia and Guatemala.

"Well, let's leave it here for the time being. Tell me about yourself, about your work . . . your women."

"I've never worked my ass off so hard in my life and I've learned a lot. But women—I swear, nothing really worth mentioning. To tell the truth, I was sort of soured on the subject. Just a little fooling around," I replied, truly unable to recall one serious involvement, one significant relationship. I told him about the garrets, the train trips, the wild binges and the long winter nights. I mentioned my article on Vietnam and my decision to return to Mexico. Then I broke off, letting my unfinished thought drift away.

Buenaventura ventured a comment about Sebastián: "He's a mixture of sarcasm and self-sufficiency. Did you know, by the way, he's the same age as José Augusto? He's a good example of the true derelict, frittering away his great talent on those all-night sprees of his."

Domingo gripped his pipe and filled it with tobacco. We returned to the subject of Laura and José Augusto—to the frame-ups and new puzzles that had just come to light. We discussed the innuendoes and malicious stories in the newspapers. Buenaventura observed that Banderas had never really accepted Laura's drifting away from him. "It's as if a vital part of him had died. He cooped himself up with his warped fantasies, getting himself all worked up over old grudges. He cut himself off from all of us and spent his time brooding over his own hang-ups for months on end."

With a vague gesture, his thoughts elsewhere, Buenaventura puffed away at his pipe. There were still any number of topics to talk about, so there was no reason to get all involved in useless speculations. For all I know, he might have been remembering a tenement in Tlatilco or the slow, painful suicide of one of his ancestors.

It was already after eleven and by now the murky sky had engulfed the whole city. Before we said goodbye, we talked some more and sprinkled our opinions with radical slogans and battle cries such as "Country or Death" and "We Shall Overcome." I visualized Laura's deserted apartment where the darkness had banished all signs of life, casting shadows on the lifeless objects left behind.

Once back on the street, other nocturnal sounds filled the air: cats leaping on tenement rooftops, the earsplitting sounds of a rock band and crude renditions of old torch songs. Construction workers were diligently digging away at the new subway tunnels on Chapultepec Avenue. "Take me somewhere, anywhere you like. I can show you a good time," said a woman standing all alone on the corner of Insurgentes. I looked back at her and imagined her more attractive, less brazen, less promiscuous— maybe she was just someone who was killing time by putting on an act. The air was so damp it seemed to cling to the doorways and the sidewalks. As I reached Paseo de la Reforma, I recalled the gatherings of rebels and other lone wolves who where brought to mind by Buenaventura's descriptions of heretics, apostates, upstarts and revolutionaries.

I recreated José Augusto's loneliness, his compulsive chain smoking, the long hours he wasted among cheap crooks and gamblers as he put it: "Sucking up my own gloom, amidst bloated faces and somber rages," without enough guts to mount an inner struggle to end his frustration once and for all. I could picture him walking down the streets on one of the many dead nights in his life—his eyes riveted on Laura's breasts and navel, and then . . . on emptiness, on nothingness, on his inability to hold her and on the rapture that had been irrevocably lost to him.

VIII

JOSÉ AUGUSTO WASN'T SURE whether they had taken him out of the city beyond the Desierto de los Leones or to the slopes of the Ajusco mountain. He thought back to the moment he had left the building that very noon. It had been muggy, the sky overcast, when all of a sudden he had been confronted by a group of thugs who started slugging him, first in the belly and then on the back. They bundled him into a car on the other side of the street, blindfolded him and drove off unnoticed. By then, the threats had become more alarming, since they were followed by a rabbit punch to his neck.

The faint voices were now directly in front of him, encircling him, bullying him. He remembered the phone call he had received that same lazy morning when he had been wandering aimlessly all around the stuffy little room. *"You've got to buckle down, dammit, work your asses off day after day! We can't afford to do things half-way." That's how you used to shout, bugging the hell out of everyone, scowling like a madman, hinting at your secret pleasures which were, by the way, your only genuine actions, the indescribable feelings you had with Laura: she alone was capable of cheering you up. You always had your own way, didn't you? Always trying to convince, to persuade others, not letting them pick holes in any of your contradictions.*

He found himself coolly analyzing his fear, his feelings of apprehension and the vulnerablity of his position at the hands of these mobsters whose faces he could only imagine and whose guns were jabbing against his ribs and stomach. He clenched his fists, not making a sound and tried to figure out what route they were taking by listening to snatches of conversation. He felt the rage inside him but also the sheer helplesness of his situation. Before the first stoplight on Insurgentes and Bajío, they made him crouch down, his head between his knees, his hands touching his feet. He was already starting to feel the pain, particularly in the left collarbone and the knuckles. The two people in the front seat hadn't said a word and the two in back, sitting next to the windows, were giving the orders, pressing their guns against his back and shoulders. He was sure they had gone around Insurgentes Circle and were now driving straight ahead. They were probably planning to take the Thruway out to the main Freeway.

During those first few minutes he tried to calm down, to control his pounding heart and collect his thoughts. He had made up his mind that under no circumstances would he be goaded into anything rash. The long pauses were occasionally interrupted by the shifting of gears as the car picked up speed, muttered curses and someone belching or blowing his nose. José Augusto remained with his head stuck between his knees, by now fully aware that anything could happen. He sensed that they had left the Freeway but at that point he lost his bearings. They might have been driving up Constituyentes past the Dolores Cemetery, and since they waited for a couple of stoplights, he concluded they hadn't reached the outskirts of the city, much less a highway. He thought of Buenaventura's warnings, of a similar experience undergone by his father, and of the past few lonely days he had spent locked up with his procrastination and sullenness, his blind rage and self-destructive, bitter attitude toward everything in his life.

Suddenly, they jerked his head back roughly, snarled insults at him but let him lean back against the seat. He gradually felt his muscles relax and the natural rhythm of his breathing resumed. They had opened the front window so that the damp air struck him full in the face. The wind smelled of pine trees and open fields, speeding vehicles and sloping hillsides. By this time his fists were tightly balled and he started thinking about anything that came into his head, not giving a damn where they were taking him. He launched into another silent monologue, twisting ideas and obsessions in his mind. *Nothing has ever been good enough for you—you've always done things in a half-assed way in that no-man's land of escapism and puny efforts—shots in the dark. All your plans have gone up in smoke and everything is falling apart—you spend the afternoons lounging around in bed, waking up every morning with your mouth tasting like shit and a panic-stricken look in your eyes. Even Laura never belonged to you completely—when you thought she was closest to you, she was already slipping through your fingers.* They had fallen into a regular pattern by now: the predictable lulls in the conversation, the curves in the road and the monotonous sound of the motor being driven at a steady pace, as if there were all the time in the world.

Much later, perhaps after twenty or thirty kilometers, the voices

60

started quarreling with each other. They argued about what happened God know when and where and then they began to smoke and curse everything imaginable: the clouds, the climate, a recent bug-infested night. They paid no attention whatsoever to José Augusto, as if he had already turned into a thing, a mere thing they were taking along just for the ride. From time to time he could feel the guns caressing his waist, his forehead, his jaw. Every single moment that passed seemed to last forever and the suspense was unbearable. He began to think that he would never see or talk to anyone ever again and that at any moment he could be faced with the final void. They were probably going through some kind of valley because the sun was blazing down on the road, spreading its rays westward. He felt like a bystander watching a dry run that was slowly falling into place, step by step, like a rehearsal for a play in which he had no part. When they opened the two side windows, he realized that he still hadn't gotten used to the blindfold.

As more and more dust kept blowing into the car he again lost his train of thought. He swayed back and forth very slowly, his head thrown back, trying to work up some saliva by sucking on his tongue. Whenever he tried to open his eyes, they immediately brushed against the darkness that had been thrust upon him and that continued to fuel his fear and anger. Then the voices died down and the car veered toward the right, first on a side road and then on a dirt path. Once in a while he could hear one of the men mumbling. At times they would slow down as if they were picking out the best place to finish their job. He figured the automobile was a dark color, had a filthy windshield and no license plates. He could feel the throbbing in his shoulder blade and his own uneven breathing.

The car lurched along and finally, after another detour on a bumpy dirt road, it came to a stop. They kept shouting as they kicked him out of the car. He strained to hear the echo of a stone bouncing down a gully, until its echoes gradually died down in the distance. He winced at the pain in his chest and neck. During the time it took to get from the last stoplight to this unfamiliar spot, he had made up his mind to stick it out as long as possible, to resist each blow and wait for a chance, however slim or unforeseen, to escape.

As soon as his feet touched solid ground, he could smell the mountains, the woods, damp shrubbery and pine cones. He felt the wind whipping against his blindfold, his tangled hair and numb hands. They all started walking and he could hear them spitting, grunting, swearing, their heels sinking into the dry grass and their holsters creaking. At times he would stumble and someone would shove him. Then for a long stretch they walked at a steady pace.

José Augusto guessed they were in for a fairly long hike and that afterwards . . . perhaps the worst awaited him, a cliff. Just one push would do it: then his blindfold would flutter in the air, he'd give a terrified shout, and finally memories and body would hurtle through infinite space. They were going up a steep incline, trudging through lush woodlands like alien beings heading for an uncertain destination. *These goons will stop at nothing—they're nothing but a bunch of morons—perfect examples of urban scum.* He wanted to scream at the top of his voice, make his echoes bounce widely and then converge. He wished with all his might for this whole business to end, once and for all.

He sensed they had left a clearing and were heading for the woods. As they pushed and shoved, the threats became more and more ominous. He tried to picture how they all looked from above, from the highest mountain peak—tiny figures lumbering along, choosing the most suitable spot to torture him, perhaps also to give him the *coup de grace*—letting him lie there like an old rag tacked to a tree trunk. The constant jostling and stumbling kept him from biting his lips. By this time the early afternoon sun was beating down on the sandy ground.

At last they stopped and they let him lie still for a while. All at once they began to shout at him; they pulled him to his feet. They pushed him ahead a few more steps, up some rickety wooden stairs and went into a room. Judging from its musty and rancid smell, he guessed it was never lived in. Most probably the windows were shut tight, leaving it always in the dark. Someone kicked him hard in the spine sending him reeling into a corner like a cowering rat, ready to accept how insignificant he was. José Augusto tried to keep as quiet as he could, though this meant choking down his fear and rage. He clung to the feeling that there was still some hope left, and that if he kept his wits about him, his chances for survival were fairly good. With considerable pain, he tried to straighten his back and stretch his arms; he felt like a piece of rubble someone had thrown away in the trash.

Then he heard a series of grating sounds which he could not quite place, since he could not identify them with any specific object. He had been leaning against a rough brick wall, his head hanging to one side, his legs spread out. They had tied his hands behind him, then thrown some iron rods into a corner. He didn't know how long he slumped there alone among the cobwebs and the dusty floorboards as the cold air crept into

62

his bones and with the darkness which to him was imperceptible. He began to lose all sense of time, to relive the entire nightmare. Thanks to an absurd set of circumstances and his own recklessness, he was being kidnapped. Why the hell did he have to put up with all this crap? It was the same old story: they were teaching him a lesson, setting him up as a warning to others.

The wind was now whistling through the cracks in the walls and windows. It swept along the floor, chased swarms of insects and searched through the piles of rubble. It invaded the small room, left its traces on the broken glass and the holes in the roof. Again and again he thought of Laura, transposing her image with others that rose up from the past. Again and again he returned to the different kinds of loneliness he had experienced; he ran through his doubts and his hates, the constant presence of his defiant anger. He imagined that by now the shadows outside the shack were like those inside; the approaching of nightfall had transformed the sounds and silence as well. Long minutes went by and then the voices returned. By now he had created a fairly complete mental picture of these goons: they'd have flabby, pockmarked jowls, buck teeth, bushy hair and lackluster eyes, broad shoulders and hard-knuckled hands—boxers' hands. He pictured them wearing dark overcoats and loud, flashy shirts. Once again the kidnappers hemmed him in, bombarding him with words coming from crude, idiotic minds. He reminded himself that they were experts in hurting, undisputed masters of violence; killers, when need be. They stank of strong tobacco, sweaty armpits and cheap liquor. He heard one of them spitting and another cracking his knuckles. Then a hand grabbed his neck, others clasped his forearms and there were still more hands pulling at his legs.

The first punch, dealt with all the gleeful expertise of a professional, landed hard on his cheekbone. Then a hard fist pounded his stomach, his liver, his eyebrows. Kicks thudded against his thighs very close to his testicles. Their spit splattered against his face and neck. His breathing became labored and, moaning softly, he swore silently at the floor, the roof, the windows and the wind which had suddenly stopped blowing as if stunned by the brutality of the scene.

It was almost a relief when the voices started up again. The beating had been terrible; millions of tiny spasms shot through his body and he could feel only his knees and elbows being dragged along the floor. Little by little, he began to pass out, his head bowed, his arms stretched wide, with blood trickling down between his skin and his clothes. He managed a feeble gesture of anger by stretching out his hands. He had been stripped of all hostility, of all amazement.

As it grew chillier, the floorboards started creaking and the branches outside crackled. In his hazy dreams, interspersed with erratic hissing sounds, he could almost see the glimmer of distant lights, recall the wisecracks he heard at some bar, the faces of Domingo and Sebastián, his father's rebukes, Laura's bare navel caressed by another mouth, her nipples pressed against another's chest, the endless plunge down an endless abyss, his vain search for a final way out. Then, all his pent-up hostilities and fantasies sank slowly to the bottom of a total, dark silence.

As the night waned and let in the dawn, he was still not fully conscious but he could hear footsteps around him. Dew was sprinkled all over the grass and furrows in distant fields and the last scattered lights were fading among the eucalyptus and pine trees. He was picked up and carried out to the meadow where he could hear the wind whizzing past him and feel the dust blowing up against his face. When they reached the car, they dumped him in the back seat like a piece of battered baggage.

The car took the same route as before; the same dirt road, the same side road and finally the highway back to the city. Cigarette smoke drifted back and forth from one window to the other. Their voices sounded listless; he imagined their eyes heavy-lidded and puffy. They were obviously testy and worn out from the long night. Fatigued or not, he was sure that beneath their dark glasses, their expressions were smug. They were proud of a job well done.

Nobody moved for several kilometers except for the driver's hands and feet, or ashes dropping from cigarettes onto the bundle in the back seat. Once in a while, he would hear droning sounds, the humdrum rhythm of the shifting gears, belches, curses and the sound of bottles gurgling against smacking lips. From a look-out point above the city they would be able to see the lights gradually dimming, the cloudy sky poised beyond the valley on the other side of Zacatenco and the Chiquihuite hill. They reached the first stoplight and then drove along the Freeway to Ciudad Satélite on the outskirts of the city. A voice—probably the leader's—boomed out orders to park in an empty lot. Near a garbage dump, in a sandy spot between scrawny cactus plants, where the ground was strewn with old tires and cardboard boxes, they flung the bundle after bidding it a final and insolent farewell.

When the motor started up again, the sun was coming out over the city, far beyond heavy tight clouds, circling birds and parched landfills. It blazed down on Lomas de Tecamachalco and a thick fog hovered over the volcanoes and the last landmarks of the Texcoco wasteland. The bundle remained motionless, immersed in isolation and in the growing shadows, its profile spread over the granite rocks and the chunks of yellowish, moldy plastic scattered about the garbage heap.

IX

AFTER TEN DAYS—the first few in a hotel on Aquiles Serdán Street, then a couple with Buenaventura and the rest in Sebastián's garret, I finally managed to reach Andrea on the phone. "Gabriel, you old so-and-so—you mean to tell me you've been here all this time and you're just getting around to calling me? You've really hurt my feelings and I won't take no for an answer, you rascal! Besides, I really mean it—if you don't stay here for a few days I'll never speak to you again." The way she said it was just as if she were right there in front of me with her turned-up nose, her brown almond-shaped eyes and perfect teeth, her hands in perpetual motion and her ability to get her way. I went all the way across the city and walked into the house in Coyoacán with the feeling that nothing had really changed.

Every single room and corridor in Andrea's house seemed to possess a life of its own. And surely those walls were the most reliable witnesses to our youthful explosions and our zealous attempts at non-conformism. It seemed that there were always histrionic poses, howling laughter, and caressing going on and sometimes the music and gentle quips and the sounds of lovers would suddenly melt together as if by merging they could weave new shapes, new images, new challenges. Our unrestricted freedom and the steady stream of ever-changing scenes were a constant presence that we never forgot.

Anything—absolutely anything could happen in that house in Coyoacán—any excuse was good enough for a party. On Saturdays there was open house, while Sundays were reserved for nursing hangovers, for late breakfasts and just lounging around. The house was always open to our select handful of regulars. Any provocation—a chance remark, a wisecrack, was enough to start the ball rolling; we'd serve drinks, put on records and everyone, in his own way, would have a great time. We did whatever we damn well pleased. We all sat on the sofa, on the carpet or on the chairs around the table, letting our imaginations run riot. First, we would discuss the latest political events: demonstrations that had been suppressed by the authorities, the recently-elected government officials and those who were just beginning to glimpse the new utopias. Later on, after Andrea had opened the windows, our throats cleared and our spirits soared and the conversations flew off on different tangents and laughter seemed to come from ceilings and venetian blinds. The voices became more and more garrulous and the guffaws more and more boisterous, and the sentences less coherent and gestures more prouounced.

"We have a million things to talk about. My, you've really filled out, haven't you? You must really knock 'em dead! I bet you have to fight the girls off. Believe it or not, the most extraordinary things have been going on here," Andrea would begin the conversation, then she would skip from one topic to another, from her new play to the crooked deals pulled by some government official; from the imminent downfall of the Rector of the University to Buenaventura's latest book.

There was no one like Andrea to make you laugh by imitating all sorts of voices and well-known people. She had them all down cold: the emotions of an unscrupulous mistress, the subservience of maternal devotion, the bright eyes of an old paralytic woman, the contorted lips of an alcoholic rummaging through a trash can. Ever since we had first known her—when we used to loiter in the halls of the School of Philosophy and in the Political Science Building—she had shown unmistakable signs of her unique dramatic talent: with just a raised eyebrow, hand motions, fluttered eyelashes, or varied inflections of her voice, she could make her personality nasal, sultry, faltering or prudish.

"She's always had the knack for making the most of a trite phrase. It's in her blood, in the very chromosomes that brought her into this world. Let's face it, this house is not only an extension of our own hangups, it's fundamentally an extension of Andrea's personality," Sebastián would have surely volunteered, had he been present, sitting as always, like a gigantic Buddha in the middle of the living room.

Andrea parked my suitcases in the back room, insisting all the while that of course I needed a woman and that I should make myself at home. Then she turned to the subject that was uppermost in her mind: Laura. As for José Augusto, she scarcely mentioned him. It was Laura who had suffered the most; how could she be expected to deal with such a horrible experience? It was Laura who in the long run would have to survive and learn to live with the burden of her own hostility.

With Andrea there was no need for questions or for detailed explanations. I listened to her version of what for me remained an unbelievable episode which I could not yet bring myself to accept. At one point, Andrea referred to Laura's fixations, to the two dominant male figures in her life—her father and her brother—to Laura's lack of experience as far as men were concerned and to those "Goddamned sons of bitches who can't appreciate a real woman." I interrupted by telling her to take it easy and that not all men were that way.

Without a doubt, Andrea was insatiable. She was totally committed to friendship, to being always the center of attention, to being admired. She offered us her own world freely: we dropped in at any hour of the day or night; often with drinks in hand, sprawled out on the carpet, we waited for her to come home.

We were the future, and it was in that house in Coyoacán, where legends—our budding spirit of revolt and our pursuit of pleasure—were born. "Don't give me any of that chickenshit, you morons," I could hear Sebastián saying as he gazed at his face reflected in the dining room window. "That's where we really got to know each other, where we really learned to drop our phony smiles and let it all hang out. Remember those long nights we spent bullshitting and making big plans and those marvelous afternoons when everyone either wound up at each other's throats or playing True Confessions?"

All of a sudden Andrea started analyzing everyone else's complexes—besides Laura's, that is. She went on about how our faces were reflected in the mirrors of the past, how age-old concepts had been revived by a seemingly eternal present, and on the damage that had been caused by the political rifts in our group. "That's what has really screwed us up—it's managed to split us in half—they've made mincemeat of us, damn it, and there's absolutely no end to petty quarrels and personality clashes. So there you have it, Gabriel, we made short work of the last organization we belonged to. They kick us out, and *then* they have the gall to say we're decadent, that we're impostors, incorrigible rebels. I'm sick of all this intrigue!"

"Come on, it's not as bad as all that," I replied. "Let's talk about something else for a change—the French Romantic poets or Gothic cathedrals, for instance."

Ever since her debut at the Caballito Theater, then at the one on Chapultepec Avenue and later in appearances at the School of Architecture, we had showered Andrea with applause and ovations from our back row seats and then with enthusiastic praise in her dressing room. Once, after her performance in *Divinas Palabras*, we all trooped over to Coyoacán to congratulate her on her success. It turned out to be one of those memorable nights—we were all in just the right mood for a real blast. We drank, danced, made jokes and clowned around until dawn. We danced to every kind of music imaginable, you name it: from *danzón* to rock, from *guarachas* to *corridos*. From then on, the parties at Andrea's were regular practice. Her house was a veritable bastion of freedom and *laissez faire*.

If anyone could picture a cross section of those gatherings—Laura's skepticism, Sebastián and José Augusto's impassioned tirades or Andrea's hilarious facial expressions, only Buenaventura would always be there in the background—sitting in the shadows behind the smoke and the breeze: alone, but not detached from the group, his attention focused on those endless discussions, on the particular tableau which contained every conceivable emotion.

When we were just getting to know each other, there were nights, especially Saturdays, when some of us became overenthusiastic and a couple of chairs would be thrown out the window and come to rest on either the flower beds or on the well-kept lawn surrounding the house. Our tendency toward exaggeration and especially our abandon in hugging each other on the rug and hurling glasses through the air, served as an outlet, for a few hours at least, to relieve the threat of boredom and depression.

Sometimes, in the afternoons or on evenings after meetings in Buenaventura's apartment where we had drawn up open letters of protest and reshaped the future of the world, Cardoso, Banderas and myself—and occasionally a few others—made the long trek to Coyoacán to lie on the cool grass and try to forget the problems and vague fears that hovered over us. At Andrea's we always felt perfectly free to drag our complexes out in the open and to clarify some of our doubts. "It was never just a pastime with us—just letting off steam and then forgetting all about it. No way. We went far beyond that. We were always ready to trample on our scruples," as José Augusto remarked once—another, younger José Augusto, still reluctant to endow the past with an air of nostalgia.

Then Andrea talked about herself, of the fact that she still hadn't found the right man, one she'd be willing to take a chance on, who'd break down her barriers, whose child she could bear. Although she was inordinately confident about her present and future, she also poked fun at herself. With a rueful gesture she observed that she had been born at exactly the wrong time: hers had been an adolescence without contraceptives. As a result, she still had qualms about not being able to prove she was a virgin to each newly chosen man. Although it was obviously painful for her, she told me of an abortion she had undergone before she was twenty. It was performed in a dreary, stinking shack in a slum north of the city. The experience had filled her with feelings of remorse and agony. She was never going to forget coming out of that ghastly place with the feeling that her womb was polluted. It was enough of a trauma that she could never discuss it without misgivings.

We changed the subject and started in on a long string of anecdotes: the time when Andrea was on tour with a road company and gave us full run of her place for a whole weekend. Of course it turned into a free-for-all. It all started around nine o'clock one Saturday night. We had had plenty to drink in a cantina downtown and were arguing with a bunch of crooked politicians about the murder of a *campesino* leader in the state of Guerrero. Then we got the bright idea of going to Coyoacán to continue the discussion there. "So we arrived with the pols in tow. By the way, they turned out to be perfect idiots who happened to have good connections in high presidential circles," Sebastián described later, frowning and licking one of his Faro cigarettes while he insulted everyone and everything imaginable. Anyway, how it happened we never really knew, but by three o'clock in the morning the kitchen was overflowing with bottles and the house with chorus girls, hookers and a long-haired rock band. The spree could have gone on for four days, but early Sunday morning, at the front door, Sebastián started a fight in which he let loose all his suppressed fury and frustrations. By the time the patrol car drove up the brawl had gotten completely out of hand. Of course the police never bothered the rowdy politicians, but José Augusto, Sebastián and I got kicked around and for no reason at all wound up in the slammer. We spent two days locked up there with nothing to do. We passed the time by arguing with drunks and potheads. I remember that the cells smelled like shit and Sebastián wondered if there were any fleas on the concrete floor. José Augusto only laughed and said: "Don't be an ass—how can there be fleas in concrete—only in the abstract, you fat slob!" A few days later, when Andrea came back and opened the door to find the rugs filthy, the sofa smashed to pieces, the venetian blinds splintered all over the floor, and empty bottles scattered everywhere, she flew into a rage. Naturally, she never left us in charge of her house again. "Come on, Andrea, don't overreact—it's not that bad," Sebastián ventured. "It was just one of those things—so what? Everyone, at least once in their lives has one helluva night to their credit."

The stories unfolded one after another, in cadence with the mounting chaos which took over the city every night. At first they blended into the walls, the rooms and the beams, but with time, our actions and experiences eventually shed their light on each corner and hallway, endowing the ivy and the shadows of the pine and jacaranda trees with new contours. Well before we had learned to disguise our personal ambitions or to control our so-called wisdom, Andrea, more than anyone else, had perceived the true significance of her house.

"Besides matters of a radical nature, we considered ourselves experts on free will and cosmic determinism. To tell the truth, we were nothing but a bunch of fools, but we just couldn't wait to change the world," José Augusto said once as we were leaving the film festival in the Roble Cinema, all set to dissect the tormented characters in a Bergman film.

Andrea's father visited her only on Sunday afternoons. They chatted for a few hours, discussing puberty, her mother's life, the after-effects of her death and the complexities of marital relationships. They laughed over Andrea's student days, with the nuns at the Incarnate Word School and at her first experiences in the theater. They gossiped about a friend or a relative who had just come into money; about group therapy versus individual psychoanalysis—without ever really agreeing about anything. Only rarely would they refer to her mother's last few months on earth—her passivity, her lethargy and her final words. Every single Sunday without fail, her father would eventually get around to the subject of Andrea's future. She would say nothing, but neither would she let his advice interfere with her own world. She always dreaded going over and over the same old pointless arguments: her early feelings of anxiety, her longing, her dilemmas and her conflicts with that inscrutable, round-faced man who had once been one of the shrewdest businessmen around—her father. Finally, they would talk about the weather—last week's thunderstorms or the heat wave—after which her father, satisfied that everything was all right, would take his leave. Never in his wildest dreams would he have imagined that in that very house a bunch of nuts was in the habit of raising hell. When he left, he always tried to take along a smile or a phrase of Andrea's to keep him going for the rest of the week.

Then Andrea turned to the inevitable topic of Sebastián and the years when our center of operation was the School of Humanities in University City. Our verbal diarrhea was boundless as we went from one cafeteria to another, from one auditorium to another. More often than not, we were busy organizing meetings and making sure we never missed

71

a demonstration. We were constantly writing articles for newspapers and magazines and we never failed to show up whenever there was a strike. Once, right in front of the Rectory Building, Sebastián was involved in a skirmish which he liked to say left its mark on our so-called revolutionary actions. It began at a rally when a bunch of goons armed with chains tried to break it up. Somehow or other, Cardoso screwed up enough courage to use his very considerable bulk to drag down one of the thugs by tackling him around the legs. We got into the act, hollering and picking our way through the crowd. There was more thrashing around and finally we managed to grab the guy. He was armed and looked like a real hoodlum. We took him to the School of Economics auditorium where we actually held a trial. Sebastián, shouting insults at the gangster, lashed out against the government and kept pointing to a bruise on his left cheek. José Augusto, standing next to me, did nothing but shake his head as if we were a bunch of idiots wasting our time on this nonsense. In spite of everything, we couldn't help feeling swayed by Cardoso's fiery speeches and his genuine gift for stirring up the masses. He stood behind the table, an impressive figure, his deep voice resounding as we cheered him on and joined him in clamoring for justice. "Those were my glorious years: my troops were always alert and ready to risk their necks, and they emerged unscathed, to a man," Sebastián had reminisced later after his bitter experience in the provinces. He had spent at least a couple of weekends in jail, a month hiding out in Morelia; he was hit in the head in Chilpancingo and was beaten up in Toluca.

Andrea chattered on about all sorts of things: the ups and downs of all our inter-relationships, Laura's loneliness, Buenaventura, José Augusto's possible whereabouts, the old days when we were "still too naive to put up a front and suffer in silence." It was way after midnight when Andrea got up to answer a phone call. I decided to unpack in the back bedroom which had been the scene of so many cathartic experiences and zany antics. This is where I used to take my catnaps, where Domingo would hold forth when there were too many people in the living room and where Sebastián let his drunkenness purge him of all his old bugaboos. Surely, Laura and José Augusto had made love in this room a number of times, adding more chapters to its history with their eloquent silences and erotic whispers.

We talked on for more than an hour about our frustrated plans and why they never seemed to jell. Somehow this led Andrea to demonstrate her proficiency at astrology and dream interpretation. She darted from Cancer to Pisces, from the universal breath of life to transcendental meditation, stressing the importance of futurology and insisting that the apocalypse was not far away. The conversation ended with a discussion of psychoanalysis and the rather unsatisfactory effects it seemed to have had on some of our acquaintances.

"Well, Gabriel, now I'm really going to say good night. Anyhow, we still have lots and lots of things to talk about," said Andrea rising, putting up her hair and heading for her bedroom.

Andrea's bedroom was the only room in the house that was off limits. It was the restricted area *par excellence*, where Andrea and Andrea alone presided. There no one had the right to meddle in her privacy by cracking jokes or telling her their troubles. This is where she studied her scripts, where every single object was linked to the act of love, to the touch of a man's hand. This is where she wandered from the bed to the dressing table, concentrated on her eyebrow pencil and her mascara. Here her lips would be moistened by cold cream or by endless wordplay, where the brush of her skin against another would lead to a feverish blending of breaths.

Every single one of us who had wandered in and out of her house as if we owned the place had remarked at one time or another, "None of us ever dared go into her bedroom. Only a chosen few were admitted and they never seemed to hang around long enough to become a permanent fixture. It was her exclusive domain, and there, at least, her word was law."

From three o'clock in the morning on, whether alone or otherwise, Andrea would sit at her dressing table slowly rubbing cream on her face, inspecting her lingerie and her pastel colored dresses. She never failed to be amused at the expression in her dark eyes which was far too naive for the disappointments and the bittersweet memories they harbored. These were the moments when she recaptured her sense of time, when she sorted out her impressions and reflected that it would never be too late for her. She would analyze the next role she was to play, such as the character of the adultress, around which she could build a whole range of emotions—the suicidal tendencies, the harsh gestures, the subtle hint or overt possessiveness. The body movements must convey the character's determination to take stock of her jealousy and her frustrations. Lastly, Andrea would focus on the adultress' more refined manifestations of lust.

She brooded over her weariness and her inconstancy, and would laugh at herself again, at her unattainable ambition, at the face in the mirror that stubbornly refused to take nothingness for an answer. Once ready for bed, in the darkness broken by tiny lights flickering through her window, she would feel, without having yet settled on one man in particular, a slow tremor run through her legs and breasts which gradually ebbed as a long silence slowly closed her eyes and eased the throbbing in her brain.

X

EVERY AFTERNOON FOR MANY years—ever since the days of the great bullfighters Armillita and Manolete, in the forties, Domingo Buenaventura went for a short walk. Turning his back on the trees and fountain on Miravalle Square, he would stroll for a while along Durango Avenue. He never failed to notice the latest evidence of the fact that the city was slowly but surely being demolished. He tried to picture it as it used to be; the neighborhoods where he had lived were still fresh in his memory.

The liveliness of his dreams shone through his eyes, in the malleable features of his face under the thin line of his eyebrows, with his whitening temples and his lips glistening from Cocoa Butter. As he crossed the small alley that led to Sinaloa Street he was leaving the noise of the traffic behind him and listening to an old *danzón* that seemed to come from a rooftop somewhere. It reminded him of a brothel in Santa María la Redonda—the couples squeezed tightly together, their cheeks, genitals and thighs rubbing against each other—a sea of boozy, laughing faces. He tried to fathom the selfish, arbitrary motives that lay behind the urban devastation. He smiled to himself, winking at his memories and rubbing his hands together as if he were priming himself to recapture invisible scenes from bygone years.

He reached the dry cleaner's shop on Sinaloa, turned left, and stopped a few steps from the door of the old four-story building where the mice skittered all around the basement and the balconies seem to gaze languidly at the street corner. He took out his worn key chain and carefully opened the door to the building, passing the shadows crouched over the stairwell as he went up the stairs. Once on the second floor, he entered his apartment, relishing every single thing that touched upon his senses: the smell of Dutch tobacco and the hands of the century-old clock, his books stacked on the shelves and the blue cushions on the antique sofa. He smiled a creaseless smile, drew the curtains, and decided to arrange the photographs on his desk.

75

Still breathing heavily, Buenaventura took off his thick sweater as if her were shedding the grime he had picked up in the street. As his fingers flipped rapidly through the books, he suddenly thought of his uncle Federico, that marvelous old man with the graying moustache who had taken him under his wing in early childhood. He could still hear that solemn voice aim at destroying all signs of prejudice; he could still picture his uncle as he sat on a bench in Alameda Park kindling his discussions with a condescending gesture that hinted at his arrogance. Although he belonged to many different worlds he had the temperament of a recluse. He was destined to die alone and forgotten, according to a carefully conceived plan for the last lucid moments of his existence—like an Egyptian Pharaoh.

Domingo had changed his mind and decided to listen to some music instead. Rays from the late afternoon sun slipped through the gap between the curtains, and came to rest on his typewriter. He filled his pipe to the strains of a symphony, and sank down on the easy chair to enjoy the aroma and the erratic shapes of the curling smoke. He paused, rocking back and forth, to gaze at the four cut-glass golbets and decanter that had gone half-way around the world with him. They dated back to his earliest daydreams, way before he left for Spain. Once and only once did the decanter ever make the rounds; filled with cognac, it was passed from mouth to mouth—of bums and whores—in some out-of-the-way bar on Bolívar street. Even before then old Federico's afflictions had all but rotted him away and his mind had been on the verge of turning into ashes. He was living in a ramshackle dump on Mina Street, fortified with nothing but his memories.

"Hey, Domingo, you've been locked up with your books long enough and you've done your share of reading. If you're really serious about writing, it's high time you started living, and getting up the guts to venture out into the world," old Federico admonished him once in a guileless but confident way as if he knew all there was to know. This particular conversation had taken place in Federico's apartment downtown on Mesones Street, where Domingo had learned his first words. It was a dreary street, teeming with the usual night people and with beggars practically glued to the sidewalks and the doorways like appendages.

After Domingo's parents had been killed in a strange massacre, Domingo had never again accounted to anyone for his actions, not even to old Federico. Often he had hazy visions of his parents, at the very spot where they died screaming at the blows of the gun butts. By piecing together the fragments he had gathered here and there from eyewitness accounts and from his own memories, he had managed to reconstruct their lives, to breathe life into their hands and faces, to make them walk, talk and smile. After years of effort he was finally able to summon them up at will. The more obscure details he left pending, storing them away in a compartment of his mind which he gradually replenished and which he resorted to only once in a while, filling it unconsciously and leaving it up to life itself to endow it with deeper meaning.

Little by little the entire room was filling up with music and tobacco, with memories of walking on Paseo de la Reforma at sunrise, of all-night binges, and arguments with bums and hangers-on. Then, against his will, the prison cells appeared, one after another: endless corridors, compounds crammed with scar-faced murderers, drug addicts huddled in grotesque positions, their gestures and eyes contorted by hallucinations. The images of Spain: Barcelona, Madrid, Oviedo, Almería all intertwined with his search for shelter, an exploding bridge and the sounds of battle. He focused on his attempts to reach the border through Gerona, Perpignan and the French Pyrenees, then the unbelievable defeat and the bombings, always the bombings, like vast dark spaces. The feeling of impotence and stupefaction had left him numb, as if transfixed. The anxious waiting and the final overwhelming defeat had remained forever rooted in his mind.

He remembered the stunning woman from Algeciras, in the south of Spain. He never saw her again; she had vanished one cold December afternoon, waving her hand upward as if it were pointed at the muddy sky. She was invested with a love of life and a total commitment to danger of any kind. This was the woman he had dreamed about over and over again, picturing her at his side, traveling through Europe. She had been able to make him forget his futile exploits; he felt constantly compelled to re-create her in his mind—her gentle face, her limpid eyes, her white skin, her black hair.

Domingo Buenaventura moved his pipe horizontally, then re-lit it and filled his palate with the taste of tobacco. He half-closed his eyes, letting the smoke ravel and unravel simultaneously into a multitude of shapes: from the insidious hypocrisy of Federico's cats to the gestures, legs, firm breasts and swaying hips that had filled him with anticipation of the full measure of sensuousness under the noon sun of San Blas and Puerto México. He let himself be carried away by his apathy and by all those episodes later transferred by his typewriter to the thousands and thousands of pages that lay on a shelf in the corner and which were now patiently waiting to be re-written in another language and with unpredictable endings.

"Don't be afraid to be who you are. Learn to take stock of what you might want to do and what you don't want to do. Pay no attention to cheap success and selfish attitudes. And above all, under no circumstances should you let time get the better of you." That had been old Federico's advice, many years ago after Domingo had shown him his first manuscripts. It was just around the time he was on the verge of deciding his vocation; he was already dazzled by the challenges of the written word.

On impulse, he re-read José Augusto's article that had appeared in the paper a few days before. Banderas had really gotten to the nitty-gritty; each phrase, each explanation was loaded with unmitigated resentment. Although he could not dispute the truth in each of José Augusto's accusations against the unscrupulous practices of crooked government officials and the murder of several workers in a Balbuena factory, there was an undertone that was not entirely to Domingo's liking: it was a compendium of grievances; it had a bitter taste from beginning to end. Still, José Augusto's deductions were accurate and the closing statement was up to the standards of any first-rate columnist. It made him think about Banderas' seclusion and his total frustration during the past few months.

Just as the needle reached the end of record, there was a timid knock which broke Domingo's train of thought. It was the son of the bureaucrats downstairs. Grinning impishly, he puffed up his cheeks and aimed his eyes beseechingly at Domingo. With a gruff, "Oh, all right, come in," Federico Buenaventura style, Domingo asked him not to get too rambunctious and to sit quietly on the linoleum floor.

"The story's going to be short and sweet today because I have an appointment, so sit still, my boy, and prick up your ears."

The tale began—an account of the most notorious pirates in history. Before long, it was sprinkled with flailing hand gestures, the same intonation as his uncle's, and exclamations: "Forsooth, Ship Ahoy! Zounds! A pox on thee, you blackguard!" Domingo went on to describe the flora and fauna of the exotic Caribbean isles, the buccaneers' insatiable thirst for vengeance—always vengeance, their boundless hatred—the scourge of both the English and Spanish crowns. The boy never budged an inch the whole time. His mouth agape, his imagination running wild, he became as totally immersed in the story as if he himself were its hero, he couldn't wait to hear the ending, he didn't want the story to end.

Buenaventura paused, replaced the needle on the record, bit his pipe and went on with the saga, which by now had shifted to a group of Basque sailors seeking Atlantis off the coast of Tortuga Island. At times, as if it

78

were old Federico speaking through him, Domingo barely heard his own words. He thought back on that long period of indecision when his feelings had fluctuated between surliness and foreboding. That was the last time he had a woman who really meant anything to him. She had died five years ago and had borne his only child, a daughter, Isabel. This woman had guided his dreams toward new—and old—horizons. She had been able to erase the thought of tomorrow with one stroke.

The sentences were now softer and slower. Little by little, the boy realized that the husky, long-fingered man with the pipe and typewriter had lost all interest in the story. He scratched his head and with a "Thank you very much, maybe I'll come round tomorrow if it's all right with you," he opened the door quickly only to bump into Laura, the woman who was now living all alone in the apartment upstairs. It was the time of day when darkness invaded every corner of the stairwell, blackening the dust on the walls and the dents on the handrails.

Domingo and Laura talked for a long time, mainly about the latest political events: the edicts from the party which they considered unacceptable, and the possibility of organizing a new group. They spent a long time discussing the dogmatic idiots who didn't understand the first thing about the new guidelines and who had failed to grasp their implications. Buenaventura made no reference whatsoever to José Augusto, not even a passing remark on the possible repercussions of the article he had just finished reading. Later, when Laura went back to her own apartment, Domingo turned off the record player, placed the pipe back on the ashtray and opened the window. The room was immediately filled with noises from the avenue outside: a goal scored by a gang of kids playing in the street, jeering pedestrians dodging passing cars, and impatient honking from the traffic on Oaxaca and Monterrey Streets. He stretched, rubbed his hands together and took an old book off the shelf. Its dusty, gray edges were getting yellowish and many of the pages were coming loose. Although it dealt mainly with the experiences of a Spanish adventurer in America whose trials and tribulations led him from convent to convent, it contained marvelous descriptions of pilasters adorned with floral motifs, the flowing, symmetrical effect of the colonial arches and the Indian pilgrims who stopped at the open-air chapel that smelled of incense and was illuminated by the faint glow from a Renaissance-style coffered ceiling.

He reached the part where a young woman disembarked on the docks of Veracruz. He was reminded of the women he had lived with: the one with the sinewy but soft body who lived on a squalid street behind the Del Carmen Market; the woman from the Claveria district whose hang-ups were exceeded only by her possessiveness; and once again, the woman from Algeciras with the sultry voice and the well-defined, shapely torso that his hands delighted in caressing, and who for so many years, when alone, he had imagined being caressed by his tongue. But perhaps no one could compare to Isabel, the mother of his daughter, the eternal gypsy who cut him to the quick; she had been the perfect foil for his rages and she had soothed his anger. She had been the last woman he had truly loved; she had eased his anguish and then faded away during the endless nights of heady midnight wine and sporadic bouts of insomnia that seemed to cling to the street lamps and the wet cries of the city after a rainstorm.

"Even memories are of no help to me now. I'm too old for surprises and I don't even have enough strength left to curse myself for it," old Federico had said a few days before his death. Once the searing pains in his stomach became unbearable, he resolved to say farewell to his thoughts and to his own face, stricken as it was by loneliness and old age. He put a bullet through his head.

Suddenly, his daugher Isabel opened the door, smiling as always; she always smiled for Domingo. She was almost twenty, wore her hair hung loose about her shoulders, and had Buenaventura's eyes, the same expression, the same distant smile, the same casual, nonchalant gestures. He closed the window and put the book back on the shelf, trying to insulate the apartment from everything outside those four walls. Isabel greeted him realizing that her presence somehow formed the atmosphere by reviving a host of invisible beings behind the paintings and photographs, the hundreds of stories lurking underneath each object; she never expected to comprehend all of them. They remained in the past and could never be retrieved, not even through the written word.

He bit on his pipe, calling upon memories, jumbling anecdotes, and measuring his words one by one. Although he spoke frankly, he refrained from doling out unwelcome advice. In this particular case he refused to assume a position of authority. He listened intently to Isabel's problems and grievances, monitoring his expressions. After a while, when they had aired their conflicting viewpoints without actually agreeing on any of them, Buenaventura knew for a fact that he was extremely proud of her and that those few minutes with his daughter made time stand still for him and restored his spirits.

"I ran into Sebastián at the University today. He's terribly worried about José Augusto. He said he's been looking all over for him and can't find him anywhere. He thinks maybe something serious has happened to Banderas. He's not in his apartment and no one has seen him at all in the past few days. Lord only knows!" said Isabel suddenly, clasping her hands in a gesture of veiled concern.

As he replaced the pipe in the ashtray, his eyes strayed toward José Augusto's article. He thought about the brazen, high-handed attitude adopted by those bloodsuckers—the oligarchs in power. He allowed himself a few thoughts about Banderas' loneliness and on Laura's assertiveness. However, he kept these thoughts to himself and decided to ask no questions.

Around eight o'clock, shortly after Isabel had left, Buenaventura couldn't make up his mind whether to go back to the typewriter or to proofread his manuscripts. He started swearing and cursing fiercely, the words sputtering out like branding irons. He saw himself in a shack in Cuajimalpa, in a brothel near La Merced market and in a flophouse on Serapio Rendón Street. From there, he felt transported to a filthy dump in Tacuba and finally to where he was now and had been for so many years: the apartment on Sinaloa. Here he'd been after Spain, after Isabel; here he waited for meetings to start or for his daughter's visits, where the objects kept piling up day after day—the mementos smelling of remembered time and the vision of endless stories waiting to be written. He always wound up settling for just a few pages, just a few facts weeded out from his own first-hand experiences. His mind went back to prison corridors, to iron bars, to the uneasy, relentless sensation of being hounded, to the sheer brutality of the thugs and prison guards and to the rotting faces suspended in the void, flanked by taunting murderers. He could hardly begin to count the number of cells, much less the years he had spent in each one of those places. Before he settled down to write, he lit his pipe and inhaled the smoke from the tobacco.

XI

ONE SATURDAY SEVERAL MONTHS after his return, Gabriel and Sebastián showed up at one of the weekly get-togethers at the Concordia Bar, in the San Angel district right in front of the monument to Obregón. The tables on the terrace faced Insurgentes Avenue where one could watch the traffic cops, harassed drivers and pedestrians. The regulars started trickling in around two thirty: Some were surly, a few others were obviously hung over, and the rest had come expressly to unwind or to massage their damaged egos.

"Well, a few heart transplants are in order, I see," remarked Sebastián, who was cold sober, as he saluted a group of discredited politicians at a distant table.

The sun along Insurgentes warmed the far side of the bar which had been taken over by the serious drinkers. Meanwhile, the dour, bald-headed pianist was driving everybody up the wall with his plodding renditions of those corny torch songs that had been standard fare in every sleazy dive during the thirties. Once in a while, someone would ask him gently not to play quite so enthusiastically. Meanwhile, the waiters could barely keep up with the clients on the terrace and in the inner rooms.

"Christ Almighty! I hope this drinking party doesn't get out of hand," called out the anthropologist from his regular table.

They started talking about all the old *cantinas* with the attractive lighting and legendary atmosphere: the Opera, the Tupinamba and the Bach Salon. They reminisced about the good old days when they had walked along the downtown streets in search of their first erotic conquests in the tacky bars of the Guerrera district. In a matter of minutes, platitudes, effusive gestures, loud exclamations and a general uproar were in full swing. "How goes it, my learned friend?" "Never better. How's it with you?" "A true scholar and a gentleman, that one." When the writer showed up, he jokingly asked the anthropologist to take a bow, adding that with his tall, beanpole figure, he could well play St. Christopher to the Child impersonated by any of those present.

"Aw Shit, that old chestnut again! Those jokes smell of the Stone Age," said Sebastián without batting an eye.

Rum, whiskey, double tequilas and steins of beer circulated freely amid interruptions from any place at every table. In less than half an hour, two or three more tables had been shoved together and the repartee began in earnest. The philosopher, who ranked high in the pecking order and had the final word on matters pertaining to human existence, didn't say one word, surveying the irreverent windbags from the heights. The enterprising politician—a perennial member of the opposition party, who had access to the lowdown on cabinet meetings and wirepulling in university circles, got the ball rolling by starting an argument and challenging every statement made. And of course, there was the self-styled comedian, always ready with a snappy comeback, a subtle pun and just the perfect timing between each quip, each burst of laughter.

"Well, I'll be . . . Look who's here . . . He's so small, there's no room for doubt," said Sebastián, quoting a Central American poet, as he welcomed the shy essayist. Gabriel watched them all closely, concentrating on their wry, spiteful expressions. It was a curious melange of parody and pastiche, of doubletalk and rabble-rousing. As far as political ideology was concerned, there was a bit of everything. They ran the gamut from the avowed enemies of private property to defenders of economic liberalism, from orthodox anarchists to progressive Catholics. Some of them were self-appointed experts in revolutionary meetings or in frustrated assassination attempts; confirmed rebels who firmly rejected all forms of power.

"Most of us here have been bitten by that bug," said the essayist placidly.

The historian, all spruced up and looking particularly thoughtful, had joined the group and took his place next to the philospher on the pontifical throne. Only occasionally did he deign to improve upon a particular sentence or to chastise some poor ignoramus. Then of course, there was the economist—a staunch advocate of the population explosion and the unquestionable stability of the Mexican peso. "Yes, Sirree, ours is a good, sound currency—accepted without any reservations whatsoever in financial circles all over the world." Then the latecomers arrived: the extroverted, moody painter, the poet with the languid ontological inner voices, and the pompous, caustic journalist, who was every bit as feisty as the politician.

Once the booze started going to their heads, their facades slowly cracked, the stereotypes crumbled and the undercurrents of old friendships came out in the open as did petty rivalries and jealousies and the stale jokes that had been told over and over again, somewhat padded here and there and brought up-to-date in the latest slang.

"We have to do away with this filthy old world of ours, it begets nothing but greed: There is scum everywhere you look," complained the journalist with a dash of irony.

Their successes, too, were shared, and provided a legitimate excuse to keep the drinks coming and the bill growing. Some drank silently, introspectively, pondering the pleasures of Bacchus. Others preferred to join in the conversation—making sarcastic comments on women's liberation and siding with those who swore that a happy marriage exists only in the minds of either the very naive or the very ignorant.

"I'm a firm believer in women's liberation. I've been married five times, so therefore, I've liberated five women," said the poet. "Down with machismo! It's a slogan I'll follow to the bitter end."

This remark immediately provoked a barrage of arguments in favor of the equality of the sexes and of the kind of women who were straightforward, willing to take risks, and seek sexual fulfillment without subjection. Cardoso, frowning, then cut in and took center stage. "We must not be swayed by misguided, cockeyed reasoning. We must always pay tribute to women, at all times, even while cursing and telling great lies!"

Their love affairs and detailed accounts of erotic experiences were a chapter in themselves. Descriptions of the breasts and hips of a diabolical gypsy filled the air. They were followed by discussions of long, drawn-out neurotic liasons sustained by some of the absentees and the incorrigible wantonness of their mistresses. "We have to hand it to the muses of yesteryear who endowed the act of adultery with a certain sense of well-being and honesty, and the most subtle and refined form of devotion," said the writer wistfully.

Sebastián pulled out all the stops. As he downed one *Cuba Libre* after another, his voice became louder, his owlish expression and his gestures more pronounced. He recounted his adventures, from his days as a party theoretician to the small empire he had established in the Mixcoac district; from the unforgettable hips of his favorite stripteaser to a "Frankly, my dear, I don't give a damn"—the classic phrase from "Gone with the Wind." He praised the superb talents of the women he had supposedly made love

84

to, describing in detail panties and bras, noting the importance of good thighs and how indispensable it was for a woman to have a well-rounded ass. As if to illustrate his point he described the blonde in the photograph facing his bed. Then, quite beside the point, he spoke of the great friends he had made in Alcoholics Anonymous.

"Boy, what a bullshit artist you are! I bet you even claim that clouds aren't really clouds at all but the faces of Greek gods or the soul of some dying poet," interrupted the essayist.

Little by little, as the bluffing subsided and everybody got fed up with the nasty cracks and sarcastic digs, someone happened to mention José Augusto Banderas. "Now, there's someone who really knew where it's at. He was wise to everything. No detail, however small, ever escaped him. Next to him, we were mere amateurs." The mind, image and shadow of the fugitive suddenly took on kaleidoscopic, mirror-like proportions. At first, Gabriel could hardly believe his ears: the sheer gibberish that poured from the mouths of that shallow group, each one portraying the anti-hero as the paragon of virtue.

For some time now, those Saturday sessions at La Concordia slowly unraveled Banderas' various personalities and the strange facets of his character from an encounter in a *pulquería* in Popotla to his role in the railroad workers' strike, from his profound knowledge of some of the works of Shakespeare to his quotations from Pérez Galdós and Valle-Inclán; they would comment his knowledge of Eliot and Malcolm Lowry, and his explanations, down to the last detail, of Obregón's death and General Serrano's assassination in Huitzilac. Fact and fiction were woven together, the vernacular of the brothels and the Jamaica Market, and the heritage Banderas had received from his Galician and Asturian ancestors, and they remarked on the influence that an elderly cabinet-maker, who also happened to be a healer, magician, sorcerer and astrologer, had exerted on him.

There was also a fair share of crude remarks about "that multi-faceted or super-multifaceted personage," as the philosopher called him: José Augusto Banderas holding court in a dump on Regina Square, the trouble-shooter who broke up a cell of militants, "all friends," added the painter; the charismatic, destitute Banderas, the recluse who haunted slums and whorehouses; "the only one of us who ever actually admitted to his mega-lomania," mused the historian. "He thought he was an expert on bull-fighting, was horny as hell, a sadomasochistic lover, an infamous, penitent son of a bitch and an incorrigible apostle of the ignorant."

85

Although the biographical sketches that came out of those Saturday meetings at the Concordia were incongruous and often overlapped, they still bore smatterings of truth, and were damnably entertaining as well. They covered every inch of the city—from the palatial mansions of San Angel to the tenements of Bondojito. And then in an endless game of challenges, José Augusto's nicknames and their interpretations would multiply to infinity.

"I used to call him the Unburied Corpse—it's the only name that fits him perfectly," said the journalist.

It seemed impossible to Gabriel that any of those impressions tallied with his own image of José Augusto; they seemed totally unreal. But little by little, these speculations began to take shape and the real thing, the real person or persons, closer to the truth than the José Augusto of the editorials and the budding political parties, slowly emerged: cagey, zealous, persuasive and brooding. It could well be that José Augusto constantly patterned himself after his contemporaries. The ideal hero of his times was the political rebel but that was just one of the many characters in that vast tableau of comings and goings, of still unsolved riddles.

"There were long periods when he kept a great deal to himself. He was shy then—and living on handouts . . . lazy as hell, smelling to high heaven and chain-smoking all the time," said the anthropologist. The essayist, on the other hand, mentioned having met José Augusto in his own element: "It was at a cathouse on Durango Street, a relic from the forties when it was the most famous house of assignation in the city, when it was really worthwhile living here. You could go for long walks and drop in for coffee on Bolívar Street, or López and Ayuntamiento and chew the fat with the Spanish refugees."

The militants who had served in the same party cell with José Augusto considered him a privileged human being, with superior intellectual powers, unique creativity, and a definite political skill; a man whose brilliant future had been ruined by intrigues and malicious gossip. The poet, however, refrained from idealizing José Augusto. "He's extremely intelligent, I'll grant you that—but he can be quite ignorant as well. Any way you look at it, he's a lively guy with the knack of picking up jargon. But deep down he's nothing but a dilettante. His superficial grasp of culture allows him to hold his own anywhere and impresses the hell out of less gifted mortals."

As usual, Sebastián had to have the last word. He scoffed at everyone by saying that all their opinions bordered on the asinine. "Your shallowness is unbelievable—it's disgusting. Banderas is like an archetype compared to any or all of you."

Everyone, even the biggest stud around, envied José Augusto his collection of mistresses. There were, just to mention a few: the much sought-after Tahitian girl he had met at the Bremen Restaurant. She was the epitome of lust, with her amply endowed thighs, dreamy gaze, provocative lips and insatiable sexual appetites. Then there was the broad-hipped mulatto girl who lived on Genova Street. By the way, she turned out to be a loyal friend at all times. The daughter of an Ecuadorian exile—the one with the haunting face and the extraordinary pelvis and breasts to match. She possessed, besides, a profound inner life. There was another one, who lived in Polanco, with all kinds of unfulfilled urges and Modigliani-like neck and arms. She was undoubtedly well equipped to make the most of her acrobatic talents in the bedroom. Cardoso underlined then Banderas' wisdom concerning the Book of Changes, Chinese culture and Oriental religions.

"This is too much. You're turning the man into a goddamned myth," ventured the painter hesitantly. "Banderas is just like any one of us. Sure, he has an incredible imagination, but his arrogance makes him insufferable. Come off it."

Gabriel did not know them well enough to voice his opinions and he limited himself to an occasional question and to a constant effort not to miss a single detail.

The main dialogue was one thing, but the undertow of more private and intimate conversation was quite another. In the latter, Banderas was referred to as "The Unmentionable" and "The Sick," and his complexity, humaneness and inscrutability all came into play. He could be downtrodden, a sadist, a would-be son of a rotten existence; but he was not a phony or a cruel person. In fact he was someone to whom everyone owed a favor. It was possible to talk about the lunatic, to describe José Augusto as a bullshitter or a book thief, but never as a sly person given to slander or uncalled-for aggression or hatred. There was at least this one, single, unshakable point: "The Unmentionable reconciled all viewpoints, brought people together, encouraged independent thinking and constantly lived up to his political aspirations," said the economist. No one raised any objections to that statement.

"Naturally, he was a real menace where other people's books were concerned. If you knew how many books disappeared out of my library . . . ," the poet broke in.

Before his disappearance, the "Great Lunatic" was something of a celebrity. You could run into him practically anywhere in the city. By weaving his own Utopias and living up to the goals he had set for himself despite the absurd world he lived in, he had justly earned—and richly deserved—each one of the multiple identities ascribed to him. "There's no doubt about it. He could speak the truth so that everyone could understand," the anthropologist's voice boomed out, "whether a woman who spent a rainy afternoon with him, or the workers of a Nonoalco factory, who listened to him intently. I saw it myself, and they were absolutely mesmerized. He calmed them down one morning when there had been riots. I'll never forget how we used to drop in on him in that hole in the wall of his. He could set up house anywhere, in any ramshackle building; there were always tons of books lying all over the place."

When they got around to the murder everyone was stumped: a kind of taboo surrounded the subject and there were a number of gaps no one could fill. Every single one of their speculations, theories and hypotheses seemed to fall apart and dangle there. "Banderas wouldn't hurt a fly. To this day, for the life of me, I'll be damned if I know why he always carried a gun in his pocket; he was peaceful enough to have been a leader in the passive resistance movement," the politician observed.

"He always seemed so cool, like a marble statue," said the philosopher unexpectedly. "He had full control of his emotions and was dead set against immoderation of any kind. His tone was always persuasive, deliberate and precise, thorough even to the most insignificant detail."

"His record was spotless," added the journalist. "Whenever there was a riot, he was merely a bystander. He usually kept his hands behind his back and had a cigarette dangling from his lips. There was always a peculiar expression on his face; I don't know whether it was fear or disgust."

Everyone agreed that José Augusto's sense of decency was a product of his upbringing. He had grown up in austere surroundings with a family background that was a mixture of both Christian and liberal ideas; repudiation of the seven capital sins was constantly being drummed into him. "Although, of course, we must not forget the days when he was the neighborhood bum. He used to hang around with drunks and hoodlums. We'd always make fun of him because he couldn't hold his liquor—he was practically a teetotaler. He couldn't handle much more than two drinks or a single beer at the most," said the essayist, smugly downing his Scotch.

However, the consensus was that perhaps his real vice—his "compulsive," "absurd," "morbid," "neurotic" vice was his passion for women, which triggered his disintegration and ultimately led to his downfall.

"What no one can deny is that he was the champion chain-smoker of all time," said the historian all of a sudden.

Although they covered practically every aspect of the murder—the scene of the crime, the apartments which most of them knew, all the stories associated with the building itself, Laura's reaction, the direction of the bullets and the blood-stained carpet—the real motives, the underlying implications such as José Augusto's possible schizophrenia, paranoia and perhaps obsessional neurosis, remained unexplained. The poet, who lacked sufficient evidence to state his case, merely sniffed, "The Lunatic is capable of anything; he'd kill his own shadow if need be."

The getaway itself generated a whole new set of enigmas. Possible escape routes were figured out: in the downtown area, in out-of-the way slums, on the rooftops of the Roma neighborhood or in the basements of the old houses in Coyoacán. "I have a feeling he's skipped the country. He could well be in Prague, in Sofia, in Hong Kong or even in Peking," said the painter, becoming more and more involved in the discussion. And so, in their minds, the Great Lunatic wandered back and forth across the four points of the globe, vanished into thin air, mysteriously spirited away. He became endowed with an amazing ubiquity—he was all over the place. His many personalities were spread out among Far Eastern landscapes or Nordic woods, the shabby tenements of Peralvillo and the miserable shacks of Ixtapalapa.

As the liquor loosened their tongues they became more and more maudlin. "We're really too much—we're pathological liars—we all made up our own versions. Look here, I knew him like the back of my hand and I can tell you that you're all on the wrong track, you got lost in a bunch of claptrap." And then new angles were brought to light which could not, by any stretch of the imagination, correspond to any real person, but only to some other lunatics who had been created or re-created by individual or collective minds. These lunatics in particular always looked hopefully to the future, did not squander their talent and let everyone give vent to their own convictions, their frustrated dreams and their vast repertoire of make-believe.

The afternoon slipped by while the pianist returned to his schmaltzy tunes, and José Augusto Banderas' intangible presence slowly faded from the scene. By now, some of them were ogling a teen-age girl with great legs and firm breasts. The essayist and the poet, somewhat pie-eyed, got up, waved goodbye and left.

Nevertheless the incoherent, bombastic remarks, the pompous speeches and the garbled reports continued. The politician suddenly cried out: "You're nothing but a bunch of Philistines, fifth-rate phonies, Pharisees, full of shit!" Then, believing himself the true representative of the proletarian revolution, he started berating the poor meek soul in front of him. He rambled on in the same vein until someone shut him up. Then he set his verbal machine gun to one side, sank into his chair and confessed that from that moment on, he was willing to turn into a sculptured rock crystal skull. "The best way to deal with these boors is total indifference," snorted Sebastián.

From that time on, every Saturday afternoon, shortly after three, Gabriel never missed one of the bull sessions at the Concordia. After the usual hassle over the amount of the bill, he, Sebastián and the scrawny writer would go somewhere else, perhaps to discuss General Obregón's rotting hand or to remember faces and lives from the past—anything to shake off their boredom. The traffic on Insurgentes grew heavier and the neon store lights were already shining on the pavement and shop windows as they left.

The subject of the Unmentionable, the Lunatic, the Madman remained fixed in their minds. Each week, the other alaises returned dutifully to their tombs only to be resurrected the next time; the Holy Terror, the Scarecrow, the Flake, the Werewolf, the Bottleneck, the Zombie. There were more, many more names dating back to the remote past, to stories they had gotten third-hand, or to legends that were barely being created: The Stiff, the Boneyard, the Blockbuster all remained in midair. The list grew longer, especially amid the stockpile of silences oppressing the regulars at La Concordia: the Sleepwalker, the Ego Trip, the Huron, the Commander-in-Chief. They, in turn, gave rise to other figures, other images, other myths which gave deeper roots to the endless controversies among the regulars.

However, as far as Sebastián was concerned, of all the names the Unmentionable and the Lunatic were the only ones that really counted.

90

XII

IT SEEMED TO HIM THAT the night had started too late. It was a dry, cloudless April day and he had spent the morning as usual—with smoke-filled ashtrays as a measure of his activity. April had been simply another month—until the night when José Augusto went for a long walk, his gun in his pocket and a bitter taste in his mouth. He walked slowly, feeling his grievances and his anger churning up inside and oblivious to the bustling activity on Insurgentes, the smell of greasy tacos sold on street corners, the hands of taxi drivers waving frantically to prospective passengers, the trolleys grinding to a stop. Then, with a resilience born of an overwrought imagination, he remembered those first few days with Laura when the apartment on Sinaloa smelled of perfume and eau de cologne, when during their last talks he had freely admitted to the destructiveness of his temper.

At last, after so many months, after his narrow escape from death at the hands of the hoodlums who had kidnapped and beaten him, he had finally seen through his own little games. He had come to grips with himself and faced up to his complexes and weaknessess. With each day, he became more and more conscious of his loss—the intimacy with Laura that he had never fully appreciated, the nightly exhilaration at the rediscovery of each other's body. *I never learned to give of myself freely—I always went to extremes: Either I wound up pissing her off or just laughed everything off... And yet, how many times I was really sure that with her it would be a permanent thing. At last I had found a woman who really reached me. And the worst part of it is that, like a babbling idiot, I am still crazy for her. It's become a fixation: this yen to have here with me, naked, to feel her hands and her mouth on my body, to open her legs and stroke her thighs.*

He sauntered across the avenue. His eyes were bloodshot, his shirt collar and trousers dark with grime. He pictured Laura lying on the sofa, learning to smoke and trying to cheer him up as he told her about some of his experiences: the first pornographic pictures he had seen as a boy, his disastrous adventures in whorehouses along the border, the risks he had taken in the company of drug addicts, barflies and ex-chorus girls.

Frowning, he swore at the neon lights and the crowd leaving the movies. He lit a cigarette as he reached the other side of the street, letting the smoke shield his face. He reflected that it was impossible to separate his goals from his lies; they seemed to go hand in hand. Thanks to his cynicism, even his dreams had betrayed him; the indescribable joy he had felt with Laura was falling apart. *Those overblown macho poses of yours — what was it someone said, you were more of a shitheel than a jock. José Augusto, the do-gooder who has to be the center of attention and who always has the last word, the big man who has to call all the shots. And at the end, you wound up empty-handed.*

As he crossed the corner of Insurgentes and Baja California, scenes of the brutal beating flashed before him — that endless night in that garbage dump in Ciudad Satélite when he finally felt himself breathe, and the next morning when two construction workers picked him up like a sack of cement and carried him to a filthy shack. Then came his slow, painful recovery, when he finally managed to get both his thoughts and his bones together, and at last, his first real glimpse of the city and his return to the apartment on Chilpancingo several days later. There was, of course, Sebastián's voice: "Where the hell have you been, you goddamned profligate? We've been looking everywhere for you and not a trace. You're a real honest-to-God asshole, you know it? Well, anyway, you know you can count on me . . . anything, I mean it."

José Augusto glanced absently at the clear sky, at the TV antennas on the building across the street, at the glum passengers on a bus. He kept walking until he reached the Américas Café, where he managed to find an empty table. Perhaps it was the same table where he and Laura had planned the decorative lighting and the new color scheme for the apartment on Sinaloa. They had talked about hanging some black and white posters and getting a new record player. Once again his mind wandered off on different tangents — their bodies merging together in absolute harmony, the words they murmured to each other just before and after sleep, lips on legs and navels, the culmination of their ecstasty. His own thoughts and senses recreated their sensitivity to one another, the infinite combinations of vitality and apathy, the cigarettes that passed from one hand to the other, their naked bodies at midday and their perennial wonder upon exploring newer, deeper forms of lust.

As feelings of jealousy — both past and present — welled up inside him, he knew how much he missed their talks, how much he missed Laura's back, the palms of her hands opened wide, her smooth knees, the undulating movement of her hips. He replayed their months together again and again—without realizing how much time had gone by since then. Their day began either at midnight or at dawn—or with the afternoon light streaming in on them. Then they would gaze at each other, giggling as they showered, the water trickling down their legs and shoulders. Sometimes they'd just fool around in the rain, watching the darkening streets and the crowds gathering on the corners of San Juan de Letrán.

He peered at a newsstand on the street through half-closed eyes, shutting himself off from the conversations at nearby tables by his own silent cries. He concentrated on reenacting the tingling sensations in their legs, the taste of perspiration on their throats and lips, their wandering, restless hands and the peculiar moisture that exuded from their bodies as the walls around them seemed to sway. *Everything seemed to gang up at me at once. Finally, there was a moment when I couldn't believe what was really happening. I felt I was drifting away from everything—like a sleepwalker—and that I was incapable of making a life for myself. Wherever I went, I heard nothing but people bitching at each other; wherever I went, I saw nothing but phony, deadpan faces. Besides, it was so easy to dream up imaginary rivals and make sure they were at Laura's side so I could witness her unfaithfulness first-hand. I was literally drowning in my own inertia, in my scars, and in the beating I'd taken, of course.*

He half-heartedly ordered a cup of coffee and was suddenly brought back to earth by smoke patterns from cigarettes, the eyes of a beggar and the white socks of a teenager. The mirror—always the mirror—loomed before him: facing them, behind them, sideways,—staring silently at their intertwined bodies—a stern, shimmering onlooker, who, even in the dark, goaded them on to new dimensions of pleasure.

Suddenly, José Augusto heard someone greeting him from behind. It was a familiar, yet distant voice, a voice long departed, a voice from the dead. First, the fellow thumped him on the back and then sat down opposite him at the table. Although he still had the same bland smile he had twenty years ago, the patronizing air was of a more recent vintage. He rambled on about all sorts of people—ghosts from the past, now scattered all over the place. José Augusto stared at him intently and remembered himself as he had been during those years when procrastination had been the order of the day. He had whiled away the time by feeding the juke-box, adopting carefully studied poses and leering at the well-stacked B girls.

The domino games had stretched on for days, and as the rum lifted their spirits, it would gradually put an end to their big talk.

José Augusto realized that while his companion was talking, he was also scrutinizing him, noticing the premature wrinkles on his forehead, the stubble on his chin and his restless fingers; his hands seemed locked together, as if seeking absolution to cure all of his anguish. Banderas had no idea how he summoned up enough composure to listen, to feign interest, to dredge up bits and pieces of dead fragments, images of obscure faces, and the standard, oft-repeated anecdotes which by now were completely pointless. *Day after day the ghosts, doubts and surliness increased. I think I even ran out of curses. I saw her everywhere—in the shop windows, in the parks, between the sheets and even in my shadow. I couldn't help thinking that she would appear at any moment and that we could go back as before. But I had also created a mental picture of the son of a bitch who was probably sleeping with her.*

It dawned on his companion that he was no longer speaking to the José Augusto he remembered. It was as though he had been talking all this time to a perfect stranger, haggard and aged beyond belief—someone who bore only a slight resemblance to the real flesh-and-blood José Augusto— his buddy from the pool halls on Argentina Street and the cat houses on Orizaba, the agitator in the Law School who used to run around with drunks and troublemakers. As José Augusto had his first sip of coffee and stubbed out his cigarette—the ash fizzling out on the ashtray—he automatically reverted to his old obsessions: the evenings with Laura lying before him or on top of him, their legs and arms locked tightly. His intruder from the past could only get up, mumble a frosty goodbye and leave.

José Augusto picked up a match at random, lit it quickly and threw it on the floor, angrily stamping out the dying flame as if he were reviving the nights they had spent in a café on Hamburgo Street or on a park bench facing the statue of Pasteur. The newspaper boys would hurt your ears with their shouts and the shoe shine boys always had a steady stream of words, a world of fiction between the hands and eyes, the trips from one continent to another, as if their imagination alone were enough to transport them to any world they chose.

The bitter taste of the coffee set his teeth on edge; he rubbed his temples nervously, his arms feeble, as tense as his own thoughts. He remembered a particularly violent quarrel, late at night, when he had shouted insults at her from one end of the corridor to the other and had kept it up when he reached the staircase. He could not bring himself to think back on the months when Laura started having second thoughts about their relationship, when she would greet his projects with reserve, and when she became skeptical about any kind of a future for them. Here again he recognized himself as the paranoid egotist that he was. *A couple of weeks after I was beaten up, I started carrying my father's gun—the one that had been stashed away in a desk drawer for so long. I kept it handy—on the night table, on the desk, in my pocket. I got used to knowing it was there; it accompanied me on my long walks and in my depressions. Its company became indispensable to me. I even got to the point where I enjoyed the bluntness of my aversions. Once, when cursing Laura got too heavy, I really got disgusted with myself.*

Somewhat disgruntled by the bitterness of the coffee, he fumbled around for some money, left it on the table and, lighted cigarette in hand, went outside. At loose ends, he mingled with hundreds of pedestrians on the avenue. The crowds reminded him of the political demonstrations, when he and Laura were always the first to arrive, raising their fists, shouting at the top of their voices and gazing upwards all around them. Then they'd hold their arms up high again and start walking, yelling themselves hoarse and braving the tear gas. As soon as the mob had been dispersed, before they reached the Zócalo, they'd run for cover, wander through the side streets and seek shelter wherever they could. Then, they'd go back to the apartment where they'd shut themselves off from the crowds to trace new paths for their lips, for their caresses and for their voices to wander through, murmuring and moaning softly in the dark in their quest for a slow, never ending and perfect fulfillment.

By now he was firmly entrenched in his loneliness and in Laura's absence. He had almost taken it for granted that he would run into her in a matter of minutes. He kept on walking north through Insurgentes, where the shops were closing for the night and dozens of people with bored, listless faces were crowded at each corner waiting for a bus or streetcar. Once in a while, he would stick his hand in his pocket and whistle a vague tune, attempting to reproduce the strains of the music that floated into their bedroom in the evenings, rippling through their bodies with a rhythm that gave more vigor to caresses and thoughts. It was nearly evening when the strings—with their cadences and arpeggios intermingled with their movements, the intensity of their gazes and the contact of their tongues; it was the image of Laura beside him and the playing of a clarinet; it was the image of her nipples and an invisible baton seeming to guide

95

slowly their embraces and the interlocking of their legs. *I had to obliterate her completely—her body, her shoulders, her navel. Then a series of distorted images kept coming at me and I'd deny the fact that I lived with her for so long. But the lovemaking, the silences piled up until I reached the very bottom of my bitterness. So many things no longer made any sense and life itself was turning me into shit.*

He fondled the matchbox, not even noticing the smoky streak of burning gasoline from an orange bus. Finally, he went back to a particular tune, to the perturbing effect of the images, to the change of rhythm in the quickened movement of her hips and breasts, to the sound of bows meeting strings and the abrupt, surprising changes in tempo of the woodwind instruments and his arms around her back and her breathtaking nude waist.

He looked up at the barren, starless sky—not one single glittering speck was to be seen. He stopped in front of a shop window, more absorbed in his own reflection than in the mannequins in the background. He could still hear the music that floated in and out of Laura's ecstasies—sometimes laconic, sometimes lascivious—the faint sounds of an oboe or a distant harp. The image of their intertwined bodies, night after night, dawn after dawn remained engraved in his visions, in his sharpened senses, in the persistence of his memory. *For the life of me, I still can't figure out how I ever got out of that beating alive. And two weeks later, once the pain diminished, I was right back at it again—the hang-ups, fixations and boredom. Except that by that time I not only hated Laura but myself as well. Everything seemed to cave in on me and that's how things stayed until a strange sort of fury would take hold of me. Then, a few hours later, I'd get back in the same old rut, the same old apathy—refusing to believe that any of it actually happened. I remember one night I started making fun of everything in sight and I finally reached the point where I didn't give a damn about Laura's cheating on me. From that moment on, I could feel the void closing in and weighing me down.*

He crossed Insurgentes and stopped to peer through the dark alley leading to Aguascalientes Street and to delve into his own enigmas from which, as if he were in a long tunnel, there was no escape. He made feeble attempts to recapture the image of their bodies swaying back and forth to the chords of a rhapsody, a symphony, an overture. He longed to return to an old or new variation, to the strings and percussion instruments, to focus all his pleasures around that small room, on their bodies, their fingertips, the tips of their tongues. He wanted to return to her endless offering of any form of lust, but this time with his eyes wide open.

He clung to the long, gloomy silence with a throbbing pain hammering against his forehead and his thoughts. He kept on walking north, imagining himself in a world of sleepwalkers, of dispossessed human beings. He groped for the gun in his pocket, feeling the handle and the trigger. He took a deep breath, trying little by little to curb the rage building up inside him.

As he plodded through one block after another, he was finally brought back to reality by the city itself. Avenida Insurgentes was slowly clearing, as if even the pavements and buildings were preparing to close for the night and getting ready to welcome the ceaseless midnight rain.

XIII

THE BEGINNING OF EACH DAY no longer seemed to drag by so slowly; there was no one beside her now, just the sounds outside her window. Laura looked at herself in the mirror: the well-defined contour of her eyebrows, her hazel eyes, the curve of her shoulders. As she paced back and forth from one end of the bedroom to the other, from her dressing table to the steam-filled bathroom, she couldn't help feeling that in spite of everything, time had lost its meaning and José Augusto's presence still lingered on.

Laura experienced a feeling of expectation, as if she were always waiting for something. *I was finally coming out of my shell, patching up the bits and pieces of what I had lost, and whatever else was in store for me.* Now everything around her—the cushions on the sofa, her underwear neatly folded inside the drawers and the oval mirror next to the bed—seemed to possess a certain vitality. The passage of time seemed to have mellowed them; they stirred the imagination and were unable to flourish if abandoned. She still missed José Augusto's voice, the voice that murmured over the curves of her hips, her neck, her thighs.

Again and again Laura had told herself that it was completely out of the question; she could not go back to that old pattern, to his verbal attacks which kept getting more and more abrasive, to his biting sarcasm. It was impossible for her to go along with the farce anymore; it should be over and done with for good—their battered dreams, the hate in their eyes. Nevertheless, *I had to start living again; I had to think of other alternatives and not let myself be swallowed up by all the that anguish—it was really getting me down.* When he was living there with her, once their outbursts had become habitual and their passion began to ebb, her own silence became intolerable to her; it had been just one more way of closing her eyes to the situation, of letting it ride.

Under no circumstances was Laura willing to relinquish any part of

98

herself ever again. This time she had to make absolutely certain that she held her future in her own hands. Finally the day came, one April morning as she left the apartment, when she realized that the empty stairway no longer bothered her.

A little before nine o'clock she set out through Oaxaca and Sinaloa Streets, which were already filled with blaring, honking sounds and nameless faces. People were scurrying along the streets, scrambling on the buses and injecting a touch of life into the orange streetcars. *I was all mixed up. My thoughts were all jumbled up in my head and I hadn't the slightest idea of how to go about being alone again. I had to erase him from my life completely—that aching need for his body, to hear his voice. But I was positive I had taken the only way out of a rotten mess.*

As she walked toward Alvaro Obregón Avenue, she remembered the first gatherings at Andrea's house, the unconditional moral support she had received from Buenaventura and her distraught state of mind before she had met José Augusto. She strolled along absently, oblivious to the shadows cast by the trees and the roar of the motors. She felt exhilarated by an undefined feeling of self-confidence. She sensed, perhaps, that soon she would meet another man, maybe even have a baby, travel, explore her other feelings and rid herself, at whatever cost, of her sense of failure. She had no doubts whatever as to her imminent recovery; she was sure she'd avoid all the pitfalls and that before long she'd even adopt a condescending attitude toward José Augusto.

The truly happy times lay just around the corner. They just *had* to, even if the memory of José Augusto's unbearable arrogance and his scornful smile still persisted. *Those last few months, I reached the point where I couldn't even stand to look in his eyes—nor any of his expressions, for that matter. They went from resignation to cockiness, from uncontrollable rage to meekness and a plea for sympathy. Sometimes for days at a time I wouldn't see him at all. Then, when he'd come back, it was always in the early morning hours—after I'd been waiting up for him—and all he would do is resort to the same old gimmicks, saying he felt misunderstood, neglected and so forth. It became so ridiculous, so idiotic.*

In her efforts to boost her optimism, Laura had not yet realized that quite inadvertently she'd been building up a series of deep-seated grudges. Still, the attitudes, images, words and impressions which were most important to her new life were being firmly imprinted on her mind.

Before she reached the publishing house, she crossed Monterrey Street. A sense of confidence enhanced the gentleness of her face; soon

99

she'd rid herself of the baggage of the past. A smug expression crept over her face as she tried to decipher the underlying implications behind José Augusto's insults. Her passivity, her growing resentment, and even her nightmares had not yet begun to haunt her. Once at work, while she scanned one memorandum after another, checked the catalogues and read a pile of manuscript evaluations, she suspected that José Augusto hadn't been able to fully enjoy any other woman, that he'd probably gone back to his old tricks—the sheep's eyes, smooth talk and so-called need for companionship. She could not believe that he was totally indifferent to her, nor could she imagine for one moment that he'd give up his penchant for self-flagellation. There was no doubt in her mind that in his futile and constant search he was sleeping around with all sorts of women. However, he had enough pride to cover up his real motives, to scoff at his own fears and devote himself completely to fabricating a whole new set of lies and empty promises.

Sometimes, even when she was hard at work, she could still remember him as he bent over his typewriter, bursting with enthusiam over his next article, an upcoming political meeting, or his constant plans to travel. He spoke of cargo ships, of exotic ports and desert islands. He was always lively then and went out of his way to please her. But afterwards, especially on Sundays, she could see that he was at loose ends again, back in the same old rut, making half-hearted attempts at a dozen different projects, indulging in the usual double-talk and pointless excesses. By this time, his plans were nothing more than mere daydreams, castles in the air. She checked off in her mind the belongings José Augusto had left at her place. They were still there, lying in the wardrobe and on the shelves, and for a long time she had felt that somehow they were hers as well. *As I got to know him better, I soon caught on to his lies and subterfuges, and that's when everything sort of fell apart. I was constantly plagued by doubts and my feelings for him wavered from pity to revulsion. Sometimes I even suspected that it was another woman who caused him to act that way—or other women—a whole slew of them. I never really found out for sure and to tell the truth I really don't care any more. One night—actually it was almost morning—I knew it was over. We'd spent the whole night quarreling and yelling at each other. I just couldn't go on being an accomplice to all his hang-ups or putting up with his lame excuses and his bluffing.*

For several weeks now, just before Laura left the office and was getting the accounts and papers in order, she'd been getting a phone call, causing her face to brighten and her tone of voice to soften. Gradually, without actually examining why, she had been instinctively seeking other outlets, other relationships. She could not afford to make any more mistakes or fall into the same trap again. One way or another she had to eliminate those bizzare, violent episodes from her life. She had to forget her previous blunders and purge herself, once and for all, of José Augusto's image. *I had to get used to another voice that wasn't his, to surrender myself to someone else without so many strings attached, to forget his hands had ever been on my breasts, on my waist, on my body.*

She left the office under the shimmering evening lights thinking that perhaps sooner than she imagined she would feel another's skin against hers, that before long her fingers would be fondling another chest—a man with strong, muscular arms who would embrace her tightly.

She walked along Tabasco Street; it was almost deserted and the leaves were falling softly. She could hear the faint sounds of the branches brushing against each other. The neon signs on the street corners were lighting up and a car was backing into an old garage. It occurred to her that maybe tonight—her forehead pressed against the pillow, her legs opened and her nipples hard—she would take the definite step and her despair would be finally laid to rest. The sick world that had controlled her emotions for so long would be buried forever.

That same dry April day Laura had taken her time to get back to her apartment on Sinaloa. She realized as soon as she got home that she was tired of dim lights, tired of darkness and of gloom. She opened the window and spent a few minutes standing on the balcony, spotting Domingo Buenaventura strolling toward Medellín Street. *After José Augusto left, I didn't know what to do with myself during those first few weeks. There were lots of times when I felt like seeing him again, when I wanted him to sleep with me. But I had to be strong; I had to adjust to being alone with myself again.*

She lay down on the sofa for a while, remembering her lonely adolescence, barely ten years ago. They had lived on the outskirts of the city, way out north near the Green Indians Statues, as everybody called them. It had been full of empty lots and abandoned shacks and was bone dry for months on end. The workmen would toil from sunrise to late evening and the clouds of dust drifted over the neighboring hills and into the houses and swirled around the street corners. She could see her father, the boss, barking out orders at the truck drivers. He had large, steady hands and never took his mind off his work. She recalled the conversations she had had with her mother about all sorts of things—religious fanatics, alcoholism, the inordinate number of pregnant women in their area, and the

101

temptations of too much leisure time. It dawned on her now that the roots of her essentially apprehensive nature had sprung from those years, from her persistent withdrawal from anything that went on beyond those four walls, from her attempts to control her budding sensuality and also her eagerness to explore new horizons.

She remembered José Augusto's strained expression the very first time they had entered this room a couple of months after they had met in Buenaventura's apartment. His outlandish talk, false humility, sarcasm, jibes and far-fetched, wild ideas came flooding back to her. *There were nights when I had to choke back my own words and I knew that my insomnia would give me away. I had to suppress my impulses. I felt as if I were split into a million pieces and was afraid I'd turn into a sort of shadow. But he was there, always there, in all my thoughts, in my fantasies, in my body, in the very fiber of my being.*

A few minutes later the doorbell rang, shaking her out of her mood. She went back to the window and threw down the key to the man standing by the front door. She looked all the way down the street to where it crossed Insurgentes, sensing that very soon she would be compensated for all the pain she'd been through. Perhaps the man coming up the stairs would sit in José Augusto's chair. Then they'd talk about the movie they'd seen last Sunday and maybe about going away for the weekend.

Laura heard some noises on Oaxaca Street. They came from the call girls in the house on the far end of the street where, night after night, their fixed smiles lured their customers until the early morning hours. On the balcony closest to her, a cat stood motionless like a dark stone idol with two shiny gaps in his head. It was barely nine o'clock and in spite of everything, Laura could not shake off the feeling of expectation, as if she were waiting, always waiting for something in silence.

102

XIV

JOSÉ AUGUSTO HAD BEEN walking along the Alvaro Obregón esplanade feeling like his own worst enemy. Once his good spirits had evaporated, he wondered whether he should go back to the stuffy apartment on Chilpancingo, call Sebastián or go halfway across the city to unwind at Andrea's. He paid no attention whatsoever to the lackluster sky or to the wind whipping around the street corners. He tried to postpone his indecision by swallowing his saliva as if by doing so he could subdue his anxieties, his inner conflicts.

He could feel his frustration piercing through his mind like restless claws which could materialize at will and without notice. His apparent indifference cut him off from the rest of the city, from everything he heard or saw, though not from himself, from his memories of past dissipations or from his smoldering rage. He had reached the point where everything exasperated him — his disjointed thoughts, his petty annoyances — even his own dirty fingernails — and he was constantly besieged by the phantoms of suicide.

He groped for the gun again and fondled it in his pocket, letting his thoughts slide on, feeling the drops of perspiration trickling down his armpits. Momentarily amused by his own steady gaze which was fixed on nothing in particular — on infinite space — he uttered a brief, fleeting epitaph in his own memory. As he reached the edge of the esplanade he thought about the invalid in the pool hall — his twisted grin, the menacing expression on his hideous face. The evil in that grotesque face was unmistakable, as was the cripple's awareness of his own monstrous appearance, his amazing talent for living like a bum and for jeering at others. José Augusto mentally changed places with the invalid, imagining himself constantly intimidating the weaklings — the more vulnerable — around him, thumbing his nose at the whole world and accepting his own brutishness as his irrevocable destiny with one definite advantage: the lifelong, unconditional compassion shown him by others.

He kept on walking as if his shadow were not his own; he couldn't help seeing the cripple's crutches reflected on the pavement and in the sewers, as if with one withered leg he not only carried the full weight of his body, but his guilt and excesses as well. He could barely make out the España Park in the darkness, got tired of looking at nothing but gloom and shadows and turned resolutely toward Oaxaca Street. He thought of calling his mother, of making up some story or of bragging a bit, to try to forget the past few humdrum days and the long time that had elapsed since he had seen Laura. This might allow him to discard his recent memories in favor of more distant ones. However, he decided against it almost immediately. He was in no mood to put up a front or to cover his obvious surliness. He came to the conclusion that tonight was not a good night for loafing around. Instead, he would go for one of his long walks, and take a careful look at all his obsessions. He would try to find some overall framework in which he could fit all of his concerns. Then he would be able to concentrate on his grudges.

Tonight was not a good night either for fixed schedules, for putting up with other people's hard-luck stories or condescending smiles. As Sebastián used to say, "I'm sick to death of those warmed-over life stories, the same old trite, rehashed monologues."

He was so engrossed in his own sullen form of introspection that he scarcely glanced at the billboards on the opposite side of the street. As he linked the immediate with the remote sequences, other voices, other images sprang up before him: the bums on 2 de Abril Street, the streetwalkers lining up and showing their garters, mangy dogs staring into the wet afternoons and the newspaper boys proclaiming the latest disasters. He no sooner had created a false illusion of relief for himself than he transformed it into inertia by reverting to trivial details such as the unconscious swaying of the trees and the dry wind pressing into basements and across rooftops.

He recreated his quarrels with his father, dredging up long-forgotten insults without feeling any remorse whatsoever. He could almost taste the bitterness in their words and feel their labored breathing as they got worked up. However, he no longer suffered from the misleading assumption that his future was stretched out endlessly before him and that someday he would get around to forgiving his father while rejecting every single one of his precepts and warnings. What had been dead and buried suddenly came to life again, like the abortive discussions when they'd invariably wind up glaring at each other and when José Augusto would mistake his own defiance for emancipation—which, as it turned out, was always short-

104

lived. He could see his father again, shuffling along the corridors, the stairs, the parlor or the dining room in the Miguel Schultz Street apartment. His hands were always clasped behind his back—those expressive hands that had accomplished so much, handled so many objects in their lifetime, grown old from rubbing against each other, and that were finally joined together in death.

José Augusto trudged along Oaxaca Avenue, submerged in a peculiar form of loneliness and into a sudden silence near the old buildings whose windows had grown tired of holding back the crisp night air, the whistles from a knife sharpener and the sporadic screeching of brakes on the corner of Valladolid Street. Miravalle Circle lay a little ahead of him; the fountain sprinkled with dim lights as if illuminated by miserly torches so that the water seemed to melt into the trunks of the eucalyptus trees in order to make tham good company in that haven for night people.

He decided to drop in on Domingo to let off steam and talk out his frustations. He abandoned his previous train of thought and tried to find some semblance of reassurance, to look at his surroundings as if they had been preordained to serve a definite purpose: either to achieve a state of perfection or else to help things rot away. He began catering to his own bitterness, brooding over his secret thoughts: how, for example, age was starting to show on his knuckles and on the palms of his hands. He concluded that his hate was not equal to his misery, that the magnitude of his turmoils could not conceivably correspond to the likes of a poor devil like himself.

He knew that Domingo was just an excuse, that he might very well run into Laura at his place. If he could meet her face-to-face he would get it all out of his system as if nothing had ever happened and their quarrels were a thing of the past. He yearned to return to her soft voice and sparkling eyes, to her parted lips and to her eager surrender. "You've got to see her again. You've got a whole lot of explaining to do," Buenaventura had admonished, just a couple of weeks ago.

At last with a definite goal in mind, he quickened his pace, forgetting his bitterness for a moment and hoping for some sudden good fortune. He was in desperate need of a lucky break; something to jar him out of his ambivalence.

He reached Miravalle Circle. It had been made to order for someone like Buenaventura. He stared for a while at the new house on the block; somehow it had always seemed old even from the day it was built. A vulgar, ostentatious mansion with tinted glass windows and tile facade, it was far less magnificent than the building that had been demolished to make room for it. As his loneliness expanded, he felt prone to surrender to gloom, to nightmares and hazy mornings-after. He remembered the nights he had spent hanging around with sordid types in Rosas Moreno and Pimentel Streets. There he had first set the course of his obsessions and learned to express his nonconformity through skillful manipulation of his facial gestures and adapting himself to the local vernacular and the penchant for exaggeration.

He lit a cigarette, thinking about the long hours of captivity that had preceded the beating, then the pains in his stomach and back, the scars that still remained and the shock he felt when he finally regained consciousness. By the time he had been picked up in the garbage with everything rotting around him, he had been a human wreck. He had been brought back to reality as soon as he saw the city, the clouds drifting along beyond the Ajusco mountain, and the birds hovering over the abandoned foothills and twisted pieces of scrap iron.

For the first time in days he felt his facial muscles relax; it was a kind of reprieve. Maybe it was only a reflex action, a manifestation of naiveté, of lunacy, or merely an unconscious flight of fancy. He slipped back into his old habit of improving upon his surroundings, mentally touching up the facades, the balustrades on balconies, the wooden partitions in office buildings and the range of sounds that dissolved into the last bright dots of the avenue. He resolved to strip himself once and for all of his aversions, of his erratic impulses, before the night was over.

He ignored the crowds coming out of a restaurant and a bus careening around the corner. Instead, he filled his mouth with smoke and blew it out into the air again as if he were releasing all his unanswered questions. At last, he arrived at Sinaloa Street. It had never ceased to have an emotional impact on him; it was so full of memories, not only of Laura but even before her, from the first time he and Domingo had spent hours talking about Spain under siege and the rampant corruption in the Mexican jails.

The impressions kept coming at him, changing his moods and unleashing his fears. By now, some of them were as transparent to him as if he were watching Laura in a mirror; she was examining her clear eyes and full lips . . . He compressed the sequences, imagining a light breeze blowing from one portal to another and an old lady around the corner reliving her past in exactly that same setting where she had lived for seventy long years. The first residents of that particular neighborhood were millionaires, and then came those who had prospered in the somber years of religious persecution. Several generals, proud of the revolution and of their new nation, proceeded to set up love nests, brothels and gambling dens on that very spot.

He realized almost immediately that there was no light in Domingo's apartment and that he would have to wait quietly in the dark, staring up at the lighted window in the apartment above, wondering whether Laura would open it, whether she would catch sight of him and hearing nothing but his voice calling from the empty street, she would finally throw down the keys. He thought of strolling along Génova Street, letting time flow through hundreds of hurrying figures and a few faces from the past. The lights in the shop windows were shining at a distance; garrishly-dressed people were leaving the bars and cafés or roaming along the streets. A few blocks away, a handful of workers were still drilling away or washing cars as scrawny beggars stretched out their brown, gnarled hands, full of relentless and forgotten wrinkles.

He longed to be walking along Oaxaca Street with Laura as they had done so often. When they reached Insurgentes, hundreds of construction workers would be digging the new subway tunnels, sloshing around in the mud. Then the two of them would spend a couple of hours talking at a café. Their conversation was invariably peppered with hand gestures which breathed life into the invisible images they described. He wanted to surrender himself to her eyes, to fill her memory with lasting wonders but he had resigned himself to the fact that he'd have to settle for just a few minutes alone with her, at the very most.

He had almost reached the door and stood motionless in front of the building, glancing at each window, each balcony, each curved arch. As he stubbed out his cigarette he felt a deceptively sudden burst of indulgence as if the weight of the cloudy sky had appeased him. Laura was probably up there right now unconcerned with the murmurs of the poplar trees or the deepening night, was perhaps getting ready for bed, as free from apprehension and strain of any kind as she was from his smooth talk. She was no longer subjected to his jeers or his foul moods. He remembered Buenaventura's admonitions, his stern reaction at José Augusto's drastic decisions, the reproachfulness in each one of his long pauses, and that profound reticence of his which conveyed both Buenaventura's weariness and his feelings of helplessness.

Listlessly he stubbed out his cigarette, scratched the back of his neck and adjusted the same dark jacket he'd been wearing for the past few days.

He heard voices from a passing car—coarse, rowdy expletives which soon faded into the stoplights. The passengers, most likely, were early customers at the bordello on the corner; there was the same boisterous clientele every single night, the same energy wasted on nothing but bawdy jokes and momentary relief from boredom. He created a mental picture of the whorehouse: the fat, giggling madam with her gaudy peacock blue dress and a long cigarette holder greeting the clients in the foyer, the well-rehearsed smiles of five prostitutes lined up in a row and the smell of sweat lingering on in the rooms, stubbornly clinging to the pillows and blankets.

He approached the building and just as he was about to ring Buena-ventura's bell, he noticed the door was ajar. The damned gloomy staircase was just beyond him. It was an unavoidable presence; it dominated his nightmares, his nocturnal wanderings, his phobias and especially those early hours when he was haunted by thoughts of suicide. As he went up the stairs, he heard sounds coming out of each apartment: the cat scratch-ing the floor in the old lady's room, the inane discussions coming from the bureaucrats' apartment on the first floor, old Caruso records that belonged to the elderly bachelor next door. The empty apartment upstairs opposite Domingo's awaited the arrival of the clandestine lovers the following day. On weekends, mornings and lazy noon hours, it was deserted except for a lurking feeling as if the invisible witnesses embedded in the walls were waiting to see the lovers when they entered the apartment, shed their clothes on the floor and made love on the carpet all afternoon.

José Augusto could hear his own steps, the creaking staircase, groan-ing beams, and his own fingers sliding along the bannister. Almost mechanically, he knocked on Domingo's door, eager to get it over with, to run into Laura now. So overwhelming was his need to see her again that he told himself it didn't even matter whether she was with someone or whether all they could talk about would be trivia, or platitudes—he would settle for anything that would make them face each other and set them at ease. He waited a while and there was still no answer. He lit a cigarette and looked up at the grime on the skylight and on the blackened wire dangling from a burned-out light bulb.

He went up the stairs slowly, more slowly than ever, feeling the ten-sion spreading through his fingers, in his breathing, in the smoke spirals drifting from his cigarette. As he reached the landing, he heard voices from the Spaniards' apartment. Buenaventura knew them fairly well; they were exiles who had arrived after the war and the endless persecutions. At last he reached Laura's door and some of his apprehension eased. He kept his cigarette between his lips, chewing at the filter, thoroughly enjoying the taste of tobacco. He could picture Laura sitting at her dressing table, dabbing cream on her fingertips, a filmy robe draped over her knees and thighs. José Augusto tried to project a note of self-assurance onto her face and strained to sharpen his senses, his powers of persuasion. Of course, he would show her that other alternatives were open to him. Even so, he knew that he had to control the sensation of defeat which wavered back and forth from self-derision to anger.

He knocked several times: the echo reverberated all through the building, sliding through the beams until it reached the tile and finally died in the cobwebs lining the basement. He glanced at his knuckles and at his yellowish fingers and then stared intently at the doorknob waiting for it to turn slowly. He remembered when he had left that place for good. He had set the keys on the night table, leaving everything in order. The sun had only started to come up through the windows; the shadows were lengthening to the rhythm of their hostilities and furies. Although he heard footsteps, he was caught off guard when the door finally opened. He confronted an unfamiliar face; the voice was self-possessed, the expression affable. Completely taken aback, he felt like a stranger, an intruder who had no business being there. But he recovered quickly and attempted to force his lips to smile as he sneaked a furtive sidelong glance at the other man.

Once again, he had turned into his own worst enemy. He had managed, through sheer astonishment, to stifle his anger. Somewhat dazzled by the lights in the living room, he asked for Laura, addressing the stranger as nonchalantly as he could by resorting to his capacity for self-control, for blending his cool, deliberate speech with silent insults, and for masking his inner hostility with the apathy in his eyes.

"She isn't here now, but she won't be long—she just went downstairs to one of the apartments to return some books. If you'd care to wait . . . " said the man; ushering José Augusto into the living room and pointing to the sofa, as if he hadn't the slightest idea who José Augusto was, as if he thought it was just some acquaintance of Laura's who had dropped in; someone with high cheekbones, a long face and deep circles under his eyes. The expression was both lazy and aloof, and the wan smile seemed to be held together by countless fears which gave his face a panic-stricken effect.

José Augusto didn't know what to do. He could not bear to think that another voice, another body, other odors were now occupying the places that once had been his and which, in his bewildered state of mind, he still considered his and his alone. It never once crossed his mind that he might be mistaken, that he no longer had the rights his imagination claimed. He stepped into the room, his eyes still smarting from the smoke, and proceeded to transpose the sequence of events. He assumed the man had been living there with Laura for several months. He sat down on the sofa with a glazed stare and, at loss for something to do, inspected the filter of his cigarette. It occurred to him that this idiot who let him in could at a moment's notice destroy him—José Augusto Banderas, the only man with a justifiable claim to these premises.

As he stretched his arm to put out his cigarette, he spotted the same ashtray in exactly the same place, on the same table, next to the same easy chair where he had so often sat talking. It was very close to the place where she had given him so much pleasure during their perfect lovemaking, boosted his ego and calmed him down. The stranger acted normally enough and seemed willing to make small talk, taking his place in the easy chair. After José Augusto tagged him as arrogant, certain he had detected a glint of defiance in his eyes, he immediately established a rivalry with the man. At the same time, José Augusto tried to mask his antagonism by not allowing either his misgivings or his fear of ridicule to show through. He swallowed hard a few times as if all his repressed anger had stuck in his throat.

He barely heard the questions the other man was asking him. He answered as if he were far away and with the sensation that all the objects in the room were closing in around him, hounding him, dragging him into a series of pointless memories: their orgasms, their murmured confidences, the proliferation of anticipated pleasures and the dim lights hovering over their legs and their bodies. The door to the bedroom was closed. He ticked off each piece of furniture in his mind and identified the two faces gazing blissfully at each other. He could recognize his own body under the feeble light from the night table, the intertwined shadows reflected on the ceiling and curtains. He recalled the nights she used to pace from one end of the room to the other, delighting in her own body, preparing to interrupt his digressions with the promise of lust, the prolonged pleasure in their tense bodies. Once they faced the mirror there was no respite; they explored every conceivable aspect of love.

The other man was right there, facing him now. His peculiar grin, which José Augusto interpreted as a smirk, was beginning to get to him. It broke through his feigned composure and aroused his rage. José Augusto could not possibly conceive of him behind that wall, assuming the right to stroke Laura's thighs. José Augusto answered absently, as if he were mimicking the other man, as if hypocrisy were still his best ally. He made heroic efforts to become someone else entirely, another person who was not at this moment waiting for Laura just so she could catch him in this ludicrous situation. José Augusto's answers were designed to protect himself from insult, and he vowed never to return here. He felt totally humiliated, his lungs saturated with cigarettes and his bravado thwarted.

Almost before realizing it, he had begun to shed each one of his defenses and whatever self-control he had left. He felt a trickle of saliva as if it were a lubricant for his expression of annoyance. He observed the other man keeping his cool and holding his head high as if he were letting him know that he was in charge here. He kept smiling a crooked smile which José Augusto interpreted as the beginning of a provocation that he never forgot. He would remember forever the very moment when he sensed that the other man had guessed who he was—Banderas, the poor fool presumptuous enough to assume that he had a claim on Laura's entire life.

He was unable to recover his outward composure. He felt like clenching his fists but stretched his neck instead, goaded on by his own conceit, and describing himself to himself in silence: Banderas, the no-good slob, the paranoid who had lived there long before this stranger had ever arrived on the scene. With his one-track mind he kept on thinking about the Bastard Banderas, the same son of a bitch who had been lived with Laura as recently as a few months ago and who was now sitting side by side, chatting with this stranger; Banderas who had used the same ashtrays, smelled the same scents and eau de cologne, and closed the same window at night: who had kissed her back and her thighs, who had moved his tongue over her knees, her legs, her nipples.

He muttered an insult and the other man was caught by surprise, not knowing how to react. The veins in José Augusto's temples stood out, a sign his jaws had tightened. He jumped to his feet, insulting him as he cocked his arm to swing, but the other man beat him to the punch with a kick in the groin that sent him reeling and shattered any pretenses he might have left. Banderas pulled out his gun and as the other man rushed to stop him, José Augusto managed to shoot him twice. The stranger's body slumped over José Augusto's legs. He got up, opened the door and rushed down the stairs. A few faces peeked out of an apartment and caught a glimpse of him as he reached the groundfloor landing.

The main door to the building was still open, its creaking muffled by the wind. The gun had been left at the stranger's feet, near the last twitch of that crooked smile, the eyes staring sideways. José Augusto dragged his unbearable pain along countless blocks and alleys to a sleazy hotel where he spent hours in a stupor, his face contorted like an idiot's at the sheer absurdity of his situation.

XV

TWO YEARS AFTER THE CRIME, we all gathered at Andrea's house once again to celebrate her opening night. While we waited for her to arrive, we proceeded to size each other up through overt stares, sidelong glances or by recognizing each particular brand of humor or laughter, each carefully rehearsed witticism. By this time, the enigma of Banderas had receded into the background and was slowly fading into a cloud of absurd speculations and rumors. Meanwhile the real truth—the obscure, incongruous facts, corroded by our own misconceptions and conflicting opinions—was made more and more inaccessible. So . . . we found ourselves in that house on Coyoacán once again, as we had so many times before, eager to shed our pompous airs and formalities.

We were gradually reverting to the way we had seen ourselves and to the old paths we had strewn with selfish interests. Although we were no longer the same people, although more than ten years had gone by since we had first met at Buenaventura's apartment, we resolved to take up where we left off, to seek a common denominator by renewing our political discussions and exploring our personality clashes. We were now unquestionably better equipped to note our differences and detect any signs of impending boredom or of serious quarrels.

Some of our faces were now filled out. Some were obviously in the middle of a love affair, while others were harboring some secret sorrow. Perhaps the best years—the decisive, the real years—were still ahead of us. The time was at hand when recklessness and necessity would be linked either to the full enjoyment of erotic experiences or to dissipation and emptiness. At least we were conscious of the fact that many of our projects would never materialize.

"No one can back out now. We're in this together. Sure, we know each other inside out but we still have a long way to go. There's no two ways about it, we just can't get away from this scene, no matter how much we grind our teeth and analyze reality to bits," Sebastián shouted from the doorway, frantically waving his right hand as always, and all set to have a better time than anyone else.

The past and present merged into the walls, the two back bedrooms and the flowerpots on the patio. We gazed at the blooming jack-in-the-pulpits in the garden where the jacaranda trees leaned over the bougainvillea. The paintings that Buenaventura had once given Andrea hung over the sofa, the same familiar photographs of nets and seascapes were still in the corridors, the fake Persian rug was in the dining room and dozens of eye-catching posters in the spare room.

The house was a reflection of all our idiosyncrasies; it had been a faithful ally that had seen us through all our ups and downs and our struggle toward emancipation. Now it acknowledged our presence once again by offering us its wide range of echoes, both old and new, and it seemed all set to add fresh anecdotes to our collection. Except for the white tablecloth on the dining room table, the copper ashtrays and a rocking chair in the living room, few things had changed. It was almost as though Andrea had persisted in clinging to the same old scenery, in playing before the same old audience: the inert and the boisterous, those seeking the support of this place and those whose voices were endlessly loud.

Sebastián—whose full head of hair seemed more wavy and abundant than ever—rambled on, gesturing with his enormous hands. He soon became the life of the party with his terse, witty epigrams and his blunt views on everything from adultery to drugs and sexual aberrations. He kept wandering back and forth from the living room to the dining room, his fist clenched, shouting for more of the good Scotch and demanding some kind of response to his verbal challenges. On the other hand, Domingo Buenaventura drank sparingly, quietly surveying the scene—the hands and faces, the wordplay, the sarcastic quips. From time to time, he would lapse into his own daydreams and brood over his own distant memories.

Once in a while, I'd throw in a comment or two, never missing a chance to bait Sebastián. I explained my reasons for returning to the School of Political Science and gave my impressions of my new job as reporter for a leading newspaper. The conversation then shifted to Latin American playboys who were living it up in Europe and to Scandinavian ladies with that special quality in their blue or green eyes. Another group discussed the May riots in Paris and their repercussions on our country, and then the radical slogans that had appeared in graffiti all over town.

Someone mentioned that the CIA and the FBI were infiltrating upper levels of police and security divisions here, that their influence was spreading to all sectors, and that some prominent politicians were involved as well. Someone else pointed out that passengers were being harassed at the airport and that there were detailed dossiers on most of us. Naturally, these observations were greeted with scornful laughter and unprintable remarks.

After that, there was no stopping us. By the time drinks were passed around again, the place was literally saturated with wisecracks, catch phrases, light banter and salty jokes; faces were either earnest or evasive, the grins sardonic. It was a dark, muggy night late in July; the pine trees and the medlars were swaying gently, as usual for that time of year, their shadows tightening around the house. The wind was subdued and awaiting the onset of midnight.

Throughout the entire room, the heat was beginning to invade every square inch of space. After a few minutes, knowing full well that an audience requires a preamble, a certain degree of suspense, and that the stage has to be set for a big entrance, Andrea finally arrived on the scene, greeted by cheers and enthusiastic hugs from all of us. Somehow, she looked different. There was a hint of smugness about her flirtatious eyes, the well-rehearsed gestures, the chiseled features, the enthusiastic, indulgent expression. Sebastián, of course, immediately started hamming it up with his grandiloquent phrases, his hands held high and tracing long, sinuous curves in the air. Domingo Buenaventura, composed as ever, gripping pipe with one hand and holding a vodka in the other, broke in by saying dryly: "Ever since I got here, I realized you just can't resist looking at the whimsical side of life." He addressed Sebastián as if he were pretty sure that the rest of the evening would go smoothly and without too much commotion.

Andrea, smiling as never before, moved from group to group greeting people, anticipating each gesture, each remark. She talked about the next performance and the staging of her next play, which promised to be sensational. We suspected that her somewhat flustered state was due to an unprecedented circumstance: Andrea, most likely, was contemplating the possibility of a serious involvement. Later on, we discovered we had been on the right track; Andrea had indeed decided to settle on one love. Her euphoria, then, was not entirely the result of her enthusiasm over tonight's success or her forthcoming theatrical ventures. She radiated a peculiar though perceptible inner glow which dispelled any trace of boredom and induced her to envision a perfect future for herself. She apologized profusely for being intentionally late and bustled back and forth from the kitchen to the dining room to the living room, making sure her guests were taken care of, asking us over and over again if we needed more chairs, or whether she should open the windows to let in some fresh air.

For a few brief minutes we let ourselves discuss the subject of Laura and José Augusto. As explanations led to more and more incoherence our uneasiness increased by the minute. Finally the phrases simply glided away as if they were unwilling to be confronted by reality and we were at last painfully ridding ourselves of all those senseless scenes that had come into our lives at cross-purposes.

"Laura's all right," said Buenaventura flatly, as if he wanted to get it over with as soon as possible. Obviously the subject could not be discussed with so many people around or in the presence of all those phantoms which our speculations had brought to the surface.

It wasn't long before the sparks started flying: rash judgments, quips and caustic remarks flew right and left as we drank up. By now, the windows were open and the cigarette smoke had drifted all the way to the ceiling. Then we began to notice that the room had been filling up with new, younger faces spouting a new jargon. These people, no doubt, were our successors. They would inherit this house, inject it with a new life, make it their haven and soon we would all be sharing new frustations, new dreams, new upheavals.

"It's high time we enriched our experience by adapting ourselves to other visions, to new ideas," said Sebastián as soon as he spotted the newcomers. He approached them at once and started bragging about his fictitious achievements and rattling off those endless cock-and-bull stories he could come up with anywhere: in sordid brothels or in the most urbane settings and before any audience—naive, ignorant or sophisticated. Sebastián always managed to get his point across through the colorful characters in his stories, regardless of his mood—unsociable or expansive.

The night wore on placidly, without incident, suspended between the lights in the garden and slowly creeping into the back bedrooms. On the rooftop, a cat leaped over a pile of rubbish. Cristóbal and Martín were two of the new faces that we saw there for the first time. They both seemed ill at ease, not knowing quite what to do or how to affect nonchalance while watching us intently. At this point, our conversation was getting disjointed, to say the least. We had regained our full-blown optimism and were feeling each other out to see how far we could go. Slowly but surely, our verbal cannibalism was getting underway.

Then Domingo inquired about the latest skirmish involving the riot squad. Cristóbal answered vaguely and tersely, staring straight ahead. After he mentioned police provocations and an alarming number of forcible arrests, he scratched his forehead and gazed longingly at a glass of rum in front of him. He had been constantly interrupted by a squeaky voice in the background that greeted each one of his observations with expressions like "Right on!" "Bad scene!" "You bet your ass!"

Then Martín had the floor. He was beardless, dark-haired and straight-nosed. As he spoke, he moved his head nervously and kept glancing at Buenaventura. Somehow he always managed to be one step ahead of our questions or comments. Martín explained that "it all started with a rumble between two street gangs downtown around the Ciudadela: the *Araños* and the *Ciudadelos* who, by the way, are a bunch of bastards—every single one of them. Then the fight, which was probably set up to begin with, spread to the neighboring high schools. When it got out of hand, the riot squad stepped in. They were combat armed and without rhyme or reason beat up a lot of innocent people, including several students and teachers. It was almost as if they had purposely intended to make the downtown area—from Bucareli to Balderas Streets—the center of the ruckus."

As soon as Andrea joined the group we immediately guessed the identity of her elect, who, most likely, was already entitled to bedroom privileges. Andrea winked at Martín, smiled, and triumphantly linked her arm through his as if she wanted us all to know. Since her expression was particularly cunning, she was obviously in the first stage of a passionate love affair. Domingo then proceeded to observe Martín more closely. He reminded Domingo of himself many years ago, before he had learned to release his pent-up anger and give in to his temptations. Domingo figured that before long this protegé of Andrea's would become one of us. He could easily fit into our incomprehensible illusions and share our common nightmares. On the other hand, he judged that Cristóbal with his petulant tone, his tendency to verbalize his fears and his pointless attempts to challenge every single statement—was poles apart from Martín. Domingo's eyes wandered to a corner of the living room where a lone pothead was communing with his own private grudges.

"See here, Gabriel," said Sebastián in that holier-than-thou tone of his, "You know, sometimes your articles are nothing but crap. You've got to do someting about it, damn it. You can't afford to be half-assed about that sort of thing. It's far better to maintain a dignified silence than to be a bull in a china shop." He went on and on with his philosophical rhetoric and his puns, obviously delighted to be back in his natural habitat where no one turned a hair at his belligerent tirades.

Andrea, still dazzled by her happiness and remarkably subdued, remained by Martín's side. Meanwhile, more people kept trooping in. Every room in the house was filled with the sound of heated conversations and laughter. The different levels of noise expanded and streamed in and out the windows, swirling around between the drinking glasses and provoking smiles and grimaces of every conceivable shape and size. The Concordia group made their grand entrance. As usual, they were bickering among themselves, tossing off anagrams, epigrams and complicated jokes in iambic pentameter, scattering their sarcasm everywhere and putting on their best facades—of feigned politeness like the proverbial wolves in sheeps' clothing. The house and the trellis outside sealed them off from the approaching nightfall and let them concentrate on the jumble of voices.

The economist was praising the "Mexican economic miracle," the journalist talked about the amazing growth of Puerto Vallarta, while the poet ranted on about the astonishing success of the Cultural Olympics and plugged his forthcoming book of verse. Someone brought up the topic of psychoanalysis in the monasteries and its repercussions in the Vatican. And of course, there was the cynic who declared that our Cactus Curtain, third-world ambitions to become first-world were strangling us to death, that everything was a sham and that Mexico's so-called horn of plenty was so much tinsel. He went on to say that there was nothing but abject poverty, destititution, and unemployment in this country, except for the tycoons who were investing in everything under the sun and getting richer by the minute with the help of front men who signed in their behalf in order to circumvent investment laws.

Domingo Buenaventura was still sitting in the same easy chair, not missing a thing. He picked out a familiar face here and there, nodding at people he hardly remembered. His gaze darted to every corner of the room—from the spaced-out loner in the corner to the flashy platinum blonde who had arrived with the poet; from Sebastián's histrionic outbursts to Martín and Andrea's interwined hands. He could almost picture José Augusto seated at the far side of the room opposite him, arguing with everybody, and Laura, aloof as always with her hazel eyes shining. He tried to imagine that no one was missing, that in spite of everything there was no real reason to despair. He tried to tell himself there were good times ahead, there'd be new horizons opening up for everybody and more exuberant nights like this. Buenaventura was entering that particular stage in life when the mind succumbs to any impression, to cyclic nostalgias, to

118

those experiences that tend to unhinge one's senses. For the first time in his life he felt as if his daydreams were finally coming true. The hubbub seemed to come from a long way off; he heard it only dimly.

Andrea and Martín were standing in the foyer where the clouds of smoke were the thickest. Although he didn't realize it, she was gazing at him, uninhibited, oblivious to everything, her lips moist with anticipation of their forthcoming intimacy. Sensuality, to Andrea, was of utmost importance at this moment.

By this time the whole house had turned into a regular sound box. Every single one of its foundations, beams and rafters were attuned to the medley of sounds, voices and tunes. New legends were created that night out of our eagerness to seek new pleasures, out of inane gossip and out of our unfulfilled expectations.

We were just on the verge of forgetting ourselves, of setting aside all our questions and the old farce of getting to know each other better, of delving into our own consciences and private ambitions when we sensed the night converging on us. It was wedged in between each piece of news: another demonstration that was broken up, another beating in Madero Street downtown, more and more people imprisoned. The dark winds were upon us, hinting at treason and torture, absurd persecutions and inordinate pressures. No one, not Sebastián, not Martín, not even Buenaventura ever suspected that at that moment we were on the the threshold of a Before and After, that we would soon be up against a series of staggering ordeals and come to know the meaning of real anguish: the image of an entirely different, besieged city, taken over by hundreds of thousands of demonstrators and then by silence and finally by infinite forms of stupefaction.

XVI

WITH THE SOUND OF gunshots and the creaking staircases still ringing in his ears and the wind whipping along Sinaloa Street, José Augusto had raced down the street in the dark. The circles under his eyes glistened with perspiration as he covered more and more ground, darting from one sidewalk to another without stopping. Now he heard nothing but his own heavy breathing and his footsteps pounding in the dreary alleys. He was unable to focus on anything except his sheer panic. That first night with fear as his companion, he spent long, anxious hours in a shabby hotel near the Buenavista railroad station. His reactions wavered back and forth from stupefaction to incredulity, from repulsion to compassion for the dead man, from horror to self-pity. Before he knew it, daylight had crept up on him and caught him with his fists clenched tightly, the invisible presence of that body sprawled over his legs and an indefinable pain in his chest. His distress, which had gathered momentum in the past few hours, had already left its mark: a dazed expression in his eyes and an uneasy, nagging sensation that he was being hunted.

He glanced at the twenty-odd cigarette butts in the ashtray, harshly berating himself and at the same time still refusing to believe the whole thing had actually happened. The deed itself not only was totally alien to what he had intended, but even to the depth of his aggression, however repressed. He was beginning to resign himself to the idea that he would be hounded by the memory of that inexplicable encounter every single day of his life. He tried to imagine his hands as extraneous objects, completely detached from his body, from his will, from his hostilities. The moment he stepped out of the hotel, the city no longer seemed to have any bearing whatsoever on his new life. As the ragpickers listlessly went about their work, he wandered aimlessly down the street, straining to break away from his uncontrollable nausea, of the urge to vomit, constantly on guard against everything around him, and particularly this infringement on his obsessions, on his future.

120

He stopped at a pay phone on the corner of Soto Street where he telephoned his mother. He took great pains to choose his words carefully and made sure he glossed over his guilt by improvising the most convincing, reassuring arguments he could think of. Then, still in an unmistakable state of agitation, he spoke briefly to Sebastián without going into too much detail. In his determination to save himself, to find a way out at any price, he sought an accomplice. He suppressed his customary arrogance and made his request firmly and succinctly. Sebastián, though throughly stunned, came forth with the responses that José Augusto had counted on: forthright, to the point, and mercifully free from evasive or snide remarks.

He waited for Sebastián on that same corner, his hands in his pockets and the lapels of his jacket turned up. By now he had run out of cigarettes and had taken to shifting his feet over the grating on the sidewalk; the shock of it all had prevented him from realizing that his world, as he knew it, had come to an end and that new, unfamiliar boundaries would determine his future. He felt a throbbing pain all through his body—in his bones, his shoulders, his legs. Each wince caused his lips to contract and paved the way for a whole new set of facial expressions of unhappiness which would soon have their own story to tell.

He remained caught in the struggle between the absurd and the rational, unable to determine the degree of blame that should be placed on the other man for harassing him in the first place. *I was subjected to every kind of fear imaginable; I knew I had to be on my guard, keep my ears open for any strange noise, the sound of approaching footsteps. I couldn't get the man's face out of my mind—the supercilious smile, the swaggering.*

In less than half an hour, Sebastián arrived. He slowed down the car without saying a word and raised his hand in a magnanimous gesture, as if he were sealing a pact pledging to keep the conspiracy strictly confidential. José Augusto knew that despite Sebastián's obvious drowsiness and bewilderment, he would eventually succeed in calming Banderas' sense of guilt, would fully understand his reticence and the sacrifices that would have to be made in the future. José Augusto also knew that his old friend would go to any lengths to keep his commitment and would even help set up the getaway, if need be. And he would share the slow, painful lesson José Augusto had learned that night that he could only survive by hanging on to something he would never surrender: his freedom.

His smugness, he now understood, had gotten the better of him; it had been responsible for tearing him away from his dreams, from the hopes he had carved out of his make-believe and his rebelliousness. As they

121

drove on, Banderas examined each circumstance separately. He thought about his mother and tried in vain to obliterate Laura's image from his mind. Sebastián hadn't said a word, although it had probably occurred to him to say something—anything at all; the sort of platitude that comes into one's head at such odd moments and which takes on hidden meanings. Sebastián, most likely, was mentally matching his own eccentricities against José Augusto's extreme anxiety, which might be bordering on madness.

The city had left its indelible marks on both faces. The prospect of a bright April day did not manage to take their minds off their immediate apprehensiveness. The sunlight, now gliding down the huge windows of the Torre Latinoamericana skyscraper and casting its rays down on rooftops and watertanks, revealed the contours of the Chiquihuite hills. They remained silent until they turned toward Hidalgo Avenue, where the demolition of buildings and streets for the subway construction was in full progress. They kept their voices low, each trying to keep his own dilemmas to himself.

Sebastián had already secured a temporary hideout for José Augusto in an old abandoned apartment building that belonged to his family. It was behind the old Military School on a dirty, lonely street in the Popotla District, with scrawny trees planted along the sidewalks and the usual kinds of slum dwellers as neighbors. José Augusto's room was on the topmost floor adjoining a small area fenced off with chicken wire on the roof. That same morning they read about the crime. The writeups in the papers were utterly incredible. The reports were a pack of lies: the so-called facts bordered on the grotesque. As could be expected, a few scandal sheets gave the story front-page coverage, screaming headlines and all. Their stories were built on a hodge-podge of fallacies and misstatements. They claimed that a gang of killers, a terrorist group or perhaps a bunch of swingers had been exposed as a result of the crime, adding that whoever they were they deserved the harshest punishment possible. José Augusto re-read each article in utter disbelief: his life story was completely misrepresented, there was a detailed account of his alleged criminal activities, and a photograph of himself wearing a white shirt and dark tie, taken years ago, when he looked very young. They even published a list of the members of his alleged gang; he had never before heard of any of those names. He began to reconstruct the whole episode very slowly and did his best to subdue his fear with self-control. He was still unable to pinpoint the motives that led him to commit the crime.

José Augusto could not picture himself rotting away in prison, cooped up inside dreary walls, pacing back and forth from corridors to cell blocks and having to put up with prison guards and constant threats from the hardened criminals who were sentenced to life imprisonment. It occurred to him that his friends would be questioned and that now he'd have to cover up his tracks and learn to live truly alone for a long, long time. He had already made up his mind to go into hiding, to mingle with strange new faces in other cities. It was still impossible for him to separate Laura from himself, to go back to earlier frustrations, to another kind of loneliness, perhaps more bitter. She was undoubtedly cursing him with a vengeance and letting all of her anger fall on him while trying to make the best of a hopeless situation.

He grew tired of staring at the same walls, at his own shadow. He spent his days waiting for Sebastián to show up and wondering at the limits of his resilience. But that only served to intensify his anxiety. Sometimes the sounds distracted him: the automatic drills, the whirring of mechanical shovels, the distant rumble of streetcars, water trickling into storage tanks, the factory whistles and the chattering of housewives. His loneliness filled the room. It was only a few steps away from the laundry area, whose tubs were full of cobwebs and garbage. Nearby were piles of boards, twisted scraps of metal and old iron rods. Everything stank of urine and decay, of rotting, rancid smells easily churned up by any passing wind.

At night, when Sebastián dropped in, they'd walk from one end of the room to the other. They'd discuss the news of the day and then the most feasible escape routes, the advisability of choosing this or that city in the provinces versus the many possible ways out of the country altogether. They considered every conceivable mode of transportation. They worked out itineraries and weighed each difficulty without overlooking a single detail such as the need for money and proper identification papers. Later on, as Sebastián lumbered slowly down the stairs silently thanking his brothers for neglecting their apartment building, José Augusto would sink back into his despondency. Never once did he lift his head to gaze at the sky or the lights flickering on all over the city. A peculiar, harsh expression would come over his face, as if he wanted to forget all his secrets, give up his will power and skip the next few days.

Before long his diversions turned their backs on him and his spirits began to dwindle; he started thinking about what was in store for him; he imagined his hands as mere things, objects. He'd start making fun of them, inspecting them with utmost contempt. *I just couldn't rid myself of all that shit and everything seemed unbearable. But there I was, looking at myself like a worthless piece of junk. I had all kinds of venomous thoughts that lasted for days on end. They'd sneak up on me when I least expected it, and then I'd get an empty feeling in the pit of my stomach. I had hit rock bottom; all my waking moments were spent cursing and brooding. Little by little, I learned to live alone in that hole and even got to thinking that I'd probably wind up living there for the rest of my life like a piece of rubble among the old iron rods and the stagnant water in the tanks.*

Day after day, morning after morning, he was feeling more substance to his anxieties, more weight to the words of another José Augusto who had gradually been absorbed under his skin—a man who was invested with far more potential and commitment than the José Augusto Banderas of rash impulses and foolish, ineffectual pride. His salvation would necessarily have to hinge on a whole new outlook, regardless of how false or how cynical it might be. There was no alternative in the face of what lay ahead but to achieve complete self-control, even though he'd much rather be strolling along the streets as he used to. He'd have to pull together a lot of loose ends—his anger, his self-flagellation, those contradictory, ambivalent feelings that constantly besieged him and seemed bent on intimidating him.

One night three weeks after the murder, Sebastián arrived with Andrea. It was then that José Augusto sensed that he was regarded with a certain degree of mistrust and realized that it was time to make definite arrangements for his next move. Sebastián and Andrea offered him words of encouragement and the three of them then got down to business of exploring the most suitable alternatives, agreeing that José Augusto should leave town as soon as possible.

Andrea wasted no words on useless chatter, nor was she carried away by an exaggerated sense of complicity. Instead, she found herself noticing José Augusto's newly-acquired tics: how he cocked his head to one side, wiggled his fingers and left long pauses between each sentence. There was a peculiar dullness in his gaze that seemed to have filtered into his thoughts as well, as if a stranger had taken over his body and his mind.

In spite of his reluctance to go into a completely new situation—and trying vainly to conceal his fear by keeping his expression aloof, José Augusto agreed. After they had left, he realized that deep down, he still balked at the thought of having to pass through many different worlds in just a few months. Then he calmly smoked a cigarette and recovered his composure, knowing full well that he'd soon be leaving that hovel with the rickety old cot that cut into his body, the winds that crashed into the wire netting of the roof and the squeaky hinges in the old doors. All of them by now had become vital elements of his nightmares.

Just as he did every single night before falling asleep, he recreated the whole scene: Laura's apartment, the dead man lying on the rug, his hasty departure and his frantic search for a place to hide. He also puzzled over Andrea's reserve. She never once mentioned Laura, as if Laura didn't exist, as if her image had retreated forever into an enchanted mirror where she was unable to move, to accuse, to shout, to demand any kind of explanation. He had also begun to perceive their silence — the silence of others, the accusations he never actually heard, the unspoken recriminations that remained only in their minds.

He decided to make room for the future, a space with cities and mountain ranges, ports and borders. He examined every square inch of it, crossing the length and breadth of it with an excitement that brought him no real satisfaction and with a passion born of his fear and supported by the full realization of his cowardice. He peeked out at the night through the cracks in the windows: the air was quiet and muggy. He could feel the tiny lights resting on his face, and his mind wandering again. He stretched his legs and smoked in the dark for a while, feeling for all the world like cynicism incarnate.

He felt more alone then he had ever been in his life and to make it worse, he'd been deprived of any kind of dissipation. He consciously abstained from any self-congratualtory feelings by analyzing his fears and his arrogance. He could not, for the life of him, believe that his memory of Laura was already so far away. *I hadn't looked in a mirror for weeks. I got to know the shape of my fingers by heart. I studied their movements, the wrinkles in my knuckles and watched my nails grow. I was constantly at odds with myself and I knew I couldn't be saved unless I defeated a vital part of myself.*

Thanks to Sebastián's determination and to Andrea's unconditional support, the details of his departure were worked out in a couple of days. Never once did they hesitate or beat around the bush. They were open and aboveboard in every way and gamely set about examining every detail. The most unforeseen of contingencies, the possible traps and unexpected pitfalls were studied from every angle. Little by little, as everything fell into place and the story was no longer news, José Augusto started comparing the previous with the present sequences: Before — when he used to hang around San Juan de Letrán without a care in the world and now — immersed in anguish. He'd taken to playing the new game of discarding his former fears and setting new goals for himself.

125

At last, one rainy Friday in May, more than a month after the crime, just when he thought he couldn't stand the strain any longer and was fed up with his mounting anger and feelings of impotence, he and Sebastián left for Guadalajara. Although it was the time of day when gloom hung heaviest over the building, once they were out on the street the shiny wet pavement reflected the lights from passing cars and managed to hold up traffic for a considerable length of time. As they left the city behind them, he began getting used to his new appearance—his hair grown down to the nape of his neck, his bushy beard and eyes strangely hard. By the time darkness had crept up on the miserable shacks in the outlying areas, he wondered at his lack of ability to rid himself of his weaknesses, his blunders, his self-contempt or to contemplate the new life he was about to begin.

José Augusto refrained from looking back toward the glittering curve of the city, the blinking red lights of the TV aerials, the cluster of dimming lights, the sharp parallel lines of street lamps and the planes vanishing toward the east. Along the boulevards, the last dark points beyond the skyscrapers were gradually fading into the background.

All through the trip, as the car sped on, the last images of Laura slowly dissolved. He strained to recover his composure—any sort of composure, to find relief at having left that danger zone, that hellhole, at having re-gained control of his senses. He refused to brood over one more compulsion, one more possible threat, over what could no longer be helped, the nightmarish experience he had never imagined could happen. He was wide awake during those first few hours and as the night waned he felt a strange compulsion to catch the first glimpse of morning.

At least I had something else to watch besides that damn chicken wire on the roof; I could breathe another kind of air and felt I was slowly coming back to life. Even the smell of tobacco was different. For a brief moment, I was comforted by the movement of the windshield wipers and regarded the rain as part of the plot. I had no way of knowing what was going to happen to me, and even then, I still had that empty feeling in my chest. His train of thought was interrupted as he dozed off, his head bobbing with the movement of the curves and the bumps in the road.

José Augusto and Sebastián hardly spoke, as if everything had already been said, as if every explanation had been repeated a thousand times without actually geting to the crux of the matter. Sebastián drove carefully, keeping his eyes on the road, gauging the curves and ticking off the kilometers in his head. His involvement in the whole affair had gone far deeper than he had ever anticipated. However, for Sebastián, this was much more than just an adventure, a risk whose consequences only time would tell. This was a way of putting his limitations and his skills to the test by carrying out a responsibility to the very end. It gave him a feeling of deep satisfaction at having achieved a common goal, of having accomplished a task by making full use of his stubbornness, his perseverance, his tendency toward the irrational, all for the sake of a cause he championed above all others: survival.

José Augusto, on the other hand, had never undergone the hardships of exile; he was unaware of the dilemmas that awaited him, the dread that would eventually splinter his personality, the gradual metamorphosis which would go by unheeded, except for a few telltale signs such as increasing reticence and selfishness. Something totally extraneous to José Augusto's delusions, to his convoluted fantasies had impelled him to escape, something he never once suspected: the belated arrival of all the other José Augustos who were huddled together inside him. Sooner or later, within the next few years, they would come out in the open. Each of them would be wary of the other; they'd be vying with each other for power, trying to outdo each other, and their quarrels would keep him awake far into the night. By and by, he would learn how to deal with them, how to handle their different speech patterns, their manifestations of youth or old age.

They whizzed by one town after another, through occasional cloudbursts, past the outskirts of the larger cities with steep mountain ranges and solitary plateaus in the distance. Fully aware of the differences that separated them as well as the contradictions that bound them together, each of them mentally reconstructed his life story or at least the high points. "We were born to recklessness and flamboyance and were meant to die cursing, blaspheming, hallucinating—with nothing but our nightmares to protect us," thought Sebastián as the first rays of sun streamed down on them. The long hours had melted away faster than they had imagined, between José Augusto's deep sleep and Sebastián's gaze riveted beyond the windshield. He was itching to push down the accelerator as far as it could go, anticipating their arrival with mixed feelings of pride and incredulity.

At last, as the sky cleared, they caught sight of Guadalajara: first the outskirts, then a wide boulevard and then the residential district. José Augusto was barely coming out of his stupor, after long weeks of being confined to walls and ceilings. As he opened his eyes a cold shiver ran through his body, clutching at his throat and neck, the aftermath of his

127

long night of muscular and emotional tension. He scratched his dark beard, his forehead and his stiff neck and somehow managed to come out with a slow grin that seemed momentarily immersed in apathy, like a shapeless, hollow mask.

Sebastián raised his fist and licked a cigarette, his eyes agleam with confidence, his broad forehead unfurrowed. When they reached the first stoplight he stretched his arms, yawned with relish, muttered something under his breath, cleared his throat hurriedly and stuck the cigarette in his mouth to help pluck up his courage and keep his anxiety from overwhelming him again. He kept his cool, stopped the car in front of the bus station, remembered every detail of the prearranged plan; then they said goodbye, taking care to keep their voices casual.

"See you around, nutso," said Sebastián, as if it were the most eloquent, unique phrase in the world, a phrase that could never be repeated, aimed at wiping away all their past conflicts and at establishing, once and for all, this final gesture of complicity.

A few days later, after a long trip north with several overnight stops at various motels, a respectable looking man in his middle thirties, wearing denim trousers and a brand new corduroy jacket strode resolutely toward the border. He carried nothing but a small suitcase and a couple of books. His dark glasses helped conceal his agitation and his cunning as he felt himself adjusting to his new name and new identity.

He left Tijuana with its dusty streets, its unbearable heat, its neon lights, its curio shops and red light district. When he reached the border and pulled out a Bolivian passport, he could feel the self-assurance sweep through his body, his face and his speech. Although he had been unaware of the gestation process, he realized, at long last, that a new cast of characters had been born.

PART II

The Real Years

I

ONE CLOUDY DAY IN JULY, after strolling along along 42nd Street, among the shadows of skyscrapers and intersections jammed with cars, José Augusto made his way back to the hotel. He had been so engrossed in sorting out the events of the past few weeks and in planning his itinerary for his forthcoming departure that he barely heard the voice of the Cuban desk clerk who handed him the key. Once back in his room on the tenth floor, he could still hear the screeching tires, wailing sirens and the ships' horns; he opened the window and gazed out at the docks. The water in the background was hidden by a thick wall of fog.

Noises coming from every direction—sidewalks, elevators, buses, fire escapes and alleys—threw his thoughts out of kilter. As he visualized himself still on the border, on a freight car, or in any of the nameless towns he had passed through, he reflected that for the time being it would be impossible to sum up, in just a few words, all that he had experienced during the past few days. He sank down in an armchair and let the sequences pile up of their own accord.

The border customs house, the dusty, parched-lipped days he had spent in bars and brothels lay thousands of kilometers away to the southwest. He relived the sensation of constant danger, of imminent arrest which had ultimately led him to self-discovery amidst jeering hoodlums and swaggering pimps; then he had realized he could easily get used to living among barflies and the bloated faces of old whores. He had spent the whole time observing every single detail, not missing a thing, adopting any expression —cheerful or blasé—that occurred to him, and changing the intonation of his speech accordingly.

For four nights in a row he had gone to a brothel on the outskirts of Tijuana. At first he was at loose ends, not knowing quite how to deal with his fears and uncertainty, and straining to obliterate images from the past, to isolate them from his confusion and from the leisurely smoke spirals around him. He stared straight ahead, his eyes motionless, and soon began to see himself reflected in the others; he'd study their facial expressions and their bodies leaning against the bar. Silently, intently, he'd notice their movements, their gestures, their eyebrows, their jaws and their hands reaching for their drinks. Never once did he tire of this interminable game of comparing voices and faces.

In his effort to understand them, he'd make fun of himself by changing places with the pimps who waited for their women. He'd see them on the dusty street corners at dawn, swapping stories and chatting for hours about nothing in particular, killing time until the women came out. Then, each man would leave with his prey in tow. Most likely, they'd head for a motel where he'd do well by her in bed, count her earnings, and perhaps wrap it up with a satisfactory beating. Then they'd probably sleep all afternoon, their chests heaving to the rhythm of their snores.

He also observed the others who crossed over from the other side of the border to where the action was. When they arrived, they were already pretty liquored up; their blond hair tousled, their wallets bulging. They'd stagger around drunkenly, not much caring that they were making spectacles of themselves. José Augusto would also spend hours watching the naked shoulders and provocative hips of the prostitutes; he had never ceased to be amazed at their capacity for sustained, phony laughter and seemingly passionate embraces. He had since discovered that this particular atmosphere was perfectly suited to his benumbered state, *which life itself had withheld from me, and which I never imagined could amuse me so much. In that place, with apparent indifference, I managed to be always one step ahead of any feelings of revulsion and I identified myself with any son of a bitch who happened to be sitting next to me. It seemed so absurd to be harshly condemning the decadence and the feigned seductions that went on, the time spent on petty grudges and trivial pursuits. Naturally, under no circumstances was I ever at peace with myself; I was absolutely certain that before long I'd have to start carving out a future for myself.*

He gazed out the window again at the forty-story building on the corner, the yellow taxis whizzing down the street and the Methodist church right across from the hotel, with urine stains and garbage piled up on the steps. It reminded him of other episodes in his life. He left a pack of cigarettes at the foot of the bed, which smelled of moldy wood and disinfectants. He looked at himself in the bathroom mirror, let the water run freely and took up the razor to trim and shave off his beard.

That face—the bushy brows, hawk nose and dark eyes—had sweated profusely in the unbearable Tijuana heat, had nonchalantly approached the border, and had looked straight into the blue eyes of the burly immigration official who had checked his passport. That face had managed to pull it off; he hadn't given himself away once by a slight slip of the tongue or a false move. A few hours later, he had boarded a bus and chosen a back seat from where he surveyed the bridges, the smooth wide highways, the yards around the houses and buildings, the profusion of billboards and the slums where the immigrants lived.

Further ahead, he had spotted the waters of the Pacific Ocean whipping against the bay beyond the bridges and TV antennas. He had spent a few days in San Diego, just time enough to face up to his fears, to try repeatedly to come to terms with his other shadowy self. After that first night he had started jotting down new words; he'd make long lists and memorize them, and then go back to the book or newspaper he'd been reading, sitting with the dictionary at his left and his cigarette on the overflowing ashtray. Sometimes—at noon or at midnight—he'd go to a movie, rubbing his hands in an outward manifestation of composure and trying to while away the time as best he could. He'd keep his eyes open at all times, always careful not to let any nervousness betray him.

In front of a San Diego pool hall—the gathering place for long-haired youths of assorted sizes and colors—he struck up a conversation with a shoeshine boy of Mexican descent. At this point he had already started to create a past for himself entirely different from his own; he pieced it together by weaving a lot of stories and anecdotes around it. He derived unexpected pleasure from recognizing his multiple personalities, in inventing fresh reminiscences and fictitious tales which not only seemed perfectly feasible but were, in fact, far more clear-cut and comprehensible to him than his own life had been. Although he was barely at the initial stage of this process its haziest aspects were already taking shape, hinting at the prospect of their own foreseeable risks, challenges, passions, pleasures—and even a whole new vocabulary springing up from José Augusto's arrogance.

One morning, feeling more calm and free than he had in quite a while, he decided to go to Los Angeles. Day after day he had tried to convince himself of his innocence by arguing that he had been provoked to violence, to a moment of blind rage. From time to time, he would gaze out the bus window at the shimmering waves and fall back on a handful of well-structured interior monologues. He spent the whole trip puffing away, absorbed in the stream of phrases flowing from his memory. From then on, it became a regular exercise which he never failed to practice; it accompanied him everywhere, in open spaces, unfamiliar streets and strange hotel rooms.

The reproaches, accusations and anxious pauses cropped up at the most unexpected moments. *Things weren't working out quite the way I anticipated. There was too much room for those hostile thoughts and I was still suffering from insomnia and the midnight jitters, the sound of footsteps and the feeling that I was being followed. There were a number of things that, for the life of me, I couldn't figure out: my attempts to become another person or persons—it didn't much matter who, but someone else, anyone who could rid me of this bummer I was on. That was the real problem: here inside where the tension never let me in peace for a single moment.*

Momentarily detached from his apprehension, he noticed his prematurely gray temples and finished shaving. All of a sudden, he felt the oppression of the great city weighing down on him in that one small room; the hotel hemmed in by huge buildings and right in the middle of the din made by dock workers and stevedores, police car sirens and mechanical shovels. José Augusto sensed at once that the old inner voices could emerge at any moment, that he was sinking back into his former isolation and that he could not possibly allow himself to be so easily swayed by every single impression, as if he were still an expatriate, a man without a country, without a fixed destination. Although he had gradually been discarding his presumptuousness and that hunted feeling, he knew full well that sooner or later he would have to confront his ingrained hostility and choose other alternatives previously closed to him. And he would have to keep on holding all those long dialogues with himself. He also realized that he would never be totally free of the harrowing images that haunted him constantly.

That fact was brought home to him while he was in Los Angeles, where he had gone after a woman who had awakened his lust. However, by the third time he had seen her naked, his hands caressing her thighs and her shoulders, he could not help feeling let down when he looked at her. He could feel only a vague pleasure, devoid of all vibrations, all excitement, at the thought of surrendering something to her that seemed pointless, as if his desire were on tenterhooks, sealed off without any possibility of attaining complete fulfillment. He did everything possible to get Laura out of his system, to set her aside. But he could only find a slight degree of satisfaction when he focused his senses elsewhere, when Laura's breasts, her legs and the memory of her scent were incorporated into his own rhythm, when he imagined her in his mouth, in his breathing, in the deepest recesses of his eyes. Then, as he became more and more aroused, he would see his hands resting on the body of the woman beside him, that distant being with whom he finally arrived at a climax only to be left with a hollow, empty feeling. Afterwards, he'd leave without saying a word and wander through the streets, spending hours at a pool hall, at a bar, anywhere at all. He'd try to lose himself among the crowds on the corners of Main Avenue, among the blacks, looking up at the neon signs lining the streets.

He rubbed shaving lotion on his face, put on a checked shirt and lit a cigarette. He sank back in the chair again and stared at the different lights reflected on the glass windows in the buildings across the street—from the stoplights to the marquees, from the violet afternoon glow to scattered shapes waving in the wind. Lately, he had fallen into the habit of comparing these streets with those of his childhood; the smells of marketplaces and the people in the parks and boulevards. Sometimes, he'd close his eyes and go in his mind from one place to another, tracing his route from the Zócalo to Melchor Ocampo Avenue, catching a glimpse of the airport and the trees along Paseo de la Reforma and the Insurgentes esplanade. Then he'd roam for a while among the pine trees in the Desierto de los Leones and listen to the amateur soccer players yelling on an empty lot near Balbuena or the Green Indians Statues.

He finished his cigarette, put on a dark blue windbreaker and went back to 42nd Street where he mingled with the blacks and hispanics, with the babble of languages and the garish outfits. *Every single day, every single hour had its own special significance; deception no longer played any part in my life. There were nights when I'd give anything to hear the sound of my own voice, even one single exclamation. I knew that by now I was totally anonymous and that little by little, other, new obsessions would eventually take over. I had to get away from that other José Augusto, the loser who wandered from street to street dying of boredom and caressing his gun. By and by, I was joined by the other José Augustos who had been flourishing all along in silence. So . . . I started providing them with a smile, a good natured gesture here and there.*

The trip from Los Angeles to New York had exhausted him; he was fed up with the foul odors, the highways, with being on the road for so long. He couldn't stand the shrill cries at each bus stop, the uniformed men—policemen and otherwise—at each street corner and the bored yawns from the other passengers on the bus. One night, somewhere along the way, he sent a letter that was never opened, the letter his mother had waited for up to her very last moments, waited in vain for as her eyes had

135

yielded to the emptiness beyond life. It arrived a few days after the funeral.

It was on this particular trip that he had started taking notes; random observations scrawled in an illegible hand: lists of places, titles of movies, headlines. He'd add descriptions of faces he'd seen along the way or events he considered especially significant. Although at first glance they appeared to be mere scribblings, random notes, he alone could understand them, he alone could decipher their real meaning. Once he tried describing the dead man's face, but came up with nothing more than a dark blot, like a stubborn stain, impossible to erase.

During his first few days in New York, he took a long hard look at his callousness and found it flimsy, hollow, lacking in substance and life. As he walked along the docks or stopped in a park he had the sensation that the whole world was nothing but a great city; that the buildings, bridges and avenues had spilled over into every inch of space, obliterating the mountains and the sand dunes, defying even the clouds and the celestial bodies.

In spite of the bustle in the streets, the people hurrying everywhere and the unfamiliar smiles and expressions that surrounded him, José Augusto never felt insignificant so long as he could concentrate on his loneliness and the range of possibilities open to him. There were times when he felt total identification with Domingo Buenaventura's accounts of his experiences in these same places some twenty years before: the dock workers, ghettos, hordes of immigrants and violence in the slums. José Augusto felt that many of these places had been familiar to him long before his arrival: there was no landmark that he didn't recognize or hadn't imagined or seen in photographs and films. He thought of the gangsters during the Depression, the Greenwich Village bohemians and the mobs of people celebrating the end of World War II.

Naturally, as far as I was concerned this was much more than just history; it was as if I had focused all my senses on that one place and let myself be carried away by everything we had heard and read; so many incredible news stories and photographs, the extremes of degradation and the sheer audacity of the master builders of its towers. Although sometimes I liked to think that nothing would stand in the way, I still could not stifle my anger. Some nights — and fortunately they started spacing out — I'd envision Laura's face in the mirror, I'd see her again, naked, and I'd feel that uncontrollable urge to take her in my arms.

He left the hotel and after catching a glimpse of the twilight on the docks he went to a restaurant where he was reminded of Sebastián Cardoso's grin the last time he'd seen him — the histrionics of that screwball who would haunt him the rest of his life. Then José Augusto wandered into a porno movie and got bored watching the acrobatics of black men and white women that bordered on the grotesque. As he went out, he stopped at a newsstand, as if it were a strategic point from which he could command a view of the entire avenue from one end to another: where he could see dark-haired, full-lipped mulatto girls and other people in multi-colored clothing, some with tattooed arms and necks inked in writhing shapes and greenish letters.

Half an hour later he had reached the Times Square subway station. He didn't much care where he went, so he headed for the first place that occurred to him, glancing at the grubby ads in the subway cars, the rubbish piled up in its corners and the drowsy faces of the old people who didn't seem to be in a hurry, as if they had already been excluded from the world. A bit later, on his way back, on 53rd Street, half a block from Second Avenue, he found himself again among the amorphous glow of neon signs. He went into a bar, greeted the same waiter he'd seen the week before, ordered a beer and started making plans for the next few days.

The smoke rose and drifted in every direction; the odors of different tobaccos merged with chattering voices and clinking glasses. People crowded around the tables, perched on stools or leaned against the bar. José Augusto, at the bar, had long since learned to sample the different kinds of drinks by swirling them around on his tongue and then down his throat. He could now let himself be transported by his thoughts and mix a number of images: lonely rooftops, broad steel beams on huge bridges, smiling lovers embracing in the parks and walking together down the side streets. For a brief moment he had the sensation that nothing but the present existed; only that particular scene he happened to be watching at the time—swaying bodies, gesturing hands and his own cigarette, nestled there among dozens of other stubs on the ashtray.

He had lost all track of time and finally went back to his hotel where he cast a scornful glance at the suitcase he would be taking with him the following day. It would break the pattern of his reveries and force him to return once more to the here and now, to the sleepless hours and to those goddamned nightmares that never stopped. *The last dawn in New York remained fixed in my mind like an old photograph in sepia where the light patches stand out, where the faces are frozen in expressions of either astonishment or contempt. Then, all of a sudden, I'd be filled with remorse and that empty feeling would come again. By the time my monologues had reached the point where they centered on vague inane issues, the other José Augustos had already learned to*

137

stand on their own two feet and were gradually forcing their way into my mind.
Anyway, I was sure of at least one thing: I was perfectly capable of coping with
the next challenges I'd be facing, and I knew I'd handle them, one after another,
even if I had to roam all over the world to do it.

Since he was running out of money, he knew he'd have to get a job—any kind of job—at his next stop. Clean-shaven, frowning at the sun shining in his eyes, he left the hotel at noon and walked toward the docks. It might be several years before he heard his own language or ran into a familiar face again. In spite of it all, he strode along confidently as if his complex mental processes and mixed feelings had no bearing whatsoever on the movements of his body.

He could only guess at what his friends and enemies had been up to all this time. He'd have to settle for just imagining the world he had left behind: Laura's new love affairs, Buenaventura's speculations and Andrea's theatrical performances. His roots lay thousands of kilometers away. So did Sebastián, drinking until dawn, as always, lost in his rages and with a trickle of saliva etched on his face like a gesture of impotence.

Before long, that other city—the same city as always, the city he could never really leave, would surely have to undergo a series of changes: there would be new neighborhoods, new slums, new freeways, more antennas on the outskirts, all of that expansion devouring the hills and forests and rocks. Although José Augusto craned his neck as far as he could, he couldn't manage to see the top floors of the skyscrapers. Just as he began to feel a certain sense of well-being he happened to spot a floating helicopter, like a huge insect, reflected in the distant water over the harbor.

II

OVER SEVERAL MONTHS, the house on Coyoacán had undergone a series of changes which transformed it into an entirely different world; it had become the perfect antidote to doubt and resentment. At this point Laura felt she had more than she could handle; the truth seemed hopelessly distorted and she was totally unable to break away from the voices which never ceased to torment her. Although she had made countless attempts to get to the bottom of the whole complex affair, she felt that her frustration had dragged on too long; she could not shake herself free from the last scene at her apartment on Sinaloa: the hollow eyes staring out at her from the body on the rug.

Over and over again she asked herself why, and invariably she would wind up with a pain shooting through her chest and throat. Her future seemed meaningless, lost in the maze of jumbled thoughts and unspoken curses.

For days on end she forgot her exhaustion. She had given herself up to the task of rejecting her memories and the awesome intensity of her fury, puzzling over José Augusto's alleged temporary insanity. Despite the fact that she was at Andrea's, in totally different surroundings with a whole new set of sounds, the old habits and reflexes still persisted. As soon as she awoke, she'd automatically look for the mirror facing her, still expecting to see the pale, ghostly wince on the dead man's face, which seemed to ward off all pain, all distress.

Still in a daze, she cursed every single experience in her life. Clenching her fists, she rubbed her neck and buried her face in her hands. The slightest sound startled her. She was constantly besieged by the outbreak of her hatred, her inability to destroy José Augusto's image, his paranoid behavior as he dashed down the stairs, his despair and the unbelievable cowardice he had displayed.

Away on the other end of town, the deserted apartment on Sinaloa was a captive of solitude. Nothing moved there, as if everything was waiting for Laura's return. The floor still bore the imprint of the body on the spot where it had fallen with hands rigid and eyes still forever; the cigarette butts in the ashtrays and the stains on the rug had given the apartment a shabby timeworn look in just the few weeks that had passed.

Laura's face had begun to show the signs of the strain, of the hard lessons she had memorized a thousand times over. Her bewilderment and revulsion seemed to converge in the vague expression in her eyes, with occasional flashes of self-denial and insight. She constantly recreated the many facets of her anxiety, her self-recrimination. The emptiness, like long, dark corridors ringing with the sound of terrified cries, would close in on her without warning.

At night, when she talked to Andrea, her words seemed to come out of someone else, like faint echoes from the past. She'd blame herself for her recklessness, for having left so many things up in the air, for not having had the guts to make a clean break with José Augusto. She had never conceived of him as a potential murderer, much less that he could ruthlessly plan the whole thing beforehand, carry it out, and then, quite calmly, rationalize his motives for doing so. She constantly reverted to the shots fired in cold blood, the bullet in the man's forehead, the irrevocable fact that it had actually occurred, and she reproached herself time and time again for not having been present. Andrea's observations, wavering between compassion and common sense, were always cautious, always aimed at warning Laura against plunging headlong into rash judgments.

A few days after the crime, after its dreadful repercussions: endless visits to the gloomy corridors of the District Courts, the unwarranted threats, the jackals and shysters posing as lawyers, and contradictory advice coming from all sides, Laura finally fled to Coyoacán. In the end, as a result of the preposterous conclusions that were drawn and the inevitable role of the police in the whole affair, her statements remained buried beneath a pile of papers which were soon forgotten. Then followed a long, quiet interlude when the windows in the house seemed to seal off her distress.

Once her apprehensions started falling into place in their feasible, concrete form, Laura decided to take an indefinite leave of absence from work. Little by little, she lost interest in the pointless arguments with herself and with others. Her futile expectations, dreams, plans and reminiscences already lay far beyond her reach. Since she hadn't the slightest idea of what would happen next, she stubbornly refused to harbor any illusions about the future.

In the mornings, after Andrea left, Laura and the house would share their loneliness. The venetian blinds in the living room were shut tight and except for the rustling of the pine branches and the jacaranda trees there was no sound at all. Every single room, each piece of furniture seemed to be possessed by a curious lethargy. Even the ivy and the bougainvillea seemed weighed down by the neglect which stunted their growth.

She would lie for hours with one hand on her forehead, her arms slack. She saw herself running through an endless forest as she had many years ago, when barely in her early teens. She had been lost and didn't know which way to go; she kept running and crying for her parents, both of whom had died of old age a few years ago in a neighborhood north of the city. She could still picture herself tearing along wildly, running away from loneliness—at least that's what she thought loneliness was at the time. She recalled her mother's stern, impassive face, as if it concealed all the secrets in the world, with a proclivity to silence always reflected in her eyes. Once, her mother had told her of an unhappy love prior to her marriage; it had been an intense, emotional experience. Laura could still see her reading in the afternoons or gazing at the rain beyond the window, the rain Laura herself never grew tired of watching. It would arrive regularly, almost like clockwork, during the month of July, awaken her in the middle of the night, frightening her almost half to death. She would be left with an inexplicable feeling of anguish. Then came the early morning light and she'd hear drunken shouts coming from somewhere beyond the house.

Ever since her adolescence, Laura had grown accustomed to staring at the horizon, letting her eyes settle on some point in the distance. Once she started living in the city, however, she had found herself torn between her delight at strolling along the wide boulevards and her longing to catch a glimpse of a natural landmark—a mountain top—on the horizon. Her father—a tall, husky man who talked and traveled a great deal, who laughed once in a while—had the same habit. She reflected that in the end, he probably reached the point where he finally understood her mother. He had aged quickly, prematurely, as if his love of life had been snuffed out in one blow.

Once, it had occurred to Laura to bring up the subject of men, those mysterious creatures her mother rarely mentioned. The replies, however, were far from satisfactory and she was right back where she started, without actually knowing who they really were, why they were so different, why they always seemed to be running off somewhere, why they traveled so much. She was also left with the impression that those vague sensations of pleasure she was already experiencing were taboo. She wondered at the real meaning of dirty words, at the lack of concrete answers to her questions and at the evasive, exasperated glances she'd receive. For years, she had taken it for granted that this was simply the way things were; it was their nature, their destiny. Her brother, much older than Laura and the first target of her erotic adolescent fantasies, had just begun to repeat this cycle by tuning himself into the ways of the world and to become what she assumed a man should be: straightforward and masterful.

Once in a great while, they would all climb on the truck—the huge monstrosity that seemed practically an appendage of her father. They'd cover hundreds of kilometers without stopping except for gas. No one would speak, as if those moments were intended only to be seen and heard, nothing else. She remembered her father's huge hands, his fingers on the wheel or waving to other truck drivers. His hands—the scarred palms and knotted knuckles, worn and calloused from hard work—always seemed to be squeezing something or other, as if they had been made to grip objects beyond their endurance. She heard her father's yells when they unloaded the cargo in dusty, desolate shanty towns where even the old people carried buckets of water on their shoulders and the ragpickers congregated on street corners. Then they'd come back home, as if nothing had happened, and leave the truck in a warehouse near the small, one-floor house in the arid, flat plain where the weeds disappeared into the hillocks and the parched land devoured the valleys.

Finally, after she'd leave those images behind her, burying them in her nightmares and in the corners of her mind, Laura would get up, wander around the room, go to the kitchen and make herself a cup of tea and then, with the dim living room lights flickering down on her, she'd start to summon up José Augusto's sarcasm, his smirk, and his petulance. There he'd be, as always, smoking one cigarette after another, never budging one inch, either in his arguments with Buenaventura or while making fun of Sebastián.

Then she'd come back to earth to face the brutal truth, to learn how to identify the sounds of that particular house, to anticipate the lights and particular shadows, to feel her quivering hands, to sense her pulse when raising or lowering the blinds as she waited for the sun to shine on the wooden beams of the front entrance.

Day by day, as she brooded over her failures and disappointments, as the objects around her came to life, she couldn't help but notice that her expression had hardened, that her trust in others and her attachments to people were waning.

In the afternoons with the sun's rays shining down on the carpets and armchairs, she'd take a couple of tranquilizers and start dismantling one scene after another, trying to visualize the flesh and blood José Augusto, whom she still could not wrench from her body: the José Augusto she had tried to replace with someone else—the man whose death had now so drastically altered any expectations she might have had. Suddenly, her thoughts went back to the last time she'd seen her mother, a woman who didn't want to waste words anymore. This time, she had just kept pressing her hand to her forehead, refusing to say even one word. Laura remembered the funeral. It had been the last time she'd set eyes on the barren wastelands and dust storms of her childhood which she thought she had blotted out of her mind forever. She could still picture the dazzling rays of the reddish afternoon sun which slowly faded away into the darkness, only to return, without fail, the following day.

Gradually, as she sat on the sofa and then on a dining room chair, her fists tightly clenched, she felt that her increasing weariness, dissociations, fears and ruthlessness were getting the better of her; hence her reluctance to face up to the future. She could feel the rancor surging through her body; it clung to her palate, tightening her face. That sensation, which she had detected sometimes in her mother's expression, was thoroughly alien to Laura. It shattered her memories and took objects out of their rightful contexts, making her head throb; it prevented her from concentrating on the more gratifying experiences in her life—a process which formerly had come to her naturally, effortlessly, devoid of self-pity, disgust or the constant need for self-justification.

She murmured a few curses to herself, knowing that now she needed to make some resolutions and stick to them. She paid closer heed to those inner voices urging her to forge ahead in order to avoid self-destruction, to shed those anxieties that clouded her thoughts and engulfed her deepest feelings. Although the crime had put an end to one world, she would have to work up the courage to live in a new one, regardless of any qualms she might have about the future.

She was totally confused, totally alone, her fingers trembling from sheer dread and her eyes moist with a curious sort of emptiness. She had fallen into the kind of long heavy sleep that often follows a serious crisis. Yet when she awoke, she would find herself even more agitated than before. But gradually she felt herself changing; she was slowly learning how

143

to cope with the pitfalls of her hostilities.

When Andrea came home, when midnight had already drifted away from the swaying pines and the eucalyptus trees, her spirits lifted somewhat, like tiny sighs of relief. However fleeting, they managed to draw the line between her fixations and her contradictions. Gradually, the less important factors took on a different meaning as she reconstructed them within a more flexible and indulgent framework while deceiving herself into thinking that she had rejected her anger once and for all. Even so, in spite of the new lies she had been telling herself, there was an undeniable glint of fire in Laura's eyes as she spoke.

Andrea would listen patiently without getting too bogged down in the details. She was always careful to distinguish between commiseration and condescension in her own attitude and to avoid expressing her real opinion of José Augusto. She would pass over the problems which seemed insurmountable by either changing the subject or letting her own pauses soften the harshness of her words. Despite her efforts and the perception of human nature gleaned from her long theatrical experience, Andrea nevertheless found herself incapable of putting herself in Laura's place, or digging into the more unsavory motivations of others.

One June day, several weeks after the scandal and the news stories died down, they spoke of José Augusto: his complexes, his belligerence, his masks and his unmitigated conceit. They also talked about his escape, his ambivalent personality and the dubious prospects in store for him; he would always be hounded by his ghosts and his arrogance. But they stopped there in order to sidestep more sensitive subjects. By this time, Andrea already knew that José Augusto had crossed the border and was learning to cope with his freedom thousands of kilometers away. She noticed that a strange silence had come over Laura and that her face now revealed the implacable verdict, her absolute contempt for José Augusto and her unexpressed desire: that he disappear forever, that she never see him again. Laura, no doubt, would have to resort to belittling his motives and smearing his image. At the same time, Andrea observed, Laura's wan face, thin hands, furrowed brow and faltering speech showed that her health had deteriorated considerably. It suddenly dawned on Andrea that up to now, Laura had lost far more than José Augusto. Although Andrea fully sympathized with her friend, she was keenly aware of the mixed feelings of pity and distaste that Laura's attitude aroused in her.

As the days went by, as Laura's scars came out into the open, her voice acquired a whole new set of inflections: sometimes dry, sometimes self-possessed or adamant, and occasionally even fierce or impetuous. As she gradually became more absorbed in the new practice of blaming others as harshly as herself, of singling out her memories in relation to the distance that separated her from her apartment on Sinaloa, she began to reject the atmosphere that prevailed in Coyoacán. Before long, Laura and Andrea became involved in all sorts of new activities—in dreaming up new projects and planning outings and trips. By now, the jacaranda blossoms were covering the grass, and the venetian blinds in the living room were opened at noon.

One afternoon, Sebastián dropped in. He reported somewhat perfunctorily on the latest political news and then proceeded to offer imaginative suggestions for the staging of Andrea's next play. He was careful to avoid any reference to the crime in front of Laura. Sebastián even refrained from mentioning the death of the old widow Banderas and the letter he was planning to write José Augusto. He had no idea then that the reply would be so terse, nor that he would, for a long time, be kept in the dark regarding the fugitive's whereabouts or the changes he had undergone in the meantime.

The following weekend, Laura decided to go to her apartment and, once and for all, get rid of that place with its memories of nothing but angry curses and sullen voices. It was early June; the wind swirled scraps of paper along the sidewalk near Miravalle Square, where the weak Saturday afternoon sun shone feebly on the old people and the cyclists.

As soon as she entered the building she felt resentment growing inside her once more. By now, however, she had well-defined, clear-cut convictions and knew exactly what she could leave behind her. No one answered at Buenaventura's door. Slowly she went up the stairs, opened the windows and cleaned the dust off the tables and the armchairs. She unhooked the mirror from the bedroom wall and left it lying in a corner without once visualizing the images recreated in its polished surface. She coughed once or twice, picked up some clothes and went back out to the street.

She had proved to herself that she had grown hard, that she was in control of her feelings. It was only her rage that made her clench her fists while the set of her mouth matched the listless, bored expression in her eyes. The following Monday, Andrea drove her to the airport, and en route to Caracas, Laura finally understood that so many memories—apparently long dead and buried—still lay submerged beneath the mirror.

145

III

BUENAVENTURA HAD SPENT that dreary night in jail with a throbbing pain in his temples. He had not slept more than three hours, thanks to the gloominess of his cell and his own restlessness. Ever since daybreak he had been speculating on the repercussions of those endless meetings, rallies and demonstrations, his sudden, arbitrary arrest and the mock trial he had undergone. The legless, one-eyed, highly intelligent character that Buenaventura had created that past week kept creeping into his nightmares by huddling in a corner of the cell and making fun of everyone. Once in a while, Domingo would have him take a few puffs of his pipe and recite the whole list of crimes Buenaventura had allegedly committed, and apply his mind to all sorts of unrelated subjects such as *The New Atlantis* and the *Harmony of the Cosmos*. Then, Buenaventura would suddenly endow the creature with a good pair of healthy legs, make him insult the guards and let him roam freely among the cellblocks and corridors.

During those few days, Buenaventura's reflections had centered around a gamut of new themes with a combination of bizarre images: One minute he'd be wandering through freeways jammed with cars or through colonial buildings, while the next he'd be in a lunatic asylum or a leprosarium, or else splashing in mud puddles in some remote plain beyond the mountain ranges. He would visualize a file of dazed, silent Indians crawling out of the underbrush, the sun beating down on them like a horizontal rainfall.

Then, little by little, he'd return to his own cell in the Lecumberri Prison where the medley of speech patterns clashed with each other and gave way to a whole new world of faces warily scrutinizing one another: from the anxiety of the pyromaniac to the callousness of the killer who specialized in back stabbing to the blasphemies of the rapist who had by now lost track of the number of assaults he had committed. Some criminals confessed to their crimes by shouting them out loud, while others were obviously incorrigible, pathological liars.

Domingo realized that here were hundreds of ready-made life stories at his fingertips, any one of which he would have liked to write by probing into the character's motivations, his individual makeup, his secret grudges. After all, they were only a very small part of the same country, or perhaps hundreds of countries within the same borders, inexorably revolving around the same, lone, worm-eaten tree trunk.

. . . I never gave it a second thought, and didn't spend too much time sitting at my desk and brooding about it. I made up my mind almost immediately and said it aloud, boosting my own self-confidence while I was at it. I knew full well that I would be coming up against my own limitations, that my flaws could give me away at any moment, and that my weaknesses, which by this time were so firmly implanted in my nature, in my body, could mean my downfall. The night I decided to take an active part in the movement, I couldn't sleep. Too many thoughts kept crowding into my head and I felt that everything was coming at me all at once. Something extraordinary was happening in our lives. It all started toward the end of July, when the rains flooded the streets and the city began to grow weary of so much sunshine. Although we were still unaware of the consequences, the alarming news reports about police provocation were spreading fast. Right from the beginning, there were already stories of people who had been killed or badly hurt and of students who had disappeared. We never imagined where we'd be going nor where our voices would finally lead us . . .

Buenaventura remembered the tenements in Nonoalco, in Guerrero, in Bondojito, and the hovels on Mesones street where he first learned to walk—the rows of washing hanging out to dry on the rooftops that seemed to fade into the horizon. It had been a world of mangy dogs and venereal diseases, of people grown old before their time and of a sense of infinite rage. Here, street brawls were routine: "Wherever the hell you want, you son of a bitch; you name it—in the alleys, on the rooftops, the dungheaps or behind the boxcars." Then came the forties, when his companions came up in the world, and generals were regular customers in the brothels. It was the era of rhumba dancers, folk singers and zoot-suiters who hung around the neighborhood movie theaters. "What's the use, you asshole. Here, we'll never be anything more than a bunch of third-rate clods." It was the heyday of the bureaucrats' call girls and the pen-pushers who aspired to bigger and better government jobs, of crowds of fervent pilgrims who flocked to the Shrine of Guadalupe and of the tattered beggars at the Buenavista railroad station.

After he recreated his travels through Spain and some well-known European cities, he went back to his old childhood friends from Mesones whom he hadn't seen for years. They were all either the fathers or even the grandfathers of the new, get-rich-quick generation who had traded in their denim for cashmere suits, cheap hair oil for French cologne. He could still see them as they gradually took leave of the slums and tenements for the minor government posts, desperately hanging on to the Revolutionary gravy train. Their descendants, the "juniors," like housebroken pups, now occupied seats in the Chamber of Deputies and brazenly strutted around the night clubs on Reforma and their new mansions in the more fashionable residential districts in the Lomas to the west or the Pedregal in the south section of town. "To hell with poverty, if we don't cash in now, we never will. In this shitty life, one has to make the most of one's chances and enjoy the cash while it lasts . . . ." Then he thought about the people who had sung the Internationale so proudly, who had pontificated about the expropriations and the government's promise to give students "a rational and exact idea about the expropriations and the universe."

> . . . We used to discuss all sorts of things in those meetings at my apartment. It was there we decided to take advantage of the situation at hand, and analyzed the different ways we could participate. One night, Gabriel and Martín dropped in. They spent hours consulting me and finally we worked it out. A few days later, we were out on the streets among thousands of other faces and arms, feeling that the city was ours. This was one of the earliest mass demonstrations after the Preparatory School at San Idelfonso was attacked by bazookas. We started from University City. It was about this time that I started reliving so many past experiences and perceiving new images as well, new prospects, as yet undefined: the shadows of the trees on Insurgentes hanging over us, voices reverberating against the windows, the people—their arms held high. We kept a leisurely, confident pace. We felt totally free from worry and fear. There was a certain kind of rhythm, a springiness in our movements that told us this was the real thing, not easily defined yet wholly perceptible in the expressions, in the flashing eyes . . .

"What country do I belong to?" Buenaventura asked himself over and over again.

He looked back at the bars in his cell, shrugging as the murals intertwined haphazardly. From the serpent skirt of the *Cuatlicue* to the flagpole on the Zócalo, from the Baroque altar in Tepotzotlán to the high, narrow towers of Ciudad Satélite, the sequences kept piling up one after another: the taco stands, the babble in the marketplaces, the colorful speech of ragpickers and loaders, the flabby B girls in bars with names like the Bombay, the Smyrna and the Gusano. He laughed right in the face of a pompous, well-groomed banker, standing at the Customs Office in Ciudad Juárez on the border watching the wetbacks as they waited, their gnarled hands, emaciated faces and baggy pants, their toes showing through their threadbare yellowish, grayish shoes which seemed to bear the whole weight of their futile, rotting hopes.

Before long, the stunning woman from Algeciras materialized before him—the myth he had built up for so many years that her sensuality had ripened through his repeated recollections. Then followed images of Spain at war: the Paseo de Gracia in Barcelona, Atocha Street in Madrid, the voices of Azaña, Durruti and La Pasionaria. "They shall not pass, the sons of bitches." He compared the other, softer, shrewder, Mexican voices and their haphazard, unfinished phrases with the jeering, histrionic shouts of the Andalusians, Catalans and Madrilenians. He walked through the old Jewish quarter which was flanked by a series of more unassuming buildings. Then he suddenly found himself in the middle of a splendid Spanish palace with Moorish doors and altarpieces dating back to the period of the Catholic Monarchs, Ferdinand and Isabella.

The scene switched to one midnight on Insurgentes Avenue. "Hey, you old coot, you'd better hand over all your money right now or we'll knock the shit out of you." He could still see the long-haired toughs with chains, brass knuckles, gloves, checked shirts and insolent looks, jeering with their half-open mouths. They had grabbed his wallet and hit him a couple of times in the face. It had happened almost ten years ago, in the late fifties, when the current presidential motto was "Work is fruitful and creative," and prior to the subsequent "With peace, everything is possible." The tunes on the jukebox had given way to high-pitched shouts accompanied by the strident noise of electric guitars. The syrupy voices of trios with guitars had yielded to the exaggerated gestures of a torch singer on a television screen. A couple had finished dancing and the seal-faced bandleader and his musicians took their bows. The mobs at the National Auditorium went wild with Beatles-type music and the wiggling of Pelvis. A voice from the crowd called, "Hey, c'mon, man, join us, this is a far out trip, man, way out."

. . . I was always amazed that the auditoriums were jammed with new faces, mobs of them everywhere. We'd cover the whole university scene from one end of town to the other: from the Polytechnic at the Casco de Santo Tomás to Zacatenco, from University City to the Normal School and then to the Agricultural School in Chapingo. Naturally, we had our share of long-winded tirades, short-lived enthusiasm and inane speeches. And, of course, there were always the inevitable, opportunistic demagogues and petty politicians who didn't miss the chance to capitalize on the situation for their own ends. Every day I'd draft at least a couple of pages and try to clarify our goals. I know that to a lot of people I was a perfect stranger who had no business being there; to them I was either a poor old fool or some kind of lunatic. By that time, thousands of perspiring faces had been congregating everywhere and our protests were being heard all over the country . . .

Domingo returned to the Indian-like faces he had seen on Mesones Street, to the peculiar murmuring sounds of some pot-smokers outside a tavern. He scorned the official version of Mexican history with its syphilitic Hernán Cortés and the ridiculous controversy over Cuauhtemoc's remains. He deplored the armchair historians who thought nothing of transplanting history from one country to another and the dilettantes who admired the Chichén Itzá pyramids and the Palenque Cross from a purely aesthetic point of view. He scoffed at the theoreticians who always had the last word on a poor drunk who risks his life by thumbing his nose at death itself and at the snobs who are enthralled by the sheer magnificence of the sugar skulls sold on the Day of the Dead. "Indian blood flows through my veins, it's the only kind that counts, what the hell," said a brown-haired Mexican at the Concordia Circle, showing off his gaudy cuff links and the blond Nordic beauty on his arm.

Buenaventura focused on the Indians coming down from the mountains near San Cristóbal las Casas in Chiapas, their faces like stone idols, their chests hairless and their hair tousled. Beyond it all — the misery of centuries, the *teponaxtles*, the obsidian jars, the wreathed columns and the Plateresque stairways — loomed the colossal stone head of La Venta. He chose to ignore Benito Juarez' presidential sash and Porfirio Diaz' bristling white moustache in favor of the sullen recriminations of the *mestizos* and the prehispanic myths that time had long since lost and forgotten.

. . . I felt again as I had during my early rebellious years, before I left for other places to devote myself to similar causes. Here again we

150

tried to keep it open and aboveboard, to discard nit-picking and leave pointless accusations aside. I had always been a sworn enemy of weak-kneed bootlickers, so now I launched into an active, wholehearted participation in the cause. I felt like a new man. I spoke before huge mobs—at rallies, meetings, what have you, and pulled no punches. I set forth new guidelines and stressed that we should not back down on a single one of our petitions. Gabriel and Martín were always at my side, offering their unconditional support. They defended us from our unseen enemies and disregarded the smear campaign that was going around about us. They matured with every passing day and their contribution was far greater than we ever imagined at first . . .

Buenaventura remembered every word of an out-dated monologue of old uncle Federico, the only one of his relatives who had ever made a deep impact on his conscience. "What can I say? I still haven't figured it out. I don't have the faintest idea who we are or where we're headed. We are, if you will, the result of too much history scattered in all directions. I swear, I can't help busting a gut laughing whenever someone brings up the subject of our so-called idiosyncrasy. It's a real mish-mash—and goes no further than that. Our past keeps crumbling every so often—with each generation, I'd say. We're constantly redescribing ourselves, morning, noon and night. We like to tear down the living and magnify the virtues of the dead. There you have it—we age our heroes, we dress them in mourning as soon as possible. Then we gussy them up, coddle them, invest them with the appropriate solemnity and then, in the end, we kick them in the ass. We bump into them everywhere, in parks, on monuments, in out-of-the-way esplanades. They could even be coming out of the sewers for all I know."

Old Federico's voice gradually became clearer, more forceful, as if he were just barely warming up for a two-hour tirade. "And, if we're going to get down to the nitty-gritty and start characterizing, I would say that we're a soft, wishy-washy people; we're a bunch of hypocrites with false modesty. We're a real pain in the ass and cagey as hell. And, of course, we have that famous ingrained snobbish streak—we're the greatest. We make a point of looking down on the living, who piss us off, and of lionizing our dead. Of course, we know how to hide our arrogance. We never make a big deal about it, but we do like to bug the hell out of our neighbor, get him in a corner, make a laughingstock out of him, and then, once we've made mincemeat of him, we pick him up, dust him off and rescue him. I'm sure you've noticed—anything more than a three-way conversa-

151

tion is sheer bedlam. Boy, are we the wise guys! We come on strong, putting on the perfect act by using three handy ploys that go a long, long way: flattery, necrophilia and bluff. To tell the truth, I really don't know. Each time we take this tack we're playing both ends against the middle. We're bogged down in quicksand, slime and bitchiness. But, when all is said and done, what the hell, we're something else. At least, that's what we have to keep telling ourselves over and over. Otherwise, we'd be wiped out. Mark my words, your descendants will have other, new experiences. They'll have to survive new twists to our national pastimes—the phenomena of hustling, hot air and chaos. One thing you can bank on—they'll be living in a world where rip-off supreme is the name of the game. Someone said the other day that we're nothing but riff-raff, but I don't think it's as bad as all that. Granted, there's a lot of chaff. But what the hell, we also have a tremendous love of life to our credit. What really ticks me off is when someone says we're living in a shitheel country. And, more often than not, the people who spout off such crap are the lowest grade of idiots around. They probably reached their conclusions after looking in the mirror. But what do I know—there are so many angles to all this business. On the other hand, maybe I'm saying all this just to size you up. And what the hell . . . one thing I almost forgot to mention, if there's something we Mexicans love to do, it's exactly that: size each other up."

Old Federico's words were slowly fading—his admiration for Melchor Ocampo, his gloomy predictions on the conflicts of a country in ruins, its excessive dependence on trade, and the longevity in office of our incompetent, boorish, coopted leaders—until at last Buenaventura turned to the events of the past decade. He covered the city from one end to the other: its gracious, colonial-style patios, the gyms where boxers trained, the terracota virgins, the priests in the godforsaken rural areas, the dustbowls and the brothels, until finally he reached Military Camp No. 1 where the political prisoners were kept. There he saw the top brass in full regalia, smiling from ear to ear, hotly denying all rumors, and shouting insults at their flunkies. Little by little, amidst the smells of greasy tortillas and rancid frijoles, poorly planned alleys and whitewashed walls, as he approached Ciudad Nezahualcóyotl, he heard the unmistakable buzz of thousands of insects. Buenaventura knew them to be the filthiest, blackest insects in the world.

. . . That night, before I was arrested, I was beset by all sorts of doubts and a deep silence. As I tried to rest in the big chair in the apartment, there were too many things closing in on me. I got to thinking that my tempestuous life story, teeming with all sorts of phantoms, could never really be summed up in just a few words. In a bit more than two months—from July to September—I have witnessed the collapse of a number of taboos and seen silence transformed into indignation and demands. But it seemed to me that all of it could fall apart at any given moment. Police provocations were the order of the day and all our petitions were squelched with an iron hand. Some of my warnings, echoed by others, fell on deaf ears and there was no turning back. Finally, tired of all the familiar noises in the building and of smoking my pipe all by myself, I decided to go downstairs to get the papers at Miravalle Circle. It was almost eight o'clock on a Saturday night and there were very few people on the street. I was arrested on the corner of Medellín, with the usual strong-arm tactics and crude insults. And without a warrant, of course. As usual, I think I rose to the occasion by keeping fairly calm and refusing to answer a single one of their attacks . . .

Domingo's thoughts were broken by a quarrel in the prison courtyard beyond his cell. There was talk of army troops entering University City. He immediately pictured the soldiers with rifles and bayonets, their machine guns resting on the benches in the Science Auditorium where scarcely ten days ago, shortly before the March of Silence, he had once again demanded that the political prisoners be released, and attacked the repressive forces in charge.

While he had been creating the monochrome monster with the one grayish eye, the maimed hand and the long, deep scar on the right cheek, Domingo Buenaventura had started counting the years, months and days he had spent in different prisons. He ticked off the Marías Islands off Mexico's Pacific coast, the jails in Guatemala and Bogotá and the Mexican provinces—Morelia, Guadalajara and Hermosillo, plus several terms in Lecumberri, "The Black Palace" where he was now. He made a rough guess—he had spent 19 years and nearly 5 months in different prisons—almost one third of his life.

"Maybe you'll never get out of this one," said the monster with a smirk.

Buenaventura stood up, leaving the typewriter behind him. He opened the door hastily and asked a couple of fellow inmates for the latest news reports. It was Thursday, September 19th.

153

IV

AT THE SAME TIME that José Augusto swore at himself while drawing the line between his irritation and self-derision, he knew that he was making considerable headway. He was now better prepared to handle the obstacles that might lie ahead. Except for his graying hair and somewhat leathery hands, his outward appearance had changed hardly at all. He had kept his past carefully hidden despite his penchant for playacting and his inability to put it all behind him. With a wary expression, he walked leisurely along, leaving the Isle Saint Louis and the Botanical Gardens behind him, relieved at having finally rid himself of the stumbling blocks in his way.

It was the month of May, the perfect time for taking stock of oneself. Though keenly aware of the interaction among the characters inside him — the charlatan and the weakling, the libertine and the smooth-talker — he could feel his spirits about to bloom again. The sun was spilling over the streets and a soft breeze was blowing beyond the Sacre Coeur all the way to the Montparnasse excavations. There still were, of course, other problems to overcome such as his search for new horizons and his need to control his inconstancy. Once again feeling a longing to prove himself, he had resolved to stop seeing the woman who wanted to move in with him. As he disappeared beyond the cobblestone streets and the faces of students and vendors, he sensed that his tendency toward solitude, toward digressions, toward categorizing his enemies and his varying degrees of apathy had returned.

In the past two years since he had left New York, he had been tearing down one barrier after another. But he was still not totally adept at handling his own subterfuges, his own deviousness, nor standing up to troublemakers and showoffs. He had been inspired by the usual dreams of lonely people and once he arrived in Madrid, he had started to make them come true — to broaden his scope and to adapt himself to other faces and other languages. During the first phase nothing had been easy. He was

154

constantly amazed at his own shortcomings, at his recklessness, and at the perennial fear of giving himself away.

His feelings had matured from self-contempt to a firm determination to control his impulses. He knew that in the long run each blunder would be to his benefit, that he would emerge from each new situation a stronger man, ready for the next, more perceptible challenges. His inner life, however, he kept to himself, as if it were locked tight in his fist. It remained there, in his conscience, waiting to be examined later on.

As he approached the Panthéon, he reflected on all the different jobs he'd held in the past few years. They had provided him with a new outlook as well as an opportunity to expand his challenges. *At first, even I couldn't believe it. It was like walking a tightrope, like being adrift. I kept rejecting every single thing around me. But . . . in this shitty, goddamned world, everything is a lesson. I'd rub my hands together—it all seemed so unreal; I'd inhale the smoke from my cigarette—and still found it hard to believe I was actually there. The only thing I was absolutely sure of was that that murderer's hands could not possibly belong to me.*

The journey by ship from New York to Cádiz had been the longest in his life. He had done nothing but brood and insult the coward that he knew he was. Not a day went by that he didn't predict a dismal future for himself. When he first arrived in Madrid, his first jobs were fairly run-of-the mill: as a waiter in the university cafeteria, as assistant in a pharmacy on Jovellanos Street, as errand boy for a hostel on Covarrubias Street where he became an expert at carrying and serving coffee, sweet rolls or grapefruit juice. He lived as best he could, by counting his *pesetas*, and remaining as anonymous as he could. Then he went through a period of drifting around; he would sleep in a small room on the outskirts of the city and wander from one end of town to the other, visiting museums and galleries and memorizing as many facts about the critics and painters as he could.

For a couple of months he lived in the most complete indolence from day to day, absorbed in dissecting and analyzing the works of art he'd seen, every detail of each oil painting. He studied his own speech patterns, each turn of phrase and nuance in his voice, attempting to achieve a more flowing quality, a more neutral intonation. He was satisfied if his accent was no longer reminiscent of the Lux Cinema or the San Cosme pool halls.

His new routine of abstinence and memory exercises had become second nature to him now, and curiously enough, they had separated him from other, more harmful obsessions which might easily hurt him and his plans for the future. As he walked around the gardens in the Prado museum, he noticed the unmistakable signs of repression all around him: the uniforms of the Spanish Civil Guards, the suppressed rage in the faces of the passersby, the memory of the Francoist salute, the chorusing of "Arriba España" and "Cara al Sol," the Fascist hymn being sung in the Plaza del Oriente. The consequences of all this had left their mark on the peninsula from one end to the other.

As he left the Panthéon, he thought of his early daring efforts, the first definite steps he'd taken toward describing paintings and sculptures to the tourists in Cuenca, Segovia and Avila. He would approach them meticulously, yet leisurely, answering questions as if he had been a guide all his life. This had been his opportunity to observe the reactions of others as he spoke; he had never had such rapt attention and it was like a link between his own body and the impressive mural or facade he was explaining. He knew that the charlatan in him was slowly emerging, that he must be fed, pampered, and provided with creative imagination as well as specific skills.

As a tourist guide he had traveled through a number of villages and cities, earning good money by taking groups around to museums and churches. Later on, as he had done every night for the past couple of years, he would take notes until his exhaustion plunged him into a series of nightmares: people being tortured, executioners tightening the *garrote*, biblical characters intertwined with visions of harlots and insane noblemen. He felt as if he were living in several historical periods simultaneously, going back and forth from the Twelve Apostles to Gothic arches, from the heliocentric universe to lush Moorish gardens, from the *condottieri* of the Renaissance period to the wealthy Florentine princes, from Spanish *conquistadores* to medieval hermits. As soon as he awoke, he'd automatically revert to his exercises by sharpening his senses, his perception, his feeling for color and perspective which gave the illusion of bodies in motion. He no longer spent those early hours mulling over his grudges or thinking how to refine his cynicism.

Although I was protected to a certain extent by my gray hair and incipient wrinkles, one day in Segovia I was almost sure I had been recognized. Besides, competition from other guides was tough, and I was in constant danger of being deported. I turned it over and over in my mind, and finally I decided to look for another line of work, a more dependable professional activity. By that time I was able to give proper priority to my decisions. It was a damned shame to give it all up. In spite of everything, that was one of the most gratifying periods in my life. Besides, I had met several women who offered me their companion ship . . . and a lot more, so there were a few nights, at least, when I was no longer completely alone.

He was approaching the Rue d'Ulm, enjoying the Parisian sun and not paying much attention to the pesky cobblestones. He remembered a particular afternoon in Madrid. With plenty of time on his hands, he'd wandered into a bookstore near the Plaza Mayor. He had leafed through a number of rare old volumes that were stacked up on a table. He asked their prices and their source, suddenly remembering an *incunabula* which somehow had fallen into his father's hands. He inquired again and carefully examined all the titles, epigraphs and colophons. Later on, he had walked around for half an hour or so, gone down to the Arch of the Cuchilleros with the smell of roasted chestnuts in his nostrils, wondering about those rare books, their small type, the hands that had printed and bound them so long ago. He was reminded of his bookstealing days in the downtown bookstores along Argentina Street and Hidalgo Avenue, priding himself on his extraordinary visual memory which rarely failed him. He'd unobtrusively pick up a small volume, carefully selected beforehand, hide it in his pocket or in his clothes and walk out into the street with complete nonchalance.

That same afternoon in Madrid, a few blocks from Colón Square, as he stared at the blind lottery ticket vendors tapping along the pavement with their canes, he couldn't stop thinking about those books. He made up his mind right then and there: the next day he'd go to a library, bone up on some specialized texts, and start doing some in-depth research. For several weeks, he did exactly that, once again abstaining from all sensual pleasures and reveling in his newly-discovered obsession. The information soon started piling up and before long his discoveries surpassed all his expectations. He began talking to booksellers, to learn the ins and outs of the business. He gathered as many catalogues and lists of collectors as he could.

At first somewhat uneasy and bewildered in his new role, he'd carefully weigh each word in his recently-acquired jargon. He had learned about all the new trends in the field and felt confident that this enterprise would soon amount to much more than a mere stockpile of isolated facts. Within two months, he had passed his first test. A seventeenth century text of the Inca Garcilaso's had made its way from an obscure bookshop to a woman staying at a boarding house on Fuencarral Street. Her accent was markedly Scottish and she happened to be the director of a Hispanic-American library in London. For this first transaction, José Augusto had

157

used up practically half of his savings. The deal proved to be highly profitable and, as a result, a more self-confident, knowledgeable José Augusto – who had long ago changed his name – emerged. He now found himself in a better position to expand his possibilities.

At first, Banderas concentrated only on Hispanic-American treatises of the Viceregal period: natural history, architecture of the Indies, documents from town councils and *haciendas* and maps of coastal regions and seaports. Gradually he branched out to medical books from the Enlightenment and finally he specialized in sixteenth and seventeenth century mechanics, where there was almost no competition to speak of and the market was solid. This also provided the opportunity to visit other European countries.

He began to learn the tricks of the trade such as how to finesse the more unscrupulous booksellers, some of whom were out-and-out crooks. He always had new titles to choose from and new goals to achieve. To increase his proficiency, he spent more time in libraries doing research. Although it was hardly necessary that he be an authority on mechanics, he did have to be thoroughly familiar with the exact terminology of his chosen field of specialization, with the names, dates and places at his fingertips. Before long, mechanical clocks, friction between objects and balanced beams became an integral part of his nightmares.

He had reached the tiny Contrescarpe Square, where a fire-eater was offering his nightly spectacle outside a restaurant. He sat down to watch the *clochards* in their whimsical poses. The scene reminded him of his first visit to Paris. It had been August, and General de Gaulle had been at the height of his power. José Augusto had visited a number of bookshops and made contact with several collectors. His livelihood, he reflected, was now intimately associated with sketches of wheels, axles and missile trajectories. Once in a while he would handle treatises on astronomy or astrology. But he preferred not to stray too far from his field and to fulfill what he had set out to do, what he had worked so hard at for almost a year and a half. He was already in another world where he could deny the image of himself as a murderer and slowly erase Laura from his mind.

Also, the revolutionary fever – the pox – as he called it had gotten into his blood. It lay in wait within him ready to burst out at any moment. By that time he knew little of what was going on in Mexico. Whatever scant information he had, he'd read in the papers. Once in a while, he'd hear of a railroad accident, of flood victims off the Pacific coast, or earthquakes near Chiapa de Corzo. Nevertheless, he kept visualizing the city growing larger, the radical transformation of its neighborhoods and the ruthless demolition in process—from the outskirts to the downtown area. Ever since he had received that first—and last—letter from Sebastián notifying him of his mother's death, he preferred to have nothing more to do with either his friends or his enemies. And he decided not to answer, hoping that some day his adventures would serve to inspire either the most absurd myths or the vilest epithets.

To tell the truth, despite my usual conflicts, I was living in the most unreal period of my life. I had more or less learned to control my shitty ways and was no longer chasing rainbows. That new venture was an extraordinary thing for me. As a matter of fact, I didn't really make too much money from it, but it proved to be extremely rewarding in other ways. Loneliness was a real problem, though. I was getting fed up with it and needed a real woman by my side. Sure, I had what everybody else has—one-night stands for purposes of releasing energy and curbing lust.

For about six months things had been running smoothly. His fluency in other languages was improving and he traveled constantly—from Paris to Madrid or from Rome to Barcelona. He always took the night train so he could arrive early in the morning and seek out out the titles he was after. He was a born sleuth, relentless and stubborn. His tenacity stood up to any test, however formidable. He himself used to say that his cynicism knew no bounds; it was free of prejudices and useless nit-picking. He hobnobbed with ex-convicts, drug addicts, white slavers and madams, telling himself that in order to attack scum you must first know it inside out. However, as friends, he preferred the company of radical revolutionaries. At last, José Augusto felt that he was living up to his potential.

One day he decided to leave the room where he lived in Madrid, a few blocks from the Atocha station. By then, he had already accumulated several paintings given to him by his artist friends, tons of books, magazines and assorted ashtrays from only God knows how many hotels and restaurants. Everything was total mess, as if Sebastián had been living there —the Sebastián Cardoso he hadn't seen for so long—spending his days and nights among derelicts and spaced-out people. It was almost as if the ghost of the old José Augusto had allowed something of the past to filter into the semi-darkness where the recluse could unwind and let his imagination run wild.

But after all—like so many other things that come to an end—José Augusto's new personalities had compelled him to move to another city. He had been in Frankfurt and Milan several times, had felt right at home

159

in Brussels and could find his way around London with no trouble at all. But, "Paris will always be Paris," he kept telling himself, and there both business and friendships seemed to flourish. He weighed the pros and cons of the move, but the balance was always positive. Besides, there were significant factors to be considered: there was an Uruguayan woman who had begun to attract him, to fill this thoughts with joy, making him feel as if he could take the plunge at any moment.

Whenever he arrived in Paris, the blonde, blue-eyed South American would accompany him in his wandering through outlying districts, back alleys, picturesque old squares and secluded wine cellars. Without too much haggling, he had managed to rent an apartment for himself on the Rue Amyot, just a few blocks from the Place de la Contrescarpe where he was sitting now, staring at an old woman dozing under a tree. He got up and walked toward his apartment where anguish was now a thing of the past and superficial amusements no longer interested him.

That first winter in Paris, the Uruguayan would sometimes spend the night at his place. She would watch him as he wrote, clenching his fists and frowning as he filled his notebooks. Finally he would come to her, caress her breasts and lie down beside her silently, his lips on her waist and thighs.

He reached the door to the three-story building where he lived and greeted the concierge somewhat diffidently. A couple of days before, he had sold an unusual volume on dynamics, complete with detailed illustrations and, for its time, amazingly well-developed formulas. He had gone back to the building and happened to notice that the concierge's door was ajar. José Augusto had knocked several times but no one came and he opened the door slowly. Then, he heard noises from the other room and managed to catch a glimpse of the concierge, stark naked, lying in bed and embracing a Hindu who was wearing nothing but a turban and heavy makeup. José Augusto had shrugged, reflecting that he had just witnessed one of the many bizarre scenes that no longer shocked anyone—not even the most prudish of old maids.

Believe it or not, I was actually sort of settling down. Laura now seemed so far away, as if she had always belonged to another man and I was merely a silent onlooker. Like the perfect idiot that I was, I imagined that everything in the world was in its place, as it should be, as if there were a universal clock— that cosmic harmony I had learned by heart and which I used to see almost every day in those books I toted from one place to another. I know now that it was only a question of repressed anger, and besides, I refused to engage in any more

disputes — however friendly — with myself. But sometimes, without my even real-
izing it, that shitty, universal harmony, that humbug, omnipotent, geometrical
god who wormed himself into my confessions and into my secrets — would blow
up in my face . . .

When he got back to his apartment, he sank down in an armchair, relishing the dark tobacco from his cigarette. He pondered over his separation from the Uruguayan when the Gardens of Luxembourg were in full bloom and he had slowly begun to detach her from his senses. He felt once more that the ephemeral was finding a place in his passions. He began to miss, once again, some of the old familiar faces. He imagined Buenaventura trudging up the stairs of José Augusto's Paris apartment and gabbing away as if nothing had ever happened, those far-off afternoons in Sinaloa frozen forever, and Sebastián, from the depths of his loneliness, dropping in to visit him, unburdening himself among the piles of books, the sounds of a *flamenco* singer or a Portuguese *fado*.

After a while, he grew tired of staring at the same four walls and set out for a bookstore near Saint Michel. He heard shouting on the corner and then spotted the piles of cobblestones like barriers blocking the sidewalks and intersections. That May afternoon he realized how the people's rage had risen to the boiling point and how clear-cut their petitions had become. He saw thousands of people marching toward the Seine; the police, machine guns and placards lined one end of the street to the other. He joined the ranks, mingling with the throng, sensing that at last something very real was taking place.

The moment he heard his own shouts he knew that his rebelliousness had come out in the open and that other, more profound goals had found an inalterable place in his life; that they would always remain there, not only that afternoon, but the next morning, the next evening, or if need be, for the rest of his life.

161

V

ONE SUNDAY AFTERNOON, fed up with the debauchery of the past few months, Sebastián arrived at his apartment in the Narvarte district. He threw himself on the sofa, intending to sleep until the following day. He was sick and tired of the endless discussions he heard everywhere, the dejection, the apprehension, the deadlock they were in, the constant threat of even harsher repressions to come. The last couple of years had seemed dismal, sordid, unfathomable. That very morning he had visited several of his friends in the penitentiary. He had spent only a few minutes with Buenaventura but talked to Martín and Gabriel for a couple of hours. They had burst out laughing at the trumped-up charges against them that appeared in dozens of official indictments: the descriptions of alleged crimes which included assault with a deadly weapon, theft, subversive activities, sedition, homicide and attacks on the general communications networks.

He was unable to sleep, still deeply moved by the impressions of his visit to Lecumberri. After a while, he decided to read an article of Gabriel's. It was lying on a nightstand on top of a stack of papers. Sebastián scratched his neck and began to read it carefully. It was an eyewitness account, written more than two years before, a few days after the March of Silence.

What had apparently started as a street fight among students soon gave rise to a series of police provocations and to the ensuing protests at rallies, meetings and demonstrations until finally the University went on strike. Little by little, each of us with a story of his own to tell pooled our efforts and our experiences. But our accusations against the aggressors and our requests for dialogue with the authorities were met with nothing but torture and imprisonment.

One July afternoon, we had to evaluate a number of reports that had just come in. The witnesses' voices rang out loud and clear. "We gave the riot police a run for their money. We were armed only with sticks, rods and stones. There were a whole bunch of students on the west side of the Constitution Square . . . "

We could all picture the facade of the Cathedral at nightfall; the two groups battling it out and people scuttling along the steets, some even darting from one rooftop to the other, while others fled through back alleys or hid in one of the buildings. The clash continued with the usual hotheaded insults on both sides and an occasional raised hand trying to calm them down. The echoes of the skirmish reverberated along the adjacent pre-Hispanic ruins, immutable witnesses of everything that was happening.

The cries and shots were sealed off within the gloomy downtown streets—Guatemala, Donceles and Correo Mayor, though they could be heard from one entranceway to another, from the stone battlements to the balconies, from the shining rifle butts to the portico of the Sagrario Church next to the Cathedral. The sky was overcast and it was getting dark; only a few bright specks could be seen to the west.

"Then the troops arrived. By that time, most of us had taken shelter in the old patios of the San Idelfonso Preparatory School . . . Suddenly, they broke the door down, shattering it to pieces. Then . . . we didn't know what to do."

The bayonets were bound and determined to break in. Inside, anxious faces waited in the long corridors, on the stairways, or in the darkened classrooms. The tanks were getting ready for action. We could see the helmets gleaming, the bared white teeth; we could hear their voices, some nasal, some high-pitched. We could visualize the enormous holes that had appeared in the exquisitely carved door of San Idelfonso as a result of the explosions. Barely seconds later—in the corridors and patios—the students were beaten around the head and on the legs, then forced to lean against the wall, and once again to face that ominous glint of hundreds of rifle butts. And that was only the beginning . . .

The city was all set for the Olympic Games. The illusion of progress was evident in the new specially-built installations all over town. Peace in all its guises—peace as a supreme goal, peace as a proof of prosperity, peace as a *fait accompli*—was proclaimed everywhere. The sparkling new pool at Churubusco, the bold design of the Palacio de los Deportes, the newly refurbished University City stadium, the gardens and buildings of the Olympic village were there for all to see. The first subway route with its brand

163

new stations and bright orange cars—the product of French technology—had already been inaugurated. Olympic symbols were everywhere: silhouettes of athletes, gymnasts, riders, discus throwers, pole vaulters, and divers. The spacious boulevards suddenly seemed restored to their former decadent splendor.

In spite of it all, the city was in a turmoil. While mass demonstrations, quickly-organized meetings and rallies broke out everywhere, the finest orchestras in the world performed in Bellas Artes and the National Auditorium. The Museum of Modern Art sponsored a host of exhibits—ranging from abstract to figurative art. An elaborate light and sound spectacle loomed up beyond the contours of the Teotihuacán pyramids while student brigades painted slogans on walls and buses, distributed leaflets and discussed their petitions and immediate objectives. They shouted, chanted and revealed their native capacity for synthesis in the pithy slogans on their banners, posters and the graffiti that appeared in industrial and slum areas on the outskirts of the city.

It was an endless jumble of scenes, attacks, posters, and motivations. Exaggerated pessimism went hand in hand with masochism, arrogance and the yearning for a miracle. Even those of us who were Council members and conducted the meetings were unable to account for many of the things that went on. There were surprises cropping up all the time: the sustained violence, the atmosphere of collective impatience and the senseless provocations. Although the situation was at a stalemate, huge mobs kept gathering in the esplanades and in the university auditoriums. From the very beginning the events themselves and the direction they took surpassed the limits of our imagination.

"Listen Gabriel, as far as those rascals and phonies in the government are concerned, we've gotten exactly what was coming to us and we deserve every single bit of notoriety—we're being buried under a heap of lies. But believe it or not, this smear campaign they've been waging against us proves they're scared shitless, and that will result in more hemming and hawing on their part, then a stalemate, and eventually, perhaps in the use of unprecedented force . . . All this goes to show that the only criticism the government will accept, if any at all, will be behind closed doors," Buenaventura observed one night in the corridors of the School of Philosophy, after we had been discussing the consequences of the May uprisings in Paris.

Our list of petitions had insisted on making the authorities responsible for their actions and on bringing the guilty parties to trial. Meanwhile, the only alternative left to us was verbal aggression in all its forms—a counterattack against the arrogance of the higher-ups and their outmoded devotion to "official history." Hundreds of thousands of students had now earned the privilege of challenging the so-called "justice" wielded by the parvenus and hangers-on who had reached the top of the ladder. They had begun to feel, at long last, in their bodies and minds the surge of rebelliousness which had been building up for centuries. This defiance soon merged with other grievances—some obscure, some inconsistent, some spontaneous, others naive or frankly dogmatic; but it never failed to face up to the verdicts passed by those vipers who were so conscious of their power. That September, the month when the country commemorates its faded champions of liberty, the inadequacy of the political system was brought out into the open as never before.

Nevertheless, in the meetings and student assemblies, there was a proliferation of histrionics and rabble-rousing, of the old-fashioned rhetoric favored by previous generations, of satirical rhymes and mottos which were improvised and delivered with the usual grandiloquence. And then, of course, there were the Judas-burning ceremonies where the cardboard, ape-like effigies of police and government officials were thrown into a huge bonfire. Amidst much jeering and taunting, they writhed and twisted among the flames until they finally melted and died away. Our own home-grown brand of necrophilia was manifest in the mock funeral rites: the black, empty coffin, the eulogies, all were geared to elicit feelings of sorrow and disgust.

The vital, effervescent days contrasted with the nights of sheer terror. Gradually, as Latin American guerrillas became legend and spontaneous contempt for the authorities became more and more blatant, the hired agitators recruited by the government suddenly seemed to turn up everywhere: burning buses, looting stores and supermarkets, and attacking pedestrians. The newspapers were always publishing ridiculous open letters from government stooges offering their unconditional support and defending the "benevolence" of the established institutions; just one more example of how such inconceivable rationalization can turn the aggressor into the victim.

One night, like the irresponsible, impetuous fools that we were, after one of the big demonstrations, and feeling giddy with self-importance, we decided to escape from reality for a while and "camp out" in the Zócalo, with blankets, tents, guitars and all. We acted as if we owned the place. We danced, we sang anonymous *corridos* and painted scurrilous graffiti on the buildings that were supposedly off limits, practically jumping at the chance to "throw so much ballast overboard" as someone remarked. Shortly after midnight, we were driven off by the army.

The accusations against us kept piling up as the officials counter-attacked. "Those bastards don't even have any national heroes. They're pigheaded, cocky, and unbelievably ignorant. Besides, they're riddled with agitators and terrorists . . . It's too ridiculous for words: no one can bring about a coup d'etat through mere insults. Sure, they managed to scribble all over the National Palace, but what gall for that bunch of vandals and hoodlums to think they can run over the legitimate government just like that . . ."

The next morning an incredible farce was scheduled to take place at the very same Zócalo: a ceremony of atonement for insults to the flag. The would-be participants, the self-styled "sheep", had been rounded up from all the government offices to pay their respects. And then came the big surprise: "The herd of bureaucrats, it turned out, was in cahoots with the students." The place was peppered with clichés such as "the government's scheme backfired." Again the troops, again the tanks, again the mob, except that this time the people running for cover happened to be government employees. Again the outrageous, unprecedented provocations.

"They're not going to let anyone out of jail, you know. If we keep this up, they're going to ram our petitions up our asses," Buenaventura remarked one morning as we were leaving the School of Medicine, after a night of interminable wrangling.

"Don't be such a skeptic, damn it. Nobody can stop this thing now," I retorted with inordinate optimism.

Martín, on the other hand, hadn't said a word the whole time. No doubt he'd already had a bellyful of the long-winded speeches, motions and calls to order, the order of the day, and the "Look here, comrades, the student brigades are the only ones who are risking their necks. In the end, the student community will always have the last word!" He was fed up with the jargon he now found so unbearable, with the pompous, bombastic voices, with the manipulation that went on in the meetings, with the demagogues who believed that the time had come to meet their executioners face to face, to have enough balls to confront the oligarchy in power.

Little by little, as we got to know each other better, once our strategies started falling into place and our contradictory points of view were reconciled, we got the idea of staging the March of Silence. We were now getting away from the spontaneous action and emotional appeal to the

166

crowds and were learning to work out new approaches. Under no circumstances could we condone the irresponsibility of some of those firebrands among us. The angry shouting and chanting of previous demonstrations would now be replaced by clenched fists, grim restrained faces and closed mouths as the most appropriate course of action at this particular moment. The student strike, which by now had spread to other institutions, was now in its forty-fifth day.

That Friday, September the thirteenth, there were any number of connotations to our silence. Gone were the grotesque Judas figures, chanting and verbal attacks. Although our silence encompassed the absence of sound and all signs of unruliness, it was not, by any means, a sign of humiliation or submissiveness. Rather, our silence served to channel our indignation in a new direction. Popular defiance increased, as expressed in a somewhat ribald cardboard sign that Buenaventura, Sebastián and I encountered at the entrance to Chapultepec Park! "Power is written with an L; Luck with an F."

Our silence was also a protest against the foul, congested slums, the narrow streets, the mazes of mud and asphalt. Perhaps our silence gave us the first real opportunity to take a stand against the deterioration of the city. The chorus of thousands of silent voices was the best possible response to the echoes of all those trite, carbon-copied official speeches, parroted from one generation of politicians to another. Our long walk along Reforma—from the Museum of Anthropology to the Plaza de la Constitución—reinforced our determination to carry through and to express our absolute contempt for decades of hollow official pronouncements. Our fingers forming the V sign, our lips covered with adhesive tape, we kept a slow pace. Our silence generated more silence, as well as applause, cheers, and the genuine admiration of the crowds lining the streets along Paseo de la Reforma, on Juárez and on 5 de Mayo. Many onlookers spontaneously joined the march. Our silence gave us the freedom to feel we were lords and masters of our surroundings: it was our chance—if only for a few hours—to make real history; to tread self-confidently on solid ground, to reiterate our claims and to defy the Pharisees. It was far from being a Good Friday procession since it was linked to sacrilege and desecration by its tacit denunciation of crimes, killings and treachery . . .

As soon as Sebastián had finished reading the last sentence, he reflected that although that September afternoon had indeed constituted a

167

successful reversal of long-standing, adverse public opinion regarding the movement, it had also marked the beginning of another long period of slander and of mass arrests. *We had left thousands of torches burning in the Plaza de la Constitución. Our return to that spot—with our contagious smiles, our dreams of Utopia and our bewildered expressions—was gullibility itself. Never before had the city seemed so completely ours. The street lights were out and there were no cars circulating. Perhaps we felt more united than ever, in a sort of trance, as we lost ourselves in the dim light and merged with some groups of scattered students. We stopped at several corners and everything seemed totally unreal, as if no one, absolutely no one, were capable of undermining our objectives . . .*

Sebastián read the last page, bearing in mind that it had been written in the heat of the moment. Although in general terms he agreed with Gabriel, he felt it was necessary to go beyond the merely emotional aspects of the episode and describe the background: the increasing corruption and police brutality, the diversity of speech patterns among Mexicans themselves, the countless strikes in all sectors that had taken place in recent years. The consequences of the growth of urban society, too, would have to be taken into account. He swore at himself for being unequipped to write a long essay on the subject. He knew, though, that the one event that would always stand out in his mind would be the massacre at Tlatelolco on October 2:

> . . . The gray skies were reflected in thousands of windows. It was shortly before six o'clock. Helicopters were circling over the buildings. Thousands of people were already gathering in front of the Chihuahua building for the big demonstration. In just a few minutes the inexorable, vindictive, vicious time would begin. It was just about to rain. All of a sudden, flares streamed out of one of the helicopters and spread daylight on the crowd below. Then there was utter pandemonium: faces went numb, aghast; the troops charged into the square from Nonoalco Avenue. Then came the first shots from the agitators—secret agents—wearing white gloves on their left hands. The shouts of our leaders could barely be heard above the bedlam. "Don't run, it's a trap . . . " Masses of soldiers trooped into the square through the nearby avenues. The human targets trampled over each other, ran wildly wherever they could, and took refuge in the colonial church close by or in the ruins of the pre-Hispanic ceremonial center. The dry, cracking sounds of the shots rang clear across the square. The first bodies were beginning to crumple, their dying hands fluttering in the air. The dum-dum bullets squashed holes

through the walls and windows. Then it started to rain. The rain made the whole thing all the more unreal. The explosions deadened the screams and both sounds could be heard across the rooftops and all the way to the shopping center and the parks. No one could even begin to count the number of corpses. The white-gloved agents did their job very well: they'd shoot or work in accord with the troops; they'd signal, shout, scatter groups of people, or else hold tightly to their machine guns. There were soldiers occupying every single building and all the open spaces. Then, the house-to-house searches, the frisking and the arrests began. The leaders of the movement would soon be stripped, insulted, beaten up, and later on they'd be taken to Military Camp Number One at the western edge of the city. When the rain stopped, a couple of floors in the Chihuahua building were on fire . . .

Sebastián could imagine Gabriel and Martín at that moment, their despair, the tortures they had undergone, the statements they made before being taken to Lecumberri. *Apparently, arrogance, mediocrity and institutionalized violence had won out in the end. But in spite of it all, the tradition of passive resentment had been broken. The inauguration of the Olympic Games was just a few days away. Once again we kept hearing all that crap on the infinite possibilities if peace prevailed. After Tlatelolco, that fictitious peace would be flaunted, with singular gall, on October 2, during the celebrations commemorating the Discovery of the New World . . .*

ONE AFTERNOON LAURA TURNED UP, quite unexpectedly, at Andrea's. During the few moments before she reached the living room door, she remembered when she had first been able to mention José Augusto matter-of-factly, after she had completely consigned him to the confines of her hate. However, although the whole episode was over and done with and she showed every sign of having overcome the past, she felt that a great deal had been left unfinished. It had been there, in that very house, that for the first time in her life she had finally come face-to-face with the true meaning of silence.

After Andrea's effusive greeting, "Well, for heaven's sake, I can't believe it!" Laura turned to stare at the wall opposite her, visualizing herself at the end of the corridor.

"I got all your letters, thanks," said Andrea, chattering away enthusiastically as usual. As she opened the living room curtains, she couldn't help but wonder where José Augusto could be now.

The years had taken their toll. It was obvious that both women were no strangers to the treadmill, that they had probed into their weaknesses and wrestled with their fears during many sleepless nights. While Andrea still attached little importance to storing up memories and considered everything on a long-term basis, for Laura, who had long since tired of trivial objectives, the present was what counted. Both of them, however, were constantly brooding over their loneliness and willing to take risks to escape it.

Although they were so totally different from each other in their outlook, temperament and speech patterns that they seemed to belong to two different worlds, both Laura and Andrea still indulged in the increasingly complex game of taking themselves much too seriously. It was as though what they had experienced was nothing but a preamble to the real thing, which would arrive in a vague and probably somewhat distant future. The best was still waiting in the wings, even if it turned out to be a furtive affair kept in the realm of untold secrets.

"Some letter writer you are! Not one single word from you the whole time," answered Laura leisurely, suddenly imagining José Augusto's smirk beyond the window pane.

"Well, you know me. I'm just terrible that way." Andrea replied, motioning for Laura to sit down. Her voice was calmer, her gestures more supple, the sparkle in her eyes brighter than ever.

Laura sat down on one end of the sofa, placed her handbag on the coffee table, took out a cigarette and lit it slowly, cocking her head to one side. She had reached the point where her skepticism had its limitations, but she still could not bring herself to accept the many interpretations of the crime. In this respect she had not changed. She owed José Augusto no explanations, much less an apology. Though she was no longer obsessed by his many inconsistencies nor her image of him as a paranoid, a fugitive or a potential suicide victim, she had fallen into the habit of repeating his name aloud when she was completely alone. Her new attitude had been the result of a long, painful search for another Laura. She had learned, after a great deal of inner turmoil, to devise a new future for herself, and perhaps, some day to look forward to new pleasures.

As she listened to Andrea's voice rattling on, "Well, how have you been, my, but you look marvelous, when did you start smoking, you look better then ever, I bet you've got at least a dozen men on the string," Laura reflected that few things in life are really permanent and that in spite of everything, she had to fight tooth and nail to preserve the little she had or would obtain—her fantasies and petty grudges notwithstanding. She rarely referred to José Augusto in public for fear of betraying herself through some involuntary gesture. She had tried to rise above it all, careful to keep old wounds from rankling. Now her hatred for him was rational, aloof; she abhorred the years she had spent with him, the stranglehold he had had over her. She also thought about the dead man, the victim who could have been only a stepping-stone in her life; the man she thought would help her overcome some of her problems—if only temporarily. With him, she would have learned to feel the body of a man other than José Augusto lying next to her.

As soon as Andrea went to the kitchen, Laura looked back at the corridor again. She recreated the room which somehow filled her with anguish. A scene with two nude bodies—the first time she and José Augusto had made love in that room—flashed across her mind: the complete fulfillment, simultaneous climax. In spite of everything, the room she was looking at now was already filed away in her mind as just one more memory. Now that she was free of anxieties or tear-filled eyes, she didn't mind going over all that again.

Laura was also there to confront the old Laura now that she had finally managed to rid herself of gullibility and bewilderment. After a long apprenticeship, she was now able to test her capacity for self-control, as she kept exercising it, strengthening it, endowing it with an appropriate indifference. She felt suddenly reassured by the hundreds of mirrors which in the past had taught her to make the most of her inner resources and provided her with new ploys, new outlets and a variety of stony facial expressions, carefully rehearsed before any prospective encounter.

With the onset of the first telltale signs of age on her forehead and hands, she had become even more convinced that time was on her side, that she was now better prepared to receive as well as to give pleasure and that, furthermore, before long, she would bear a child. That was her latest, overwhelming obsession; it gave a whole new perspective to her life. She turned to gaze at the dining room window with its curtains opened wide allowing the sunlight to reach the chairs and a vase full of red carnations, when Andrea broke into her thoughts. "Honestly, Laura, you look wonderful, you have no idea how I envy you. From your letters, I gather everything's going great for you," Andrea said as she placed the cups on the coffee table.

"We've got lots and lots to catch up on. And how about you? What have you been up to? As far as I can tell, nothing's changed. Everything seems just the same, as if it were only yesterday when you took me to the airport," Laura replied, knowing deep down that she was lying, that she could sense the barrier that had sprung up between them, and that although she was indeed back in exactly the same place, Andrea's house, everything seemed totally different to her now. There were unfamiliar facets to each object, an iridescent quality that no longer belonged to her.

"Don't you believe it," Andrea retorted. "It may not look like it but too many things have been going on, much more than any of us could have imagined. But, we've managed to pull through, and here we are, better than ever, if I do say so myself. Listen, once I get started talking, I swear I'll never finish. Besides I have the feeling that there'll be a lot more changes before long or maybe it's just my imagination. But I swear, I don't think I can take much more of all this commotion. I'm worn to a frazzle already."

"It's just as well; that means you're an optimist at heart," said Laura earnestly. She realized then that they had barely scratched the surface, that Andrea did, indeed, have a great deal to report. However, except for a casual reference to José Augusto or about old friends, under no circumstances was Laura willing to thrash over the whole subject of the crime. She wanted at all costs to avoid stirring up old feelings of resentment which by now were well under control. She had no desire to start choosing her words, or to put on a cool front, and have to listen to herself for the first time.

They chatted about their work, their trips, gossiped about recent divorces, affairs, adulteries—and the imaginary complexes or hypothetical frustration one usually tacks on to others. Andrea's voice took on a sharper tone as she lashed out at men in general, "those extraordinary, hairy beasts, who are so expert at making it tough for us women." They talked about the city, of the brutal changes it had undergone in the past few years, of how impossible it was to live there anymore, to enjoy it; of the new slum areas that had sprung up overnight, of the floods downtown, the traffic jams and the power failures that lasted for several hours. "At least Coyoacán is free from all that—so far," Andrea observed. "It's sort of an oasis where one can live fairly comfortably without all the hassle with traffic or fear of being mugged. Of course, in time, it'll probably go the same route."

The inevitable subject of Sebastián came up in the conversation. He was only one of their group who was a genuine, *bona fide* madman, an original, whose dissipations knew no bounds. They discussed his latest affair—with a girl twenty years his junior. It seemed that things weren't going too well between them and he had taken to playing the role of the jealous, neurotic lover whose illusions had been shattered. Clearly, Sebastián was not prone to either the sullenness or the maudlin, emotional displays of the lovelorn.

"Cardoso is quite a guy," said Laura, remembering how he used to put José Augusto in his place by merely referring to the "arrogance of all boors" and "spineless cowards."

They switched to the subject of Domingo Buenaventura, his loneliness and numerous illnesses, the aftereffects of imprisonment and how impossible it now was for him to write. They pictured him brooding, absentmindedly holding his pipe in his left hand, as always. Andrea immediately launched into a tirade against "the goddamned scum, the sons of bitches in this country, those despots who have complete control through sheer nepotism, rip-offs, and all that crap that goes with corruption." Buenaventura was a case in point: he did nothing but sit in his armchair patiently listening to his daughter Isabel and he hadn't even the right to grow old like everyone else, "because Buenaventura's first obligation is to tell it like it is, to write about our times. He's the only eyewitness with enough insight to understand, explain and analyze it more perceptively than anyone else." They recalled his stories about the massacred workers in previous uprisings, the vengeance of the *caudillos* in the provinces, and the backstabbing among politicians in the top ministries whose expectations hinged on the sealed envelopes which determined their fate, for better or for worse, at the end of each presidential term.

Then they talked about Isabel, of the great comfort she had been to her father while he was in prison, of her independence, her spunk and her freedom to do as she pleased. Since her circumstances, the times she lived in, were so totally different from theirs, she had fewer taboos or complexes than they had at her age. "Isabel had the chance to make her own choices; she was no longer taken in by all the virginity crap. I bet you anything that at her age she's already had experiences we never even dreamed of. She knows a great deal about pleasure and who to share it with, although of course she has her share of problems and her own little quirks. On the other hand, for us, it was a long, hard road," Andrea observed. "By the way," she added, getting up to bring coffee and cookies from the kitchen, "Gabriel's been sort of lonesome lately. It's about time he got himself a girl."

Laura was alone again. The doubts and apprehensions had vanished. She was now capable of resurrecting, almost painlessly, all those people who had taught her to enjoy life and to benefit from her experiences. After all, she told herself, not everything in her life had been bleak. She also remembered her long sojourns in Lima, Caracas and Bogotá, the work that she had grown tired of: mingling with publishers and booksellers, deadlines, orders that had to be filled on time and all those little routine chores that went with the job and fell under her responsibility. She was tired of holding back, of the future she had imposed on herself, of the tic-toc passing of days, the trips, the same itineraries, the nameless faces at the airports, the people who, like everyday objects, had passed through her life without leaving a single impression.

"Have you heard anything about José Augusto?" Andrea asked casually as she poured the coffee, as if it had been an ordinary, run-of-the-mill question and designed to skim over the obvious implications or to test Laura's mettle.

174

"I haven't the slightest idea," Laura answered dryly, her face almost expressionless. Although she made no attempt to avoid Andrea's gaze, she could feel the anxiety fluttering inside her. She stubbed out her cigarette, staring steadily at the ashes, making every effort not to know, letting her silence be the best possible answer.

Andrea quickly changed the subject. She herself had heard nothing about José Augusto. Vague speculations and contradictory rumors were all she had to go by. They talked about Sebastián, Gabriel and Buenaventura and that terrible year when they had been hiding out for months at Andrea's, sleeping on the floor or on the sofa, and about Andrea's weekly visits to them in prison after they were arrested. Each one, in his own way, had tried to blot out that particular period that had been riddled with false accusations and unspeakable atrocities—it had been a time impossible to erase. Although they did their best to conceal it, it was always there, pursuing them in their loneliness, embedded forever in their senses.

. . . I saw Laura only once, about a month after we were brought from the jail to the airport and sent to Santiago, Chile. Undoubtedly Laura was an entirely different person. I had heard dozens of contradictory versions about her side of the story. "Gabriel, what are you doing here? It's so good to see you. It's been a long time, hasn't it?" she exclaimed when we ran into each other on Bulnes Avenue, right in front of a big publishing house. We went to a little cafeteria a couple of blocks from the Palacio de Moneda. She talked about the South American cities she had visited, her new experiences, her impressions and added that some day she'd like to live in Valparaiso. She was considerably more attractive. Somehow, the tone of her voice and her gestures seemed more defined. But now that she had set new sights for herself she seemed more aloof, as if she looked at everything from a distance. Her conversation was sprinkled with "buts" and "who knows." She approached some of the things we discussed like her mind was a card catalogue, which she could automatically open and shut at will. On the other hand, everything else about her gave the impression that she was open to everything; she showed no signs of regret over the period in her life when she had lived on Sinaloa Street. But it seemed to me that she had lost her capacity for receiving compliments, as if she were constantly trying to prove her self-sufficiency. And . . . she had lost something else as well, something I couldn't quite put my finger on. I don't know if you could tell all this from the harshness of her face. Her eyes still had the same old sparkle, but I could guess it was pretty hard for her to admit to her own contradictions or anxieties. I mentioned the possibility of my returning to Mexico and that was the last thing we ever talked about. We said goodbye with a warm but vague "See you." I had the distinct feeling that she wanted nothing more to do with any of us, that a great deal had been lost, and that whatever it was, it could never be recovered. I also faced the fact that I too had changed and that before long we'd be reaching the stage where we'd be comparing stories and making up new nightmares. I think it was that same day in Santiago when I started idealizing José Augusto. A favorite phrase of his flashed across my mind. "Aw, go on, you son of a bitch, don't sweat the small stuff."

Andrea, as usual, got on the subject of men with a capital M, a gimmick she could never resist. She declared that as far as that was concerned, she had been at loose ends for a couple of months now. She ticked off her profits and losses and came to the conclusion that she hadn't done so badly after all. Since she knew full well that she still had a great deal going for her, that she could pick and choose and was lucky enough to make her own decisions, she poked fun at herself with a certain self-congratulatory air, not bothering to dwell on possible future successes. Laura listened placidly with a cool smile but she preferred not to pursue the subject further.

"Maybe you remember Martín. Well, I've had my eye on him for quite a while now. He doesn't say much, but there's a lot to him—he has guts. I think maybe I'll make a play for him," gloated Andrea, putting on an act as if she were all set to snare him right then and there. She was obviously bound and determined to reconstruct an erotic experience that had never quite materialized, but which perhaps she could resume at any moment, one that would serve to cure her loneliness and channel her energies in one direction.

Laura mentioned a couple of brief affairs—nothing she had lost any sleep over. She let it go at that so as to avoid revealing her true feelings. For the first time, Andrea noticed how tense Laura looked; there was an expression on her face that hadn't been there before, except perhaps only fleetingly—but it had wound up there as a permanent reminder of her suppressed rage and anguish.

Just before Laura left they talked about the house, the new plants in the garden and the humidity in the back bedrooms. They both had the feeling that on that night in particular the darkness would weigh heavily upon them and that during the next few hours they would be wandering among vague memories of intertwined faces and hands; they would be constantly threatened by the need to mull over their most intimate thoughts and the prospect of a dialogue with their own images. Laura persisted in her obsession to have a child; perhaps, on her next trip, she would make up her mind. By midnight, when each was alone they'd take stock of their regrets and ostensible success, still fully convinced that they'd be waiting patiently for their real destiny, and come what may, they'd take whatever was in store for them without complaints or regrets.

VII

GABRIEL HAD MANAGED TO TURN in his article—an exposé on a high-level real estate racket—before the deadline, just as the editor had requested. He had committed himself wholeheartedly to the task by digging up as many facts as he could lay his hands on and he was positive it was going to be a bombshell. He also had the hunch that it would be the subject of a long and heated debate at the editorial staff conference that night but, in the end, that he'd be reading it the next morning—right on the front page. It had required several days of hard work: pouring over files, records, archives and documents, interviewing people and then, finally, long hours at his typewriter. In any event, he seemed to have gotten over his long ordeal: the threats and torture, the feelings of impotence and despair. The years spent in prison and his fierce hatred of the rotten system with its increasing overtones of violence and its never-ending vengeance had left their mark on him.

When it was finished, he had read the article to Sebastián. They had gone over it in detail, touching it up here and there. All in all, Gabriel was convinced that in spite of the pressure, the time element and the fact that he had so much to say, the article was a damned good piece of work. It was all there in print: the statements by those who had made their fortunes in real estate as well as those of the rightful owners who had been forcibly evicted from their land, all complete with photographs and signatures of the front men who had made the deals. "You've really got something, Spook; there's enough substance here to guarantee your smooth sailing through the stormy seas of journalism," Sebastián had declared warmly.

Gabriel turned in his article and went out into Bucareli Street, strolling under the flashy neon signs of the National Lottery Building. He decided to cross the city, go to Andrea's, unwind with a couple of drinks and maybe block out a couple of other sensational stories he planned to write. He had every intention of coming down hard on all the influence peddlers scrambling for jobs in the forthcoming presidential administration and of putting Cristóbal in the hot seat because of the thoroughly objectionable position he had adopted lately. Gabriel walked aimlessly along as he had done that night many years ago after his return from Europe, way before the movement, before prison, when he had grown tired of the superficial Parisian life and his half-baked projects.

Although it was almost eight o'clock, there was still no threat of rain. Suddenly, he bumped into Isabel, Buenaventura's daughter, on the corner of Juárez and Reforma. For some reason he felt a certain sense of well-being, an optimism he had long ago forgotten, and he immediately discarded his original plan of going to Coyoacán.

. . . In barely a few moments, as we made our way toward Colón Circle, I realized that Isabel was under a tremendous strain and in a real state of frustration. However, I did everything I could to cheer her up. Ever since I had known her, I had noticed that she kept herself at a distance from the rest of us. I knew she never quite trusted us, that she considered us a bunch of oversexed hotheads. Like a lot of other people, I guess she imagined we were gloomy nihilists who spent all our time spouting sarcastic remarks and going around in self-destructive circles. Although she already had that restless quality, the spark that responds to the first feeling of suffocation and she was able to go beyond seeing things in black and white, Isabel was still not quite prepared to understand us. She was too prone to generalizations and sweeping statements, and occasionally lapsed into an extreme self-absorption by adopting an air of superiority to which she was not yet entitled. I saw her lots of times in Lecumberri during those visiting days which meant so much to us—it was an outlet for all our tensions. She spent most of her time talking to Buenaventura and never bothered too much with the rest of us. Once, on one of her visits, I remember I was struck by the sensuous tone of her voice and her expressive hands. We went to the Café de Paris for a while and I told her a little about my experiences in Chile and of the first few days here after my return. Just as I was getting ready to leave, she suggested we drop in on Buenaventura. I promptly agreed, and off we went to the apartment on Sinaloa. I can't remember exactly what that night was like, but even now I can still see Isabel breaking into a grin as she walked along beside me. I still have the habit of wandering along aimlessly, stopping in all sorts of places and letting

179

the passage of time be engulfed by the sounds and images of the city . . .

That night, Domingo didn't say much. He sat in the easy chair facing his desk, puffing away at his pipe and listening attentively. The unusual listlessness in his movements was a clear indication that his health was deteriorating considerably. He seemed to be deliberately playing up his introspective mood by staring at a wastebasket stuffed with papers, as if all his usual talkativeness had ended up in that particular spot. Once in while, when his pipe happened to be resting on the ashtray, he'd comment on the recent turn of events and the possibility of amnesty for political prisoners. He kept brushing his forehead with his hand, yawned and finally sank back into silence, probably reverting to scenes of his own time. Although for others those images were already part of the past, for Domingo they remained very much alive and represented a source of very real grief, of rage; they were a constant reminder of the wrongs that had been inflicted on him, forcing him to brood over them again and again with that far-away expression on his face.

"How's your manuscript coming?" asked Isabel, anxiously seeking some vague though meaningful response.

"It's coming along, more or less," Buenaventura answered, pointing to the wastebasket crammed with half-finished pages and sentences he had rejected because he thought they lacked substance. One could detect the determination in his eyes that showed even through the thick glasses, that streak of inordinate stubbornness that was Domingo's trademark.

Gabriel sat quietly at one end of the sofa, staring at the photograph on an end table—the Buenaventura of thirty years ago, his eyebrows dark, a fist raised high—and compared him to the other Domingo, the Domingo he'd known so well in prison, the Domingo of the endless discussions and staunch convictions. From time to time, Gabriel would glance at Isabel, imagining what her adolescence, her hang-ups, and her loneliness might be like.

"You look a lot better," Isabel remarked simply, without overdoing it.

"I'm getting along, I think things are picking up," said Domingo dryly.

Gabriel broke in by saying that if Domingo needed to be hospitalized, Cristóbal could lend a hand. Buenaventura bit his pipe, stroked his forehead again and muttered a grudging disspirited "Yes." Though the look

180

on Isabel's face was clearly one of disappointment, she let it go at that. Gabriel then mentioned his aricle and how much it could mean to him personally and to the newspaper as well.

Half an hour later, after they had exhausted the subject and had turned to the question of the amnesty, Buenaventura's concentration started to wane, so they decided to leave. They walked to another part of the city, trying to piece together their mutual experiences and telling each other something about their lives. When they finally reached Alvaro Obregón Avenue, the street lights seemed to glare even more brightly on the sidewalks and streetcar tracks.

. . . I really don't know exactly how many hours we spent together. We wandered quite a way and finally wound up on the corner of Insurgentes and Tlaxcala. I guess I did most of the talking—explaining some things that had happened in the past few years. We remembered that night at Andrea's, when the political situation started getting really critical: the beatings, provocations, and violence, the first few days of the strike and our final decision to join the movement. Isabel had stressed the importance of the list of petitions, particularly the points on releasing political prisoners and removing the police chiefs. Later, we talked about the notorious article concerning "social dissolution," which was specifically aimed at squelching any possible dissension. At that time no one had the slightest inkling of what was to come. While I was describing the consequences of the whole chain of events to Isabel, I was also trying to figure out the answers to a number of questions in my own mind. Strangely enough, although I had lived through it all the whole thing still seemed quite unreal to me. I had only met the problem halfway, as if I lacked the necessary perspective to view it all dispassionately from a safe distance. I had too many things preying on my mind and the problem of my pent-up rage was still unsolved. Sometimes I caught myself swearing at the damned air we were breathing. Martín's words came back to me all of a sudden. "You know, we're nothing but a bunch of morons. We refuse to face the fact that when you play politics you're in the big league. What you need is real power, not this naive, messianic crap." Isabel asked about Banderas. She had met him briefly at the Sinaloa place and had heard a lot about him. By that time the ghost of Banderas was slowly fading into a mass of contradictory rumors and legends. People assumed either that he was dead or that

181

he was leading a miserable existence somewhere in Europe. I suggested that Sebastián was the person to ask; he knew that whole jigsaw puzzle inside out. Then we talked of our past love affairs, our disappointments, our indecisiveness. I told her a little about my obsession for that woman in Paris whom I had been with when I read about the murder that Banderas had supposedly committed. She had made a real fool of me and almost destroyed me. Since I was aware of my growing interest in Isabel, I was careful not to say too much. She told me about her studies, her plans for the next few years, and of her father's rundown condition. I looked at her closely for the first time: her loose, straight hair, her full mouth, her olive skin and brown eyes. To me her voice was unique; its tone was both soothing and voluptuous but it had a remote quality as well that made you want to cling to it and never let it go. I left her at the entrance to a building on Quintana Roo Street, near the Chilpancingo Circle, after promising her that the next day I'd try to get hold of Cristóbal . . .

When Gabriel came into his apartment on San Antonio Avenue, half a block from Insurgentes, he found the television set going full blast and the window, which overlooked a corridor, wide open. The television screen was a luminous rectangle with wavy lines made up of tiny quivering black dots. It looked like a negative of a snowstorm in some godforsaken arctic region, with the muffled sound of static as background music. He heard someone snoring in the bedroom, and ventured a pretty good guess: Sebastián, his face all puckered up, was sprawled full length on the bed. Gabriel looked around the room. A pair of shoes had been tossed onto a stack of old magazines and a poster of a naked woman was draped over the typewriter.

Sebastián was dead to the world, the slow rhythmic snoring no doubt keeping time to his hallucinations. When Gabriel slipped into the bedroom again to gather up a few of his things, Sebastián didn't even blink. Gabriel controlled his anger, went back to the living room, turned off the television set and closed the window, knowing very well that as soon as he woke up the next morning, he'd be trying as usual to figure out the reasons behind Sebastián's erratic behavior, which was probably linked to some deep-seated feeling of regret or disappointment.

He lay down on the sofa in the dim light thinking about Isabel and making her part of his dreams by recreating her face, her hands and voice.

182

His feelings wavering somewhere between anticipation and enthusiasm, he had begun to perceive a need for a new kind of obsession: to give himself fully and unconditionally to another person. In less than half an hour, Gabriel was dreaming of Isabel, her smile, her thighs, her breasts.

"Hey you lazy bum, get up, don't sleep so long—it's almost ten o'clock!" shouted Sebastián, who, still bleary-eyed and dishevelled, had already gulped down three glasses of water and paced around the room griping about the light streaming in through the curtainless windows. When he finally realized that his attempts to wake Gabriel were useless he opened the door and scooped up the newspaper.

"By God, Gabriel, you did it!" he whooped as soon as he spotted the article on the front page; it was a full spread, photographs and all. In his efforts to conceal his envy, he kept raving about it, making altogether too much fuss.

Little by little, Gabriel opened his eyes, yawned a couple of times and stretched lazily. He was just about to give Sebastián hell but restrained himself when he noticed the newspaper in his hands.

"This is a real blockbuster," Sebastián said, getting more and more worked up as he re-read Gabriel's accusations, his eyes sparkling mischievously. Despite Sebastián's inner conflicts, the sincerity and genuine admiration that poured out of that misshapen body were unmistakable.

Gabriel kept staring at him, still trying to shake off his futile dreams with one last yawn. At last he got up, shoved aside the shoes on the floor, and sighed contentedly. Everything had turned out much better than he had expected. Nevertheless, he instinctively crossed his fingers as he went to the stove to heat up some coffee, reflecting that perhaps it would be his selfish motives that in the long run would serve to get him back on his feet. They might just solve the problem of his wasted talent as well as his tendency to put things off.

Sebastián gave him a capsule description of the gathering at Andrea's the night before. "Martín and Cristóbal almost came to blows, I swear, Gabriel, things got really hairy there for a while. It was the same old story —they kept needling each other—the most vicious gibes you've ever heard in your life. Just so you get the whole picture, Andrea finally kicked us all out. Even *I* kept my trap shut the whole time, that's how bad it was."

. . . I knew Martín and Cristóbal very well, way before the Movement. They were both a couple of years younger than I. I never had any doubts about Martín and though at times his arrogance was

183

unbearable, we'd always been good friends in spite of it. He never said much and always had a chip on his shoulder. Cristóbal, on the other hand, was something else again. He talked a blue streak and was a slick, ambitious rabble-rouser—a two-faced double-dealer who changed his tune whenever it suited his purposes. He always seemed to be watching us and he could be a real pain in the ass, particularly when we were having our morning coffee. He was a mover but he wouldn't stick his neck out for anybody—except himself. However, whenever we were in a jam, there he'd be, offering us jobs or helping out someone who was really hard up. Once in a while he'd drop in on Andrea, putting on his big impresario act. He also fancied himself as something of an intellectual since he held a plum job at the Education Secretariat. He was always taking part in some round table discussion or other, pontificating in the language of the opportunist which he handled so well. Although Andrea claimed that he was a ranking politician and that he'd go far, Sebastián had him pegged as a son of a bitch who only gave away whatever he didn't need for himself . . .

Gabriel and Sebastián, now raring to start the day, sat down at a table at the Cascada Restaurant, which lately had become their favorite hangout. They looked at the streams of water gushing out of the fountains in the background and at the billboards to the left, announcing the construction of a new shopping center. Just as they were ordering breakfast, Martín arrived, carrying a sociology book under his arm. He was unshaven and he was already showing signs of premature baldness. Obviously in a surly mood, he made no bones about his contempt for idle chatter by shooting scathing comments right and left.

"What's with you, you maniac? Have you taken a look at Gabriel's article yet, by the way?" Sebastián greeted Martín, gleefully anticipating the harsh retort he guessed was coming.

"It's all right," said Martín curtly, cutting Sebastián short and perceiving Gabriel's silence. Martín was clearly playing a game—he was on the offensive, demanding sacrifices from others and trying to gain their unconditional support at the same time.

They talked about what a big farce the recent election had been, the new set of lies that went with it, and the reports of rural land invasions in the northern states. The three of them expressed feelings of rage, pride and an unwillingness to admit defeat in spite of what happened. They went round and round, giving their own interpretations of recent events, a favorite pastime which served either to pull them closer together or to split them further apart. They discussed last night's absurd quarrel and Cristóbal's offensive remarks which had touched it off: "The so-called heroes of '68 can go screw themselves. They're dead ducks," and Martín's sarcastic comeback: "With your civic spirit we're sure to go far. With you, the word 'honesty' takes on a new, crystal-clear meaning, pure as the driven snow! Right?" Gabriel glanced at his watch and got up quickly, tossing a quick goodbye over his shoulder as he ran to the next corner to grab a taxi. Sebastián and Martín, who were accustomed to the noise on Insurgentes and Pensilvania Streets, lit up cigarettes. Since they had nothing much to say to each other, they exchanged pleasantries, letting the morning drag on, and eventually wound up commiserating with each other over their past mistakes and present misfortunes.

Once in the taxi, Gabriel barely listened to the driver's complaints about the low fares and measly wages, the muggings in the Oriental District, the lastest sloppy playing by our Mickey Mouse soccer team. Instead, as Gabriel thought about Isabel, a series of erotic images rose before his eyes. He started making plans to see her again and working out a strategy so as not to blow it. "I must learn very soon how to enjoy her," he kept saying to himself over and over again. He knew that Cristóbal was waiting for him at the entrance to a downtown restaurant on 16 de Septiembre Street, opposite the Olympia movie theater. He stopped speculating about future plans and turned to look at the city: the buses stopping at the next corner, the clear sky beyond the Freeway. He thought about his article, about the language he had used and the irrefutable facts he had furnished. They had, no doubt, already been discussed at length by flabbergasted investors and politicians. As he reached Reforma, the sound of Isabel's inimitable voice came back to him again.

VIII

WITH THE DISTINCT FEELING that this gloomy January morning would be no ordinary day, José Augusto got up leisurely and with a clear head. Still in the dark, he thought of the long journey that lay ahead. In addition to his underground activities, he still continued with the same work he had been doing for several years now—selling those old books which had become part of his daily life. He found himself alone again, this time in an apartment near Montparnasse Station, with only his thoughts and eccentricities to keep him company. Before he turned on the light, he had a sudden impulse to break his routine and he wondered whether to shave first or pack his bags.

Some six months ago, he had left the building on the Rue Amyot, just half a block from where he was now. That was shortly after he had been picked up by the police and had felt the imminent danger of losing his freedom. That particular episode had had its tragicomic overtones. One day, as he strolled along the Place de la Contrescarpe with plenty of time to kill and had stopped to watch the *clochards* holding court and gesturing wildly for no reason at all, he ran into an Italian he had known in Madrid. The fellow greeted him effusively with a "Ma guarda, chi si vede, da dove spunti, che strano incontrarti!" and promptly invited him to lunch. José Augusto had suggested a Vietnamese place. They ate and drank lavishly, chatted for a couple of hours and then went back to José Augusto's apartment where the Italian fell asleep on a rickety old sofa among the stacks of books. Early next morning he dashed off to catch a plane that was leaving from Orly for Rome. The following day, right on the corner near the Vietnamese restaurant where José Augusto used to pass every day, he was suddenly detained and immediately taken to the police station. In the beginning, he had imagined the worst, that from one moment to the next he'd be deported and that soon he'd find himself with other murderers serving a long sentence. Finally, after a number of inquiries and discussions, he found out that the Italian had turned out to be a real son of a bitch; he'd had the nerve to pay for their lunch with a worthless check.

José Augusto not only had to pay the full amount for the meal, but also a fine for contempt of the authorities. That cute trick cost him plenty: practically half the money he had made on a treatise on optics, a transaction that had taken him more than two months to complete. But more serious than that was the sensation of being trapped and the inevitable follow-up investigation of his real identity which would, of course, put an end to all his plans. Once back in his apartment on the Rue Amyot, as he swore at everything and everybody, the rooftop on the Popotla building came back to him clearly. There, a few years before, the wind had churned up those different smells and he had done nothing but wait impatiently for Sebastián to bring him news. As soon as he was able, within the basic rule he had set up for himself, he dropped in on the Vietnamese, had a fine meal, left a generous tip and then walked out as nonchalantly as if nothing had happened.

Things really looked black for me then—much worse than that time on the Spanish border: the sinister faces of the French police, their undisguised contempt for foreigners and their unwarranted insults still remained very much in my mind: that place was a veritable shithole with its long, gloomy corridors, the skimpy and filthy furnishings and the rough treatment I received . . . I think that for about a week after that, I still went around with a panic stricken look in my eyes. And all because of a stupid mistake. All my hate and my fear suddenly came to the surface again.

He finally decided to turn on the light and went to the bathroom to shave. He discovered a few more gray hairs at his temples and noticed that his hair looked somewhat more oily; the furrows between his eyes were much deeper. He counted up the number of trips he had made in the past few years, knowing full well that this one would be the most important of all. Now he was not only involved in tracking down old books, but he also had other interests: his clandestine activities took him to a number of places: London, Amsterdam, Frankfurt and Edinburgh. Besides, the bookselling business was limited and the money-hungry book dealers were too much for him; they had a whole staff of apprentices and salespeople at their disposal while his was strictly a one-man operation.

José Augusto caught himself grinning in the mirror, telling himself that the steadiness of his gaze was proof enough that he had his future well in hand. He was no longer drifting through the dreary tunnels of his past nor lying low in some sleazy hideout. The search for a book of Torricelli's suddenly came to mind—it had led him to the daughter of an aristocratic Roman couple who were willing to pay a handsome price for such an extraordinary volume. She had been in charge of handling the transaction and before he knew it, thanks to the glibness which by now was second nature to him, they ended up chatting over coffee in a café on Babuino Street. They talked about all sorts of things: the Roman catacombs, scorpion bites and the rampant syphillis among Spanish *conquistadores*. Too late, when he was already involved, and they had slept together several times in his Paris apartment, he found out that she was just about to marry a wealthy Sicilian tycoon and that he, José Augusto, had been nothing but a pawn in the game she was playing. Nevertheless, his solitude had taught him not to take it too hard, *to take things in stride, and let them work out by themselves.* The girl kept visiting him off and on, and he made the best of the situation by letting her sleep with him and then leave as if nothing had happened. All in all, the situation was rather pleasant and for a while it presented no real problem. It relieved his sexual hunger, an emptiness so acute that at times it was almost excruciating. Besides, she was the prototype of the modern woman—attractive and open-minded. She had a tendency to talk too much but the next day she'd be gone again, back to her old stamping grounds. Then a couple of weeks later, she'd come back to him, her lovemaking a combination of largesse and vanity.

After a fairly placid winter, when he had finally gotten used to the situation, the girl started spacing out her visits until she just never returned. One unusually sunny afternoon, José Augusto received a letter written in her old-fashioned, slanting hand, effusively expressing her gratitude and her deep friendship. Although it had succeeded in disconcerting him, he turned to look through the window at the cloudless sky, shrugged, and decided to enjoy the landscape rather than curse himself for having lost her. *I proved to myself that in these situations, one always has to be prepared for the unexpected. And like the fool that I was, I thought is was just one of those things, one of life's little jokes. Naturally, it took me some time to get over it. She had such soft skin and extraordinary thighs. Fortunately, I had become pretty hard-boiled by then and no longer brooded over my regrets or the blows to my ego. One day, I happened to see her in a café on St. Germain with her husband and two children, one of whom could very likely have been mine, I guess; but frankly, I couldn't detect the slightest resemblance. We greeted each other like life-long friends. Deep down, we were grateful for what we had so generously given one another. Believe me, if this had occurred to me a few years before, I would have felt like the biggest sucker of all time. But after all, when you're over forty-five*

you get more thick-skinned about this sort of thing, and so I stored it away in
a corner of my mind, keeping it there to gather dust and then blow away along
with the other ashes of the past.

He finished shaving and, still grinning, started packing. This time, besides the clothes he always took with him, he slipped in a number of magazines and documents that were of some importance to his underground work. Since he had embarked on that course, tactics and strategies were of the essence. His involvement dated from that May in Paris when he had mingled among thousands of demonstrators and had rediscovered his long-lost Utopias. After that episode, at first every two or three weeks or so, he'd started holding rap sessions in a park on the Isle de la Cité, from where he could see the Pont Neuf. His audience was a group of gangling, long haired, jean-clad youths, and he'd invariably suggest certain texts and standard works for them to read, never failing to point out the importance of concrete actions that could be carried out as soon as possible. His alter ego, the restless dreamer constantly seeking new horizons, the sworn enemy of establishments and counterestablishments, the diehard who had finally discovered new and workable methods to bring about social change, had succeeded, for long periods at a stretch, in warding off attacks from his other personalities. The radical group had been set up for less than three years and now José Augusto started demanding action from its members as conclusive proof that their objective could really be accomplished. He then began testing each recruit and discarded those who showed signs of too many inner conflicts. His ongoing search for new incunabula and tracts on mechanics also provided him with deeper insights into such issues as Spartacus' uprising in ancient Rome and familiarized him with the prophets of the Industrial Revolution and the daily life of the early experimental communities.

Once his baggage was in order, José Augusto checked his passport and the signature he had practiced so often in that Tijuana motel years ago. He never failed to be slightly amused at the sight of his own photograph and at the fictitious names he had chosen for himself. He placed the documents in his coat pocket, recalling a time on the Spanish border near Fuenterrabia, when he had traveled with two other militants, a Peruvian and an Argentine. There was subversive propaganda in the trunk of the old car he was driving and he had come within an inch of being arrested. José Augusto had gotten out of the car first and was just on his way to the sentry box to make sure there were no problems, when all of a sudden a patrol car drove up beside them. Inch by inch, the police inspected the motor, the seats and trunk. Although the other two were arrested on the spot, José Augusto decided to keep right on walking. He presented his passport—the same one he had just now placed in his pocket alongside his plane ticket and managed to cross the border with no trouble at all. Within a couple of weeks he had been able to get the other two out of jail. Although for José Augusto it had been a matter of little consequence, he had learned to be on his guard at all times and to be more conscious of even the slightest detail. Meanwhile, the group had stepped up its secondary activities and the organization had expanded considerably. Little by little his regular work—books on statics or kinematics—were linked to other objectives. His next important move was to set up a travel agency as the most suitable front for his operations. *By that time, I felt like a new man. I'm not quite sure to what extent I had managed to stifle the presence of the egotist in me, but more important than anything else was the fact that I no longer felt the world was crushing me. Those emotional hangovers at dawn and the usual midday depressions were a thing of the past. One day, I just got fed up with the same old shit, and decided to move to another apartment in a large building next door to the Montparnasse Station. Naturally, since I still had the same problems, I just took them right along with me. In spite of everything, though, at last I felt that I wasn't on the run, and that the constant temptation to become my own worst enemy was slowly fading.*

The travel agency, which on the surface looked like any other office building, was located half a block from St. Michel. Its tours were moderately priced and the work did not require a great deal of special skills. Besides, after the first few months, José Augusto no longer had to run the whole thing single-handedly. The principal objective of the business was not really to make a profit, since it functioned mostly as a drop. Money and instructions arrived from other places and a large portion of them were, in turn, sent to other countries across the sea where they were picked up by contacts in tropical, coastal or mountain regions.

It had been a long, hard pull, but finally, José Augusto had managed to shake himself free of his defeatist attitudes and to put down the other Banderas within him who could very likely—all of a sudden—set him against himself and destroy the goals it had taken him so long to reach. He no longer avoided the people he had known in Mexico and whom he ran into occasionally, those whose faces reminded him of the past. Although he didn't go out of his way, he now could look them straight in the face or call to them from afar. Life had finally fallen into a pattern. But he still longed for a woman, a real woman of true passions, one who would transport him to "the hellish depths of agonizing rapture," as Sebastián would say. There were friends, there was plenty of work and there was the revolution. As far as his love life was concerned, he made do with fleeting affairs and the like, but there was nothing that really touched him very deeply.

One Saturday, while he was going over the weekly accounts at the travel agency and was preparing some sample packages for future trips, he met Ana Elena, a Peruvian girl who appealed to him immediately. She was tall, slender, perhaps twenty-five years younger than himself. She had come in with a fellow who always wore a leather jacket. José Augusto knew Ana Elena's companion fairly well; he was one of those pseudo-revolutionaries who always seem to turn up in that part of the world. That was a minor question, however; the real problem was how to approach her under more favorable circumstances and give her enough time to know him better. Little by little, he found himself thinking more and more about her and being stirred by these thoughts.

José Augusto picked up the telephone and called for a taxi to take him to the airport. Then he lit his first cigarette of the day and got to thinking about the events of the past few months. The travel agency was now merely a sideline and since it was managed by members of the same group, he no longer devoted much time to it. His next enterprise was a news agency, as if he was finally coming back to the project he had so often discussed with Buenaventura and Gabriel: the importance of the written word, of news as reports or the impact of a first-rate editorial. Every single day he'd go from Montparnasse to the news agency on the Rue Mouffetard and spent hour after hour typing away and discussing the most important news reports of the day with his colleagues.

One afternoon, as he approached the gateway to the Jardins de Luxembourg, he spotted Ana Elena from a distance. He was able to look at her without her noticing it; he studied her narrow waist, long hair and graceful hands. While he was watching her, he knew then and there that he had to find an excuse to get to know her better, to work nuances into their conversations and to make an impression on her.

José Augusto's thoughts switched to an entirely different subject: the long trip he was to make in an hour's time. After years of being away, he would be crossing the ocean again. He had worked out every step beforehand, the contacts had been set up in advance as well as the itineraries for the two months he would spend in major cities as well as smaller towns. He then recreated part of the conversation he had had a few days ago when he happened to run into a friend of Sebastián's at the Cardinal Lemoine metro station. This time he didn't hesitate at all and stopped to chat, to inquire after his friends, about the scene at Andrea's these days, and who had been arrested and sent to prison.

That had been the very first time—he had told himself this over and over again that night—that José Augusto Banderas had introduced himself by his real name, listened to its sound, and discarded his old roles and his ever-present wariness. *To a certain extent, I was already someone else, as well as those other persons who had consciously been growing within me for so long. I was sure the sources of of my anger had disappeared. Though I knew I could always go on creating new lies for myself, I was careful not to let them bother me too much. Those two hours I spent with Sebastián's friend in a café on Guy Lussac convinced me I just couldn't keep running away forever. Naturally, the fact that I'd grown more thick-skinned helped me considerably during my inevitable nightly reflections. I was sure that by now I was no longer the subject of exaggerated speculations back home, that my name was slowly melting into the rubbish heap of collective memory.*

In the taxi, he stared at the bare trees and gray buildings, thinking about the tremendous upheaval in Mexico over the past few years. He knew that things had gone from bad to worse; he had seen photographs, compared the news reports and clipped out the open letters and manifestos in the newspapers. He found it hard to believe that things had reached such a point. He thought about Buenaventura, and then, although he tried to recall Laura's face and body, he was left with nothing but the vision of a solitary mirror that was no longer waiting for anyone.

He sat in the waiting room of the Charles de Gaulle airport reviewing a list of volumes on optics and improved telescopes of the Enlightenment period. At that particular time, he hadn't the slightest idea that in a few moments he would be seeing Ana Elena again, and that for the next few hours, as they flew over the Atlantic to Caracas, he would be drawing her more and more into his lustful imagery. It was to be a singularly important event in his life, a definitive form of optimism and, as he was soon to discover, it would mark his reentry into a new world of pleasure. Nor was there any way for him to know that a few hours later, while he was falling under the spell of Ana Elena's smile, Sebastián Cardoso would be back to his old tricks with the other regulars at the Concordia in Mexico, denying there had been any other crimes and announcing that the Great Lunatic, the Unmentionable, was alive and well, free from all strain and all ready to welcome his friends in his apartment on Montparnasse.

IX

CRISTÓBAL TOSSED AND TURNED between the sheets, knowing full well
that he was sick and tired of hearing the big shots in his department repeat
the same orders over and over again, of being pushed around in the various
offices, of the crass stupidity around him and of listening to the same
clichés all the time. Even so, his ambitions had been whetted at the prospect of a secure future and the chance to get his hands on easy money.
His outward appearance was all set for the masquerade. He knew that his
was a flawless, beautifully camouflaged act, ready to undergo any quick
change—however drastic—that might be required to continue swimming
along effortlessly, like a crocodile, with the slimy tide he moved in.

Every day for the past three months, the first thing he laid eyes on
as soon as he woke up was the telephone. He thought about his enemies,
the constant backstabbing and wondered whether he could get even by setting one against the other—like that idiotic assistant in his own department, for example—just tell him to go to hell and settle that particular
piece of business once and for all. He glanced absently at his wife lying
next to him, noticing her pencil-thin, practically nonexistent eyebrows, the
faint layer of cream on her face, the odd movement of her lips and her
jerky breathing.

Cristóbal glanced at the telephone again, checked the time and got
up reluctantly, swearing softly under his breath as always. He rehearsed
a series of facial gestures—astonishment, disdain or flattery so that he would
be prepared for anything.

The round of meetings last night had left him feeling rotten: he had
dizzy spells, his eyes were still bleary from the smoke, and he felt exhausted
from putting up with the unbearable din, manipulating other people's words
and trying to interpret each glance, each facial expression, each seemingly
bland smile. He was sure that by now he had learned to read between the
lines, to perceive the slightest innuendo behind a chance remark, and then,

to sort out the information he had gleaned by spreading it into various jig-saw puzzles, shifting the pieces around here and there but never allowing his personal feelings to get in the way, as if his own destiny were enclosed within a perfectly traced circle.

He left behind the sleeping body of his wife, a body which had been so much a part of him for over eight years, a body with muscles, bones and meaning well before the birth of their two children, and which day by day became more attuned to his own goals, to the essence of his daily life. She remained there, enveloped in her distant dreams. The unmistakable scent of her eau de cologne blended into the sheets and blankets and floated out through the bedroom door into the corridors.

He drew aside the curtains to make sure that his staff was waiting for him in the garden, his chauffer had washed the car and the skies outside looked promising. He could almost predict, step by step, what his day would be like, already sensing his boredom and imagining the number of favors he would be asked, the pompousness of all those half-wits—climbers like himself—who were also clawing their way up to the top, that bunch of half-assed clods that he had to contend with by stringing them along, meeting them halfway when necessary, saving the biggest concessions for more auspicious occasions when he'd have the last laugh—in just the right tone: patronizing and slightly indulgent. After all, by now he was firmly entrenched in that shadowy, unpredictable world where everything seemed to hang by a thread.

For Cristóbal, concrete, objective reality lay in his surroundings; it was everywhere—in the material goods he had acquired after each of his promotions, in his expensive aftershave lotion, in the contraband wines and liquor he drank, in the echoes of his children's voices as they romped in the Canadian snow, in his magnificent home, in the bougainvilleas that covered the walls of his villa in Cuernavaca. Perhaps before long, whether he admitted it or not, he too would have access to what others had already obtained: large investments in packing or canning companies, a hefty dollar account abroad and sound, reliable stocks, carefully distributed among his relatives and front men. The bad times—the really bad times—had been left far behind. They had been buried—quite painlessly—a few years ago, way back when his silence and lack of self-confidence had lasted into the early hours of the morning, only to disappear gradually with the day.

He stared at his chin, at his cheeks—which seemed to grow puffier every day—at his round face, at the spindly but trim moustache, and at the eyes which somehow never managed to conceal his obsessions. In time

194

to the vibrations of his electric shaver, he proceeded to expand on his repertoire of curses, a habit he had cultivated in order to keep his perspective. It allowed him to compare himself favorably with others, to proclaim his status and thumb his nose at the world by bragging to himself that others had to come to him, not he to them, that he and he alone counted, and that everything and everyone else was pure shit—scum who had been crushed by the very aimlessness of their existence. He thought again about the imminent phone call, the voice he had been anxiously awaiting for several days, the words notifying him of his reinstatement, a guarantee of his incorporation into the new regime.

All of a sudden, the memory of his confrontation with Martín at Andrea's house came back to him—the sarcasm and cutting remarks, while Martín "slipped into the comfortable role of victim, that goddamned prig who's never in the wrong, because that bunch is something else—they're always encouraging each other to play the martyr, but it's all just sour grapes. Before long, they'll go back to their old ways and take up where they left off: their verbal violence, the plotting and planning behind closed doors, just asking for trouble, as if they were begging to be sent back to jail." He thought about Domingo Buenaventura, his gutsy writing, particularly that story of his where the main character, a politician with a huge persecution complex, wound up talking to himself, swearing to take revenge on those who had stripped him of his power, while at the same time switching back and forth in his mind to scenes of murders and thefts in which he had been involved.

Cristóbal was constantly haunted by all those people who were now so far removed from his immediate goals, those shadows from his strange past whom he repudiated as "that bunch of licentious, subversive fanatics." He gave passing thought to "their incredible debauchery" and forgot about his own, as if the clean-shaven image in the mirror was the epitome of pulchritude and sobriety. It was, however, Martín's haggard face that always loomed most distinctly before him, shouting at him from the darkness of his cell, writhing with stomach pains and a face of infinite fatigue. With a tinge of nostalgia and malice, Cristóbal made flippant attempts at deciphering the "naivité, the sheer transparency, the outdated principles that governed Buenaventura's life, that prudishness of his which bordered on the ridiculous. His hopes were always pinned on unattainable and preposterous ideals: an uncompromising messianism and a concept of an ideal human being who never existed and never will. He was always babbling on about the altruism, the greatness, the heroic feats of those who managed to alter the rhythm of history."

Once again, as he checked over the day's appointments on his agenda, Cristóbal anticipated a fairly uneventful, dull day. He could almost visualize the different sections of the city, the amorphous masses who lived in each one of them, the anonymous petitions he received, the eyes of the hangers-on wistfully riveted on the entrance to the government offices, and the practically foolproof format he had devised for dealing with such interviews. As he left the bathroom, he put on his shirt and light blue suit, knotted his tie, and was unexpectedly brought face to face with his own conceit, with an urge to speculate on the whole question of human relations by placing them on a huge electronic panel, pressing different color-coded buttons, working out all kinds of combinations and finally, letting all the petty grudges come to the surface once and for all. He had scarcely realized that by this time his wife had opened her eyes almost submissively, as if she were just about to ask him for something, anything at all, as long as it remained with her all day to keep her company. She had absolutely no doubts in her mind about her hold over him, about her ability to give him, at the precise psychological moment, the perfect compliment or well-timed apology.

Cristóbal bade her an effusive goodbye and hurried out, eager to get his appointments over with, to get the conversational ball rolling, to make a splash, to be on the go all day until the moment when he came home that evening to stroke his wife's body. The women beside him would be waiting for him as always, her sights, like his, set on high places. She was his ally in any circumstance, even when he was away from her. Theirs was a coolly calculated relationship that had been nurtured within the framework of two perfectly structured lives. Together they had learned not to make excuses for either their compunctions or their setbacks.

During the lonely hours she spent in their home in Lomas de Tecamachalco, she had learned to weave her husband's aspirations into hers by idealizing them, embellishing them and giving them her own, very personal, very whimsical interpretations. Exhilarated by their newly acquired affluence, she would spend hours gazing out of the enormous picture window in the living room. A couple of barren hills seemed to have been placed in front of that particular spot with the express purpose of remaining there forever, to grow old along with the rains and the dust storms.

Cristóbal stared at his chauffeur's back, at the pimples on his right cheek, and then settled down to read the morning news. For some reason, his ego always seemed to get a lift as he scanned the paper for items that seemed to be just begging to be interpreted. He picked out a familiar name here and there while reading the attacks on the newcomers in the government, the greenhorns or the has-beens whose wheeling and dealing had been their undoing. Just as he exhaled contentedly, he happened to spot Gabriel's article. He read it anxiously, half-expecting his name to crop up at any moment, no matter how incidentally, whether he were actually involved in this particular case or not. He finished reading the last sentence and almost laughed out loud. "Poor devils, they haven't the slightest idea that they're actually playing into the hands of other crooked government officials who have their own little rackets and are delighted to have a red herring thrown in their way." Just the same, it occurred to him that Gabriel might be on to something big and that he could be dangerous. It wouldn't be a bad idea to keep an eye on him, give him a break, maybe find him a job and if possible, keep him happy. One of these days, when least expected, Cristóbal himself might well be the target of this "type of sensationalism" which, of course, would mean the end of his political career. "As a matter of fact, this particular affair is small potatoes. What these poor suckers seem to forget is that, in the end, when the chips are down, we're really all in the same boat."

He remembered Domingo Buenaventura again, the sound of his voice ringing throughout the auditoriums, his naive illusions of building a new tomorrow, his "rabble-rousing exposés of the tactics employed by the upstarts in the government." And once again, Martín appeared before him, always a nervous wreck, always living in squalid dumps, with his blind faith in the historical importance of all those nameless heroes, always churning up his old grievances in concert with those freaks, those dyed-in-the-wool fanatics he hung around with. Nevertheless, there was a great deal about Martín that Cristóbal could not account for. He'd go round and round without ever arriving at any definite conclusion except, perhaps, for a grudging acknowledgement of Martín's superiority, a twinge of envy, and a vague longing to strip himself of his own phoniness and go back to wearing his old mask, which at least was a lot simpler, more straightforward, and free of present trappings. And then, of course, there was Andrea, the extraordinarily gifted Andrea, his confidante for so many years, who could give of herself so lavishly, so unconditionally, who so captivated Martín as well; the Andrea of the unforgettable sanctuary in Coyoacán; Andrea (whom his wife loathed with a passion) and only Andrea was capable of understanding him, of lending a sympathetic ear to his conflicts and his outpourings.

197

They had long since left the Paseo de la Reforma behind them and had reached the Freeway. As the traffic grew heavier, Cristóbal scanned the rest of the news, only to discover practically the same statements that had been made half a century ago, the same gibberish, the same misleading statistics on the country's extraordinary development and its economic and financial miracles. He smiled shrewdly and turned to look at the entrance to the newly inaugurated sections of Chapultepec Park. He tossed the newspapers aside, vowing that he would never be the main character in an article like Gabriel's, and that never, absolutely never, would he be caught red-handed.

At last they reached the Hotel Diplomático, where before long, he'd have to launch into his glad-handing act: waving greetings, patting people on the back, doling out hearty *abrazos* and handclasps, and then engaging in convivial small talk with his fellow politicians. Here, once again, he had to be on the defensive, watch his step at all times, and make sure he projected the right image through his carefully rehearsed gestures, by his reading of the degree of ruthlessness or anxiety conveyed by others, and by giving just the right inflections to his voice while casually resting his chin on the palm of his right hand. On the whole, he was totally convinced that his natural superiority made him a winner, particularly in a situation such as this—a testimonial breakfast where he was surrounded by other hopefuls in what was nothing more than a backscratching ceremony. He had a strange sensation, right then and there, that he had an innate ability to do this kind of thing, that he had a natural capacity for assuming the right disguise to match the mental and physical requirements of the moment. Every now and then, amid the light banter and the double entendres, when he felt the boredom descending on him, he would immediately catch himself and adjust by faking a series of expressions ranging from flagrant adulation to innocence to astonishment, always making sure that he was once again pushing the right buttons on his imaginary panel.

As soon as the breakfast—with the corresponding backslapping, strained expressions, wary eyes, taut mouths and smiles—both encouraging and dutiful—was over, he went back to the car and gave his orders, trying to summon up what little patience he had left and making great efforts to give an impression of serenity. As he looked out at the high rises on Insurgentes, the bushes on the esplanades and the swaying trees along the avenues, he thought about the phone call again. The car stopped at a red light on Alvaro Obregón Avenue, where the image of Domingo Buenaventura flashed across his mind—the long walks through these very streets, the frequent references to "that José Augusto Banderas and his amazing getaway—that cheap fairy tale concocted by a bunch of ding-a-lings who were bent on turning a common murderer into a legendary hero. They thrived on each others' lies, creating their own private labyrinths, weaving their little intrigues, whiling away their existence by acting out a series of outlandish scenarios and whodunits which, like images in a carnival's distorting mirror, were devoid of any authentic import. They spend their time brooding and poring over their memories of the past with other dropouts like themselves."

Although he was fairly certain that all the pieces on the political chessboard had already been set up for a final masterstroke, he never lost sight of the fact that the whole thing could come crashing down with just one flick of a finger. Only the lickspittle could ever claim it was all in the bag. He was still savoring the spicy taste of his breakfast when he finally arrived at the Education Secretariat, catching sight of a group of students demonstrating noisily in front of the building and the gloomy pedestrians on Argentina Street. He got out of the car, greeted a couple of bodyguards and made his way through the main courtyard, reading the graffiti as he went along. The slogans were everywhere: on the columns, over the balustrades, under the murals and even on the landings of the main staircase. He shrugged, telling himself that those problems no longer concerned him; they would probably be postponed and, in three months' time, it would be up to the incoming administration to deal with them.

He entered his office, wishing he could have some time to himself, have a nice leisurely smoke before he started his routine of meetings, haggling and dictating his proposals. He took one last puff, assumed an official-looking air, and got down to business. The sea of faces came and went, one after the other, their outlandish requests a combination of shrewdness and servility. Then came a group of shabbily dressed women with drawn expressions and repressed anger, fed up with being sent from one waiting room to another and clamoring for more schools for their children. Next were the people with letters of introduction, their faces gleaming with perspiration as they poured out their last-minute requests, complaints and petitions in their flowery, pretentious language. "A good job, sir, please; it's my last chance, you know, to get ahead and to allow you the satisfaction of having my life-long gratitude, of knowing I will forget your great generosity." During these interviews, his feelings moved back and forth from distaste to rage, and as he expressed his most profuse apologies, he tried, at the same time, to get a complete picture, as objective as possible of how the other half actually lived—how they worried, how they were always demanding something as if it were their right.

Since he knew his own position was transitory, barely at the threshold of his career, he didn't go out of his way to explore each case too deeply. Cristóbal recalled the long, hard training undergone by himself and his colleagues in the official party, the discipline that forced them to show feigned interest, to lie saying a solution was coming: "Your case is under consideration, and now, it's just a matter of time. Just sit tight, and please don't worry. We'll let you know as soon as we have word . . ."

Finally he left the office, leaving the peculiar combination of odors behind him: the musty air of the bureaucrats' baggy trousers, a whiff of liquor here and their, the peculiar smell of crowded cross-town buses and factories. He went upstairs to say goodbye to the higher-ranking officials whose stylish suits and natty ties were similar to his, and whose smiles he returned with a conspiratorial grin.

A couple of fawning bodyguards were waiting for him at the elevator, bound and determined to follow along while keeping the prescribed two meter distance away from him; one of them carried his briefcase and the other a bundle of magazines. It was only when he sank into the back seat of the car, half closed his eyes and gave the driver his instructions, that he realized how tired he was. He caught a fleeting glimpse of the main balcony of the National Palace, the crowds pouring out of the subway station; then he yawned, indulged in a brief, erotic fantasy, and before he knew it, the car had arrived at the restaurant on 16 de Septiembre Avenue. He had braced himself for his meeting with Gabriel and planned to congratulate him for his superb article. After all, he must be encouraged; no sense in creating more trouble. He renewed his self-confident pose, and just as he got out of the car, he came face to face with Gabriel, who, in spite of everything, always managed to unnerve him and shatter his composure.

They talked about securing a bed for Domingo in the Cancer Institute by pulling all the necessary strings, so that he could live out his life as painlessly and comfortably as possible and without having to bite his lips from the searing abdominal pains. Cristóbal forgot all about congratulating Gabriel and they parted curtly, as if they sensed their mutual distrust.

Once he had been assured that his instructions had been followed and he knew for sure that there'd be a room for Buenaventura that same afternoon, Cristóbal went into the restaurant where he recognized some voices from the group sitting at the next table. As he sat down, wondering whether his greeting had been appropriate, a bombastic voice ranted on

200

about all the blunders and inconsistencies of the outgoing regime. Someone with an angular face, who cocked his head to one side so as to appear
more important, claimed that the peso had just been devaluated, and that
a peculiar floating exchange rate had been established instead. The statement, of course, provoked a great deal of angry controversy. At last, after
the customary leave-taking, Cristóbal, his brain a bit fuzzy from the alcohol, came out to the brightly-lit marquee of the Olympia movie theater
across the street, heard the cries of the news vendors and saw the blank
gaze of his chauffeur in the background. All of a sudden he felt a queer
sensation of nausea, as if the smell of vomit was momentarily cutting him
off from all his ambitions.

X

ON THE SURFACE, it was almost like any other Saturday noon at the Concordia restaurant, with our crowd showing the usual blasé expressions and mouthing the same old platitudes. It was a crisp, gray day in early January with uncommonly heavy traffic for that early in the day, and spirits were low. Everyone was sick and tired of all the scuttlebutt that had been going around during the past few months since the new president had taken office: the sinecures awarded to newcomers, the rampant corruption in the previous regime and the short-lived expectations harbored by the more gullible among us. No one, however, was being taken in, either by promises of a rosy future or by the radically different style of government; and much less by the prospect of a new team composed largely of technocrats and administrators. We were fed up with the jumble of contradictory statistics on the country's economy and the misleading statements from government officials and private investors alike. Even the devaluation had worn thin as a major topic of conversation. Also, we were especially careful not to tread on anyone's toes by coming out with a malicious remark, a contrived witticism or by cracking the same old political jokes. As a matter of fact, everyone was late that day, a sure sign that no one was feeling particularly loquacious.

We sat there for a while, answering listlessly when spoken to and not picking up on the obvious differences of opinion among us. We also refrained from indulging in our usual flights of fancy and in the well-worn reminiscences which had been torn to tatters. There were a great many empty chairs inside and no one on the terrace; only a few scattered voices could be heard at the nearby tables and even the bar seemed unusually quiet. Outside, the noonday ritual was in full swing, with drivers stuck behind the wheel at the Insurgentes intersection, people waiting for buses along Alvaro Obregón Park and several scruffy beggars planted at the entrance to practically every restaurant and store in sight. Nevertheless, we

202

stuck it out, bound and determined to while away the time with small talk occasionally sprinkled with desultory comments, despite the general feeling of despondency that could not be shaken off. Our bored expressions seemed to mirror the full extent of our inertia, our wandering thoughts and our lofty pretenses as they gradually surfaced.

The economist arrived looking very down in the mouth and completely oblivious of the fact that for months he had driven us up the wall by proclaiming that this new administration would finally give him his chance to make his dreams come true, that soon he'd have it made. The philosopher, his face seemingly darker from constant brooding and apparently skinnier and more absent-minded by the day, reminded him of his incessant wire-pulling, the unexpected telephone calls from politicians at odd hours and his alleged automatic *entreé* to all government inner sanctums which he had bragged so much about. The economist ran his fingers through his graying hair and announced that there were still any number of changes in the wind, many more than we could possibly imagine, such as new systems and logistics, the implementation of electronics to streamline bureaucratic efficiency and the reinforcement of government centralization by establishing new supersecretariats. Naturally, this statement was greeted with the customary snickers and sighs of resignation. An oppressive sensation of futility seemed to have suddenly descended on us all.

The historian started ticking off a long list of the cushy jobs he had had—and lost—over the past few years. He went on and on about the thousands of pesos that had slipped through his fingers, all because of the tremendous turnover in the government: There was that job at the Social Security Institute, another in the Education Secretariat, a third in the official Political Party, another in Public Works. Of course, someone pointed out rather facetiously that he had forgotten to mention two other posts: one in Pemex, the National Oil Company, and another in the National Properties Office. The historian admitted his oversight quite readily and then proceeded to name yet another two or three minor government agencies where he had been employed at one time or another, thus provoking the first round of spontaneous laughter of the day. However, he remained perfectly straight-faced through it all, ordered a stiff gin drink, and sat back, totally unruffled, as if it didn't really matter anyway. "What the hell, after all, mark my words, the country will get back on its feet in less than two years' time," he added primly.

Around 3:30 or so, just about the time when some people were getting ready to leave and started their sentences with "Well, what can one do, there's no way to change people's minds overnight," Sebastián showed up, looking very self-satisfied. Although he seemed somewhat aloof, he was obviously out to disrupt the whole gathering by dredging up old feuds and grudges. He began by needling his neighbor to the left, the hawk-nosed painter with the large Adam's apple. Although to all intents and purposes his remarks were harmless enough, they were just a little too hearty. He laughed jovially at some witticism with the man on his right and joked with the person opposite him about the pleasures of the flesh, "that bewitching magic of lust, before you know it, turns into dust." No one actually paid too much attention to him, though, since we were all either too engrossed in our drinks or were looking in other directions.

In any case, Sebastián was not put off so easily: he kept the wisecracks coming, one after another, modulated his voice, pounded his fist on the table repeatedly until it gradually dawned on us that he was, in fact, perfectly sober and that his garrulousness was actually some sort of an outlet. There was no doubt in our minds that there was something he was dying to tell us, but he wanted to relish it just a little while longer by putting out feelers to gauge the degree of our curiosity. Then, once he was positive he had won our undivided attention, and still unable to get over it himself, he finally broke the news. After all these years, he had finally received a message from José Augusto Banderas through a friend of his. His emphatic gestures, his calculated pauses between each bit of information, coupled with his sustained excitement and his determination to take us with him back into the past, eventually got to us, and we wound up in a series of digressions on the subject. "The Great Lunatic," Sebastián observed as he licked one of his rice-paper cigarettes, "was living under the weight of our full oblivion."

As the various personalities of José Augusto evolved from diffuse to more concrete shapes and as we heard more about the tremendous changes he had undergone through his sheer will-power to keep going, we made our own private forays into the past, as if in a matter of a few minutes we could go back to strolling along the old streets and through the slums, once again visiting the hangouts of our adolescent years. We had momentarily recovered those long-gone days by pausing in front of the crumbling buildings, empty balconies and peeling doors we had known, and standing in the shade of the eucalyptus trees and burgundy-colored bougainvilleas. "I swear to God that nut Banderas is living in Paris and he's in great spirits, never been better; he's a regular optimist now, believe it or not." Sebastián kept repeating this over and over although he realized that for the rest of us the whole story seemed like something from another world, a world of alien beings totally unrelated to our own. Nevertheless, we started dragging out all those forgotten tales, feeding on our nostalgia as if we could once again see our reflections in the puddles in the parks, the wide boulevards, in glittering shop windows or in the mirror of the very first brothel we ever visited.

Now, more than ten years later, when we had grown weary of hearing our voices, of burying our frustrated hopes and our minor accomplishments which had been largely unnoticed, Cardoso had revived a long forgotten chapter which had introduced us to a new set of enigmas and involved a cast of characters who no longer played a part in our lives. A great many Saturdays had passed since our talkfests had been enriched with new material, and there was a large backlog of anecdotes waiting to be heard. Although we had reached a point where we no longer bothered to pat each other on the back, now, all of a sudden, this announcement that José Augusto was still wandering around in our world as the materialization of a phantom whom we thought had surely vanished forever, began to take on the significance it deserved. It stirred our consciousness and a great many memories as well, and consequently we drank up even more boisterously than ever until well into the afternoon.

A peculiar atmosphere seemed to have pervaded the bar. An eerie glow flickered in every corner, on the terrace, on the whiskey glasses and it even seemed to merge into the shiny-pated pianist's unsuccessful attempts at musical romanticism. The long string of anecdotes about José Augusto, along with his multiple identities, soon blended into one in the course of our long odyssey through the whole city, with its rooftops and basements, its flophouses and its dreary pool halls. Unquestionably, as the stories about José Augusto's eccentricities unfolded, it was really our city that dominated our thoughts, the city that had been reconstructed and defiled a thousand times over; its streets that had been retraced again and again and had grown old before their time, but still had managed to survive each new attack and every attempt at demolition. Although it was true that we were very fond of that outlandish character who was our friend, we cared even more about what lay beneath the surface—what we had given and received from each other, what we had experienced together in a past that seemed to be centuries ago, before and after World War II, before and after the railroad workers' strike; and most of all, what we had gone through during José Augusto's absence during the fateful year of the Olympic Games—that period of intense frustration, of infinite loneliness, and of our gradual decline into crass cynicism and apathy.

If our penchant for stretching the truth was brought into play by José Augusto's shadowy image, it was another, perhaps more distinct presence that hovered over those long conversations, over our mental trips from past to present as we recalled our distorted impressions and even our most recent blunders. It was the transfigured image of Laura, who also seemed to have disappeared from our lives—Laura of the clear eyes and olive skin, who unwittingly stirred in us and others around her the most varied and farfetched erotic fantasies and obsessions.

Sebastián attempted a description of José Augusto as he most likely was now: his hair would be more gray but that would not alter his determination to leave his mark on the world at all costs. "That son of a bitch has it all over us, that's for sure. Some balls he must have! Compared to him we're nothing but a bunch of amateurs, cheap caricatures of the Great Lunatic. Fugitive or not, he will never go back on his word; his loyalty is beyond question," he added without even bracing himself with the glass of rum in his hand.

"Come on, come on! Granted, we practically invented the legend of José Augusto, but don't put us down as a bunch of shitheads! What the hell, we have our own stories to tell, and damned good ones at that," interrupted the essayist as he tried to fit the pieces of this particular jigsaw puzzle into the right places.

At this point, the stories started pouring out of us in rapid succession, with everybody getting into the act, although naturally no one could agree on anything and each one of us stuck to his own version. Nevertheless, in the end, our collective imagination won out by providing the background to many of the frictions that had existed between José Augusto and Laura, as well as their devotion to each other. Once in a while, forgetting the fact that they were flesh and blood human beings like everyone else, we'd send them out on long walks through avenues and boulevards, quarrelling in front of a shop window; or else, we'd picture them lying together on a cozy chaise lounge with their arms around each other as they watched a spectacular sepia and orange sunset. However, we'd always come back to the murder, to the jealousy that caused it, and to José Augusto's meticulously planned escape. "There is no truer lie than the collective imagination, the conjunction of apparently incoherent facts that engenders heroes, and where the riffraff comes into its own by singing its own praises," observed the poet.

For us, those two phantoms represented a great deal more than a mere attempt to recapture the past or to seek a parallel with our current ambitions; above all, they stood for something we had half-perceived within ourselves as a feeling of nonfulfillment, of dissatisfaction at not having accomplished what we had set out to do. They were a symbol of our frustration at not having lived life to its fullest, a constant reminder of our misgivings and of our unfulfilled pipe dreams, or as Sebastián so aptly worded it, "the lucid awareness of expecting the unexpected."

As the bickering, gibes, drinking and boisterous laughter were stepped up, José Augusto's personality seemed to grow in stature. Every single one of his roles was stretched out as far as it could go, the slightest detail was blown up to overwhelming proportions. The most insignificant item about him tended to provoke the most violent of controversies, and a mere casual gesture of José Augusto's was dissected as if it had been performed by a great actor, the star in a play requiring a number of disguises that ranged from the egotist to the victim, the *bon vivant*, the redeemer of the destitute and even the sadomasochist. Now and then the idealist was transformed from a lost soul whose tireless pursuit of freedom led him through a maze of slums, into the cynical chain smoker with a bleak future ahead of him, and then into the eternal wanderer roaming the alleys and cobblestone streets on the outskirts of the city.

The extrovert, the dialectician of both the written and the spoken word, was also, at times, the poor devil who, with his stubble-bearded chin, his rheumy eyes and his bitter, inexpressive face, had become the laughingstock of whores and ragpickers alike.

On the other hand, as we talked ourselves out, Laura's personality emerged more clearly, regardless of whether she was at this very moment in Tierra del Fuego or in some out-of-the-way Pacific resort, perhaps making love to one man after another, doing exactly as she pleased with her sexuality, and soaking up all sorts of new experiences. "Someone, I can't recall exactly who," the historian remarked, "told me that Laura is in her prime; she's apparently turned into a real stunner. That's my kind of woman, straightforward, unpretentious, none of this woman's lib crap about her." He was immediately squelched by the anthropologist, who after bluntly calling him an idiot, added that the historian had absolutely no idea of what he was talking about, that he didn't know what Laura was like at all.

Laura and José Augusto would have found it hard to believe the buildup they were getting as a result of the barroom gossip, the dim tavern lights, and the effects of countless vodkas, whiskeys and assorted spirits, and the extent to which the ups and downs of their relationship were recreated. For a few hours at least, every one of us had managed to escape the fact that the city as we knew it was tumbling down around us and that the ghouls it had engendered had been let loose. The revival of the José Augusto myth had served not only to link our conversations together, but it had also given us plenty of food for thought, "those endless corridors of the memory, like open doors to an empty room where all visions shrivel and decay . . ."

Time had slipped by quickly, what with our poetic license while interpreting and gathering up the loose threads of the puzzles of the past. Our disbelief grew with each new discovery and at the revelations that kept cropping up one after the other. We kept going back again and again to our sketchy and most probably inaccurate reappraisal of that whole chain of events and intertwined lives. At a given moment, by the time the huge picture windows had prevented the afterglow from streaming directly in and everyone had expressed his opinion, however noncommittal, illogical or restrained it may have been, we all fell silent, keeping our thoughts to ourselves and particularly our refusal to believe in the reappearance of the Great Lunatic. The journalist pointed out that there were still a great many gaps in the story to be filled. While some of our theories had been shattered in the process, others had remained up in the air. And a few of them had left us with the conviction that deep down, in spite of everything, we actually envied the character we had created, whose superiority, latent but unrealized, lay dormant in each of us as well. We also were aware that if José Augusto were present, he would certainly have picked holes in our harebrained conjectures. But at least this whole episode had given us a chance to relieve our minds of the fantasies we'd been harboring and to unburden ourselves of any guilt feelings we may have had.

A while later, we were back to our unanswered questions, to our stories, to our speculations as to Banderas' exact whereabouts at this moment, analyzing the personalities he had generated in his new life and the events leading up to the crime, as well as the getaway itself. We discussed the consequences of his frustrated adolescence which had doomed him from the start, and the disapproval he had brought upon himself as a result of his contradictory, inherently suspicious nature. The journalist reminded us of the brutal beating José Augusto had suffered at the worst possible time in his life, just when his whole world was caving in, when he had been left all alone without Laura's comforting presence and with the feeling of failure so characteristic of the militant; all of this earmarked him as a potential suicide. The essayist added, as an afterthought, that ever since those episodes, José Augusto had gotten used to violence, led an even more solitary life than before and was always seen with that pistol in his pocket; he was at odds with the whole world and felt that it had cast him out. The philosopher mentioned that a good many leaders in the fateful 1968 Movement had known José Augusto at his best, when he was a voracious reader and no one doubted his political expertise, when his conversation was much more profound and no one was able to refute his theories. According to the painter, several high-level politicians had also been on friendly terms with Banderas; as a matter of fact, their names had appeared in this morning's paper—two senators, a secretary of state and a top executive officer in one of the important secretariats.

Sebastián, who in spite of a little more hair and a double chin had the practiced air of an Oriental sultan, was perfectly aware of his capacity for whetting our curiosity. However, he refrained from telling all he knew as he reminisced about the last time he had seen the Commander in Chief, the Superlunatic. "He lived up to those nicknames, all right," he mused. "We were right to accept him at face value for exactly what he was. How many of us would have given anything to have earned the right to such titles, to be identified with a character who never had the slightest doubts about his own weaknesses or who never spent all his time concerned about that sort of death called oblivion—which is the same as being everywhere without actually being seen." Once in a while, he'd remember José Augusto standing in front of the bus station in Guadalajara, after that long night's drive, when they had compared notes on their respective lunacies and had vowed never ever to give up their freedom. Sebastián was jolted back to his present and major concern, wondering what José Augusto was up to at this very moment and what new dangers he might be facing in his misguided pursuit of a supposedly great destiny.

They could hardly believe that so many hours had gone by. Although some faces were already rather bloated and the conversation was still going strong, the journalist got up, left a couple of bills on the table and mumbled a curt farewell. Little by little, the chatter died down, paving the way for any unfinished business to be resumed within the following week or the next few days if necessary. This was the early evening hour when another type of clientele started arriving at La Concordia: young men with carefully tousled coiffures; bright-eyed young girls wearing jeans and colorful T-shirts; and spinsters, probably still virgins, who, despite their makeup, were obviously in their twilight years.

Sebastián waited until everyone had gone, leaving him alone with his reflections on the inexorable passage of time and on the fleeting sensation of redemption that long conversations seemed to provoke. He dwelt at length on their unsuccessful attempts to recapture something that had been irremediably lost to them forever. He listened to a wistful melody while gazing at the balding pianist who seemed to be consumed by some unrequited passion and apparently struggled with his inner emotions as if he had no idea how he could possibly have wound up in a place that was so far removed from his original expectations. Cardoso swore under his breath as he realized that he still had a couple of hours to kill before he met me downtown that absurd night, filled with new projects we dreamed up in order to make our lives more bearable, to surrender to the proverbial twists of fate and to indulge in the game of deciphering still more enigmatic, mysterious personalities.

XI

ALMOST EVERY MORNING, once his pipe had been filled with fresh tobacco and he had sorted things out mentally, Domingo Buenaventura would type a few sentences. Invariably, as he reread them, he'd feel both excitement and disappointment. Over and over again he'd struggle with the words, cursing the phrases which failed to convey the power of his feelings. He'd think about the anguished faces and hear again the "silent" voices mingling with the thunderous shouts of anger which seemed to drift in every direction, reverberating against buildings and monuments, and carrying every form of human agony clamoring to be heard.

Although it had been several years since 1968, since he had experienced it firsthand, his own recollections, and others' as well, were somehow not enough; he couldn't capture in words what he desperately wanted to tell. At best, he could shed light on a few of the facts; what was beyond the facts seemed to dissolve between the typewriter keys and the tension in his fingers. During all those months he had spent in the hospital, Domingo had not wanted to think much about those years; they were too filled with threats and violence.

But since coming back home he had tried many times to write a personal account of his experiences, a kind of brave autobiographical sketch, a testimony where each and every word was wrenched from his guts. He did not pay too much attention to grammatical structure, allowing images to flow freely by linking each sentence to his impressions of prison cells and walls, extortions by the prison guards and the black despair of the prisoners. Even so, in spite of his intense effort and the time he had allowed to pass in order to gain a proper perspective, he'd find himself fiercely clenching his fists as soon as he'd written a couple of pages. He was like a helpless bystander as his sentences floated away from him and his curses stuck on the tip of his tongue and strangled in his throat. Then he'd get up from the desk and walk over to peer through the curtain as he tried to enjoy the odor of the smoke from his pipe.

The sensation that the days were speeding by much too quickly, that time was closing in on him, plunged him into a peculiar kind of inertia. He could almost feel the burden of his wasted body weighing down on him, its gradual deterioration as a result of the torrents of blows and curses it had withstood in a lifetime.

Buenaventura wound up his old-fashioned watch, slowly inhaled smoke, and paced the room from one end to another, his hands behind his back. He'd open a book at random, flick listlessly through a couple of pages and then recall the first indications, the earliest symptoms of what was to come: the vague provocations, the attack on the Ciudadela, the rifle butts glistening in the stately colonial patios. He could see himself among thousands of faces gazing upwards. He'd rub his hands together and look absently out the window as he tried to analyze his characters and identify the different sounds of their voices.

He recalled a scene he and Gabriel had witnessed, almost by chance, at the National Auditorium a few weeks ago: a rally of thousands of workers wearing overalls and caps and carrying placards, cheering so loudly you could hear them in the very last row, while blownup photographs of the most powerful labor leader in the country were hung all about the stage. The arrival of the man himself, a husky figure in distinctive dark glasses, was greeted with even more displays of enthusiasm: a flurry of banners, noisemakers and signs to which he responded by languidly half-raising his right arm, poker faced and treading carefully, as usual. The ceremony continued with the usual long-winded speeches, lavish praise and empty rhetoric. "I'm willing to bet," said Gabriel, clenching his fists, "that he's survived at least a dozen attempts on his life, and yet there he is, cool as ice. He's the real enemy. What would the government have done without him?"

Buenaventura took a long, hard look at the man who had stirred up so much controversy over the years but somehow always managed to remain in power, always in the limelight, ever since the rule of Cárdenas. The perfect image of a sphinx, he had an amazing ability to adapt to the circumstances, although his terse, almost incoherent statements, which betrayed his incapacity for linking two sentences together, elicited withering criticisms from his enemies. The white-haired, bushy-browed, well-dressed personage stood practically motionless at the center of the stage, whispering orders to one of his aides. Once in a while, he would turn to look at the crowd who applauded and revered him as their supreme and lifelong leader. Not a single one of his gestures escaped Domingo. There he was, erect, expressionless, clean-shaven, standing like a rock but for a slight flick of his thumb, and occasionally a raised eyebrow, as if he had control over everything, even over silence itself. He was both a springboard and a bulwark, the quintessence of subterfuge. He symbolized the present, the concrete and real present, and could easily be the main character in a sinister political novel. Although Buenaventura couldn't see the color of the man's eyes behind the smoky lenses, he guessed at the cunning, unpredictability and acquiescence they could reveal at any given moment. Others could come and go, get rich, die, or fall back into their old ways, but only he remained. There he was, in exactly the same post he'd held for years, outlasting them all, holding fast to his inexorable destiny with a tenacity that could well last for a long time to come. It was as if he were somehow entitled to grow old more slowly than those who fawned over him, bowing and scraping incessantly. That old war horse was a veritable genius when it came to manipulation; he could invent imaginary enemies or pull them out of his sleeve at any strategic moment as the political circumstances required. He had calculated, almost with mathematical precision, exactly how far he could go on his precarious tightrope. He knew the rules of officialese backwards and forwards, the evasions necessary in order to achieve his ends. He was always prepared for unforeseen contingencies, to withstand any low blows enemies aimed at him, to respond to attacks with absolute equanimity. He had a knack for measuring the fears and hates of his opponents, for knowing innately what was at stake at any particular time. In view of his status as the perennial and most powerful labor leader of all, one who could demand wage increases, prevent strikes and start them as well, he could well afford to laugh to himself at the efforts of the so-called historians of the labor movement . . . After about half an hour, when Gabriel and Buenaventura had had their fill of mealy-mouthed rhetoric, they decided on a change of scene. With the sounds of cheers still ringing in his ears, it occurred to Domingo that here was material for an extraordinary story which he hoped to write some day.

Domingo sank into his armchair and ran his fingers through his hair, trying to blot out past scenes from his memory: the Spanish Civil War, his travels across two continents, the series of strikes that had broken out in the northern section of Mexico City, the years that were finally catching up with him. Despite the fact that so much time had gone by since his last imprisonment, that so much had happened both to him and to the others since then, the time before Lecumberri seemed to be cut off by a huge barrier, like a lengthy preamble to the moment when he had finally confirmed, beyond any reasonable doubt, that he had been deceived all along; viciously, callously and most brutally deceived.

He could never forget the ruthless stupidity of his jailers, the preposterous accusations and the premeditated negligence of his accusers, nor much less the trumped-up charges against him, the absurd distortion of the facts. He'd pick up the newspapers, read an item or two, and then start feeling a strange pain invade his stomach and legs. He'd regret once more all the years he'd wasted on debauchery and procrastination. He waited for his spirits to rise a bit by mentally making fun of the people who still believed either in the existence of miracles or in worlds that could someday turn into Utopias.

. . . When I was in the hospital, I resurrected several of the monsters I had created in Lecumberri. They never left my side for a minute and we'd have a ball, laughing our heads off at any old thing. They were all over the place, climbing up and down the walls, adjusting the bottle of saline solution and closing the door gently when necessary. They knew quite well that my life was their life too, so by the same token, they could either make fun of me or disappear into the anonymity I'd called them from. It also occurred to me that perhaps in that imaginary afterlife, I'd at last be able to meet them in the flesh. As soon as the doctors told me I could resume my normal life and I left the hospital, I left them behind, too. They were magnificent specimens, believe me, a veritable gallery of freaks: hunchbacks, one-eyed, one-legged cripples, you name it. It's really too bad I can't take advantage of them, write about them now, when I'm staring blankly at my typewriter, when once again I've postponed my covenant with the Great Beyond . . .

The typewriter keys were waiting patiently for the ideas to start pouring forth. He'd type a couple of sentences, rub his hands together, let the smoke drift across his palate and wait until some of the street noises died down and the series of visual images came back to him again: the objects that seemed to cling, like flotsam, to the sheets of rain, the defiant expressions of the demonstrators confronting the bayonets: their fists raised, unflinching, adamant, demanding their rights and refusing to be held in subjection.

He'd frown, bite his lip, tear the page out of the typewriter, crumple it up and toss it into the wastebasket, confronted once again with his incapacity to give the proper focus to his descriptions and forced to reject

214

what was barely beginning to fall into place. He'd wander into the other room, rummage around for the notes he'd taken in prison, ponder for a while on the absurd orders from the big shots in the government and the tactics of the unscrupulous prosecutors in charge of his case. Then, once he'd found the notes after digging through piles of old magazines and papers, he'd clutch them firmly in his hand, go over them carefully, and place them next to his typewriter.

He never gave up even though he was perfectly aware of the fact that the task he had set for himself was far too much for the scant energy he had left. Buenaventura went over and over the various aspects of his mock trial: the statements by both friendly and unfriendly witnesses, the fabricated evidence, the trite wordiness of the corrupt government officials. A while later, when he'd grown tired of puffing on his pipe and of being cooped up, he'd go out for a walk and try to figure out a way to get exactly the right words on paper.

. . . When we were in prison, despite the vast differences in background or opinions, and our occasional rifts, there's absolutely no doubt in my mind that we all faced up to the consequences and that none of us ever tried either to play the martyr or to elicit admiration for being unsung historical heroes. When we finally got over our self-imposed silence and reached the point where we could actually talk about the whole thing openly, I discovered two very good friends in Martín and Gabriel; they turned out to be the best possible allies in these troubled times. Those years, when we experienced the full meaning of the unexplainable, are sealed off in a corner of our memories . . .

He left Durango Avenue behind him, scarcely noticing the people hurrying from one street corner to another, streaming out of stores or office buildings. Domingo kept remembering the slow, painful suicide of old Federico Buenaventura, the relative who lately had never been far from his thoughts. "Truth always bring one a great sense of relief. Only idiots can affort to sing out loud and clear in the chorus of phonies," old Federico used to say. Domingo stopped for lunch at a restaurant on Yucatán Avenue and then relaxed for a while at Miravalle Square, thinking about his quest for the literary dimensions that eluded him: the precise quality of language he needed to express his characters' motivations.

As soon as he reached his apartment, the problem of atmosphere, dialogues, monologues, and the scenes involving huge crowds slipped away from his mind, his fingertips and the ringing in his ears. At times, during those very moments when his head seemed about to explode, he was almost sure he had finally recaptured it again. But then, there he was, back in the same old rut with only a few sentences typed out, barely half a page full of settings, hearing percussion sounds he was at loss to describe, seeing long open tunnels leading to a deep chasm, or motionless bodies lying in a huge open square. All his visions soon became distorted, as if frozen in glacial despair.

Buenaventura did his best to give free rein to his emotions and his ideas, to let the voices and bodies run wild and join together at their own pace. At this point, it didn't matter too much if the images remained in the shadows, since he knew that gradually the bloodstained mouths and scarred cheekbones would eventually emerge more clearly.

> . . . I never kept track of the days that passed nor checked on my own testimony. What did matter most of all, though, was that the events of the last few years have affected a great many lives, and it's obvious that they've taken their toll. Even among ourselves, the doubts and contradictions seemed to multiply with each misleading report we'd read. They were bound and determined to break us by sowing dissension among us and preventing us from speaking out, from telling the truth, shouting it out. And since we couldn't possibly turn a deaf ear to all the lies which were linked to our helpless situation, we reacted by making fun of the judges, spitting on the documents and faking broad grins when we found out what was really in our dossiers. We made up other lives for ourselves, other adolescences, and revealed our most secret longings. Each one of us had his own story to tell; we had all allegedly committed some kind of crime and had even been guilty of mass murder. As a result of the whole farce, we got to the point where we thought we'd never get out. We felt that we were doomed forever behind those walls, doomed to learn the grim stories told by other cellmates, to hear the shrill, distant echoes from other cells, to see the bitter faces and gnarled hands of our fellow prisoners . . .

Finally, the ideas started flowing: the curses of the half-crazed prisoners mingled with the sly, lewd faces of other characters. He wrote without stopping, each phrase, like a mainspring, touched off other vignettes, a new imagery, of human beings with nervous grins and sweaty foreheads. After an hour had passed, he decided to take a break.

216

He was brought back to a closer reality as he glanced at his watch and realized that it was just about time for Isabel's visit. He prepared to come out of his shell with his daughter and listen to the sound of his own voice for a while. At first, they'd always make small talk and then they'd exchange views on current topics of interest such as the amnesty for prisoners and wind up scoffing at the hypocrites in the government and at their blatant inconsistencies.

Buenaventura shrugged and laughed to himself. He knew that by now he was endowed with infinite, almost immutable patience, built on long years of suffering and coercion. Later on, Gabriel would be dropping in as well, another one who, according to the government, had made the transition from common murderer to ordinary citizen, one who had also learned to measure the depth of his aversion by pitting it against his own inner resources.

> . . . I really could not believe that we were getting out of jail and that another world was waiting for us with a new kind of freedom. We'd look once more at the trees and parks, the crowds along the boulevards, the city we thought we'd lost forever. I kept staring at my fists, then at my fingers. I squinted and somehow even the light seemed different to me. The nightmares we had lived through that had kept us from sleeping had finally been left behind. All our frustrations, it seemed, had remained locked up in those long corridors, those display windows where every conceivable form of depravity and vice was to be found. On our departure from prison we were neither meek nor insolent. It took place with embraces and the sound of our friends' voices; we marveled at being able to see more than a few meters in front of us, at the number of automobiles in the streets, at a series of images that seemed to fade into the pavement. We went around greeting our old friends, looking forward to sharing our lives with them again, *our* lives, which nevertheless, had to go on. I can still remember that as soon as I got to my place, using the very same key I'd had for the past thirty years, I rearranged my books and set to work right away. Ever since then, every time I open the window, every time I breathe this air, every time I see the rain pounding against the balconies, every time I hear the noises in the street, every time . . .

When he was left alone again, as soon as Gabriel's and Isabel's steps echoed down the stairs, he went back to his armchair, lit his pipe and listened to music for a while. As he reread the pages he'd written, he was filled with the old doubts again until it dawned on him that genuine revulsion cannot possibly be transmitted to paper, that no words could even begin to express the bare outlines of infamy, nor mirrors reflect the depths of degradation.

Those last pages he wrote were never to find their way into print. They were lost forever, swept along by some anonymous wind and then burned to ashes in a city dumping ground.

XII

"CUT IT OUT, you clod!" exclaimed Sebastián, his cigarette dangling from his lips and his enormous hands squeezing the long billiard cue.

On the far end of the table, Gabriel, who had just completed a run of six, was making one carom shot after another. Martín, standing opposite him, remained silent, staring intently at the green bands of the table beyond the red ball. Then he glanced at his watch, noted the veins visible around his knuckles and thought about Andrea. A few days ago, he had finally held her in his arms, naked and glowing with pleasure as they both watched the dawn break.

"Well, I'll be damned, you really had a lucky streak today," remarked Sebastián, scratching his beard. "This son of a bitch is giving us a run for our money."

Gabriel remained unruffled and continued stroking the ball confidently, bending his body the way he used to in the old days in the Argentina Street pool hall, which was just half a block away from San Idelfonso. Finally, he managed to close with a run of twelve. When it was Sebastián's turn, however, his missed his shot, kicked disgustedly, and ground his cigarette underfoot with an air of resignation.

The pool hall on Universidad Avenue was a veritable anthill: the tables were jammed, several women were sitting on the benches, a couple of middle-aged kibitzers hovered over the domino players while a group of teen-agers, carrying soft drinks, clustered near the entrance. The voices bounced back and forth from one end of the room to the other, as the sharp, staccato sounds of the balls rang out incessantly. A huge photograph of the late president Lázaro Cárdenas, gleefully hitting the red ball with the white one, hung prominently over the main table.

"I sure gave you guys a good screwing," said Gabriel smugly as he replaced his cue in the rack.

Suddenly, apropos of nothing at all, Sebastián launched into a tirade about these apocalyptic times we were living in and the sheer futility of waiting around for the Messiah to return. He ranted on and on about the crap that had been proclaimed on the Second Coming ever since the beginning of time, dating back to the ancient Biblical predictions, and on the impossibility of ever regaining an earthly paradise. Martín kept looking at him and saying to himself, "this ding-a-ling never changes; he's hopelessly incorrigible." Finally, the three of them decided to hit the road and see the way of other worlds.

"Let us go out, my good fellows, and make ourselves the masters of the night," said Sebastián, with a perfectly straight face.

Once out on Universidad Avenue, under the glare of the street lights and the neon signs over the shop windows, they piled into Gabriel's car without knowing where they were headed. They drove around aimlessly for a while, debating over whether they should go to the *cantina* on Revolución Avenue or to Andrea's. While Martín was still thinking about Buenaventura's latest book, which he had recommended to his students that very afternoon, Gabriel, with Sebastián's tacit approval, came out in favor of having a few drinks first. It was a dry day in early April, with the winds sweeping stray papers along the sidewalks.

En route, they discussed the reports on alleged CIA intervention in various local organizations and the fact that some well-known militants had turned out to be paid agents who had informed on a lot of people in the movement. They went on to predict more devaluations and guessed that during the new presidential administration, the same old payoffs, rackets and stealing—although in a slightly different style—would still go on. When they reached Insurgentes, Gabriel was reminded of the severed hand of General Obregón (now a yellowish-green color that permeated the fingertips) which looked as if it were still moving, as it lay in a niche in the monument nearby. They arrived at the Providencia Bar just as the traffic along Revolución Avenue was getting heavier and when a couple of beggars were approaching a small grocery store.

The bar was crammed with sluggish faces, rum glasses and hot air, but a couple of corner tables were empty. They settled down, ordered two vodkas and a tequila, and, as Gabriel lit his cigarette, Sebastián gave him a sly look and blurted: "Aha, so you made it with Isabel! That's the way to do it—no beating around the bush, no crap, just straight to the point, right?"

"Everything's going well," replied Gabriel, "better than I thought, actually, though of course Isabel's got a mind of her own and sometimes it's

220

hard for me to understand her." He remembered her as she had been almost eight years ago when she used to visit Lecumberri every Sunday—her dark skin, her chiseled profile, the unmistakable tone of her voice—at once vehement and sensual. Gabriel merely smiled, not caring to go into details and decided instead to watch a drunk who was weaving his way to the men's room. Martín, still with a faraway expression in his eyes, that guarded look which never left him, scratched his cheek, remembering those long nights in jail, the wheezing sounds from the other inmates that seeped through the prison bars in the dark and seemed to engulf him, jolting him out of his nightmares and digressions.

The waiter brought their drinks promptly and as they drank, Sebastián kept harping on his remarkable and unexpected comeback: his lectures on the sociology of literature to hundreds of new faces, to young people with new life styles and different outlooks, students who were not seeking easy ways out or professing blasé attitudes; they had no fear of appearing ridiculous and did not resort to the put-ons affected by cynics and phonies. "You know, this new generation understands me far better than you bunch of morons ever did. I've already forgotten those lean years, when my days were a chain of hungers," Cardoso observed. Martín glanced at him skeptically, not believing a single word. He preferred to link his own past to the incredible fact that he was still alive, still actually there, living in the present and proving to himself, day after day, night after night, that he indeed continued to exist, that the whole thing was real. Gabriel, whose obsessions were similar, but who was more adept at reading between the lines where other people's conversations were concerned, fully sympathized with the nature of Martín's anxieties, the barriers that constrained him, and most of all, with the world-weariness that afflicted him.

While they both downed their drinks, Sebastián went back to his admonitions, gloomy predictions and vast repertoire of invectives. Then he turned to Martín, trying to draw him out of his obviously apathetic mood. "Come on, what the hell, snap out of it, we're here, aren't we?" Sebastián urged, with his ingrained habit of always trying to be the center of attention, to hear the sound of his own voice and know he was being listened to. He liked to flaunt a slightly supercilious air which elicited not only admiration for his nihilistic poetry, but also a certain deference to his age and his bluntness which so often was nothing more than sheer arrogance.

Martín blotted out his thoughts, mentally rejoined the group, gripped his glass of vodka and smiled genially. He spoke of Domingo, of his latest frustrations, his dismay at not being able to write and at those migraine headaches that pierced his temples and paralyzed his thoughts. Gabriel mentioned that one of Buenaventura's short stories would probably be made into a movie and that he'd read in the papers that his most recent work would be published on Saturday.

"And what about yours?" asked Sebastián. "It's high time you devoted a good article to Domingo, don't you think? Yes, come on now, don't play dumb. You know damn well you have a commitment to your past, even though I wouldn't like to be in your shoes. Fortunately, devil-ridden kooks like myself are not generally in the public eye."

Although his words were left hanging in the air, they had an immediate impact on Martín and Gabriel. Their past experiences, which for others had become an inexhaustible source of speculation or of gossip with fictional overtones, for them had remained in a state of brooding suspense, separating them from the rest of the world. They gulped down their drinks and decided to visit Andrea.

For the first time that evening, Sebastián was strangely silent, puzzling over the conflicting reports on José Augusto's latest activities. Sebastián longed to see him again or at least to write, and find out if it was really true that he'd been beaten up again, or whether this were merely a carefully planted story or one more unfounded rumor. He imagined that Banderas had aged considerably and pictured him with his hair completely white and with deep creases in his face, but still adept at jaded contempt pouring out of his speech and his convoluted imagination. It was becoming increasingly difficult for Sebastián to keep that whole story to himself, to live up to his oath of secrecy, to conceal his complicity in the whole affair. It was like a labyrinth that separated him from his own people and from which he could extract only bits and pieces of the real adventure, weaving new stories around it, so as to keep everyone happy and make a good impression.

Startled by the headlights and the shouts of vendors in the street, Cardoso came back to earth again. He decided, for a while, at least, to stop speculating about Banderas' enigmatic existence; then he noticed the hundreds of floral arrangements piled up in the market stalls alongside the *cantina*, pointing them out to Martín and Gabriel. He stuck his hands in his pockets and emitted a long, uninhibited belch.

Once back in the car, they swore at the traffic and the crowds of people in the streets. Then, somehow, they got to the subject of Cristóbal, now a big shot in the government—the patronizing air he had assumed lately, his delusions of grandeur and the innumerable fringe benefits that went with his new job. "I hear he's also one of the president's special advisors," added Gabriel, remembering Cristóbal's moon-face peering out of the crowds during the rallies and meetings, his expression of feigned concern and unconditional support to the movement. Martín, on the other hand, didn't give a damn, since he never bothered to analyze the more devious motives of those sympathizers who never actually became real leaders, and yet who later on used that particular set of circumstances as a springboard toward bigger and better things. They disregarded all their previous verbal commitments to dash off *in open pursuit of one sinecure after another. God Almighty, they were always hanging in there, making damn sure they got a piece of the action, that there'd be something in it for them.*

As was usual under these circumstances, Sebastián assumed his wise-guy attitude and suggested they take advantage of Cristóbal's influence, *particularly now when anything could happen, and we could very likely be screwed up for good. Shit, we've got to be on our toes. I pity the poor devil who happens to get caught in the middle.* It was not only himself Sebastián was thinking of, but the rest of them as well. It occurred to him that this might just be the solution to José Augusto's problem. It was quite possible that his dossier had been mislaid in some bureaucratic shuffle, and lay buried among thousands of other files, and that he might be able to return to Mexico any day now. Why not? He also thought about Buenaventura's predicament: his chronic illness and the possibility of his being hospitalized again soon.

When they reached Taxqueña Avenue, the wind was still swirling the dust clouds along the esplanade. Although it was fairly late, they still had a couple of hours to kill. They headed toward Coyoacán and drove along a narrow street where people swarmed around the taco stands. They turned right, leaving behind them the church and Cortés' palace.

"From what I gather, you're the only one who calls the shots around here," said Sebastián to Martín. "Come on, you sly dog, you don't even have to say anything; it's written all over your face, so don't open your mouth or you're liable to trip over your own tongue."

"Knock it off, for God's sake," retorted Martín, although he knew quite well that in a few days he'd be living in that house, and that for several years now, ever since she used to visit him in prison he had often contemplated the possibility of sharing his memories and his problems with Andrea. They had indulged in mild flirtations which gradually led to a more serious relationship that in turn slowly merged into more solid dreams of a future together.

With her eyebrows perfectly made up and her hair arranged in a bun, Andrea was sitting on the sofa in the living room reading a scenario and trying to immerse herself in the character she'd be portraying, striving to perceive the selfish motivations behind her sharp words aimed expressly at disconcerting others: her inner conflict as a woman at grips with her desire for another woman, and the paradoxical behavior of a schizophrenic. Just as she was becoming totally involved in the bizarre personality she was to play, Sebastián walked in, shattering her introspective mood. They exchanged a significant glance, as if they agreed there was a great deal to be discussed later when they had a chance. Their thoughts were on the same track, divided between the garbled reports they'd heard and the tense moments they'd shared almost eleven years before.

"Well, hi, what a pleasant surprise!" exclaimed Andrea when Martín and Gabriel came into the living room, where so many encounters, both hostile and friendly, had taken place. It had served as an escape hatch for them; here, all the experiences they had shared had given them the chance to pat each other on the back now and then, if only by reflex; to wrestle with their own petty ego-trips and frustrations and to keep on in their quest for fulfillment and cohesion as a group.

Martín greeted Andrea, seeing her in an entirely different light than the other two—her slim waist, firm thighs, smooth shoulders and the swell of her breasts. Although it was some days ago, it seemed only minutes since he had left her sleeping naked between the sheets, her face radiant. On the other hand, Gabriel's greeting was more exuberant. Adopting Sebastián's tone of voice and mannerisms, he puffed up his cheeks and came out with "And how are you this fine evening, you magnificent enchantress? We are here, dear Madame, to pay homage to your great talents and to your boundless generosity!" His imitation was almost letter perfect, and then, as his eyes fell on the drapes and the walls, the dining room table and the paintings hanging over the sofa, he was carried back to the day, several years ago, when he had first met Isabel, then to the interminable debates with Buenaventura and finally to those harrowing weeks and silent mornings, with all of them smoking like crazy and still not able to grasp the magnitude of what was happening. Then came those tense hours in Tlatelolco before they were taken to the Military Camp, the long nights of violent beatings, and the incredible humiliations they had suffered.

The four of them discussed the tragic consequences of the electricians' strike in Puebla, *whenever these bastards in the government want to solve any problem, they beat the shit out of everyone.* Sebastián announced to Andrea that a book of his poems would be published soon. They had been dashed off at odd moments, during his all-night binges with his scruffy bunch of cronies—in cafés, *cantinas*, or some sleazy bar. He then proceeded to give Andrea a few pointers on her craft, suggesting that she become thoroughly familiar with the great playwrights and with the historical background of their characters until she felt she was actually living in that particular period and thus could reproduce the emotions of those characters as faithfully as possible by experiencing their anxieties and their failings as if they were her own. He stressed the importance of keeping her composure at all times and of remaining detached from whatever reactions—whether indulgent or derisive—her performance might provoke in her audience.

"Ease, my dear lady, that is the secret. Remember that ease does not necessarily mean simple," Sebastián added, raising his hands. "Ease in everything, in you voice, in your body movements. Let the most intimate contradtions in your character flow through you; let them become one with your consciousness, so that you feel envy, pride, lust, as naturally as possible. Even the most complex emotions should be spontaneous, so search no further, this is the key to it all."

Andrea said nothing and only laughed resignedly without telling him that she no longer cared about such trite observations, since ultimately the only thing they developed were her own patience and forbearance. She had a fleeting thought: the best—and the worst—part of man is his tongue.

And gradually, between cups of coffee, sips of Scotch, cigarettes and jokes, the house once more became a silent spectator to a group of people who no longer sought different forms of pretense nor to spend their time in silent brooding or in their all-too-apparent angers. They no longer bothered to cover up their complexes or their past mistakes. Their main concern at the moment was to rearrange a world which had deep roots in their past and never ceased to remind them of victories and failures. They managed to keep their spirits up by telling each other their life stories; each one, in the process, becoming more of an individual in his own right as reflected in their tales which ranged from the weary old anecdotes to those which were just taking shape then and there. They talked a great deal about the constant disasters that befell their city, the apparently interminable burgeoning of its slums and outlying areas. There was no longer any room for sham or playacting, since every single ploy, every single gimmick, was by now eminently predictable. There was, of course, still ample opportunity for everyone to show off.

225

At one point, when Gabriel and Martín had discussed the incredible courage it must take to commit suicide and then began to talk about dialogue as a game with set rules and a necessary outlet for boredom, Andrea and Sebastián went into the kitchen to sort out the latest contradictory information they had received about Banderas: the farfetched stories that had been spread about him—of new identities and persecutions, and particularly the disturbing rumor that there had actually been another murder, that he was allegedly drifting around from one place to another as if he were quite capable of adopting a whole new set of voices and personalities.

Sebastián reported that according to a friend of his who had seen José Augusto several times in Europe, that nutty Banderas was once again up to his ears in revolutionary activities, was "stuck on a girl much younger than himself, and was willing to risk everything and to become a new man."

Later on, other people, also eager for the chance to build up their own legends, to "remember themselves out loud," started dropping in. As they began dancing, their bodies became more supple. They let themselves go in a more abandoned and uninhibited fashion than usual, as they gradually ignored the nocturnal sounds outside and their own reflections in the windows. Sebastián watched each one of them in turn and then stared at a couple petting in a corner, sensing that tonight would be fairly uneventful, and that, for a while at least, he'd stifle the rabble-rouser in him, *that no-good son of a bitch who's always screwing me up and hounds me so senselessly, the great double-crosser who has no respect for me whatsoever and only points out my hang-ups—the very worst part of me.*

For the first time in his life, it dawned on Sebastián that his best years were on the wane, that despite the fact that Andrea's house was coming alive again, he now belonged to another world, to the world of the extraordinary, the world of legend; he would have a string of imitators and be incorporated into that charmed circle of stereotyped lunatics who can afford to make mistakes knowing that before long they will have their place in the sun—a much higher one than they'd ever imagined.

226

XIII

DAY AFTER DAY, as on this April morning, a hatchet-faced man with buck teeth and dull eyes, wearing a gray suit and striped shirt, would stroll along a block on the Rue Mouffetard just a few doors away from Saint Medard. He'd pause briefly on each street corner, inspecting the shop windows, balconies, and all entrances and exits of the street. He focused on one particular building in the middle of the block and scrutinized anyone who happened to enter or leave the place. Little by little, his memory began registering more concrete information such as the exact time the lights were turned off in the building and names of the people who stayed on there till midnight. He carried out his assignment with absolute dedication, weekends and holidays included.

A few days later, a second man, wearing bifocals and a dark suit, took over the evening shift. He too, took note of every detail. One afternoon, both men checked into a third-rate hotel opposite the ordinary-looking building that housed the news agency, and where, apparently, nothing unusual ever happened. During their stakeout, both men kept a close watch and took notes on what went on beyond the shop window across from them. Since the weather was balmy, crowds of people bustled along the avenues and strolled about the parks and squares.

By this time, José Augusto's sole concern was his underground work, mainly the management of incoming funds from Eastern Europe and Southeast Asia, which, in turn, were dispatched to countries in the Caribbean, South America or Africa. He was in charge not only of keeping accounts and arranging itineraries, but also of setting up periodic meetings in several countries, and of updating the news to make it more inclusive. By mid-April, his plans for a business trip to London and Edinburgh were nearly complete. Ana Elena's prominent role in José Augusto's life was by now an uneqivocal fact, and he felt confident that the worst was over and that finally, after so many years, he had made up his mind, once and for all, to take a chance and do away with the ambivalence·that had been reflected in both his speech and his attitudes.

José Augusto had never felt better in his life; he no longer gave in to distortions caused by his multiple personalitites nor to his pretenses of boredom. He'd managed to control his tendency toward ridicule and his fear of being found out. Strangely enough, it was the incorrigible loner in him—put to the test day after day—who, in the end, turned out to be his best ally. He had stopped calling himself a coward and was no longer disposed to the icy calm that belonged to his former self, the one who, more often than not, concealed his intentions from the real José Augusto.

He knew his decision regarding Ana Elena was a big gamble, probably the most important step in his life. But he was also convinced that in spite of everything, and after all his misgivings and so many years of loneliness, he had found someone who would willingly follow him anywhere. He was totally oblivious to the fact that the dull-eyed man and his bespectacled partner had been watching his every move or that they'd leave the hotel several times a day to observe him at a distance as he went into his apartment building. They'd spot him whenever he stopped to chat on a corner or as soon as he ran down the steps to the metro station. He was also completely unaware that the others were being watched as well and that, after putting two and two together, the agents had already been in touch with several embassies. Their minds, like their suits, ran along similar lines.

One Saturday noon, José Augusto and Ana Elena arrived in London. Since they were barely at the initial, sharing stage of their relationship, they took their time, allowing themselves the luxury of frank, appraising glances. He no longer cared to keep rehashing his past mistakes or to dream up new guises and games. Although once in a while he'd laugh at himself, he refused to harbor any more doubts—either about the José Augusto he once was or about the vulnerability of his position. On a few occasions, however, he felt he should not forget his former tactics, that he should keep his distance and think carefully about the consequences of his actions.

Although he still smoked steadily, his demeanor was calm, and he lost no time dredging up old memories. He glanced at Ana Elena and then looked out at the green rectangular fields and the factory smokestacks sliding past the window of the plane. They talked about all sorts of things, of days spent together strolling through the streets of Caracas, the port of Ancón and the picturesque Miraflores district in Lima. As his thoughts wandered, José Augusto concluded that the main objectives of his two-month trip to South America had been successfully accomplished. Picking up his conversation with Ana Elena, he then described his friends in Mexico who had just been released from prison, their different personalities, and wondered what their lives were like now and how he would react had he been with them. He reminisced about Domingo Buenaventura, their impromptu rap sessions and their frustrated hopes. Gradually, over the past two months, ever since the first time he had slept with her in Bogotá, he had begun to confide in Ana Elena. As far as the crime was concerned, he had held back nothing: the initial provocation, the insults, his pent-up rage, the feeling of the gun in his hands and the loneliness he had felt on the stairwell.

He felt he was gradually weeding out the antagonistic elements in his nature, laying aside the masks he'd worn so often and that subtle brand of cunning he'd made his own. Quite often he realized that the remnants of his former life were still there and when he least expected it, the slightest slip-up, the slightest gesture, could give him away and put him on the defensive, *tear me to pieces at any moment . . . What the hell . . . those last months had been absolutely crucial for me. The midnight jitters and my nightmares were a thing of the past and I no longer blamed anyone—not myself, nor much less Laura—for what happened. It finally dawned on me whenever I swore at my father, it was really myself I was insulting. I was no longer willing to keep on with my so-called persecution mania. Besides, I was sure that my dossier had been forgotten long ago or that perhaps it had even been destroyed, that no one really much cared about my case anymore. My nights were no longer anxiety-ridden, nor did they rob me of my sleep.*

That same Saturday afternoon, after lunching in a Haymarket restaurant, they went directly to the railroad station where they boarded the train that would get them to Edinburgh in about seven hours. They wandered for a while along the platform amid the black porters, the swarthy Hindu faces and the soccer fans who were on their way to an out-of-town game. Walking leisurely, they amused themselves by listening to the variety of English and Scots accents, the screeching of the wheels on the tracks and by watching the orderly queues of travelers lining up for their trains.

At times José Augusto wondered about the hang-ups that sooner or later he was bound to discover in Ana Elena. He sensed that under no circumstances should he spoil those few days together which meant so much to them. As they boarded the train and wandered through the aisles, looked for their seats and arranged their luggage, neither of them could possibly imagine that at that very moment, the dull-eyed agent and his partner had already broken into the news agency in Paris where they were checking every single paper, document and file in sight, following all possible leads, tying up loose ends, and finally estimating the amounts of money involved and the possible contacts that had been made. Little by little, the fact that they had uncovered a clandestine network came to light.

Once they knew they were on the right track, the two men set to work even more diligently than before, knowing that someone might turn up unexpectedly since it was likely that a meeting had been scheduled for the same night. They left a few minutes later, taking the revealing documents with them, then crossed the street to their hotel room where they made a few phone calls, reporting the names and possible rank of each member of the group. After a short break, they returned to their vantage point at the window, careful not to miss anyone who might be arriving within the estimated half-hour's time.

On the other side of the channel, the train to Edinburgh had started moving, giving Ana Elena and José Augusto a chance to enjoy a view of old bridges, breweries, rugby fields and villages dotted with brick cottages, sloped roofs and graceful arches. Their lighthearted, carefree mood was reflected in their obvious lack of tension and in their earnest, frank conversation which revolved around their commitment to each other and their efforts to eliminate all trace of distrust from their relationship. At one point, José Augusto recalled the first jobs he'd had in Madrid and how, gradually, as he became more sure of himself and free of his old grudges and self-reproach, he'd eventually given up the rare book business. He made no mention, however, of his real line of work—the most important incentive he'd had in the past few years—and about which Ana Elena knew absolutely nothing; either about the existence of the underground organization itself, or the magnitude of the operation and the wide-ranging activities it comprised.

As was the case so often in the past, despite the experiences and concealments he had undergone, despite his painstaking efforts to construct his present plans on a long-term basis, José Augusto was still unable to reconcile his intentions with reality or to measure the consequences of his actions with the inevitable stumbling blocks that never quite disappeared and which could once again lead to his destruction. José Augusto the dupe, José Augusto the visionary, José Augusto the wolf in sheep's clothing, and the echo of "you're more of a son of a bitch than a handsome devil, you know"—even now under entirely different circumstances—still continued to

230

weave an interminable maze where they all vied with each other, grappled with each other, and at very best, lived in a permanent state of conflict.

As night came on and they could see their profiles clearly reflected in the window, they recalled their first real meeting, their astonishment at running into each other on the flight to Caracas, and their first sustained conversation. At the same moment that they were expressing their mutual determination to make their future lovemaking as intense as possible, a young man was slowly opening the door to the news agency in the Rue Mouffetard.

I kept staring at Ana Elena's hands and her lips and her legs, listened to her for a while, letting her express herself freely without any interruptions on my part. She seemed so totally different from Laura — the Laura of eleven years ago, who necessarily was so far away, the Laura it was now so impossible for me to imagine. I also knew that Ana Elena was just beginning to taste the real temptations of deep pleasure, but I never fooled myself for a minute. I knew quite well that either of us was liable to get caught up in an absurd, intolerable vicious circle. At any rate — and this was the most important point — I was not thinking so much of the future on a long-range basis but only of what the next few months would bring. I had deluded myself into believing that this episode marked the beginning of the best years of my life — however belated they might be.

That afternoon, José Augusto's apartment in Paris had been ransacked as well. The two men spent a great deal of time going through a pile of papers on the desk and a number of documents they had found in drawers and closets. They disregarded, however, the journals José Augusto had kept over the years, and left the pages scattered over the sofa.

The train arrived in Edinburgh when it was already dark and only a handful of pedestrians walked along the main streets. By then, José Augusto already knew that Ana Elena had made up her mind to move in with him in his apartment on Montparnasse as soon as they returned to Paris on Tuesday. They stubbed out their cigarettes and calmly gathered up their luggage, melting into the crowds along the platforms. They wandered around for a couple of blocks under the bright lights of Princess Street and the distant glow from the Castle gardens until they found a quaint Victorian hotel. Ana Elena couldn't help smiling when José Augusto signed the register with the assumed names Andrea and Sebastián had dreamed up for him. Although they still appeared on his passport and identification papers, he only used them when he had to write them down.

Ignoring the subdued noises that reached their room, they spent the rest of the night entwining their bodies, trembling with the sound of their own words, feeling each other with their hands, embracing once and again until they reached their mutual climax. Afterwards, José Augusto slowly, ceaselessly caressed her body, gently going over her shoulders, breasts and mouth.

Well after midnight, a number of people had already been rounded up at the Paris news agency. There was no need to go beyond a minimum use of force: when one of the suspects lashed out at the police, he was immediately rammed against the wall and silenced with a couple of punches. The two agents, who were still keeping watch across the street, made a couple of phone calls and gave further instructions.

A few blocks from the raided premises, a student in a leather jacket strolled along the Panthéon, occasionally rubbing his hands and spitting at random. He knew the raid had been pulled off successfully and that only minor details were still pending. He bit down on his cigarette and, as he turned into a dark alley, he suddenly remembered Ana Elena and the day he himself had introduced her to that fellow Banderas.

That night was extraordinary. To tell the truth, I had not experienced anything quite like it in years. By then, I knew by heart every inch of Ana Elena's body and I was sure that it would continue to be a source of joy to me for a long time to come. But that night was a real milestone for another reason: I had finally gotten rid of that persecution mania of mine, of my constant fear and foolish pettiness, of all those masks I'd been wearing. I think I was even getting fed up with the shadow of the other José Augusto. I felt that suddenly a lot of my self-delusions had been stripped away, that I was gradually drawing closer to the real me, and that at last, I could once again appreciate the sheer beauty of two bodies waiting, of thighs opening to love, the incomparable joy of being one with the other person. Naturally, not everything had been entirely erased from my memory. There were still times—at dawn, especially—when I'd wake up and imagine there was still some kind of barrier there in the darkness—a nagging sensation that there'd be more failures, the awareness that my own ingrained selfishness still persisted. Those obstacles remained invariably rooted, firmly entrenched beyond Ana Elena's white, vibrant body, as if they were fated to accompany me for a long time to come.

The next morning, after confirming his appointments, José Augusto waited for Ana Elena in the hotel lobby. He sipped a cup of tea, smoked a couple of cigarettes, and as he gazed thoughtfully out the window at a winding hill, the bridge near the station, the trees swaying on the nearby sloping terraces, the clouds floating over a Gothic church, he speculated on the dirty tricks fate was in the habit of playing. A few minutes later, he and Ana Elena went for a long walk, giving themselves a chance to express their awe at rediscovering each other and noting with delight that their shadows walked along together as they felt the wind sweeping along the gardens and side streets.

Ana Elena chattered on about all sorts of things—that her studies in Paris would be over in a few months, and the beauty of the colonial churches and extraordinary balconies that studded the Jirón de la Unión in Lima. The afternoon slipped by leisurely, and as José Augusto contemplated the double-decker buses and the weather-beaten old buildings, he realized that this time he hadn't resorted to his old obsessive habit of modulating or changing the tones of his voice. His totally relaxed mood seemed to endow him with a sense of superiority; it made him impervious to the damp winds which were blowing about them and to the threatening rain clouds which hovered over the Castle beyond the Royal Mile on the opposite side of the avenue, where the train tracks were hidden among the trees and the winding curves of the hill.

They made unabashed references to last night's lovemaking which had come about so naturally and which, in time, they would no doubt learn to enhance. Then he told her of the infinite loneliness he had felt when walking around the streets of New York and of how much Laura had meant to him. Abruptly, he erased the image of the dead man's eyes staring up at him in the Sinaloa Street apartment and then went on to recall his adventures as a guide in the museums and cathedrals of Spain. He pointed to a church in the background, just beyond where they were standing, and stressed the importance of the arches, moldings, belfries and vaults in its overall design. He realized, for the first time, that he was now able to talk to someone else about his past without the slightest hesitation and listen to the sound of his own voice without flinching.

José Augusto's spirits lifted, and, as he tried to transmit this mood to Ana Elena, he laughed to himself for no reason at all except perhaps the realization that he had finally confronted the invisible inner enemies he had learned to overcome. It seemed to him that at this particular moment in time everything—the biting winds, the treetops, the rain slapping against the railings and dark cornerstones of old buildings—had come to a standstill. They watched a couple of old people come out of the church and then turned at the next corner.

Since it had started raining, they took shelter in a small restaurant where again, in eager anticipation of their next erotic experience, they talked of the rhythm of pleasure, the search for perfection in the movement of hands and legs, of thighs in close contact. In those brief moments of creative imagining when the mind strikes unique chords and only the present contains reality—José Augusto's attention momentarily wandered to the thoughts he'd had at dawn, to his former apprehensions, to that goddamned skepticism of his that never quite left him, to those amorphous barriers which he must tear down at any price.

He looked into Ana Elena's dark eyes, at her white skin, at her delicate features and compared her to other women he'd known. The enormous differences between them, both in age and in experience, never crossed his mind. They drank their coffee leisurely, inhaled their cigarettes, and felt exhilarated at the prospect of the pleasures that awaited them, at their need to hold each other once more. Suddenly the rain stopped and they decided to go out into the avenue again. They crossed the street, watching several middle-aged women sitting placidly on benches or walking toward the sloped garden paths. The sky was still cloudy and the castle towers seemed to melt into the haze.

On their way back to the hotel, they passed what looked like an abandoned stone monument with the railroad station in the background. They spotted several statues on the right, and a group of shabby, drunken vagrants leaning unsteadily against the railing. There were very few pedestrians on the opposite side of the street; the stores were shut and most windows were closed, except for a few in the upper stories. José Augusto talked about the old books he had come to know better than anyone else—their origins, the hands that had made them, the various techniques used to restore them. His words, however, did not manage to conceal his mounting desire for her, the image of their mouths coming together, her erect nipples, their bodies caressing each other, and once again their inevitable bliss, the slow release.

Before planning to visit other parts of the city, they decided to return to their hotel, to recreate their newly-found delight in each other. On the way up to their room, José Augusto was stopped by a stranger, and before he had time to think or speak, or even clench his fists, a second man stepped up and flashed his identification. Ana Elena had no idea of what was happening; the astonishment on her face was there for all to see.

234

XIV

AFTER ADJUSTING HER HANDBAG and the books she was carrying, Laura stepped into the elevator and pressed the button to the ninth floor. Since she had already gone over her accounts, she was fairly sure that the check would be enough to cover a few days' vacation in San Miguel Regla with her two children, who were waiting for her upstairs. First she half-closed her eyes and then glanced absent-mindedly at the panel. All of sudden, the lights went out between the third and fourth floors and the elevator came to a stop. Guessing there'd been a breakdown of some sort, she set her purse and her books down on the floor and pressed the alarm bell insistently.

It was after five o'clock and the afternoon sun beat down on the Baja California Street building, half a block from Culiacán Street, where Laura had been living for the past two years. Since she could hear no sound, it occurred to her that perhaps there'd been a blackout. At first, she was at a loss; she tried sliding her fingers all down the buttons, while her shoes bumped against the books on the floor. Although ostensibly she was now at peace with herself and the world and didn't feel at all tired, she was in no mood to face a long delay. There was total silence and total darkness around her and soon the minutes started ticking away. A few seconds later, she thought she heard faint noises around the pulleys above her and out in the corridors and then pictured the gaping holes yawning above and below the elevator. Although she felt like banging against the door, she decided to wait, hoping that the time would pass quickly and that the lights would go on again. She ran her hands through her long hair, and slowly closed her eyes.

Laura had the sensation that everything around her had become invisible; she started thinking about her own blind spots, her perennial expectations, and her carefully worked-out plans for the future. But she could not long distract herself from the darkness that enveloped her. The darkness was becoming oppressive, peopled with images and episodes from her past. She opened her eyes and beat against the door. She could hear herself breathing, and decided to wait a while longer by leaning against the back wall. Then she rapped with both hands but no one answered. It seemed to her that everything had gone awry, that midnight had seeped into that place. Once more she hammered on the door and again there was no answer. The darkness seemed suspended in the air around her, pressing in on her thoughts and isolating her even more. There was no space left to sort out her words, no way she could listen to herself as the darkness that was not really night set up vibrations in the hidden corners of her memory and slashed into the savage fury she had felt in bygone times.

Six floors above her were her two sons, the children she'd borne in South America. They had helped make bearable the long silences that enveloped her and had appeased the furies that still smoldered within her. She placed her hands on the aluminum rail and kept on listening to her breathing. At last, when the darkness came to a standstill, she resolved to control her fear, to keep calm and curb her uneasiness and impatience. She began to weave a string of random thoughts: the heavy rains of the past few days, the traffic jams at every large intersection, the flooded tenements of Tepito. Then she focused on her work, adding up a series of figures in her head and estimating the total amount still owed her by the publisher, the debts and overdue accounts in different establishments and the constant haggling with booksellers and distributors. Now, after more than ten years of it, she had grown heartily sick of such chores. She shut her eyes and summed up the deferred payments for each agency. Nevertheless, the darkness seemed to beckon her again; she could feel its presence, its overwhelming and constant weight. Black dots flickered before her eyes, intertwining, expanding, enfolding the entire space.

Before long, despite her resistance and her refusal to brood about the most hopeless of situations, the unavoidable came little by little, that something she was trying to hold back and not think about. She opened her eyes and wondered about José Augusto. She pictured him sitting in the armchair in the Sinaloa apartment, the last time she had ever heard his voice, when there was finally no turning back. The scene shifted, first to her children, then to herself in an airport, staring at the snow on the Andes; and finally, to her Santiago apartment on Ahumada Street near the Alameda, where her life had taken a radical turn and she no longer had time for idle thoughts or rationalizations. Now the darkness about her had become impassive, wordless, devoid of creaking or grating sounds. When she slid her foot on the floor, she managed to break the silence and disperse the flock of images crowding her mind.

A distant sound, like a skate skidding along the tiles, drifted up beyond the hollow spaces above her and seemed to rise all the way to the rooftop where the sun beat down on the water tanks and on clotheslines. She visualized José Augusto's eyes and hands, saw his mouth in constant movement, always belittling her, always questioning her and always with that angry, supercilious expression on his face. It had been a long time since she had felt anything like that or recalled the memory of those tense months at Andrea's which now returned to stir up her emotions with such force. Now, though, there was a big difference: gone were the dead-end streets in her mind, gone was the deep hatred she had felt for the first time during her stay at Andrea's. As she clasped her hands together, she was once again confronted with old doubts and regrets. However fleetingly, the sardonic laugh and taunting gibes of José Augusto were also back.

She moved her hands forward as if she could actually touch the darkness and push aside the invisible objects that encircled her, the stifling air that heralded the approaching night. She remembered the birth of her first child, her nerve-racking pregnancy, then the second baby, their first smiles and their first babblings, the cloudy days at the foot of the Santa Cecilia Hill, the docks in Valparaiso, the ships waiting for their cargo and the mist hovering over the ocean. She hit the door hard again and again, but the sounds disappeared among the gaps above her and melted into nothingness. She tried to imagine a chapter in José Augusto's present life, a desperate man in search of himself, still clinging to the same old lies and pretenses of astonishment. She saw him as she saw the darkness around her; as someone fumbling around in a dismal world without even the faintest glimmer of light to guide him.

Suddenly, a grinding mechanical sound trickled through the walls and vanished into the cables. She leaned against the corner of the elevator with a feeling of claustrophobia she had never experienced before. It felt as if the elevator was about to come crashing down at any moment. She cursed every inch of its walls and floors. She clasped her hands together as if to shake off her symptoms of anguish. Gradually, she regained her composure and stopped herself from going endlessly around in impossible circles by telling herself that soon she would be out of there, that perhaps those dark tones around her were only the same kind of flickering specks that seemed to dot the sea at midnight. She thought back to an afternoon in San Antón on the Chilean Coast where she had finally recovered her hope and regained her self-confidence. It had been raining day and night and finally she had managed to detach herself from her immediate surroundings, from what she could see before her eyes and from the sounds of waves crashing against the rocks.

She heard footsteps on the floor above her; they stopped abruptly. Perhaps it was just someone entering an apartment or going up all the way to the eighth floor. She clung to her hope that sooner or later the lights would come back on and that she'd hear the creaking sounds of cables and pulleys. She felt sure that only a few minutes had actually passed, and that quite soon someone was bound to come along and reassure her somehow. She remembered a gas leak one winter night in Viña del Mar, when both she and the man she had married—the man whose children she had borne —had come within an inch of losing their lives. Luckily, they detected the danger just in time. The next morning, their fear had dissolved into light banter and smiles of relief. Gradually, other faces appeared before her: there were her brother's petulant expression and her father's scowl, there was herself, an adolescent, standing in front of the window, noting the brittle cobblestone streets; and there was her growing estrangement from her mother. Once again she saw her brother and her father, heard their blustering voices and their unbearable authoritarianism.

Finally, she decided to cry out, making sure her scream was loud enough to reach beyond that square box so that it would reverberate on the building's ceilings and windowpanes. Although she went right up to the door, her first shout immediately died away, sealed off between the bricks and concrete. By now, she had gotten used to the darkness which hovered before her eyes, lurking. Her second shout pierced the walls, seemed to reach the light bulbs and bounce off the elevator's panels. She ran her right hand over the buttons again, struggling to stay calm. She thought about the South American cities she'd visited—Quito and Lima— about her discussions at work, the long hours she'd spent in hotel rooms and offices and about the man she'd slept with—in Panama—several months after she'd left Andrea's.

She was still undecided as to whether she should sit down, let time slip by, or let her thoughts drift and the images rise before her eyes. A third shout, stronger, more penetrating, rang out clearly, floated upwards, and even created an echo which resounded between each floor and pillar. Although she realized that her breathing had become labored, she was spurred on by her eagerness to erase the past and get out as quickly as possible. Her confinement had become unbearable, and all the while, a couple of José Augusto's familiar phrases kept running through her head:

the most caustic, ruthless, verbal thrusts imaginable. She was reminded of the old, sturdy elevator in the Ahumada Street apartment, where she used to go up and down every day with one child in her arms and the other clinging to her skirts. The snowcapped Andean mountains loomed over them, and below, they could hear the shouts of the demonstrators, proclaiming Allende's victory and the beginning of a new era.

She heard the sound of approaching footsteps from somewhere below, shattering the silence and enabling her to measure the distance between the ground floor and where she stood. However, as soon as she shifted her feet, she stumbled over her books as she strained to hear the footsteps again; but the silence, the uncertainty and the night returned. One phrase in particular hammered in her head: *"We've lived by dint of blows, by dint of anger, by being kicked in the ass."* After her fourth yell was ignored, her loneliness became acute, and the darkness weighed more heavily upon her. She decided to sit down for a while and rest. She would cheer herself up by remembering the happy times she'd spent on Isla Negra in Chile, with the sun shining over the ocean. She relaxed her arms and then pictured her children racing around Quinta Normal. The void right there in front of her, in front of the door, had started breathing again, swirling around the ceiling and the walls.

She recalled that time in the Crillón Hotel in Lima when she entered the incredibly swift and noiseless elevator—so quiet it seemed to have been wrapped in cotton. She was on her way up to the twentieth floor when she had been accosted by an unctuous, conceited fop. Laura closed her eyes and leaned her head against the wall, feeling as if she were falling down a bottomless pit, peered at by strange and mocking eyes. If José Augusto had been in her place, she thought, most likely he would have remained perfectly calm, making the best of the situation as he listened patiently to the medley of distant sounds and waited for the footsteps to come nearer.

The words pounding in her head clashed with each other, throwing her thoughts into turmoil. She could neither curb her distress nor ward off the implacable nightfall which closed in about her. The nervous tremor that spread throughout her body began to upset her to the point where she began to have serious doubts about what was actually happening. The sensation of emptiness seemed more real than ever; it was right there in front of her, alive, hounding her, pushing her over the brink. Scenes from the past streamed on: the dead man's eyes staring at the rug, José Augusto running down the street, the cracked mirror beside the bed; then her children upstairs, and always the threat of the approaching void hanging over her. As her panic mounted, she half-opened her mouth and squeezed her hands together tightly.

Just as she was about to shout louder than ever, she heard footsteps on the fourth floor, just above the elevator shaft. As soon as she heard voices, she didn't wait any longer to shout as loudly as she could. That done she muttered a stream of curses at the strange confining cubicle that held her, at the blacked-out bulbs and at the baseboard that she could feel with her left hand. When the voices began to answer back, she felt that the darkness had retreated, become static and aloof. One of the voices shouted that there were blackouts in several blocks through the neighborhood and probably others in entire districts all over town. Laura also learned that the power had been out for only a few minutes. Yet in that brief time her mind had been forced to stand before the distorting mirrors of her past.

One of the voices sounded very much like that of her children's father, whom she had met in Santiago and who, later on, gave her such a bad time that separation was inevitable. She took a long, hard look at herself, at her tendency to blame others and to minimize her own shortcomings. She deplored her mercurial, suspicious nature, her useless perfectionism, the cold-bloodedness of her decisions and her inordinate fondness for making scenes. As she stretched her arms and moved her legs nervously, she jeered at the make-believe nightfall and the empty spaces around her, at the images that had been wrenched out of her own vague fears. Her left hand was still quivering, and she desperately longed—for a moment at least—to draw a long deep breath again.

Gradually, her pulse returned to normal. She went over some of her previous thoughts, insisting that José Augusto was not, after all, the perfect semblance of masochism, nor could she any longer hate him so intensely, any more than she could feel she was exempt from all blame. She reached out and touched the darkness, feeling it with her hands, staring at it with her eyes wide open as she examined the series of defense mechanisms she had built up over the years. She lowered her arms with a faraway expression in her eyes where dreams and frustrations were mixed together. She saw herself in the airport, arriving in Mexico after that last month in Chile when she had witnessed the persecutions, reprisals, brutality, curfews and those corpses strewn over Bulnes and Ahumada Streets. This, she reflected, was the real, the most intense manifestation of darkness—one that borders on the inconceivable; it lies somewhere between utter anguish and absolute

240

impotence in the presence of infamy.

After a great deal of effort, she succeeded in blotting out a few unpleasant memories, letting the seconds slip by and melt into nothingness, into anything at all, into the objects on the floor, into the book she had opened, into the hand that was groping for the wall and lingered on a corner of the elevator. She was interrupted by the murmur of other voices, by other footsteps which she no longer had to listen for, going up the stairs and fading away on the next floor. She thought about the passing of time, about aging, about the opportunties that had slipped away from her. Then the scene switched back to the Mexico City airport, to the slums near El Peñón, to the grinding poverty all around her and to the endless double talk she read in the newspapers every day. She let her arms go slack, recalling some of her children's most characteristic expressions and the terrible loneliness she always felt around midnight.

Later on, after making sure that her anxiety had subsided, she thought about her screams and realized that she had just experienced a new form of despair. Then she resolved to keep watching for a light—any kind—and to reach the ninth floor as soon as possible. She relived some of her old anxieties and then set her sights on her immediate goal: to flee this darkness, this closed-in space that had grown so large and which she had sworn at so many times in such a little while. She imagined how she would tell her story first to her children and then to the man—considerably older than herself—who was a frequent visitor. He was pleasant enough, to be sure, but a bit on the mousy side and full of many little quirks that annoyed her no end. She pondered over her inadequate sex life, her repressed sensuality, that brief affair she'd had with a married man and the insistence of an insipid young admirer.

Now the noises were different; they had another pitch, other tones that seemed to resound more distinctly before fading into the naked brick walls. She remembered Andrea's house and all the other places she was reluctant to return to, all the people she never wanted to see again. The faces flashed before her eyes: Buenaventura, Gabriel, Sebastián at a farewell party they'd had for her over ten years ago. She made a mental tour of the Sinaloa apartment, and although she was still there in the elevator, crouched in the same corner, stretching her legs again with one hand on the floor, she could almost hear the concierge's voice and her own listless reply. It suddenly dawned on her that every trace of nervousness had disappeared. She began retracing her own features in the mirror—that mirror in her mind that could be relied upon to reflect the cold hard facts,

241

the naked truth which was corroborated by the first tell-tale folds on her neck, the slight wrinkles at her temples, and above all, in the awareness of her own loneliness, a loneliness that was impossible to share. She wondered what the next few years would bring, with her children grown and only her work to look forward to. Perhaps there'd be a man, some special man she could really communicate with, who would share her interests and her memories, who might even succeed in reawakening the old passions and make her feel whole and fulfilled again. The dead man, her long-lost chance for a new lease on life, was now a blurred memory, along with (as she told herself over and over again) the resentment she had buried long ago. She was convinced that at least she could picture José Augusto without that sullen expression on his face or his fists clenched.

She stood up with a sense of doubt which grew stronger and made her lips tremble and her eyes close. In spite of everything, in spite of the fact that her inner struggles had surfaced, she was determined to cling to her love of life and not let herself sink into inertia or be overwhelmed by skepticism. As if the gesture would help her forget, she automatically touched the buttons in a reflex action to get the elevator moving again. Since by now she was thoroughly familiar with the dark cube suspended in the air, she paid no attention to the sounds around her. At least she managed to free herself from a series of memories and overcome several of her weak points such as physical fear and the sensation of nothingness.

At last the power came back on, the elevator lit up and started rising and the door opened on the fourth floor. She went out into the hall and found other kinds of light; there was the afternoon glow streaming through the windows and brightening the staircase. On impulse, she ran up the stairs at the same rate as the elevator, keeping time to its echoes, to its lights as they flickered on each floor. Gradually, as the machinery started working normally again, she was left behind. She didn't mind at all having to climb all those stairs or having to pause at each landing to regain her breath. Little by little, she rid herself of that darkened cell that teemed with those strange vibrations, intertwining and distorting her memories.

However, as she went up the stairs the notion of time crossed her mind once again. It was a recently acquired habit of counting the days and the ages of her children; of watching for wrinkles in her hands and testing the rhythm of her pulse. She stopped on the seventh floor to view the dingy sunset she had imagined would be so radiant. Slowly, she went up the rest of the stairs, then remembered her chldren were waitng for her and hugged her books tightly to her chest.

XV

DOMINGO BUENAVENTURA, IMMERSED IN boredom and insomnia, rocked back and forth with an involuntary smile on his face. Gradually, his expression turned into a protracted grimace more in tune with his own inner sounds. He felt totally alone, abandoned even by his rage, his bitterness and by the long years he'd spent pouring out his anger while exposing all the misery in the world. His furtive smile, devoid of any illusions, at times turned into a grim expression which conveyed his well-controlled vindictiveness and his total familiarity with each and every one of his silences—to the point where it had become almost second nature to him. Then, without even bothering to gaze at the smoke drifting from the pipe in his hands, he reflected that everything around him seemed out of kilter.

Harshly berating himself and disregarding any form of delusion, he started ticking off a series of names in his head while glancing at the old clock out of the corner of his eye and then studying the Cape of Good Hope on the map. He placed one hand on the map and bit his pipe. As he carefully closed the book, he felt the slow throbbing pain in his forehead and the onset of a listlessness which promised to be relentless. Before long, the words and images in his head gradually crumbled.

At times, he was barely conscious of the fact that his thoughts had fragmented, that his sense of wonder had remained frozen in his memory and that the voices were slowly fading away. The Saturday night noises outside—distant whistling sounds, youthful shouts along Oaxaca Avenue, a bottle smashing against the trunk of a poplar—somehow seemed far off to him and totally unrelated to his immediate goals. He got up to close the window and wind the clock, trying to separate his pain from his muddled thoughts.

He became engrossed in the smoke from his pipe, as if the spirals contained all his past experiences and were, like himself, grappling with the temptations of worldly pleasures, with selfishness, with the words which

243

once again seemed to slip away from his original intent and lacked the substance to be transferred with the proper intensity to the blank pages in front of him. He reflected, somewhat wryly as if it were a long-standing joke, that the smoke was really freedom personified and that life itself smacks of tobacco.

... When we were in prison, there was never a morning when we didn't find time to get involved in some discussion or other; sometimes while walking along the corridors or just leaning against the walls. As a starting point, we'd pick up on only those remarks which succeeded in stirring up our doubts and passions. I discovered that neither the evasiveness nor the incoherent ramblings of others fazed me any longer. One of us would start talking, another would break in, and so we whiled away the hours inside those walls without letting ourselves be carried away by phoniness or feelings of self-pity. We learned the sounds in our cells and the shadows in the corridors by heart. I knew that Martín's eyes were always there—with their uncompromising, hard, reproachful gaze that saw through our blunders and contradictions. I knew that under other circumstances, Martín would be even more demanding and would not be easily dazzled by momentary victories. Gabriel, the less complex of the two, was just the opposite. Although he too rejected all those lies and muttered to himself all the intentions of anger, he was less severe in his judgments and tended to focus on constructive rather than on negative thinking. But, in any case, there we all were, and there was nothing to do but to size up our fears and try to take a mature attitude toward the threats and hostility that hemmed us in. While in the other cells it was pure hell—we heard occasional screams of pain, the sounds of bloody vomiting and of brutal beatings—I was able to write dozens of pages. With my imagination working in high gear, I'd write nonstop for hours ...

After Buenaventura leafed through the book again and found the map, he scanned the Costa del Sol and then the Adriatic. He thought momentarily of some scattered images: men and women trudging through the snow toward the Hendaya border and a solitary flagpole standing forlornly in the middle of a godforsaken village. Then he surrendered himself to a medley of sounds and images: the silhouette of an old woman bending down on one of the banks of the Manzanares River, the planes swooping over the broad avenues in Barcelona, and a dreary concentration camp in the south of France. The riddles of the past kept breaking into his mind, filling the past with gloomy shadows and unpleasant memories.

Now the bemused faces, the muffled sounds, the torture chambers, gave way to the rhythmic beat of the pendulum, the hands on the clock, the lasts wisps of smoke. He breathed deeply and turned to look at the floor lamp with the realization that everything he'd seen, everything his hands touched, was already tarnished beyond repair and could never be scrubbed clean again. He cleared his throat a couple of times and closed the book. Coughing, he groped around in his mind for some source of stimulation, anything at all, whether it lay in a memory leading him down an obscure alley or in a photograph that set his doubts in proper perspective. Reverting to his old habit of rocking back and forth, he suddenly felt the words surging up again and sensed that at last a real smile had spread across his face.

> . . . I never dreamed that those first few days would be so rough. The headaches and fear of open spaces set in. I was in a state of permanent contradiction: reason told me I had to stay shut in here, looking at the walls, arranging my books and magazines and becoming reacquainted with the sounds of my own silences. On the other hand, my body demanded that my senses find solace by resuming my walks through the old landmarks which I'd assumed would be there forever: the squares downtown, the esplanades on Durango Street, the colonial buildings and the milling crowds on Juárez Avenue. More often than not, the sharp throbbing in my temples became more acute, boring into my thoughts and leaving me limp and exhausted. I'd lie down for hours at a time, as if I hadn't slept in days, rubbing the back of my neck and my face. Gradually, I'd feel myself getting over it and becoming my old self again, mastering the simple tasks of getting to my feet, of looking at the clock, or of filling my pipe. Although I had absolutely no desire to see anyone, I kept seeing myself among a lot of people. I've never quite figured out if the loneliness I felt after I left the hospital was forced on me or was acquired as a result of stigmas attached to all those years in cells. There was a direct contradiction between the past and the present, I had no chance to make excuses for myself, . . . to justify my actions or to listen to anyone else. Gradually, however, I found my way out of those empty spaces, that strange kind of prolonged absence. Once, as I walked from the metro station to Insurgentes, just a few blocks

from here, I happened to notice a man talking and gesturing to himself. He seemed to be making fun of everything: the very air, his cane, and the people around him. I watched him closely and felt a twinge of envy. That image remained fixed in my mind for several days. By that time, I had already managed to step out on the balcony for a few minutes, or else I'd walk for a couple of blocks, watching the pedestrians and the cars. I decided to imitate that man and not take myself so seriously, to laugh at myself and not go around always worrying about everything. It goes without saying that I didn't make much headway. Not a day goes by when I don't feel that old anxiety again, feel those pains shooting through my temples or when I am not hounded by the memory of those cowardly, brutal beatings I suffered . . .

He placed the book on the table, blocked out the next couple of sentences in his head, and started typing slowly. The lamplight streamed diagonally over the typewriter, making the veins in his hands stand out even more clearly. Only a few strokes on the keys corresponded to the sum total of hundreds of personal experiences, reduced to one alone. He'd rest for a moment, peer down at the letters, and in his mind he'd summon up the colors on the map. He could almost hear the explosion alongside old Federico's forehead, like a *coup de grace*, which, of its own accord, had snuffed out all traces of enthusiasm. Later, in a matter of seconds, he had traveled over seas and continents, pausing on the Mediterranean at Almería as he thought about a certain ship on its way to North Africa. Once there the Moors, their hands and faces covered, were lying in wait, as if hidden in the darkness.

After he had adjusted his glasses, he leaned against the back of the chair and noticed how his fingers seemed to obey his every command; as his hands flew over the keys, the words kept spilling out, linking the images together. The real years, with the ruptures, the broken promises, the disaffections, were all there in black and white. Strangely enough, he had forgotten all about the taste of tobacco.

. . . One afternoon, Gabriel dropped in carrying a bunch of newspaper clippings. Although he didn't pay too much attention to me, I kept insisting that it was common enough to see compliments and words of praise turn into a smear campaign. I also explained that as a result of my disenchantment with that sort of thing, I had grown thick-skinned and urged him to stop being so solemn and not to be so eager to write me off so quickly. I'd stopped showing off a long time ago and it really wasn't worthwhile to bother with such trifles. I don't know whether he believed me or not, but at least I wanted him to see that everything comes in its own good time and that he should be on his guard against petty vanities. There are other kinds of vanity we feed on and maybe, in the long run, we care more for those kinds that come to us from women and travels and enjoying the pleasures of life; or from the feeling we get when witnessing the uneasiness of our enemies. We chatted a bit and then recalled some of the arguments we'd had a few years ago. We discussed the events leading up to the two recent massacres—in Hormiga Park and the Corpus Christi riot—and their consequences without really arriving at any important conclusion. We talked about the differences between the many millions of inhabitants, between the country and the city, between the slums and the residential neighborhoods of the new rich. I mentioned, as a case in point, my own rapidly deteriorating part of town, where some of the buildings had been taken over by large oil companies, and where, at the same time, the same pious old maids were still living in the house on the corner. Once I was alone again, I started piecing things together and working over stories from here and there. I reread a couple of paragraphs from some unfinished piece I'd written more than twenty years ago and, much to my surprise, I discovered that my predictions were not too far off the mark; I'd spent all my life writing about events just about to come true. Sometimes I could foretell weeks ahead of time what eventually I was to see with my own eyes. I came across descriptions of what I was to live through more than twenty years later. When I went to bed that night, I had an eerie feeling. The next day I rummaged through a pile of papers. Luckily, I didn't find any description of my own death or of my funeral, nor of the oblivion to which our ashes most surely will be consigned . . .

By now, Domingo Buenaventura was grinning broadly. He was determined to expose the trumped-up charges, slander and intrigues of the groveling cowards. Nevertheless, now that most of the sequences seemed to fit into his original plan, and to match his vehemence and the intensity of his emotions, he felt his eyes growing tired and bit his lips while waiting for the stabbing pain in this head to subside.

At last he launched into a description of a scene he had witnessed

247

over a year ago, one dismal afternoon when the parking lots of University City were empty. The wind swirled back and forth between the buildings and the esplanades, among the trees, and along the avenues, and beyond the library murals, then back again to the auditorium gate. Only one streak of blue could be seen over the stadium and there were no reflections at all on the windows of the Rectory Tower. Little by little, cars started arriving and people began to talk in low voices on the staircases and in the corridors, obviously discussing the writer and his last works. Some of them mentioned his sudden death in the hospital after the gradual deterioration of his body had been caused by a combination of dissipation, years of torture and imprisonment and of being so badly misunderstood.

As his thoughts poured out and the typewriter keys responded, the tension in his hands was transmitted to the written word. He returned to the auditorium again and recalled that after five o'clock a hush had fallen over the people as the coffin was carried forward. The cortege went slowly down the stairs between the seats where the former prisoner, the creative writer, the polemicist, the loner, had so often spoken, his powerful voice ringing out as he pounded the table and fixed his eyes on the hundreds of faces from the front row to the last. The casket was finally set down in the center of the main aisle, where it was received with impassioned speeches and eloquent silences.

While the lamps shone over the ripples on the ceiling and on the wooden paneling of the auditorium, those present recognized each other's faces and the events of more than forty years flashed before them. Then, there was a long pause during which all thoughts and eyes were riveted on the center of the auditorium and crowded memories of historical events and turbulent scenes of both city and country streamed forth. The first guard of honor was made up of old radicals, refugees from different countries and the writer's former cell mates. There was a mingling of generations, of roots, as if everyone had been swept back to those hostile days of the demonstrations. Only the clarity of their purpose remained: a new vindication, devoid of morbid overtones, and eulogies for the man who had made himself master of the word. It was their attempt to clarify and understand the ways in which even suffering can be corrupted.

A few minutes later, after the last mourners had paid their respects and the coffin had been carried up the main aisle, everyone stood and applauded. The cheers bore echoes of times gone by, resounding through the walls, the prison cells, and through the vipers coiled around each other. The applause lasted longer than any of the silences or any of the speeches.

When the coffin finally reached the main exit, the afternoon was grayer than ever, as if it suspended momentarily for many of the mourners an essential part of their past, the accusations against them, and their defiance of insults and offenses. Meanwhile, the wind continued howling about the buildings and along avenues.

. . . We went in and out of that auditorium as if we owned it; we practically lived there for several months. Right from the beginning and to the end, we got to know each other better than ever—sitting on those benches and confined behind those walls. We had, of course, our share of agitators and the inevitable stragglers—deadbeats with nothing better to do. Later on, it would serve to house the bayonets and the rifles of the soldiers. We learned how to work the overhead lights and the lower lights as well, and we'd memorized the corridors as we wandered around them during the early morning hours, discussing all sorts of things. Even after we got out of prison, we returned to that auditorium. It was in these seats that many of us learned to speak up, to denounce openly the violence and repression around us. We also knew that those benches had been the forum for the debates about our trials and our sentences. Our statements had been read there and the alleged kidnappings and lies about us had been reported in this place. For almost three years we thought we would never return, that never again would we be able to raise our voices and our hands. A long time later—perhaps for many of us, longer than we every imagined—we saw our own faces appear on the screen in that auditorium, the scenes of our imprisonment, the faces of our friends and families during visiting hours and the stupid expressions on the faces of the prison guards. We know that those walls have a long story to tell; that we shall keep going back to them; that there we shall talk of long silences and dark passages, of our stupor, of our memories, of the vilest of scum we had encountered. We shall never tire of talking about our tormentors, men who at all costs attempt to impose their own decrees and their own judgment arbitrarily, without common consent. Once the lights are out and the doors have been shut, thousands of slogans will remain invisibly engraved on those walls. They rose from our endless debates and from the insults that still pour out of our rage and of our intense hatred for those who persecuted us . . .

Buenaventura kept pounding the keys more and more forcefully, feeling the unquenchable vitality in each word. When he had written half a page, he left the cheering in the auditorium and started describing what had taken place the following day, north of the Social Security Park, beyond the din of the Alemán Viaduct. Crowds of people streamed into the French Cemetery. The same coffin and the same cellmates led the way. A few sleek automobiles had parked along the street, formerly known as Calzada de la Piedad, while the bodyguards and chauffeurs waited impatiently on the sidewalk.

Little by little, hundreds of people crowded around the grave site. Their faces mirrored their indignation and disgust. Just before the casket was lowered, the voice of a former fellow prisoner was heard. The words were aimed directly at the enemy, reciting again the the litany of charges and challenges, mercilessly accusing the government officials there present of paying homage only to the writer, of conspiring with the iron-fisted policies of the government while never lifting a finger or intervening in the release of the man they were now mourning. The speaker's voice was firm, lucid, eloquent; he kept one fist raised the whole time and never took his eyes off the unwelcome intruders.

Suddenly, while someone tried to silence him, another took up the cries and still a third hurled even more insults at the men in dark suits. The voice of the fomer prisoner, who had also been charged with murder, gradually prevailed as the midday sun beat down on the gravestones and monuments. Discord set in again, and other voices were raised, shouting down those who had no business being there.

Although the shouted recriminations continued, the government officials remained impassive, their faces stern, accepting the insults, not moving a muscle. One last voice, even stronger and harsher than the others, stood out above them all because of its emotional and sarcastic tone. When he finished, he was greeted with shouts demanding that the official opportunists be thrown out. As the atmosphere became more and more charged, the protests became more insolent, more aggressive. A common voice seemed to mount in volume until it reached the distant walls and outside avenues. As others intervened, as the name-calling was reaching its peak, the casket was being lowered. In view of the increasing hostility, several of the government officials began to leave; one gestured helplessly while another walked straight ahead as if he were on his way to yet another funeral.

There were a few last words of farewell to the old rebel, to the harsh critic, the enemy of sinecures and of the repressive apparatus set up by the ambitious profiteers. At last, when the last handfuls of earth had fallen on the coffin, silence reigned once more. The officials reached the gate with insults still ringing in their ears. Those who stayed behind were immersed in their reminiscences, in their need to continue to challenge, in the midst of the provocations they had suffered, and the enduring rage they'd felt for so many years with its roots lost in the timeless past. The clouds were casting more shadows and more and more darkness among the gravestones and epitaphs.

Domingo Buenaventura managed to write one more page and left it in his typewriter as if those phrases could stand by themselves. He walked toward his armchair, bit his pipe, and stopped for a few minutes to gaze at the clock where the big hand was nearing ten. He wondered whether he should curse the pain that was closing in on him again, threatening him, forcing him to sit down slowly and wrestle with the jumble of ideas in his head. He was already miles away—in Murcía, in Oviedo, in San Sebastián, strolling through the streets of Bogotá, stopping over in Guatemala. Then he walked around an intersection on Mesones Street, on Regina Square, along the slums of Peralvillo, until his own image began to fade among the whistles of the trains at the Buenavista Station and the shouts of an old sailor along the docks of Veracruz.

As the traces of his past were suspended in mid-air, his face took on a dreamy expression. He could no longer keep on stirring up old angers nor delve into the depths of his hatred. There was no one on the streets; the doors were shut tight and only a few lights were to be seen on the balconies and porticos. Even when the last of his thoughts was fading away, when the last moments were descending on him, he refrained from hurling one more insult, one more accusation. He had left them all there, on the last bending page he'd written, as if it were struggling to remain standing. As he lost consciousness, the pipe slipped from his lips onto his chest and fell to the floor. Finally, Domingo Buenaventura's eyes stared into nothingness.

XVI

ANDREA RAISED HER ARMS and ran her fingers through her hair as she paced up and down. Terrified, she stopped in her tracks and clutched her throat, then glanced sideways and then upwards, her gaze fixed on a distant point beyond her dreams, at something that was slowly dissolving into the purplish lights and nebulous barriers. Her face reflected a mixture of tears and distress—sorrows borne in silence. Staring straight ahead, she looked relieved and then smiled mechanically. Her eyes opened slowly, as if all her hopes had suddenly been shattered and slipped through her fingers in search of a hiding place, perhaps beneath a mound of ashes or under a rubbish heap in some dark alley. Once again she skirted the edges of the bizarre as a peculiar grimace crossed her face, overshadowing the few words she had yet to speak.

She barely managed a low, unintelligible murmur, which nevertheless conveyed her gradual descent into numbness, with undertones of frenzy. Her reluctance to accept the inevitable was accompanied by a series of intense staccato sounds drumming within her head, by the fear in her eyes and in her half-opened mouth. She resumed her pacing, allowing a final moan to escape her lips and seep into distant shadows among other echoes, only to return and transform her despair into a hollow laugh as she seemed to ridicule everything around her. She felt that she was learning to touch the limits of the unbearable; it was precisely those last few moments which intensified her anguish and marked the last chapter of a predictable destiny. Although at last, as her entire body went limp, she contrived a gesture of arrogance. She seemed, at last, to have been totally enveloped by the void.

"Bravo! Bravo!" Sebastián boomed out just as the curtain fell.

Andrea, smiling more radiantly than usual, took her bows and then one, two, three, five curtain calls. Martín, who was sitting in the last row, joined in the applause. Far better than anyone else, he knew the seclusion, nervous tension and endless rehearsals Andrea had gone through in the past few months. The comments on her performance were, to say the least, enthusiastic, and Andrea bowed in acknowledgement with delight radiating from her face. Gabriel and Isabel were seated in one of the front rows, while Cristóbal, right behind them, raised his hand and then applauded even more enthusiastically than before.

"Long live *La Chacón!*" Sebastián shouted, never dreaming that from that moment on the nickname would stay with her and would always resound at the end of every one of her performances, after each of her increasingly demanding roles, on other stages and in other settings.

As soon as the ovations died down, her friends and admirers gathered in the foyer for the customary backslapping, handshakes, smiles and catty remarks, greeting each other just as they had in the old days. They then trooped to Andrea's dressing room, chattering away while they waited for her, making plans to go somewhere to relive their own world and recapture their long-lost dreams.

. . . Martín had invited us over to the house in Coyoacán. It was early in May, with Buenaventura's funeral behind us. By that time, the José Augusto myth had been practically forgotten and we rarely talked about him anymore. Nevertheless, I myself had been unable to shake off that particular obsession and couldn't help feeling that some day, sooner or later, I'd run into him again. Perhaps it would be in the very same place where, one lazy unpleasant morning in the Mexican consulate in Paris, I had read every news report I could get my hands on, where the game of multiple personalities had originated. On the other hand, I was reluctant to keep going round in circles, in the same rut that often made me feel uptight and depressed me no end. I was seriously thinking of going away again and getting a job somewhere as a foreign correspondent. Now that the restrictions for people with my kind of record had been lifted, it was much easier to travel, and besides it was very likely that I would be in extremely good company. Things were going very well between Isabel and me. Although we knew quite well the essence of our lust and some of our personal shortcomings, we still had to learn how to let off steam and keep our tempers under control. Perhaps because it was an extra-special occasion—or because all of us shared wholeheartedly in Andrea's success or because of the indescribably cheerful, expansive mood we were in—we were all there, waiting for "La

Chacón" and warming up for the same old stale jokes, determined not to fly off the handle over some petty comments that usually set us quarreling. I can remember everything very well—from the moment we left the theater with our usual boisterousness, to the faces of our friends staring out of the car windows, to our arrival at Andrea's with the threat of rain hovering over us. As usual, there were the roars of laughter around the table, Sebastián's special brand of sarcasm and Martín's aloof, detached expression. There was plenty of gossip and light banter, particularly jokes about our double chins and noticeable wrinkles. We even went so far as to avoid pointless discussions with Cristóbal. Although we did not agree with Andrea's opinion that "Here, all of us have at least one thing in common and sooner or later we're bound to run up against our very same vices," on that night we refrained from making innuendoes of any kind. By that time, I felt I had a great deal to say; that I was, at last, emerging from a long tunnel and had finally overcome my tendency to screw things up for myself. It goes without saying that my prison memories still bothered the hell out of me; they were always there, like some slimy reptile, always horning in on my thoughts. Still, the really important point was that Isabel had now become an extremely significant part of my life and I made up my mind to give up all those passing fancies, which never quite materialized anyway, hanging in the air . . .

In another part of the city—in an old house on Tabasco Street in the Roma district, José Augusto was sitting on a straight-backed chair, putting up with the barrage of insults and endless grilling as best he could. He made efforts to control himself and not let anything slip out. Once in a while, he was allowed to light a cigarette, which he smoked at leisure, inhaling it deeply, his face stony and expressionless, despite his shock at the way things had turned out. After a while, he started making up the answers off the top of his head. The voices crowded in around him, taking him back many years to the brutal beating and the dungheap in Ciudad Satélite. As drops of perspiration glistened on his forehead, José Augusto seemed to have aged considerably in just a few days.

It had been a week since he had been brought to this place directly from the airport, after a long trip which had been no more than a big blur to him, with the hours slowly dragging by. For the life of him, he still could not grasp what had happened; he could not imagine what possible blunder or oversight or trap had led him here, how it was conceivable that so many things had fallen apart so suddenly.

The invectives, aimed at the criminal, the agitator, at the son of a bitch, and the dissolute life he'd led in Paris, kept coming at him, twisting out of shape, clashing with one another, trying to wear him down and corner him. In an attempt to embellish his past experiences and gloss over the actual facts, he kept on improvising his answers. Most probably, he reflected, no one knew he was here, and yet, there was the city—both real and imaginary—the city he had been irremediably forced to accept.

Since it was practically impossible for him to hold out indefinitely, he couldn't stop wondering if they were about ready to give him a good working over, and if the blows to his neck and testicles would finally break him.

Little by little, as he managed to overcome his tension, he assumed an unmistakably resentful expression. *Lots of times I'd catch myself clenching my fists; I'd stare at the cigarette smoke and at the eyes all around me. It was really me in this place and I still couldn't believe it. It was as though a premonition— something I had imagined so many times in my loneliness—had suddenly come true—all too soon it had materialized as a palpable reality. Once in a while I thought about Ana Elena, about self-delusion, about the foolish hopes that had been built on such flimsy foundations, on so many goals that had vanished into thin air. There were times when I was utterly convinced that I was at the end of my rope and then I'd imagine I was slipping down into the biggest escape hatch in the world. I had absolutely no idea how I would get out of this one. During the whole time I was there, I found it impossible to grasp the fact that I was actually there, as if the hands of a dead criminal had been reborn.*

. . . After the first few drinks and the compliments and effusive praise for Andrea's *tour de force* had died down, Sebastián launched into what he called the "game of massacred biographies" by injecting a new vitality into our long lives of dissent and dissipation. Although at times his frankness overstepped the mark—even for him—he nevertheless managed to be on the mark more often than not. "La Chacón" was merely an excuse for him to start telling a lot of stories about each of us—no matter that we'd heard them all before. He ran the gamut—from ancient history to the present, from the peanut gallery in the neighborhood cinemas of our youth to the *cantinas* on Donceles Street downtown. He exaggerated our successes and our failures; he drank toasts to everybody imaginable, including the long dead and the very much alive, and even to lost and nameless souls we'd never heard of before. He gave Martín an enthusiastic bear hug while at the same time holding him up as the perfect example of the misanthrope. He gave Cristóbal the back-slapping embrace that was standard procedure in the Chamber of Deputies. Cristóbal, unperturbed, gave back as good as he got, with his incredible self-presence completely in control. As for Andrea, she was in her own element, happier than ever, after those months of strain and apprehension. The rain was approaching the house, with the wind barely rippling through the branches of the pines and the jacarandas . . .

And so there we were again as we had been so many years ago. But now there was no way we could kid ourselves about a new beginning nor could we deny the fact of our obvious deterioration. We had reached the point where even old gibes or sudden flashes of wit had lost their punch and had become nothing more than commonplace remarks punctuated by appropriate gestures. Our moods were far more revealing than our words. Complicity was unspoken but real; we had long since grown tired of looking into the mirrors of time, which had been clouded over by our phoniness, lies and complexes. Our faces already showed the telltale signs of age: dark bags under our eyes and graying moustaches. Even so, we were bound and determined to reclaim the house in Coyoacán which had served as an outlet for both our troubles and our unbridled enthusiasm.

We kept needling each other mercilessly, sometimes to the point of sheer verbal cannibalism, although we knew that some of us had more than our share of suffering. After a great deal of soul-searching, of exchanging views and of comparing our relative achievements—and though we were very much aware of our inner conflicts—we had already managed to lose sight of the distances that separated us from our common goals. Instead, we preferred to heap our criticism on the outstanding personalities of the moment or on our own individual weaknesses. However, whenever we got together, a peculiar mechanism seemed to provoke almost automatic reactions in each one of us, as if all our voices had joined together and become one. And this in turn gave way to a whole chorus of tones which were ultimately absorbed by the walls of the house.

It had finally started to rain and the downpour was particularly heavy on Chilpancingo Circle, several kilometers from Andrea's house. On the next to the top floor, in an apartment building on the corner of Baja California and Culiacán, the telephone rang insistently, rousing Laura from her sleep. Finally, she got up, switched on the light and padded into the living room to answer. She had a hard time shaking off her drowsiness and her annoyance while still fighting off the shapeless forms in her dreams.

Laura was still yawning as she lifted the receiver. Abruptly the voice on the other end jolted her back to reality. At first it seemed inconceivable to her: ghosts, the darkness, the old breathlessness had returned. But as she listened, everything seemed to confirm the fact that the irrational, disturbing confrontations with unforeseen circumstances were being inflicted on her once again, taking her back to the image of José Augusto, to the hatred and the despair she had buried so long ago. Although the voice was firm, it only requested that she clarify a few points and provide some additional information.

"Yes, yes, but that was over eleven years ago," Laura stammered, pressing her forehead against her hand as if it could help dispose of her bewilderment and her mounting agitation.

When she hung up, she didn't know quite what to think; she tried putting the pieces together—the events that had led up to fateful consequences, to her old grudges and her blurred memories; and now the knowledge that José Augusto was definitely under arrest. Before calling Andrea, torn between self-pity and resentment, she stared at the lines of her hands for a long time until her thoughts fell into place. She rose to see if the door to her children's bedroom was closed, and then, with a half-indulgent, half-stern expression on her face, she tried to pull herself together.

Through the window, she caught a glimpse of the lights glittering over the city and of a plane disappearing toward the east. Finally, she dialed Andrea's number.

. . . No doubt about it, Sebastián was in rare form that night. With no sign of his usual malice, he had taken it upon himself to cheer up everyone and he got us all laughing our heads off and clowning around. By then, a whole bunch of people had dropped in, and through the windows, one could see the rain pounding down on the grass. Without a trace of embarassment, Cristóbal was trying to brainwash me by congratulating me on my viewpoint and insisting that what this country needed was precisely my kind of outspoken criticism. He added, as a clincher, that many government officials like himself were in dire need of these articles which served as eye-openers, and that the misery and injustice in our country should most definitely be brought out in the open. I merely shrugged and

257

said, "The cynicism of you people is not to be believed; what's more, if you'll pardon the trite expression, it's bigger than your mouths." He chuckled as if I had just given him the greatest compliment in the world, and then, believe it or not, we drank a toast to the buzzing of the flies around us. Later on, when the party was in full swing, Andrea announced she was pregnant with Martín's child. Once again, Sebastián outdid himself by piling it on and we went along with him. Even Martín cracked a smile which was, in itself, almost a miracle. The entire Concordia contingent milled around in the hallway, greeting and congratulating each other. Sebastián managed, without ruffling any feathers, to enliven the conversation by describing them jokingly as the chorus in a Greek tragedy. One of them—I think it was the poet—retorted that Sebastián was overdoing it; that he should not confuse real tragedy with high camp. A few minutes later, Isabel murmured to me that something peculiar was going on; apparently Andrea had gone to answer the telephone in the pantry, and had then continued the conversation on the extension in her bedroom. In fact, an ashen-faced, subdued Sebastián had joined her at the end of the corridor; I'd never seen him like this before. Later on, they both called Cristóbal over and the three of them huddled together as if they were involved in some strange conspiracy. Despite his efforts to conceal his apprehension, Sebastián's face revealed his mixed feelings: perplexity, impatience, revulsion and anger . . .

"Don't worry, we'll find out exactly what's going on right away," said Cristóbal to Sebastián. "First, we'll try to get to the bottom of the situation and of course we'll do our best to help him out as soon as we can." He added with absolute certainty that at least José Augusto would not be beaten up.

Later on, as the party was getting rowdier, they went into Andrea's bedroom where Cristóbal telephoned several VIPs asking for advice and more concrete information about the case. Sebastián, his eyes flashing, kept clenching his fists angrily as he remembered Banderas strolling toward the bus station in Guadalajara. It was beginning to dawn on him that the fate of the Unmentionable was irreversible, and that other, more significant capitulations had already been made, starting from the moment when he had been taken from Edinburgh to the London airport en route to Mexico.

After five phone calls, Cristóbal began to link up some aspects of the case that were not clear to him: there was talk of conspiracies, of an international espionage network, of funds that had been transferred from one country to another—a very touchy business that was not within his power to handle. He explained that later on certainly something would be done, but at the moment, the most urgent matters must be attended to at once, such as conferring with lawyers and complying with the necessary legal procedures and formalities, such as the appeals, the trial and especially pulling the right strings. "I'll be perfectly frank with you; right now there can be no immediate solution," warned Cristóbal. He added that, so as not to complicate matters even further, Banderas would be held for the charges he had pending against him in Mexico rather than for the more recent affair he was implicated in abroad. Sebastián's initial reaction was a crooked grin, as if he were making fun of "all those jerks who screw things up by splitting hairs and beating around the bush. What we really need around here is guts, to learn to be real men who know where it's at." He fell silent and his eyes seemed to glaze over in a peculiar fashion.

The news spread around soon enough, casting a pall on the gathering and provoking endless speculation. Another myth had just toppled, breaking into empty words and generating gestures of resignation and disbelief. Andrea couldn't stop thinking about Laura: so many old ties to the past had suddenly returned to haunt her. For a long time, while everyone else had apparently calmed down and, under the influence of liquor and other sources of inspiration, were giving their own interpretations of the situation, Sebastián sank down on the couch and thought about his forthcoming encounter with José Augusto. He visualized himself strolling outside beyond the windows, under the jacarandas, soaked to the skin and opening his mouth wide to taste the rain.

"Come on now, you bunch of kooks, we'll go crazy if we keep this up. Life must go on, and we must keep on stripping the world of all its masks," said Sebastián as he rose to his feet, drained his drink and dredged up the old memories and vague premonitions.

Two days later, José Augusto had been consigned to the newly built prison north of the city. A number of riddles had already been cleared up and once again rumors made the rounds among malicious gossips. The thousands of pages which José Augusto had written night after night over so many years were on their way home, crossing the seas above the huge masses of clouds and with the sun shining against the side of the motors and the plane windows over the North Atlantic.

XVII

JOSÉ AUGUSTO, NOW white-haired, though still black-browed, with his features more aquiline than ever, stared at the walls of his cell. By now he was already well into the initial stage of yet another long apprenticeship, bound and determined to overcome the new obstacles that faced him and not let depression get him down. After all, these were circumstances he had anticipated long ago and had often imagined as possible.

His face was unlined and only his hair, his yellowish teeth and a certain vacant look in his eyes—a cautious, guarded expression—betrayed the experiences he had had in so many different places. Now he had resolved to eliminate any trace of self-deception, along with those multiple identities of his which were constantly at odds with each other. He hunched over a small stool, watched the smoke rise from his cigarette and then started to analyze his case; he reflected that in this country, justice is a commodity to be bought and sold. He thought too about the long sentence in store for him. However, another thought—about his prospective reunion with Ana Elena—stirred up all kinds of unexpectedly mixed emotions.

Banderas was fully aware of the fact that his was no ordinary dossier; it added up to a great deal more than just plain homicide and there were a lot of other incriminating circumstances as well. Doubtless anything could happen. He also concluded that it would be foolish even to think of bribery. Anyway, that resort was beyond his limited financial means. Now, once again, he had to be the soul of patience, transform himself into the ever-present character who lived off of him, who was bent on following him for the rest of his life, who screwed him up, hemmed him in, stirred up his old rages, jeered at his other personalities and bragged, at the top of its voice, about each and every one of its previous successes. Even so, that bastard Banderas, with the help of perhaps the only accomplice who could no longer compete with him, would not give in to despair; he was fated to run up against not only his own obsessions but also against his amazing resilience.

Most likely, that Banderas who was a defeatist, the Banderas of the premature decline, who was totally incapable of perceiving the vibrations that separated him from others, the Banderas whose bitterness rankled inside him like an open sore, that son of a bitch, had stayed behind, perhaps even died, on the staircase and in the mirror of the Sinaloa Street apartment. Nevertheless, he was now confronted with the years that had passed, with the shadows of time and all they implied and, perhaps, even with the impossibility of ever recovering from his present predicament.

. . . He greeted us as if nothing had happened. At the beginning, he had exactly the same voice and mannerisms: his restless hands, the face behind a cloud of smoke, the same familiar expressions, the eyes that darted back and forth as he expressed his firm determination to get out of prison as quickly as possible. We did not mention the crime, the dead man, nor Laura. He talked about a few of the women he'd been involved with and of his frustrations, his travels through England and France, his narrow escape in Hendaya and different types of work he'd done in Madrid and later in Edinburgh. He'd rub his hands together, laugh somewhat halfheartedly and then tell us of the problems he'd had with other inmates here—the worst scum he'd ever met in his life. He explained the various means he'd used to try to keep them in line. "Shit, remember I'm here with a bunch of vicious, cold-blooded murderers. Naturally, there are always one or two morons you wouldn't believe. Here, Gabriel, I swear, you have to fight tooth and nail to protect yourself," he'd exclaimed over and over, his palms spread wide. He described the favorite weapons of the convicts in the adjoining cells: lead pipes, razor blades, jackknives, metal rods, belt buckles and forks. Then he mimicked the speech of both the prison guards and the gang leaders. At times his account seemed surreal. After he described the house where he'd spent several weeks before he was imprisoned, he told us about the yelling he'd heard in this prison, how it increased in volume after midnight; and the shrieks from the other inmates he'd hear at dawn and the pain that lingered for a long time after in their bones and eyes. He spoke of his travels, of the day he met Ana Elena and his complete giving of himself to her—something he had thought he'd never experience again. He'd scratch the back of his neck, screw up his eyes and swear at his cigarette. He insisted on telling us all about the ordeals he'd been through, his fears and the dangers threatening him now. He

261

laughed at his other self, whom at last he knew he could not escape. Most of his conversation was closely connected to his physical appearance, his struggle to overcome the agitation which had somewhat altered his arrogance. At one point, Sebastián interrupted him: "We will never be reduced to mere skeletons, you know. By God, our rebelliousness will live on in others until the Day of Judgment!" . . .

Once again, José Augusto was overcome by doubts, as if they had the power to mock the anxiety in his eyes, to envelop him in his own disgruntlement and self-subjection, *in that goddamned, shitty humiliation which I tried to bury so long ago.* There were moments when he had almost persuaded himself that everything was going smoothly, that he'd be out of here soon, and be able to see for himself the unbelievable changes the city had undergone. Nevertheless, at some point the goddamned anxieties, the misgivings and the random thoughts would flood in on him once again. He'd stroke his smooth forehead and his stubbly chin. With unremitting courage he refused to accept the circumstances that would force him to remain in this place for several years, where perhaps he would lose his sanity and never again be able to gaze upon the esplanades or the wide boulevards.

The gradual conditioning process was accompanied by a proliferation of sequences which sooner or later led him to a continuous struggle with the other José Augustos within him and with his surroundings. As his self-confidence mounted, however, he tried to listen to the only Banderas he could truly respect. Then he could concentrate on the immediate business at hand: the allegations, statements, depositions, appeals, the vague promises and the hopes he'd had for his unfinished projects.

He went over his case again and again, as coolly and as objectively as possible, careful not to let himself be swayed by his own selfish motives nor by outwardly convincing arguments. He visualized himself twenty years before, making the rounds from one newspaper to another, handing in articles and stories, arguing at political meetings and distributing instructions, as if he had the situation well in hand. He had been too inexperienced then to notice all the backstabbing and the cover-ups that went on around him, *but that was all in the past. Even then, I had to take my laziness and irresponsibility into account. I was just a poor jerk who had absolutely no idea of what he was doing. Now, I'm an entirely different person; I've grown thick-skinned, and I don't see why I should be made to pay a heavy price for my past mistakes.* He marveled at how the others inside him had matured, and recalled the first inkling he'd had of the existence of those bizarre characters who constantly harassed him with their diatribes. He remembered his escape with Sebastián at his side, the day he crossed the border, when he finally learned to control those hidden voices, the tones and gestures that ranged from twisted grins and tight-lipped grimaces, from apparent fatigue to the cunning subterfuges of the bullshitter he had become.

. . . While Sebastián kept plying him with questions, I studied him closely and compared him over and over again with the Banderas of Bucareli who rarely agreed with Buenaventura on anything, the Banderas of the uncompromising views, who knew just how to set us against each other and then pick holes in our arguments. "Self-criticism, my friends, self-criticism is the only thing that can ultimately save us," he used to say, somewhat scornfully. I found it almost impossible to believe that he was there in the flesh, that he was actually setting us straight on all those half-truths and far-fetched stories about him, demolishing them with that old familiar sarcasm, flicking his fingers nervously and sprinkling his conversation with a combination of fact and fantasy. He kept cocking his head to one side and biting the filter of his cigarette, rambling on and on about all sorts of things: the places he'd been, his interpretations of what we had imagined his life was like, the experiences he would like to have had, and his most immediate problem. I was absolutely convinced that he was on the level; that he had held back nothing, not even his bewilderment, by putting on an act. After we had gotten over the initial shock and Sebastián kept shooting questions at him, he described the last trap he'd fallen into, like a perfect idiot, gradually drawing us into his own world and coloring our own experiences by reminding us of a number of things we'd long forgotten. He knew much more about us than we'd ever imagined. It was as if he had predicted not only the direction our lives had taken but our own individual frustrations and weaknesses as well. While we were looking at him we were also seeing ourselves as we really were, and gradually, as we opened up to him, we found out a bit more about what made us tick. We spent a great deal of time discussing Domingo Buenaventura, the aftermath of his funeral, his unusual epitaph and the tributes that arrived all too belatedly. Sebastián kept harping on Banderas' role in the railroad workers' strike, the day when we all met for the first time, the all-night bull sessions that lasted until dawn and the long strolls through the downtown streets . . .

263

José Augusto never tired of analyzing his real motives for the murder; once again he began regarding his hands as things, as objects completely detached from the rest of his body, with a will and feelings of their own. In spite of the time that had passed, the scene had remained crystal-clear in his mind and he was still able to reconstruct effortlessly the steps, the voices, the creaking sounds, the days before and after the crime, the gun-shots he'd fired point-blank, his hasty departure, and finally, the dim staircase and pitch-black street. Then his imagination would run wild as he tried to justify himself as a solitary man, a loner, with violent tendencies, full of despair and a persecution mania which saw nothing but deceit at every turn and fueled the deep resentment raging inside him.

All of a sudden, he would hear another prisoner snoring loudly, or the distant rattling of drainpipes, and the sounds of doors, locks and hinges. He stared at the ceiling and at the shadows of the iron bars reflected on the floor. He realized, in his eagerness to unmask his own characters, that there was no longer any room, either in his mind or in his senses, for José Augusto the coward, nor for José Augusto the loser nor, for that matter, for that whole cast of characters ranging from the cynic to the rebel to the restless adventurer. As far as everyone else was concerned, he had no valid grounds for defense; he was and would continue to be an outlaw in every sense of the word. But in the face of his own loneliness, his need for justification became imperative and hinged on his vision of himself going through a particular phase where his extreme susceptibility, bordering on paranoia, triggered his almost total involvement in the essence of the absurd.

When he realized that he had been defeated at the end of a long match and after a considerable period of time which was suddenly terminated, he started swearing at all those José Augustos who had shared both his face and his shadow, who had already shown him their ability to handle any kind of situation as long as he was pulling the strings: the lecher, the madman, the victim, the neurotic or the martinet. He thought about resorting to his extraordinary adaptability, to instant metamorphosis by adjusting his mannerisms and his expressions to the specific performance which seemed most appropriate at the moment. Once again he would have to achieve freedom by becoming his own best accomplice.

. . . All of a sudden we started talking about many things we'd been through together, from our first political meetings to the endless bar-hopping, from the destructive infighting to endless knock down and

264

drag out fights. Both Sebastián and I were astonished by José Augusto's exceptional memory. He could remember, down to the slightest detail, Sebastián's little rooftop room on Colima Street. He then ticked off, one after another, the names of streets and districts all over town, never forgetting a single name, not even those of the hardware store owners or shopkeepers in the area. He wondered why Sebastián no longer licked his cigarettes with the same relish as before and then asked me if I still had the habit of scratching the back of my neck whenever I was nervous. Little by little, it dawned on me that we were dealing with a mature human being and that despite the fact that he was getting along in years, the former José Augusto was a carbon copy of the present one, as if everything were interchangeable, with the epilogue at the beginning and with this José Augusto as the genuine article. As I saw myself in Lecumberri, far away from the new prison where José Augusto was now, I glanced at his long, bony hands and found it impossible to believe they could be those of a murderer. I also observed Sebastián: the double chin had grown to almost insulting proportions and there was a peculiar glitter in his owlish eyes. He was unusually ill at ease, and for once, he was at a loss for words. Not only did he refrain from his customary wisecracks, but he kept tripping over his words and opening his mouth wider and wider, getting hopelessly mixed up over names and dates. In haphazard fashion, he kept prodding José Augusto with a series of totally unrelated questions. José Augusto remained unperturbed, resting his elbows on his knees as if nothing had happened, just as if we were passing the time of day in some café on Insurgentes.

Although he had been in prison for a few days, the nights still seemed to stretch out before him. He tried to remember Laura, to separate her from all the other lives that had since been incorporated into his world. Long ago and over a period of time, each one of his senses had been able to discard her and remove his old need to have her by his side, to caress her olive skin and make love to her in the evenings. It seemed almost as if he were in an entirely different country and that another José Augusto had undergone those experiences, perhaps even a stranger who had run into him one afternoon in Paris and told him his troubles, someone who had nothing to do with his new sources of anger nor with his new outlook on life. *I could only manage to come up with a couple of blurred shapes: my murmuring to her, the image of a guy with a huge chip on his shoulder wander-*

265

ing around in a daze. That was the only time in my life—and I have the scars on my back to prove it—when the idea of suicide had become my inseparable companion, hounding me all the time, like a malicious bitch, when I least expected it, but particularly during my sleepless nights and in the early hours of the morning. I had to explode; I felt I had to get it out of my system, to tear out those complexes once and for all.

Nevertheless, a vague sensation of uneasiness would suddenly jolt hm out of his nightmares. As soon as he guessed that it could well be Laura's voice, he was suddenly confronted with old doubts, with his inability to remember her face, her hands, her nipples, her body. He could not conjure up even one impression of her—however dim it might be—such as watching her silhouette at a distance or her strolling along as if seen through a picture window. It was the only great mental void he thought he still had left, like a hazy netherworld, a peculiar sensation of the inaccessible that seemed buried in some hidden corner of his memory. Even so, despite this great blank, he never once had any qualms about justifying his actions; he was fully convinced that he would never be faced with either feelings of remorse or with a long prison sentence. His innate shrewdness and inordinate confidence in his capacity to handle problems had endowed him with built-in defenses and with a somewhat smug conviction that he could always snow people when he had to, that he had been born to take risks. It was way after midnight and a hush had fallen over the cells and corridors.

> . . . We spent practically all Sunday morning with him. It was a weird experience meeting him under totally unforeseen circumstances, as if the whole thing were nothing but a big farce or some sort of dream. I tried as hard as I could to relive the impossible, to isolate those years, to do away with the old riddles and wounds, and go back to parroting the same expressions which would turn into a cheap parody of José Augusto. Although we had shared a number of experiences, by now, our perceptions of them were either distorted or clashed with each other, or were considerably watered-down. Perhaps José Augusto—and this was the strangest thing of all—was the only one of the three of us who seemed to have both feet on the ground. Sebastián and I were in a state of total bewilderment in the face of this incomprehensible reality which we had long ago ruled out as unthinkable. At the same time, we were in no mood for ridiculous nostalgia trips or indulging in vague reminiscences. I happened to spot a stack of papers in a corner of the cell and sud-

denly imagined that one of the many Banderases was handing them over to me. "They're yours," he insisted, "Take them. They were written in a lot of places—hotel rooms, brothels, on shipboard—everywhere and anywhere. I thing they're worth saving. Maybe you can do something worthwhile with all of this." Before we left, when two other fellows came to visit him, I noticed that the very instant he started talking to them, José Augusto underwent a complete transformation in his intonation, his facial expressions, his hand gestures, the sarcastic nuances. I'm sure it couldn't have been more than just a few minutes, but during this brief time span, while he spouted off about dictatorships and spurious democracies, it suddenly came to me that there was no end to his experiences, to the stories he had to tell, and that he would always be listening to his own voices and manipulating his other personalities at will. We said goodbye as we used to in Buenaventura's apartment, using the catch phrases of twenty years ago. When we finally left the new building, we were overwhelmed by all sorts of conflicting reactions that needed sorting out. What's more unusual, Sebastián didn't open his mouth for well over half an hour. We headed back to the city, winding through the shanty towns that seemed to be stacked on top of each other, and finally made our way into the devastated streets under construction, the traffic jams on the Freeway and the city itself, which, judging from the descriptions he'd heard and the information he'd read over and over again, José Augusto knew like the back of his hand. He had reconstructed it, day after day, by resorting to his imagination, his resourcefulness, and his amazing memory. "One more chapter has ended. No doubt about it; life goes around in a full circle. Births and deaths are meaningless shit," Sebastián remarked, breaking his silence. From then on, there was no stopping him.

José Augusto stretched his arms and leaned his head against the wall. He was still perched on the stool, thinking about Ana Elena and knowing that he was not completely alone and that she would come to visit him as often as possible. He began counting up the number of years he had to remain there and attempted to assess the limits of his patience, seeking comfort in his utopias. He went over the most recent advice he'd received from his lawyer and wondered once again about his own capacity for recovery. He had to protect himself from himself and keep his hopes up, no matter what happened; he could not afford to be dragged down by depression and by the constant manipulations by all those people inside him—those broken-down facsimiles of Banderas as he had been either a decade ago, yesterday, or that same evening, for that matter. At last he lit his last cigarette, begrudging his cellmate's sound and apparently untroubled sleep.

XVIII

IN HIS JUMBLED, CATHARTIC nightmare he had witnessed the demolition of
the old Lecumberri prison, then seen the plans for new model prisons and
finally, watched husky convicts ripping apart iron bars, struggling to get
out. Finally, Gabriel shook off the memory of the gloomy corridors and
noticed that the Saturday morning sky was exceptionally clear, with only
a few clouds to the north and the sun streaming through the windowpane.
He decided to get up and spend a couple of hours at his typewriter to
record some of his most recent impressions or maybe even to resume his
descriptions of Domingo Buenaventura's last few days. He went over a few
of the pages that he'd written, reading them carefully and making a few
corrections that were not altogether satisfactory. He knew that José
Augusto's criticism would be ruthless and that most likely he would regard
many of Gabriel's metaphors as meaningless and only a few as truly
genuine.

Gabriel's last few pages, which Domingo Buenaventura never had a
chance to look over, were there in front of him. They had been left for
weeks in the Sinaloa apartment which had been deserted since the funeral,
as if that particular afternoon had marked the final chapter in the history
of the building. Somewhat apprehensively, Gabriel started writing, allowing the ideas to flow freely and not bothering too much with the rhythm
of the monologues or his retrospections, but preferring instead to concentrate on characterizations. Abruptly, the voices of Laura and José Augusto
mingled with the shouts in the auditorium and public squares, with the
crowds at Constitution Square around the flag, and finally, with the rifle
butts and the army tanks.

He wrote three pages without stopping and gradually began to feel
more confident that he could continue without further stumbling blocks
and that the story would flow to its inevitable denouement where a number of lives would be rounded off with only a few loose ends left dangling.

Perhaps in another story he would follow up on Cristóbal and Martín, and later, focus on Andrea with Cardoso as the main character. There would be many other opportunities, he was sure, to rehabilitate the dead and retouch the image of those still living. When he noticed that the rhythm of his pulse was uneven, he realized that he still had a great many pent-up emotions to deal with.

He remembered that Sebastián would be arriving at any moment and that he still had to go halfway across the city to meet Isabel. He had a great many people to see that day and the following day would be just as crucial. He began to shave and discovered a few grave hairs in his moustache. When he started reflecting about all their lives, he tried to reassemble them by placing them in order where they seemed to belong for the time being, according to whether they could actually be written about or were best kept to himself. He had a cup of coffee and spent some time analyzing the last few pages: the birds-eye view of the city, which, before long was to become the most densely populated and polluted city in the world, its public parks teeming with people, the poverty belts spreading all around the city limits, the filthy air and the deterioration of old neighborhoods. He studied Andrea's house as if he were gazing at it from the terrace of a ten-story building. Later on, his mental camera closed in on an anonymous, enigmatic stranger who, like an invisible witness, silently made his way from one place to another: from the Canal de Miramontes to the run-down shacks in Ixtapalapa, strolling through the squares, dropping into bars and *cantinas*, whiling away the time in some brothel, staring at the shop windows on San Juan de Letrán or else just sitting on a bench on the Paseo de la Reforma.

Just as Gabriel had discarded the idea of describing Buenaventura on one of his walks along Miravalle Square, he heard Sebastián's voice at the door. As he opened it, he came face to face with an unrecognizable Sebastián, sporting a brand-new suit, an impeccable tie and even a vest. His attire was a total about-face; it clashed with his personality, with the outlandish gestures of the rabble-rouser of La Concordia and of the house in Coyoacán.

"Don't say a word, my dear Gabriel. You know, once in a while, it's not a bad idea to put on a monkey suit for a change. Sometimes it's a great feeling to be considered respectable by all those vipers outside," he said, adopting the old familiar mannerisms and exaggerating the hoarse tone of his voice, which bore a tinge of self-satisfaction.

They went out into San Antonio Avenue, half a block from Insurgentes, leaving behind the building where, for the past few years, Gabriel had been living almost like a recluse. The streets were deserted as if they were totally indifferent to this first weekend in June. As Sebastián started up his car, a trolley bus stopped on the corner where an old man on the opposite side of the street was reading the headlines about a kidnapping in Spain and the murder of several guerrillas in Angola.

. . . The books Buenaventura had been reading were all there: a collection of César Vallejo's works, an anthology of subversive literature, some of his own short stories, and a biography of Tolstoy. When Isabel opened the curtains in the apartment, the pipes all around the ashtray, the posters on the left-hand wall and a sheet of paper with a few typed sentences lying over the typewriter keys suddenly seemed to glow. The pendulum clock had stopped, and there were piles of books and magazines on several shelves which seemed just about to topple over. The photographs of the Spanish Civil War and of the Sunday visits to Lecumberri were still there, in their usual place. Everything—the easy chairs, the metronome, the floor lamp, the worn old carpets, a reproduction of Picasso's *Guernica*, and a sketch of a crusty old revolutionary—was quickly disposed of. From the bedside table, Isabel removed a poem of Machado, written on a piece of blue paper. We stayed there until Domingo's apartment was completely empty. While Sebastián stood on the balcony, staring at the shadows of the buildings opposite us and at the pedestrians headed for Oaxaca Street, Isabel kept stuffing more and more things into the boxes. I helped Isabel and the movers, who kept trudging up and down the stairs carrying the boxes and the furniture, making the stairs creak louder than ever. No one said a word, as if we were carrying out an indispensable ritual which perhaps could have been delayed for a while longer. In less than two hours, the task was finished. Nevertheless, I still couldn't believe it. It was as if these walls didn't deserve to bear witness to a series of empty rooms . . .

"Believe it or not," Sebastián remarked, straightening his navy blue tie, this sort of thing gives me the willies, it really gets me down. Come on, you big jerk, don't look at me like that—I was expecting that you, of all people, would understand. You know that I'm just not cut out for situations like this."

They were in the car again, exchanging memories and enjoying the taste of tobacco after saying goodbye to some friends of Isabel's who lived

271

in the del Valle district and who had agreed to store the furniture and some of Buenaventura's personal effects. All during the ride to the south side of the city, the silence hung heavily over them, throbbing with intensity and seeming to endow the past with more clarity by helping them retrace the paths they had traveled together so often and reminding them of past accomplishments they had forgotten and of the goals they had never attained. Around two o'clock, just as they were approaching Avenida Universidad, Isabel decided she might as well spend the night at Andrea's.

"I'll see you tonight," Gabriel said to her when they had reached Coyoacán and the sunlight had started to fall on the branches of the pine and jacaranda trees, streaming directly on the trellis of bougainvilleas.

Once on Taxqueña Avenue, en route to Insurgentes, Sebastián started rambling on about the joys of having a good memory and about the gradual deterioration of the physical body, this "goddamned prison where all mortals fail, where something or other is bound to distort us and where the unexpected is always just around the corner—in ourselves, in our unpredictable behavior, in our stupid mistakes. I really don't know if we're just too complicated, but at any rate—and this goes for those of us still on this side of the grave—we're at odds with the world every waking moment of our lives, and with the goals set by this shitty cosmos. There are so many conflicting emotions that split us in two: our zest for life, our bitter experiences, the sensation that we're no more than puppets, those brief moments when life is truly extraordinary, and those long nights when we lose ourselves in phoniness and emerge empty-handed. It reminds me of the poem, 'I'm nobody's nursemaid, nor procurer of Death, nor go-between, nor God's lackey, nor graveyard eulogist, nor, much less, father confessor to people's sorrows.' Shit, I think I got carried away, didn't I, although, let me tell you, at least, in this most recent phase of mind, I'm finally coming out of my shell. I swear I have a whole new set of delusions to work with. I'm only hoping they'll last for a couple of months, at least."

"Look, there's La Concordia," Gabriel interrupted, inwardly turning a deaf ear to Sebastián's monologue. He was in no mood for pointless discussions. He felt they belonged to the past, to the demise of the omnipresent, to the years when nothingness and the infinite weighed upon them, day after day, playing on their emotions and uselessly prolonging their sleepless hours. Only the idea of delusions remained with him; the prerogative of making up a future for himself, one he must cling to at all costs.

. . . That Saturday afternoon almost everybody had gathered at La Concordia, stunned at the news of José Augusto's sudden reappearance, his imprisonment, and his imminent conviction. Naturally, there were a variety of opinions, both for and against. There was talk of an informer, of crimes of passion, of political involvements and of José Augusto's hopelessly psychopathic tendencies. Once again, Sebastián became the center of attention; he made the most of the information he possessed by juggling the facts around arbitrarily, fully aware of the fact that this incident had invested him with considerable importance, and consequently, with an opportunity he certainly could not afford to pass up. After he described José Augusto perfectly, imitated some of his expressions, and talked about Ana Elena as if he had known her all his life, he provoked a heated argument by comparing each version of the story and accusing the poet and the essayist of making deliberately misleading, malicious statements. He also mentioned Laura and the fact that she was willing to stick up for Banderas to the bitter end. He was drinking even more heavily than usual, his eyes lighting up with each gulp, and he kept rubbing his hands together as if he could wash away both his personal problems and his obvious pretenses at the same time. There was, of course, the would-be lawyer who analyzed the case in detail and concluded that José Augusto would be sentenced to at least 15 years; and then there was the know-it-all who declared that with a couple of million pesos, Banderas would be out in just a few months. Someone else added that Banderas would surely rot in jail for the rest of his life. Sebastián gradually became more and more withdrawn, until finally, after his fifth *Cuba Libre*, he quit talking altogether. I kept watching each one of them and imagining each of the Banderases they had known or would come to know in the future. There were a number of things I couldn't quite figure out. I realized that precisely because there were no concrete facts to go by and nothing but speculation and uncertainty at hand, it was fairly easy for the collective imagination to erect the pedestal and put the finishing touches on the statue of its idol. Most probably, now that the long gap between so many years had been filled, many of them were entering a state of calculated egocentricity and chronic incredulity. No doubt, some of them believed that although José Augusto would continue to be a topic of conversation for many more Saturdays to come, before long other subjects, other sources of stimulation would replace the Great

Lunatic, the gaunt, sharp-eyed, white-haired, dark-browed chain smoker who was pushing fifty, now locked up in a cell in the modern prison north of the city. I was convinced that it would be impossible ever to exhaust the topic of José Augusto; his saga would last us a lifetime. Perhaps in a few years, when I saw them again upon my return, they would prove me right . . .

"Will you get a load of that?" exclaimed the philosopher, pointing toward the end of the railing on the terrace.

A young, dark-haired woman with bedroom eyes was slowly making her way to our table. One of us who remarked on her extraordinary anatomical structure was immediately interruped by someone else who claimed she was much more than just a body; as a matter of fact, he added, she looked like an interesting person and maybe she was really searching for a familiar face at our table.

"Don't poach on my territory, my esteemed sons of bitches," said Sebastián, getting up with an insufferable air of self-assurance.

Gabriel kept staring at the vest, at the natty tie, the gray suit, the shrewd eyes and the head cocked to one side, noticing the drops of sweat on Sebastián's forehead. It suddenly came to him that here was a thoroughly unfamiliar Sebastián, one who looked for all the world like a seedy parody of a literary lion. In spite of his efforts, his ensemble was totally out of place; it had been designed for an entirely different face and voice. Cardoso approached the woman with flamboyant courtesy and out-dated manners that led him to introduce her to each member of the group one by one. Then he made a triumphant exit, as if he were aware of the fact that he had vindicated himself in the eyes of those who regarded him as nothing more than a consummate liar whose only merit was to spout the verses of deranged poets and to create metaphors based on the good old days—when he went hungry for weeks on end.

"That bastard is nothing but a troublemaker. He's the kind that loves to flaunt the merchandise. Who'd ever have thought it? Well, I suppose it's just a case of good old-fashioned envy on my part, don't you think?" said someone with a high-pitched voice as Sebastián was still waving good-bye from a distance and wearing a broad smile that he reserved for very special occasions.

A few minutes later, once the subject of José Augusto had been ex-hausted and the voices had become slurred or totally incoherent, Gabriel decided to head for Andrea's and on the way to spend time strolling on

274

Insurgentes Avenue, watching the beggars and the lottery ticket vendors lolling about the streets. He could hardly wait to see Isabel again, and was looking forward to spending the last few hours of this, his last Saturday night in the city, with her—his last Saturday night here for many years to come. As he crossed the street, he imagined that the make-believe ghost of Banderas had just breathed its last.

. . . That last night at Andrea's was fairly calm. There were no other voices, no new faces, no midnight phone calls to interrupt us. Our suitcases, Isabel's and mine, were all packed and ready. The air, too, was pleasant, moistening the grass and plants and seeming barely to graze the branches of the trees. Martín, with that invisible anger of his that always tormented him, didn't say much. Despite the fact that he was already a militant member of a newly-formed political party and that he was slated to be editor-in-chief of a prominent publication, his skepticism ran deep; it permeated his every idea, word and gesture. Andrea, on the other hand, was a different person. Judging from the determination in her eyes and in her smile, she was thoroughly enjoying her pregnancy and kept making a big fuss over any witty remark as she repeatedly ran her fingers through her hair. I might have been wrong, of course, but I had the impression that Martín wouldn't be living in that house much longer; that one of these days he was bound to explode and get rid of his stigmas once and for all. Even now, whenever he had a few drinks, he always gave vent to his anger at the whole world. We talked for a couple of hours about all sorts of things, without getting excited or lapsing into our usual ambiguous silences. We spent a great deal of time talking about Cristóbal and putting him down. Isabel and I slept in the back room, to the left of the corridor. I woke up practically at the crack of dawn and once again started separating this house from the city by re-creating a number of vignettes and remembering the first time I had ever been here, and then the weeks we had gone into hiding, the violence which had become an everyday occurrence, the constant meetings, one after another, and, of course, our all-night binges when we struggled to stay awake and steered clear of all premeditated slander or subservience. I thought about those long nights after our return from Chile, when I had no idea how to regain my love of life, nor how to piece together all those things that had suddenly seemed so trivial. Over and over again, the past kept rushing back at me until I found myself wavering between feelings of self-confidence and loneliness. I kept brooding about this house, about its sturdy walls which had always protected us, as if they had become an essential and vital part of our lives . . .

"You can count on me; after all, what are friends for?" said Sebastián as Gabriel handed him the keys to his apartment. They had been standing at the doorway of Andrea's house that first Sunday in June, when the sky was clear and the streets practically deserted.

The two of them hopped into the car, knowing that José Augusto was expecting them. All during the long ride, while Sebastián was describing, in great detail, his adventures of the night before with a sensational woman who had soft, milk-white skin, incredible nipples and soft, flaxen down all along her thighs, Gabriel was trying to imprint on his mind every single thing he was looking at, without bothering to add up all the years that had gone by nor indulging in nostalgia. He recalled again the mysterious character who appered in the last few pages of his novel, silently strolling along the colonial streets and the slum areas, admiring the reddish walls used in the new constructions and the terra cotta images in the altar niches ensconced in walls blackened by rain, then pausing to gaze at the wrought iron gates and lonely railings. He couldn't stop thinking about that obscure nobody who gradually had grown in stature before his eyes, as he drank in the constant mutations of the city: its wastelands, its blend of historical periods, the gray dome set in square columns and the long August rains.

Gabriel had the sensation that he was running away from himself but at the same time taking stock of himself as he mentally wandered past adobe shacks, grimy derelicts and thugs in some hangout, and through the memory of a mad chase down cobblestone streets, to the brave, clenched fists at rallies, to the interminable, deferential applause in the Senate and the Chamber of Deputies for the current president, to the faces of the roustabouts and truckers in a San Jerónimo whorehouse. He was barely listening to Sebastián's account of his erotic experiences.

"Fine, fine, Cardoso, that's just what you needed. But don't overdo it, hear; otherwise, you'll never get out of those booby traps you've set for yourself," Gabriel rejoined when he finally spotted the rectangular buildings of the new prison.

I sensed that José Augusto was watching me closely, as if he had guessed at each and every one of my conjectures about his life. He gave me a number of places I should visit, names and addresses of people to look up, and urged me to make up my mind on certain personal matters, which, under no circumstances, was I to leave dangling. For the first time in the thirty-odd years I'd known him, I realized at last that I had him pegged and that I was playing along with him. All the while that I was sizing him up, I was more conscious of his gestures than of his words as I tried trying to get to the bottom of his other personalities: the man who lived with Laura, the subversive in South America, the rare-book dealer, the man who expected Ana Elena in just a few hours, and the man he would become in the next couple of years walking out of that place and resuming his strolls around Bucareli or arguing in any one of the new bookstores in the San Angel district. I didn't ask him a single question, making him feel as if I still acknowledged his natural superiority. At times, I had the feeling that the whole thing was unreal; that Banderas was, in fact, nothing but the sum total of all our blunders, or perhaps, only the projection of either my own fantasies or of my deeply buried complexes. Once in a while, Sebastián, now freed from all his rhetoric and gruff poses would interrupt, laughing helplessly. As I left behind José Augusto's lanky figure with his cigarette dangling from his lips, I realized that his intelligence was way beyond mine, that he had read my mind and that, in fact, I didn't have the slightest idea as to what he had really gone through. The pile of papers, which I would have given anything to unravel, word for word—the stories that perhaps would never be published—remained there. In any case—and this was the most important thing of all—some of us bore a marked resemblance to a few of his personalities, and although it may not have seemed important, José Augusto knew that a Lunatic or an Unmentionable had, at some time or another, either lived in us, or would eventually grow within each one of us . . .

"All set?" Andrea asked, as she stood beside Martín in the airport waiting room.

"Well now, you've got to start sending us some damned good articles, and putting some balls into whatever you write, hear? Well, that's life for you; once again, traipsing all over the globe," added Sebastián, screwing up his eyes somewhat apprehensively and running his fingers through the long wisps of hair at the back of his neck.

Gabriel looked towards the back of the waiting room, still struggling with his doubts and his hopes. Then he turned to smile at Isabel, encouraged by the challenges that still awaited him in the immediate future. Then came the inevitable farewells: the embraces, the hands waving from among the stream of passengers on their way up the ramp.

Isabel was still smiling as the plane left Mexico City. Below, glimmering lights were beginning to emerge; luminous lines that formed what seemed to be an endless network. A few hours later, while Isabel was already fast asleep beside him, Gabriel reread a couple of his passages describing the grand mansions in Tlalpan, the hovels around the Merced market, the volcanic rock below Ajuscos peak, and the archways and doors in the Plaza Santo Domingo. When he reached the description of the junk heaps, and the houses of the old *conquistadores* that were up for auction, he reflected that time does not pass in vain.

Once again, the stranger appeared before him, the only witness who had seen Laura lying naked next to José Augusto, who had made up all sorts of paradoxical reconciliations between them, and who, one Monday, in the very same cell, had seen them surrender to each other after so many years, as if they could eliminate all trace of bitterness and live their lives all over again. Later on, the stranger greeted the members of La Concordia with a sarcastic series of gibes, enjoying himself thoroughly, knowing that he could be everywhere and anywhere without being seen. He eavesdropped on the conversation between Sebastián and a prominent lawyer in a bar in Tacubaya. The decision was definite: Banderas had been sentenced to twelve years in prison. Little by little, the stranger approached Domingo Buenaventura's epitaph: "A rebel always, even when delivering up his soul in ashes."

While the stranger left behind the cheers from the Azteca Stadium, lost himself among the bloated faces in a dimly lit café, Andrea and Martín were standing in front of a pyramid at the Olympic Village, reflecting on the passing of time, at the relentless hours which gave no quarter. At last, the character vanished into a screen, above the lights of the city, beyond the shadows and the rocks worn away by the centuries.

Finally, Gabriel opened a page at random and stopped at a description of his devastated city and the chronicles of his dead. Once again, the paths chosen by his friends and by his ghosts seemed to fade away and he felt as if the squares, the alleys, the buildings, the entire city, with its silent voices, belonged to him alone.

SHADOWS OF SILENCE

ambitions and fears at the heart of the massive protests that racked Mexico City in 1968. Arturo Azuela's works have been translated into six languages. *Shadows of Silence* is the first of his novels to appear in English.

Elena C. Murray is a freelance translator in Mexico City.